Praise for #1 *New York Times* and #1 *USA TODAY* bestselling author Robyn Carr

"Carr's new novel demonstrates that classic women's fiction, illuminating the power of women's friendships, is still alive and well."

—*Booklist* on *Four Friends*

"A thought-provoking look at women…and the choices they make."

—*Kirkus Reviews*

"The captivating sixth installment of Carr's Thunder Point series (after *The Promise*) brings up big emotions."

—*Publishers Weekly* on *The Homecoming*

"In Carr's very capable hands, the Thunder Point saga continues to delight."

—*RT Book Reviews* on *The Promise*

"Sexy, funny, and intensely touching."

—*Library Journal* on *The Chance*

"No one can do small-town life like Carr."

—*RT Book Reviews* on *The Wanderer*

"A delightfully funny novel."

—*Midwest Book Reviews* on *The Wedding Party*

"Well-rounded characters, a plot rich in emotion and humor and one sweet romance make this a great read."

—*RT Book Reviews* on *A Summer in Sonoma*

"Carr has hit her stride with this captivating series."

—*Library Journal* on the Virgin River series

ROBYN CARR

never too late

A NOVEL

MIRA

Recycling programs for this product may not exist in your area.

ISBN-13: 978-0-7783-1803-3

Never Too Late

For questions and comments about the quality of this book, please contact us at CustomerService@Harlequin.com.

www.MIRABooks.com

Printed in U.S.A.

This book is dedicated to Denise and Jeff Nicholl,
with deep affection and heartfelt thanks.

Dear Reader,

Have you ever been a little nervous about a trip you're going to take? Whether it's to a family reunion—meeting with relatives you haven't seen in a decade or three—or to some exotic land you've only read about, wondering if you packed the right clothes, if you'll understand the people, if you'll get lost? Eek!

Writing a book can be a similar experience—an adventure. It's a journey I meet with a little trepidation every time. The only difference is that writing a novel is a little like a board game. If you make a wrong turn, you can go back to the beginning and start again, until you make all the right turns.

Never Too Late, one of my very favorite adventures in women's fiction, was no exception. And it's built around one of my favorite themes— second chances. Central to the story is Clare, about to turn forty and in serious need of a "do-over" after a youthful heartbreak, a bad marriage and near-fatal car accident. What would give her a fresh start? A sexy younger man would be good. Maybe a love from the past to complicate things. And then to make a real mess—because we're all about getting our characters out of messes and on the right track—the ex-husband is desperate for his own second chance... with Clare.

But of course Clare isn't in this alone. She has an older sister and a younger sister, and as chance and adventurous journeys would have it, they both need a fresh start, too. Ambitious and successful Maggie needs to pump some energy back into her stale marriage and young Sarah, who has been watching life from the sidelines, would die to get even a smidgen of the attention that her big sister Clare is suddenly enjoying from men.

But wait—men are real nice, but the presence or absence of them is hardly a panacea in a woman's life. Especially a woman in search of a second chance. At the core she must find herself, come to terms with past mistakes and build herself from the inside so she can emerge stronger, more confident and ready to take on the world. Once a woman is secure in her heart and mind there's almost no more powerful force in nature. Make that three women and it feels like an explosion of passion for living. And loving. But is it too late?

Nah. It's never too late.

I hope you enjoy reading *Never Too Late* as much as I enjoyed writing it.

Robyn Carr

chapter one

· ·

CLARE DROVE THROUGH the March rain to the house that had
been hers, the house she left when she separated from her husband, and she felt a little guilty. Her trip was another of those
nighttime forages for things she missed, something she only
did when she knew Roger was going to be away. At least this
time she'd brought a birthday card to leave behind.

Maybe she was too easy on Roger, as their son, Jason,
maintained. Her leniency also dismayed her sisters. Maybe
she should try to be tougher, less tractable. Maybe everyone
was right—he didn't deserve it and she was a fool.

Today was Roger's fortieth birthday, and she felt a little
sorry for him. He was clearly having a problem with aging,
as someone like Roger would. He'd said as much. So Clare,
being the accommodating almost-ex-wife that she was, had
offered to make him dinner for his birthday. It would give
Roger a chance to spend a little time with Jason, which Roger
very much wanted even if Jason did not. But Roger said he
had to be out of town on business, holed up in a hotel alone
after some boring meeting.

It was probably for the best that the dinner hadn't worked—

Jason was still so angry. She had forced Jason to sign the card, and would leave it on the breakfast bar for Roger to find when he got back to town. She had wanted Jason to come along tonight, but it turned out that signing the card was as far as he could go.

Right before dropping Jason off at his friend Stan's house for the night, he had said, "You're going to get back with him, aren't you?" There had been such vitriol in his tone, she didn't even dare to respond. Which only led him to accuse, "You *are!*"

"No!" she had insisted. She had said it as strongly and firmly as she could, adding, "But I think it would be good for all of us, especially you, if we just get along."

"I don't want to get along with him! I hate him!"

Oh, how that caused her gut to clench.

Roger had brought it upon himself. In his naiveté he'd imagined that his adultery would be a secret from his son forever; that Clare would be the only one hurt by his actions. He'd really screwed up with Jason and it was a pity. For both of them.

Jason was fourteen. Just budding into manhood, struggling with puberty, freckles giving way to pimples, his overly tall, big-footed form gangly and awkward. And he was, to say the least, pretty touchy. Take one irritable teen, one self-centered and adulterous father, mix, watch explosion in a matter of seconds.

A plethora of responses had sprung to her mind, but she squelched them. She had some experience with these comebacks, and knew they didn't work anyway. *You might not always hate him. No matter what you might think, he doesn't hate you. He screwed up, he knows it, and he's sorry, Jason.*

Clare didn't care that Jason was mad at Roger—Roger deserved it. But this *hate*. This wasn't good. She didn't want her son to be in pain. So when Jason had refused to even go by the house with her to drop off the birthday card, she had said, fine. I'll do it. No big deal. I'll drop you at Stan's on the way. Call later, before you fall asleep. If you think of it.

Clare admired her old house as she pulled into the drive—it was a fine-looking, two-story brick, carriage lights shining at the three-port garage and around the walk to the front door. She sat in the car, gazing at it, thinking. Thinking how much she missed it.

This was her fourth separation from Roger. She thought it would get easier, since the reason never changed. Roger was habitually unfaithful. This time when Clare caught him with someone else, she had decided to be the one to leave. She thought she'd finally had enough. She was pushed so far that she didn't even want to stay in the house she had shared with him, though she loved the spacious four-bedroom home. She thought a fresh start would do her good, but this had been harder than she expected. She had labored over every detail of the interior, having done all the decorating herself, and it was like parting with an old and dear friend.

Right on cue, Roger had immediately started making noises about wanting his family back and a chance, one last *chance,* to start his life over and make amends with Clare and Jason and all the peripheral people wounded by his behavior.

"I'm about to be forty, Clare, and it's pretty traumatic," he had said. "Don't think I don't know what I've done, how stupid I've been. I do. And I'm going to prove to you that I can change. I'm going to get help. I'm in counseling now."

"I don't think I have one more chance in me," she had returned. "And even if I did, my family doesn't. Our friends can't even take any more."

"That's your doing," he had shot back. "You haven't been able to keep even our most private problems to yourself!"

Well, that was true. But if Roger thought that was hard on him, he ought to try being her. Once people knew what he'd done, they couldn't believe she'd taken him back again. And again. And again. Their recriminations had run from astonished disbelief to what felt like a crushing lack of respect. Needless to say, the people she loved most had all but given up on her. In this relatively small town of only fifteen thousand, she was sure everyone knew.

And why had she caved in and taken him back, anyway? Because there were things about Roger. He was handsome, funny and very often kind-hearted. He was generous and a wonderful dancer. There were times in her life when she'd been shattered—like when her mother died and her little sister, Sarah, had plummeted into a frightening depression—and Roger had been completely there for her. He'd always been a good provider and while not a doting father, he loved Jason. He'd never been a coach or Boy Scout leader, but he'd enjoyed his son's games and achievements. Truthfully, Roger only had one screwup—it just happened to be about the biggest one available.

She just couldn't seem to get past the notion that this was all her fault. Her inability to make her marriage work; her failure to leave it. She couldn't keep him from straying and she couldn't seem to keep herself from letting him back in. She wasn't sure if trying to keep the family together had been a good thing for Jason, or the opposite. Clare just couldn't win.

She had officially moved out three months ago, right after Christmas, and into a town house the perfect size for herself and her son. She had taken only what she needed, but over time she transferred more of her things. She retrieved them in small increments on days and nights like this, when Roger had said he'd be away from the house. If he noticed the linen closet or kitchen getting emptier, he never mentioned it. Tonight she was in pursuit of a Bundt pan, slow cooker, her favorite red-trimmed dishes, the kitchen rug from in front of the sink and a bunch of Williams-Sonoma dish towels. Leaving the card on the breakfast bar would give her secret away, but that was all right. It was time Roger figured this out. Time to make this split official with the big *D*.

With a sigh, she turned off the engine and stepped out into the cold drizzle. She pulled the collar of her jacket up around her neck and shivered—possibly from the cold, or from the prospect of stepping back into the house she loved. Clare was a little surprised that the house alarm wasn't set, but then Roger had never worried about things like that in this nice little town. The only lights were those built into the walls of the foyer and hall, but that was all she needed. She knew every inch of the house; she'd obsessed over every countertop, cupboard, baseboard, floor covering. She'd just go straight to the kitchen, prop the card on the breakfast bar, get her things and go home. No lingering. No looking around. Seeing the house perfectly tidy always depressed her a little. It was kind of hard to see Roger getting along so well, especially given all his protesting that he needed her back in his life.

This house, after all, had been her domain. All the more reason to leave it in the past and start over.

She heard a squeak and froze. A creaking floorboard upstairs? Her heart pounded. Was someone in the house? A burglar? Then she heard another noise, kind of like that high-pitched moan the water pipes made when the backyard faucet was turned on. She thought about bolting. Then she heard it again, louder. This time it was followed by an undeniably female giggle.

The son of a bitch!

She was enraged on so many levels, but star billing went to the fact that she had asked Jason to come with her! My God, how much counseling would it have taken to get him past *this?*

She crept up the stairs without making a sound and saw the slit of light coming from the master bedroom; the double doors were just slightly ajar. She peeked inside and saw the long slim back of a blonde riding Roger. The woman rocked back and forth while beneath her Roger moaned. The woman giggled again. At the foot of the bed was a wine bucket with an opened bottle sticking out of it; on the bedside table, two glasses.

She gently pushed the door open and stood there, watching. She cleared her throat. It took a moment for them to realize they were no longer alone. The woman glanced over her shoulder, spied Clare and dived off Roger and under the sheets. She only glimpsed her but at least she wasn't someone Clare knew. Thank God.

Roger, at a disadvantage, struggled to prop himself up on his elbows. "Clare…"

She walked toward the bed. "How's that boring old business trip going, Rog?"

"Clare, it was cancelled. At the very last—"

"Oh, shut up, Roger," she yelled.

"But Clare, we're separated, and I figured—"

She plucked the wine bottle out of the bucket, tossed it on the carpet and lifted the bucket full of melting ice and water off its stand. She doused Roger and company. He was lifted off the bed with a yelp of pain and the woman under the sheets screamed.

Clare turned and fled the house, deliberately leaving the front door standing open, hoping there had just been an escape from the zoo and several lions and tigers were loose in the neighborhood. Or maybe a serial killer would be passing by and see a prime opportunity.

She jumped in the car and screeched out of the driveway, changed gears and zoomed down the street. And she cried.

She didn't cry because she loved him so much, but rather because she was so bloody sick of being humiliated like this. When would she learn?

Despite the fact that Roger had no discretion whatsoever, this was the first time she'd actually caught him in the act. She'd found evidence, like hotel charges, receipts for gifts not given to her. There had been strange phone messages and there was that time a woman had called and begged Clare to free him. Once confronted, he'd always come clean. He was a charmer, a flirt, a philanderer and a lousy liar.

She'd asked him more than once why he didn't just embrace bachelorhood. "Seriously, Roger—why not just be single? You act like it anyway. Just go for it. Knock yourself out."

Then he would hang his head and say, with pathetic sincerity, "Because I love you, Clare. I've always loved you. I know I'm screwed up, but I just don't think I can get beyond this without you."

She hit the steering wheel in blind fury. That's when she saw the flashing lights in her rearview mirror and looked down at the speedometer. Damn it all, she was speeding.

She slowed down and pulled to the curb, then she let her head drop and she fell apart, crying painful tears. Familiar tears.

It was a few minutes before the officer's flashlight shone into the window and he tapped lightly on the glass. She lowered it and looked up into the handsome face of an overgrown boy who wore a paternal frown. "Got an appointment?" he asked.

She wiped the tears off her cheeks. "I'm sorry," she said, though even as she said it she knew he wasn't looking for an apology. "I was angry and careless. A bad combination."

"Angry, careless and dead is an even worse combination."

"I found my husband in bed with another woman," she blurted. There, she'd done it again. Roger wasn't the only one with no discretion. She just couldn't keep her mouth shut.

"Whoa," said the police officer. He shined the flashlight on her face. "He must be crazy," he said.

"We're separated," she added. "I walked right into it. I should have been smarter. I should have *known.*"

"I'm going to need to see your driver's license and registration."

"Sure," she said. She fumbled a little, but got the papers together and handed them out the window. "Proof of insurance, too."

He looked at the documents. "Are you drunk?" he asked.

"No. But I'm not going to kid you. I'm going home to fix a nice big one."

He had a dazzling smile. Wonderful dimples. Good-looking guy, she thought. "Hey, if I weren't on duty, I'd buy you one." He handed back her stuff and said, "Look, I don't know anything about this man of yours, but you're a beautiful woman and it would be a damn shame if you got yourself killed on account of him being a loser. Know what I mean?"

"Yes," she said contritely.

"Think you can make it home safely? Stop at stop signs, drive slowly, all that?"

She nodded, confused. "Aren't you going to give me a ticket?"

"I think you've been through enough tonight. Don't you?"

"But I thought once you started a ticket, you had to finish it."

"I've always wondered why people think that," he said. Again that smile. "I'm the police—I can do what I want. Go on. Be careful. And don't punish the bastard by hurting yourself."

"Of course you're right," she said, surprising herself with a weak laugh.

"Of course I'm right. I could tell in thirty seconds, you have a lot to live for. Drive safely."

He went back to his car and she put hers in gear. She signaled, looked around and carefully edged away from the curb. She was only five minutes from home. He followed her, she noticed with some amusement. She came to the traffic light and stopped on the red. She gave him a little wave in the rearview mirror, but couldn't tell if he returned the gesture. The light turned green and she cautiously entered the intersection.

And the lights went out.

Sam Jankowski went back to his squad car. Whew, he thought. What a dish. If he'd met her anywhere else, he'd have asked her out. Even with the tears, that was one good-looking woman. She was a little older than he, but he liked that. The women he was accustomed to dating tended to be younger, often immature and a little flighty. He liked a woman who had lived a little. A woman who was clear on what she wanted and where she was going. Clare Wilson, five foot four, one hundred and eighteen pounds, brown hair, green eyes, stupid ex-husband.

She pulled away from the curb, blinker and all, and he moved off right behind her. She stopped at the traffic light on the corner and when it turned green, proceeded into the intersection. Then, from out of nowhere, bam! An SUV ran the light and broadsided her, shoving her car all the way across the intersection into the light pole. "Holy Jesus," he said.

He lit up the squad and moved into the intersection behind the collision to stop any approaching traffic. He keyed the radio attached to his belt while jumping out of the car. "Control, DP-thirty-five, roll medical. I have a 401 at the intersection of Winston and Montgomery."

"Copy. I have them en route."

"Can you copy for two plates?" he asked, as he went to the trunk for flares.

"Copy."

"Mary Nora Paul seven six nine," Sam said, repeating Clare's license plate from memory as he ran toward the collision. A young woman was getting out of the SUV. "Ma'am," he called, "please get out of the intersection if you can. Stand on the sidewalk." He lit and threw down a flare.

"My baby," the woman cried.

"Control, advise medical we have an infant in the vehicle."

"Copy."

"Copy plate Union Zebra Henry two two nine." He went to the woman, who was looking in the backseat. The rear windows were intact, the baby was crying, a good sign, and the broken glass of the windshield was contained in the front of the vehicle. "Ma'am, leave the baby in the car seat until medical arrives."

"I have to pick him up," she said in a panicked, shaken voice.

"It's better if you don't move him."

He lit and tossed another flare. "Ma'am!" He heard sirens. "Leave the baby for paramedics to examine before moving him." He ran to the trunk for his fire extinguisher, then to Clare Wilson's little, destroyed Toyota. There didn't seem to be a fire, but he'd be ready.

The driver's side was crushed against the light pole, which, thankfully, hadn't broken in half. The right side was destroyed by the SUV. He couldn't get to her, but he could look in the driver's window. Her hands still gripped the steering wheel, her head lolling to the side. She moaned. He reached through the broken glass and took her left hand into his. "Clare," he said. "Can you hear me?"

"Uhh," she moaned, eyes closed.

God almighty, he thought. This is bad. Bad. He held her hand. "Try not to move, Clare. Just try. It's going to be okay."

"Jason," she said.

"Be still, Clare," he said.

"Mike. Mike!"

"Shh," he said. One of those must be the ex, he thought.

He was moved away from the wreck by paramedics, so he backed up and went into the intersection, directing traffic. It took a long time for them to remove the SUV, pull the Toyota away from the pole, and then it required the Jaws of Life to remove her from the car. He heard her scream as they put her on the stretcher and the sound ripped through him like a knife.

After the ambulance took her away, he asked the fire captain, "She going to be all right?"

"I don't know. Her vitals are iffy. You see it?"

"I was right behind her. She had a green light. The SUV ran the red. I'll put it in my report." And then, he thought, I'll call the hospital.

Clare was wandering around in a fog so thick it was hard to move her limbs. She wasn't sure if she even had her eyes open. There seemed to be a dim light in the distance and she did all she could to move toward it, but it was difficult. She felt as if she were restrained. Something was pulling at her.

There was a figure coming toward her, a shadow. As it neared, the light behind it brightened and he came into view. She gasped as she recognized Mike, the love of her life, still wearing that Air Force flight suit he'd had on nineteen years ago. He stopped several feet in front of her and treated her to one of those bright smiles that just made her melt. "Mike!" she gasped. "Oh, Mike! I knew you'd come back!"

"Hi, Clare."

"Oh, God," she said, weeping, trying to reach for him.

But he didn't come closer. His hands were plunged into his pockets and he kept his distance but he looked so perfectly at home, at peace. "You have to go back, Clare. You have things to do."

"I want to be with you! All I've ever wanted was to be—"

"I can't stay, and neither can you. I'll see you next time." And he turned his back on her and began to walk back into the fog.

Terrified of losing him a second time, she screamed. At first nothing came out, then only the weakest groan. When she tried to reach out to him, to follow him, she was prevented. The force that held her was filled with fear and anger and though she tried to escape it, it held her fast.

So she screamed again—but had no voice.

The fog began to thin, then lift. A light was beginning to penetrate from above and she struggled against it, pinching her eyes closed. The power that was drawing her away from Mike was so jagged, so raw with emotion—not pleasant at all—that she began to thrash in protest. Then her eyes suddenly popped open and there above her was the face of her son.

"Mom!" he said. "Oh, Mom!"

Jason was instantly pushed away, out of her line of vision, while people in scrubs moved in and took over. A woman was injecting something in a tube that dangled above her, the surface she was lying on was being jostled and a man was shouting, "CT's positive. Give her a hundred mics of fentanyl and send her upstairs, stat."

And the world went dark again.

The next time, she woke from a dreamless sleep and looked up into the face of her older sister, Maggie. Nothing was ever more beautiful to her; Maggie always made her feel safe, even when she was chewing her out for something. She tried to smile, but wasn't sure she had succeeded.

"We're all here, Clare," Maggie said. "Dad, Sarah, Jason, Bob. But we're not going to crowd around your bed."

Clare tried to explain that she'd seen Mike, but only a guttural sound escaped.

"Don't try to talk. You're going to be fine, but there will be pain. Just let them drug you out of your mind and try to sleep. Bob and I will take care of Jason. We'll be here."

That woman, who she now knew must be a nurse, was fiddling with her tubes again, and then sleep came. The tube was magic.

She was in and out from then on, having no idea of the length of time in between. Once she lifted a hand to see how much her nails had grown, wondering if it had been days or weeks, but they looked the same. She became increasingly aware of pain, in her throat, back, pelvis, gut, legs.

The last thing she could remember was not getting a speeding ticket. Had she done something wrong? she wondered.

The pain was terrible, but just as terrible was not having

any idea why she was here. She opened her eyes and there was Maggie again. Maggie was so busy—too busy to be sitting around the hospital for hours. Or was it days?

"Hey, 'bout time," Maggie said.

Her hand rose shakily to her neck. "Ugh. My throat."

"I know. It's from the intubation. Here, have a little sip of water."

The cool liquid was welcome but swallowing was very hard. "What? What?" she asked.

"A car accident, Clare. Do you remember anything?"

She shook her head.

"You got broadsided in an intersection. Your injuries were the worst—you lost your spleen and your pelvis is cracked. You're lucky to be alive."

"Oh, God," she moaned.

"You're going to make a full recovery, but it's not going to be an easy road."

"Who hit me?" she was able to ask. "Drunk driver?"

Maggie shook her head. "Nothing as cut-and-dried as that. A young woman in an SUV was fussing with her baby in the car seat while her light was green. When she looked back at the road, it was red and you were in the intersection."

"Oh, God," she said, closing her eyes. "The baby?"

"They're both okay—baby's fine, Mama had a few bruises. She had the SUV. Your Toyota is toast. They had to use the Jaws of Life to get you out. You don't remember anything?" Clare shook her head. "Well, your head is all right, so I guess it's just a stroke of luck that you can't remember."

Clare nodded off again and when she woke Maggie was still there, holding her hand. She stood from the chair she'd been using and leaned over the bed. Seeing her there made Clare feel so cherished. Maggie, a lawyer, wife and mother kept a killer schedule. She couldn't imagine that she'd just drop everything. "Have you been here long?"

"Just a few hours. Today."

"You don't have to stay," Clare whispered.

"I'm going to leave soon," Maggie said. "I just wanted to be sure you're back."

"Did I almost die?" she asked.

"I don't know about that, but your injuries were definitely life threatening. Is the pain terrible?"

It was, but she shook her head. "Roger?" she asked.

Maggie got a look on her face as if she wanted to spit something out. "He's been here. Do you want me to leave word that you want to see him?"

She shook her head. "I want him to stay away."

Maggie obviously couldn't resist a satisfied smile, but all she said was, "Sure."

As time passed, so slowly, Clare saw the faces of all her loved ones leaning over the bed at one time or another, but they were careful not to tire her. Jason was very emotional. He cried and laid his head on her hand and said, "God, Ma, I was so scared. If you died, what would I do?"

She said, "You don't have to worry about that. I'm not going anywhere." And she had it on firm authority from the other side. She had things to do. Things to do?

Her younger sister, Sarah, was holding up, but she looked a little wild-eyed behind those thick glasses, as though this close call had terrified her. She had been twenty-one when their mother died and definitely took it the hardest. Clare touched her hand and said, "It's okay, sweetie. It's going to be okay."

Sarah gave a wan smile. "That's so you," she said. "You're in the hospital, but you're comforting *me*."

Looking at Sarah now, dishwater blond hair pulled severely back, black-rimmed, old-fashioned glasses, no makeup—it was hard to imagine the younger wild child. Maggie and Clare used to call her slut-in-training. Their mother's death had changed all that; had changed Sarah completely.

But another trauma had changed Clare. It was no coincidence that she'd be thinking about that quite a lot while in the hospital. After all—she'd just seen Mike in that ghostlike, after-life appearance he'd made. It caused her life to literally flash before her eyes, sending her back in time over and over.

Right until she was twenty-one Clare had lived a charmed life. She'd been a happy kid from a happy marriage, even as the middle child. Maggie was bossy and Sarah had that sense of entitlement that comes from being youngest, but Clare had good looks, humor, intelligence and luck. She'd done well in school, been popular and was never afraid. She'd hung out with a great group of friends who had all grown up together and at the age of fifteen she fell in love with the star quarterback and homecoming king, Mike Rayburn. He was two years older than she and went to college in Reno, just a short drive from their hometown of Breckenridge, Nevada, a beautiful little town nestled at the base of the majestic Sierras below Lake Tahoe. With the green, plentiful valley filled with crops and grazing animals under snowy peaks, it could pass for Switzerland. It was a sweet life in a magical place where they had played at the lake all summer, skied the mountains all winter.

There was no question but that Clare would go to school in Reno, too, and their romance was hot and steady right through college. After Mike graduated he went into the Air Force, separating them for Clare's last two years, but he gave her a shiny big diamond and told her to spend her last year of college planning their wedding.

Then there had been a hiccup. Er, earthquake.

Mike's younger brother, Pete, who was Clare's age, had been one of her best pals and buddies all through high school. They had graduated together. Pete had never been much on school while Mike had been an honor student. Pete concentrated on having fun. He and Clare would get laughing so hard and so long that Mike, annoyed, would threaten to pound them both. And like big brother, he was a gifted athlete. But because he was more of a fixture in detention than the honor roll, after graduation he had taken a full-time job and some classes at a community college in Breckenridge. Then at the age of twenty-one, ready to finish a degree, he was university shopping. He went to Clare's campus and she was more than thrilled to be his hostess while he looked around.

In the way young men are a bit slower to mature than young ladies, she always thought of him as a kid—skinny, lanky, goofy. She'd been busy doing other things while Pete was maturing and she was a bit shaken to find this kid came to her a grown man, just as handsome and sexy as his older brother. Maybe, just maybe a little more so.

Pete stayed with her and her two roommates while he toured the school, met some of the teachers and coaches, talked to counselors and in general had a look-see. She introduced him to her friends and took him out to the local pub when it was crowded with people and he had a wonderful time…and all her girlfriends went gaga. Then her roommates left for the weekend. Clare fixed Pete a nice big spaghetti dinner and he bought a jug of Chianti as big as a horse's leg. They ate, drank, laughed and told stories late into the night.

Then something happened. She began remembering how much she liked him; realizing how much she'd missed him. They were a little bit drunk when she felt the vibrating tension of his muscular thigh against hers. He touched her hand, he looked into her eyes, he kissed her. He kissed her again. To this day she wasn't sure what happened. It wasn't exactly the first time she'd had a little too much wine, nor the first time a guy had come on to her. She had never cheated on Mike, had never even been tempted. But she was suddenly swept up in some kind of crazy passion right there on the couch with Pete, who was no longer a little brother but a very strong, able and experienced man. Every kiss sent her soaring; his touch thrilled her and she responded with need of her own. Her brain and her judgment took a hike.

Before she knew it she was beneath him, opening herself to him, begging him to come inside, to finish, to give her everything he had. He told her he wanted her, that he couldn't stop, and the fact that he seemed slightly out of control only made her want him more. He thrust and she answered each one with wild craving. He nibbled, caressed, teased and brought her to a shattering climax right in time with his own.

They came slowly to earth and suddenly she was stunned. Mortified. She gasped in horror and said, "Oh my God!"

"Clare, I—"

But she couldn't listen. What had she done? To Mike? To Pete? To *herself?* She fled from that apartment couch into her bedroom, slammed the door and was racked with sobs of remorse through the night. All the while she was thinking that if she felt that terrible, he must hate her for what she'd encouraged him to do to his brother. After all, she had begged him! In the morning when she got up she found a note under the aspirin bottle. "Let's never talk about it. It didn't happen. Pete."

She didn't talk about it, that was for sure, because she was thoroughly ashamed. Clare froze up inside. She had trouble putting together the wedding guest list, couldn't stand to talk about the reception, didn't register her gifts and when she went for a bridal gown fitting, she burst into tears. She was completely miserable and a long way from getting over it. Of course she didn't hear a word from Pete—and she didn't know if that made things better or worse. And if he didn't hate her, at the very least, he would have lost all respect for her.

Mike seemed not to pick up on the trouble during their phone conversations, either because he had so much going on at flight school that he was preoccupied or maybe she was becoming the master of deception. Either way it hardly mattered because just a couple of months later his F-16 went down and he went with it.

Clare was plummeted from despair into a deep well of grief and regret. It was the blackest time of her life. She wondered if she would die of it. She never once met Pete's eyes during the memorial services, not even when she embraced him and they sobbed on each other's shoulders. It was a long, long while before she stopped feeling she had killed Mike with what she had done.

It was two years before she could even manage a girls' night out with her friends, and she adamantly refused any fixing up. There was such an ache in her heart. She wouldn't consider letting herself be that vulnerable again. When she ran into Pete, she could barely talk to him, and he ducked his head away from her eyes. It was obvious to her that his pain was equal to her own.

And then she met Roger; smooth, good-looking Roger. She was lifted up out of the darkness, laughed, looked forward to events and dates. He was such a clever flirt; he could charm the paint off an old Buick. He pursued her with such gusto. She didn't even know she had it in her to be seduced and she felt alive for the first time since Mike's death. When she realized that days passed without her thoughts turning to Mike or her sin against him, she saw in Roger a chance to start her life over. More than that, she fell for him, hard and fast. That was the Roger she had always had trouble leaving—the sweet, sensitive, fun-loving man who pulled her up out of the darkness and into the light. Clare would be forever grateful to him for that. Her friends and family were so relieved to see her smile again, they wholeheartedly encouraged them. They loved Roger, and so did she. She accepted his proposal, which came a little too soon into their relationship, but he had always moved fast. Jason arrived immediately.

Then came the late-night meetings, the trips out of town, being unable to reach him during the day because he was tied up with a client. Once he was home, he could smooth things over with ease—he had this way about him. Irresistible and always so desirable, he banished her edginess in no time.

But it was not how she thought it would be, not how it had been with Mike who was far less charming and fun loving but more reliable. There were lonely times in the dark of night when she rocked her baby—often waiting for Roger to come home hours later than she expected him—that she would fantasize she was waiting for Mike and that she rocked their child. Because of that dirty little secret, because of what she had done before, she worked as hard as humanly possible at being a good wife.

Clare felt guilty about fantasizing Jason was Mike's, until years later when she learned that Roger had first been unfaithful while she was in her pregnancy. There had been a reason why he was always unavailable and late, and her name was Jill. As far as Clare knew, Jill was the first one.

Instead of being her knight in shining armor, Roger became her cross to bear. Her penance.

Much of her adult life had been manipulated around the mere fact that she had made love to her fiancé's brother. Every time she ran into Pete she remained aloof and cool and he looked at her with the saddest eyes—it appeared neither of them would ever recover from what they'd done. She even tried counseling and was honest as a heart attack during her sessions, but still she floundered on in a marriage that wasn't true.

That was another reason she kept taking Roger back—because if she couldn't be forgiving, she couldn't be forgiven. That, and she wanted her life to be worth something. She wanted the family she'd made to survive. And of course there was the fact of Roger, a seductive and charming flirt to the end—and it had worked on her for years.

But then she woke up in a hospital in Reno with every inch of her body throbbing in pain and for the first time in almost twenty years, she realized her marriage had gone on long enough.

It was time to move on.

chapter two

· · · · · · · · · · · · · · · · · · · ·

IF THERE WAS anything on par with being dragged half-dead out of mangled car, it was physical therapy. Every step shot through Clare like dynamite, every stretch came with the agony of the rack. The first thought she had upon waking in the morning was that she was going to suffer the torture of the truly damned. All this was administered by a devilish little creature no bigger than a wood sprite. Her name was Gilda and one should not be fooled by the fact that she was a mere slip of a thing. She had a black heart and the strength of a herd of dragons.

"One more step, come on, one more. Good! Good! Okay, one more…"

"I…hate…you…so…much…."

"Ah, yes—sweet talk. You'll thank me when you're up dancing the rumba again."

"I'm…taking…out…a…contract…on…you…."

"One more, no whining. Good! Good! Okay, how about just one more."

"You're going to suffer. I swear to God!"

Gilda kissed her cheek. "You're tough stuff, Clare. Good

thing you were in such great shape when you got hit—it's paying off."

"You are a mean-spirited witch."

"Yes, so they tell me."

The payoff was that after being abused by Gilda she could have a pain shot, a sponge bath and a nap. Then the company would start to arrive. And with them always the same dilemma—she was bored and lonely in addition to wretchedly uncomfortable, and she was too tired to endure too much visiting. Still, she wanted them to come.

Her younger sister, Sarah, dropped by daily and Maggie came for a little while most afternoons, often bringing Jason with her. Her brother-in-law, Bob, usually made a quick swing by in the evenings—he spent a lot of his workday in Carson City, the capitol of Nevada. And her dad, George, still went to his neighborhood hardware store every day, retirement not even a part of his agenda despite the fact that he was in his sixties. One thing had changed in his schedule—he was now taking a lunch hour, which he spent at the hospital. And he would sometimes stop by later in the evening on his way home from work. And George's cleaning lady, Dotty, made it a point to come to the hospital most days with some kind of sweet treat meant mainly for the hospital staff. "Soften them up," Dotty said. "They'll go easier on you if you feed them."

Clare's mom, Fran, fell ill with cancer when Jason was only three. It took her quickly. Sarah was devastated by the loss and at twenty-one, moved back into her dad's house, but she proved to be no help at all. Both of them grew thin and messy, so Maggie and Clare pooled their resources and hired Dotty to clean twice a week and stock the refrigerator with nutritious meals. George protested, but soon he gained some weight and his stained clothes were clean and pressed. Sarah, so lost there for a while, had a maternal figure to watch over her.

Dotty was a widow just a couple of years older than George. When they first found her, she had a total of four families she worked for, but now she was down to George, who she said would have to bury her to get rid of her. "I don't like him that much," she said, lying through her false teeth, "but it's obvious he is useless on his own. And if I can do one kind thing for his departed wife, it will be to make sure he doesn't join her too soon."

The one person in Clare's life who hadn't put in an appearance was Roger. But in the way things that seem too good to be true aren't, he showed up. He got past the sentries at the door. He waited until evening, just before visiting hours were over, and brought with him that pathetic face that said, *Oh I'm such a bad boy, you must take pity on me for I suffer so.* What poor Roger didn't know was that the second she saw him that vision came into her mind—of a slim blonde on top of him. And it infuriated her anew.

"Clare," he said. "I've been trying to see you, but your sisters said you didn't want to see me."

She put on her call light. "That's right, Roger. Go away. I'm an injured woman and you're making the pain worse."

"I want to talk to you about Jason," he said.

She turned off the call light.

"I think he should be staying with me," Roger said.

"What on earth for?" she asked, genuinely perplexed. "You're busy all day and most evenings. What's he supposed to do?"

"We'll get in the car pool for school. I'll lighten my schedule. He can have his old room."

She thought about this for less than ten seconds. "No," she

said. "He's fine at Maggie's and, in case you haven't noticed, he's still very angry. You're going to have to give him more time and make up with him before you coax him home."

"How can I make up with him when he doesn't want to see me?"

"I'm sorry, Roger, I know it makes you feel bad, but he's adamant, he doesn't want to spend time with you."

"You can talk to him about that."

A few days ago, pre-cracked pelvis and major surgery, she probably would have. But the cause of this current separation had created such terrible anger in Jason. This had been a long time coming; she had always dreaded the day her son would find out that his dad, the object of such admiration, was screwing around on his mother. Jason felt completely abandoned by his father, though Roger kept trying to reconcile with him.

The night it happened was awful beyond belief. Clare had chosen the time specifically because Jason wasn't going to be home. He was spending the night at a friend's house. Clare confronted Roger about his latest affair, which she had researched thoroughly. He denied it and she laid out her proof—copies of bills, cell phone calls, et cetera. She knew exactly who the woman was—one of his many clients to whom he sold insurance. A lot of regrettable things were said, but the worst were:

"Okay, maybe I did have a stupid, meaningless little fling—a guy can make a mistake!"

"A meaningless little fling? There have been over a dozen. Maybe many dozens!"

"Well, you're not exactly welcoming in the sack, you know, Miss Ice Queen."

"What do you expect? I've had to worry about disease!"

"When have I ever given you—"

Roger's eyes had grown large as he looked past Clare and his expression became stricken. She whirled to find Jason standing there, the in-line skates he'd come home to fetch dangling from his hand.

"My God, Jason," she had said, chasing him as he fled from the house.

Roger rattled the bed rail to regain her attention. "Clare? You'll talk to him about that? Tell him, regardless of our family problems, his place is with his father."

In her mind she saw that blonde again; she remembered the night Jason overheard their fight.

"No," she said. "No, Roger. We don't have 'family problems.' You have a problem. I'm not sure what it is—sex addiction? Being a pathological liar? Doesn't matter. The fact is, I don't have a problem and Jason seems to be doing fine. He's had a big scare with my accident and I'm not going to make it even worse by forcing him to go to your house. We'll deal with your relationship later."

"My house? It's still our house, Clare. And there are legal—"

Her hand came crashing down on his and he yanked it off the bed rail with a yelp. "What the...?"

"Listen to me, Roger. Don't you *dare* fuck with me now. You leave Jason alone or, so help me God, I will make you pay! Now go home and leave me alone. No one will bother you—you can screw your brains out with any hoyden you can find!"

He looked at her as though cut to the quick. "That's nice, Clare. Very nice. As though your accident hasn't been a big shock to me, too?"

"Oh bite me, Roger."

He shook his head sadly. "I don't know what's happened to you."

"It's very simple—I got smacked up the side of the head and

all your bullshit fell out and some sense seeped in. Now *go!*"
She flipped on the nurse's call light for emphasis.

"Fine," he said. "Fine." He turned and left.

It was amazing how good that felt. She didn't seem to even
want a pain shot. It was as if drawing that line in the sand with
him, firmly for once, was all the narcotic she needed.

She saw someone peeking in the door. George had a real
evil grin on his leathery face. "Oh, Clare," he said. "That's
the best entertainment your old dad has had in ages."

So how did they get past that trauma of Jason overhearing?
He skipped the night at his friend's house and Clare took him
with her to the Hilton in Lake Tahoe where they got a plush
two-bedroom suite. She bought them bathing suits in one of
the shops there, and ordered room service and a movie. They
went swimming at midnight. She told him as much of the
truth as she thought he could bear—but she could see it really didn't get through his anger.

The real credit went to George, both for being there for
Jason and somehow managing not to kill Roger. George explained to Jason that Roger was a screw-up when it came to
flirting with women and had really disappointed and let down
Clare. It was probably a good idea for them to separate, but
what George wanted Jason to understand was that while Roger
seemed to have this weakness, he had many strengths—he'd
been a pretty good father and was proud of Jason. He cared
about him and was suffering, terribly, because he'd disappointed his son. "So what? He should have thought of that
before," Jason had said.

"You're right, he should have. But none of us is perfect,
so let's not throw stones. I know you're all bent out of shape,
and maybe I don't blame you, but don't nurse this too long,

Jason. Your dad loves you, and you're only as mad as you are
because you love him."

"You're saying I should forgive him?"

"I'm saying I hope we get to that pretty soon, yes. Because whether you believe me or not, the two of you need
each other."

Clare topped that off by getting Jason in a counselor's office, too. She intended to do all she could for him, feeling so
damn awful about not bolting the door that traumatic night
against his possible surprise return. What they finally came to
learn was that once Jason knew his father had been unfaithful, he immediately felt that Roger had cheated on Jason, too.
No wonder he was pissed.

Lying around in a hospital bed, Clare had plenty of time
to think about her family, especially her sisters, her two best
friends. Maybe they hadn't been best friends growing up, but
they were in adulthood. As Clare spent so many long hours of
the day in pain, her sisters putting their own lives on hold to sit
at her bedside, she was reminded constantly of how lucky she
was to have them. She couldn't get through this without them.

George and Fran McCarthy had three pretty green-eyed
daughters. Maggie came first, Clare three years later, and then
Sarah, the caboose, who was born six years after Clare. They
couldn't be more different if they had been born on different planets.

Maggie was a typical firstborn overachiever, who had excelled in high school and college and attended law school,
graduating with honors. She married a lawyer and had two
daughters who were now thirteen and fifteen; they were sometimes Jason's closest friends, sometimes his bane. Hillary and
Lindsey.

Maggie, age forty-two, lived in a perfect world and though she worked hard and put in long hours, her clothing was always chic, her shorter-than-short light brown hair impeccably cropped, her nails immaculate and there were never circles under her eyes. She had the wonderful high cheekbones that can carry off that coiffure and looked sexy as hell, except that she downplayed the sex appeal with conservative suits, tools of her trade in court. She had household help, of course, in that not-so-modest Breckenridge manse of hers, but even on Ramona's days off, there was never a speck of dust or so much as a throw pillow out of place. Maggie was all about perfection and control. Yet she was loving—but in a very crisp and unflappable way. Nonsentimental. Maggie was the one to call if you needed something taken care of; if there was a problem to solve. If you were wallowing in self-pity or feeling fat or in love, forget Maggie. She had no time for petty self-indulgences.

And then there was Sarah, thirty-three. As a teen, Sarah had been in constant trouble. She lied to her parents, broke curfew, went to parties she was forbidden to attend, lost her virginity at fourteen and found school to be a gross inconvenience so she dropped out in her senior year and moved out of her parents' house the second she turned eighteen. Sarah smoked, drank to excess, wore tight, provocative clothing, and when she did come home for family gatherings, she always managed to find a guy to bring along who looked like a member of a biker gang. Sarah knew her mom was hopelessly disappointed in her; Sarah and her mother had been locked in a bloody battle over Sarah's wild and loose behavior since Sarah was fourteen. Then Fran fell ill and died without that being resolved and Sarah crumbled. She hit bottom and suf-

fered through a frightening depression that required medical
attention.

In therapy, Sarah discovered art. She eventually went back
to school, got a degree in art and began to create and do some
teaching. She painted, threw pots, sculpted and wove deco-
rative rugs, throws and tapestries. A true gift emerged, and
also a focus so intense she would become lost in her work.
She opened a small studio that grew into an art supply shop
where she also gave occasional classes to small groups of as-
piring artists. With that avocation came not only renewed
health but a disinterest in those bad habits and slutty clothes.
She tossed off the contact lenses in preference for glasses so
her eyes wouldn't dry out if she was consumed by a project
for hours and hours, chose clothes that were loose and comfortable to work in, had no time for makeup and pulled her
hair back into a severe ponytail or bun. At thirty-three, still
living with George, she had become dowdy and spinsterish.

Of the three daughters, Clare lived the most average life.
She was a stay-at-home mom who did some volunteering
and substitute teaching. She had become an excellent decorator, chef and homemaker. A terrific wife. For what good
it had done.

Clare loved her sisters deeply. She was probably closer to
Maggie, given that they were nearer in age and both tended
to mother Sarah. Much to Sarah's annoyance, they still worried about her and protected her whenever it seemed like
what she needed.

It was only Maggie to whom Clare confided the events
preceding her accident. In earlier times she had felt the need
to explain reasons for her separation from Roger to her sisters
and dad, though they were hardly surprised. They'd taken
him for a hopeless philanderer long before Clare put a name

to it. She hadn't said anything about the night of the accident, however. She had already left Roger and her family patiently, hopefully, awaited the divorce. No need to drag him through any more mud and risk having the whole shoddy experience further damage Jason.

But when they had a moment alone in the room, she told Maggie.

"He said he was going to be out of town on business, so I went over to the house to grab a few kitchen things and leave him a birthday card I forced Jason to sign. I was actually feeling kind of sorry for him—alone on his birthday. I'd barely arrived, standing in the foyer, when I heard a sound from the bedroom. He was banging some blonde."

Maggie surprised her by letting go a whoop of a laugh. "My God! How can one man be so predictable!" She leaned closer to the hospital bed. "Is that why you never saw the SUV coming? Your mind wandering back to the scene of the slime?"

"No, that's just it," she said. "Just a few minutes before the accident, I was pulled over for speeding. I didn't get a ticket, but the officer followed me a little. I remember stopping at the red light and I remember it turning green. He was right behind me."

"He must have seen the whole thing! That's how the police got the witness report that she had blown the light!"

"Probably. I should thank him. But maybe if he'd let me speed..."

"Yeah, then maybe it would've been *your* fault."

"I hadn't thought of that."

"Let me ask you something. Does Roger think he upset you enough so that you weren't paying attention and got broadsided?"

She took a heavy breath. "I don't know what Roger thinks

and I don't care. He's great at acting guilty, but since his be-havior never changes, it's probably all crap."

"Oh man," Maggie said. "I think you've finally suffered enough."

"We're not going to tell anyone about that night."

"Are you protecting poor Roger?"

"Hell, no. But I think Jason has enough on his plate."

Maggie nodded resolutely. "Agreed. Time to let the kid heal."

Clare had been in the hospital for over two weeks and the rains of March were giving way to the sunshine of April, which Clare could only view through a veil of pain. Within a week she would be released, though she would be on crutches for a while and back for physical therapy, probably lasting months.

Maggie let her know she'd be coming into money. She was using her attorney skills to negotiate with the offending driver's insurance company for a settlement. "I'm not going to have to sue her, am I?" Clare asked.

"Not a chance," Maggie assured her. "You're badly hurt, a police report puts her in the wrong and believe me, they're going to settle generously. I'll see to that. You should have a nice nest egg—which is the least you deserve. The details will take time."

Police report. She was reminded about finding and thank-ing the police officer who stopped her, though she wasn't sure how to go about that. And then, late in the day after company had gone and the lights in the ward had begun to dim, he ap-peared in her doorway. It took her a moment to place him as his dark blue uniform had been replaced by a sweater and a pair of jeans. The absence of the bulletproof vest didn't seem to diminish that broad chest, thick neck and strong shoulders. As she studied the young face that peeked in her doorway, it wasn't until he flashed that winning grin that she realized who it was. "You!" she said.

He came into the room and pulled a bunch of flowers inside a cellophane wrap from behind his back. The kind you'd pick up at a convenience store. "Hi," he said. "How are you doing?"

She struggled to lift herself in the bed. "I'm... Well, I've been better. But coming along. I was just thinking about you."

"Well, that's something. You've been on my mind, too."

"About that night... I think I need to thank you. I was going to track you down, but I don't know your name."

"Sam," he said. "Jankowski." He glanced about the room. "Is there anywhere to put these? I'm such a dunce, I never thought about a vase...."

"Don't worry. Just put them here," she said, touching the tray table. "One of the nurses will bring an extra water jug later. So, thank you."

"For...?"

"I don't really know. For catching me speeding before I *caused* the accident. For not giving me a ticket when I deserved one. For— Were you the witness who said it wasn't my fault?"

"What I saw was in my report. It was an awful wreck. I sure was relieved you made it."

She giggled stupidly and then covered her mouth. "Sorry," she said. "I might be a little loopy. I just had a pain shot."

He stood right over her bed, where her sisters and Jason had all done so much time. But his presence seemed out of place.

"How much longer do you have to be in the hospital?" he asked.

"Actually, I'm going home in a few days. Depending on the

doctor. And then I'll have physical therapy for a long time. Probably months."

"Jeez, good thing I stopped by. I didn't want to miss you."

"Thanks. But as you can see, even though I look like hell, I'm going to be fine. Eventually."

"You look pretty good, as a matter of fact. Total recovery?"

"Probably. Ninety-five percent chance, as long as nothing weird happens."

"Fantastic. Damn, that was lucky."

"Well, depending on your perspective...."

"I mean, you could've been killed. Do you remember the accident?"

"Not a bit. Not a piece. I remember the light turning green. Otherwise, nothing."

"Good."

"I was unconscious...."

"Not the whole time," he said. "You drifted in and out. Asked for someone named Jason."

"My son."

"And...Mike, I think."

"Oh, God," she said weakly.

"The husband?" he asked.

"No." Could it be she was seeing Mike at that moment? At the accident and not later, in the hospital? Was time altogether different when visiting the other side? "Mike," she repeated. "An old fiancé. Many years ago. Nineteen. He was in the Air Force and was killed in a plane crash."

"Wow. He must be someone you think about all the time."

"No. No, I don't anymore. Years ago I did. I couldn't seem to run him out of my mind, but then I married, had a child and... Listen, can I tell you something crazy? And you wouldn't burst out laughing or tell anyone or anything?"

He shrugged. "If you want."

"I saw him. Mike. Right before I woke up in the trauma center. I was in a foggy place with some light out there in the distance. And he came right out of the mist, said, 'Hi, Clare,' and then when I cried out to him and tried to reach for him, he said, 'You have to go back. You have things to do. I'll see you next time.'"

To his credit, his eyes didn't take on that bug-eyed, shocked expression that said he thought she was nuts. Instead, he smiled. "I heard that sort of thing can happen."

"Maybe I dreamed it," she offered.

"Or maybe it happened," he said. "I never rule anything out."

"Thanks," she said, smiling back at him. "That's nice of you to say."

"Oh, I wasn't trying to be nice. Seriously, I've heard those stories. You never know, huh?"

"Yeah."

They were quiet a moment, looking at each other. Then he cleared his throat. "Mmm. This is kind of awkward, but maybe after you get a little better, maybe we could meet for coffee."

Dumbfounded, she stared at him, gape mouthed, until she realized she must look as if she'd just been hit in the back of the head with a two-by-four. "Coffee?"

"Whatever." He shrugged. "How about you give me a phone number where I can reach you. At the very least, I'd like to check up on you, see how your recovery is going."

Oh, that was it, she thought. Her features recovered. It wasn't as if he was asking her out on a date. He was bonded to her by that accident, which probably shook him up. "God, forgive me," she said. "It must be the drugs. I thought you were asking me out on a *date*."

There was that smile again. Dazzling. "Just coffee. Something like a date could take as many as two coffees." Then he laughed. And she laughed.

"If you don't mind my asking, how old are you?"

"Twenty-nine," he said. "And you're thirty-nine."

"How do you know that?"

"I've gotten really good at that driver's license thing," he said. "So, when you're up to coffee?" She nodded. "How about that phone number?"

That was kind of cool, she thought. That fantasy, though brief, that this drop-dead gorgeous young guy was asking her out, even though she was feeling really old, not to mention greasy haired and makeupless. But, he didn't really look all that young. He could even pass for thirty-two.

Thirty-two, Clare? she thought. Get over yourself. The guy wants to have coffee to assure himself that the banged-up heap they pulled out of a wreck was going to be fine. Just fine.

"Sure," she said. "Got a pencil?"

The nurse stuck her head in. "Visiting hours are ending, sir," she said.

"Okay," he said. Then to Clare he said, "I thought about badging her so she'd let me stay longer, but I'm really not here on official business. And you probably need the rest." He reached over to the bedside commode where the clipboard and pen sat. Then like a kid, felt-tip poised over the palm of his hand, he said, "Shoot."

She gave him a number and added, "That's a cell phone."

"Good then. So, take it easy and I'll be in touch."

Clare nurtured that little fantasy about the younger man for a good twenty-four hours. Then when Maggie dropped by the next day it got wiped away by a bigger matter. "Oh, I keep forgetting to tell you—Pete Rayburn called me. He heard about the accident and wanted to know if you were all right."

Clare instantly turned her head away, almost a reflex now. That discomfort, that shame. She wouldn't want anyone to see it in her eyes.

Maggie touched her hair. "Does Mike's death still hurt so much? Even after all these years?"

Clare looked back at her sister. "Sometimes at the strangest moment it will come back—a suggestion, a name, like Pete's—and I remember how much it hurt then. You know?"

"Sure."

"What did you tell him?"

"That you were going to be fine—but there would be some serious recovering to do and it could take months."

"Good. And how is he?"

"You know, I didn't even think to ask. But I assume he's fine. Divorced a few years ago I heard, and still teaching and coaching. Do you ever see him or his parents?"

"I've run into him a few times," she said. In fact, if there hadn't been that terrible indiscretion, she might've spent a lot of time with the Rayburns, when they could have helped each other get through Mike's death. "That was nice of him. To call."

And that's another thing to take care of, she thought. Put it on the to-do list. Get divorced, find a job and make a point of seeing Pete to put that whole business finally in the past. He probably needed it as much as she did.

chapter three

· ·

SARAH'S LITTLE SHOP was in the center of town, and she typically put in very long days there. It was customary for her to open the art supply store at around ten in the morning and close at six, but after dinner with her dad she would go back to work in her studio, which was behind the store, sometimes until quite late. In fact, she could get lost in some project—a woven throw, an oil painting, a sculpture—and forget time altogether, looking up only when her eyes burned with exhaustion, finding suddenly it was two or three in the morning. She was so focused when creating, the outside world seldom intruded.

That was before the accident, three weeks ago. Since then, Sarah had spent minimal time at the shop. She put a sign in the window: Illness In The Family: Call 555-2323 For Today's Hours Of Operation. Most of her customers were regulars who knew the family and were aware of the accident. Most of the town had heard about the accident—it made the papers.

Sarah opened the shop for the sale of art supplies a few hours a day, spending the rest of her time with Clare at the hospital. Worry had clouded her usual single-minded drive to create.

But today, a beautiful and sunny April day, as she closed the shop before five, there was a special lift in her heart because after three weeks, Clare was finally coming home. Clare's town house was out of the question, given the stairs to the bedrooms, so George was bringing her home to his house. His and Sarah's house. And the relief Sarah was feeling was tremendous. The whole family would be at George's to welcome her.

Of course, Clare wasn't well yet. She was up walking, but still in pain, unable to sleep through the night without drugs. Sarah would gladly get up to make sure she was medicated and comfortable. The bed in her old bedroom at Dad's was too soft and low, so George rented a hospital bed. It could be a long and difficult few months, most of the summer at least, through which Clare would struggle with pain, physical therapy, making slow but steady progress; Sarah would do anything to help.

But Clare would be *home*. After nearly losing her, this was paramount.

Of course Jason was coming to stay, as well. He'd been at Maggie's for three weeks and Lindsey and Hillary were on his last nerve.

When Sarah got home she was so happy to see all the cars in the drive and on the street. It looked as though everyone was present and accounted for, including Clare. No one would ever know how much seeing Clare in that hospital bed had shaken her. Besides her art and her shop, all she had in her life was the family. She didn't have girlfriends or boyfriends, and that was perfectly all right with her because her days and nights were busy with her little business and her creative projects. Her dad, sisters, nieces and nephew were everything to her! Her sisters were always trying to coax her into being more social, but she honestly didn't know where she'd find the time. And she certainly wouldn't take it from family.

Her sisters were her best friends.

When she walked in the house she met that wonderful noise of family making things happen in the kitchen. She spied Clare at the end of the long oak table in the large kitchen. She'd spent many an hour studying there, before and after what she'd come to refer to as the dark years. Clare was sitting on a pillow, a strained look on her face, as though she might be in pain. Sarah went straight to her, leaned down and kissed her forehead. "I'm so happy you're home. Are you okay?"

Clare grimaced. "My pain pill hasn't quite kicked in yet. I'll be okay."

"Can I get you anything?"

"No, thank you, honey."

Sarah went to the stove, where Maggie, George's housekeeper, Dotty, and Maggie's thirteen-year-old, Hillary, were surrounding a big pot. "What's happening over here?" she asked.

"Stew. Aunt Clare's request." She lifted a spoon. "Taste?"

"Hmm," she said appreciatively. "Not enough salt."

"Told you," Hillary said to Dotty.

Maggie slipped an arm around Sarah's waist and kissed her cheek. "How's the shop, sweetie?"

"The same." She shrugged. "Fine."

"Are you losing weight?"

"You ask me that once a week."

"Are you?"

"I don't think so." But she was, and she knew it. Thing was, she could get involved in some art project and forget to eat. She could be consumed by a bust or throw or painting. Her work didn't bring in a lot of money, but she did have a following. And her major accomplishment of late was to have a tapestry of a towering brown bear on a snowy ledge hanging in a ski lodge in Lake Tahoe.

But it wasn't art that had cost her a few pounds. It was the fear and worry Clare's accident had brought on.

Jason came into the kitchen with a sweater for his mother, draping it around her shoulders. "Hi, Aunt Sarah," he said.

She smiled her greeting.

Maggie got her girls setting the table for nine. This kind of gathering didn't usually happen during the week, but it was a tradition to have Sunday dinner together whenever possible. While Maggie had the biggest house and Clare's home with Roger had been larger than George's, everyone still liked coming back here every week, cooking together, spending a few hours with family, sitting around that long oak table. A few years ago they had started having Dotty from time to time, as well; she was as much family as anyone.

Maggie's husband, Bob, came into the kitchen carrying two drinks. He handed one to Maggie and dropped an arm around Sarah's shoulders. "How's my little artsy-fartsy?"

She merely leaned against him. Bob was so steady, dependable.

No one had to be called. As the plates began to land on the tabletop, George appeared from the living room with Lindsey, and people began to take their places. Maggie and Dotty brought the stew, salad and bread. Bob poured milk into the kids' glasses; George fetched himself a beer. There was a little scuffle between Jason and Hillary for the seat next to Clare; Jason won. Sarah could've gotten up and yielded hers next to her sister, but no. She wouldn't give it up.

Before the plates were full, someone's cell phone chimed.

Lindsey looked at her phone and said, "I have to get this," and jumped up from the table.

"'I have to get this,'" Bob repeated, humorously. "She's fifteen."

"There's a guy," Hillary said, clearly having no intention of protecting her sister's secrets.

"What guy?" Maggie asked.

"He's a junior," she said meanly. "A football player."

"Christopher Mattingly," Jason said. "He's gonna start next year."

Sarah felt herself smile. Her nieces were so gorgeous and smart, there would be no shortage of young men. Hopefully they would handle these years better than she had. With the force of Maggie and Bob to watch over them, surely they would be safe.

There was passing and chatter, except that Clare, who was often talkative, was quieter than usual. That was okay, Sarah thought. Because she was getting better; things were getting back to normal. She folded her hands over her plate and let her eyes gently close for a moment, enjoying the sounds of her family around her.

"You okay, honey?" Clare asked.

"Yes. I'm just so relieved that everyone is back together again."

"You don't do so well with change, do you, kiddo?" Clare asked.

"Oh, I'm not as fragile as everyone thinks," she said. But because of this close call in her family, she realized she had kept herself too isolated. Too safe. She vowed to take more chances. A little risk now and then. Maybe open up her life a little so that art and family wasn't the totality of her existence.

However, she wasn't sure how that was done.

★ ★ ★

Leaving the hospital was far more complicated than Clare imagined. First of all, when she left Roger months before, she found herself that cute little town house to rent—a town house full of stairs with a community washer and dryer. She didn't know how long it was going to take to be pain free. "Everybody is different, healing time varies," the orthopedist had said. No one knew how long a person's cracked pelvis was going to hurt, how long walking and lifting and climbing stairs would be impossible and then merely difficult.

Because her recovery would involve many weeks, maybe months, Maggie immediately and without being asked, stepped in on Clare's behalf and negotiated with the landlord to cancel her lease. It was very quickly done. Clare had rented the town house as a temporary base anyway. Part of her plan had been to eventually find a larger, more permanent home for herself and Jason, with her share of equity from the house she and Roger shared, an amount to be determined later, in a divorce. Now there would be more than one settlement to help pad her purse—one from the accident, one from the divorce. Both of those would take as long to settle as her recovery would be, if not longer. Maggie had warned her that dealing with the insurance company would be simple, but not fast. And she hadn't even filed for divorce from Roger yet.

But as May came in bright and warm, Clare found that living with George, Sarah and Jason, with Dotty ever present, was getting a little crowded. She liked her space; she'd get a little bristly when surrounded by too many people. Yet, the prospect of house hunting was too daunting to even imagine.

Dotty came to George's place almost every day, to make sure Clare had everything she needed. But she talked constantly and bleached Jason's undershorts with such gusto they turned into mere threads in no time. When the good house-keeper went out to replace them, she bought them too small. "I don't know if I'm better off going commando or having my nuts squished all day," he complained. "Besides that, if she doesn't quit asking me who I'm talking to on the phone, I might kill her."

"Patience," Clare said. "This is temporary."

After a month with George, Clare could see that very soon she could live on her own with a little help around the house, a problem she could throw a little money at—preferably Roger's money. But she had no house.

Except, she did have a house. She had walked out of it with practically nothing, assuming that in the divorce settlement she would get to take some of the things she treasured plus a tidy settlement out of the equity, investments made during the marriage, plus half of the nest egg accrued during their sixteen years together. Roger screwed around, but he had been a successful businessman. He'd made plenty of money. It might've been shortsighted of her at the time, leaving so suddenly, but since seeing the blonde in her bed, the thought of that master bedroom she had once found so luxurious and comfortable had lost all its appeal.

However, there was a guest room and bath on the ground level. She could live there, manage the downstairs easily with her crutches, and rely on Jason to get up and down the stairs as necessary.

She could not live with Roger, though. And neither could her son. Just trying to get him to visit his father had so far proved impossible.

If she'd thought it through, she could have suggested that she and Roger temporarily trade homes—he could have her town house, she could have the home she'd lived in for ten years. But thinking things through while lying in a hospital bed in excruciating pain had not been possible.

She called Maggie and said, "I wonder if you could do me a favor. Would you be willing to suggest to Roger that he move out of our house and let me have it when I'm ready to live on my own again? That's going to be real soon."

Maggie didn't respond at once, but finally in a voice both surprised and pleased said, "I'd be more than happy to."

Maggie had always felt a bit underappreciated by her family. Here she was with her degree in law, a successful practice, an enormous number of important contacts, and they not only rarely asked her for help, they sometimes eschewed her advice. It was exactly the opposite to what other attorneys complained of. In fact, her own father was going to pay another lawyer to do his will and living trust. Sometimes it was insulting.

Every time Clare began making noises about divorcing Roger, Maggie tried to counsel her. Clare had always been more than willing to complain about her marriage, but she was never prepared to discuss doing something about it. But the accident had changed everything. Clare needed Maggie to deal with the insurance company, the lease on the town house, and now this. Maggie was secretly thrilled. And she was going to do right by her sister.

She took a large chunk out of her busy day, putting paying clients on hold, to track down Roger. She went to his office in downtown Breckenridge, not really expecting to find him there. Roger liked to be out and about and did most of his business, and his running around, all over this town and those nearby. At least that was what she expected—to have to chase him down at a restaurant or client's home. But his secretary reported him home sick.

Hah! she thought. She decided her trip to the house would be a mere formality, for he would not be there. His illness was an excuse given to the secretary, surely. Roger was probably in some no-tell motel. Or... Maybe with Clare pinned down at their dad's he was using the house as some trysting place. All the better. She'd love to catch him in the act and make him feel like the lowlife he was.

So she rang the bell and banged forcefully on the door.

It opened quickly. "Maggie?" he said in question.

She did a double take. There stood Roger looking worse than she'd ever seen him. His clothes looked as though he'd slept in them, his thick mane of golden hair was on the greasy side and his eyes were red rimmed.

"Jesus, Roger, you look like hell," she said in surprise.

"Yeah? Well, what did you expect?" he asked, turning and walking back into the house. He headed down the hall toward the family room where the television could be heard softly droning.

She was left to follow, thinking this was an odd twist. Roger was handsome, damn him. And he pampered his looks, especially that Robert Redford hair. He was fussy about his clothes being both stylish and perfectly kept. And what was with the watery, pink eyes? Maybe he really was sick. He had that look of a killer cold.

She caught up with him just as he was sinking into the sofa and picking up a drink of amber liquid that was not apple juice. For a moment she just stood there, looking like a lawyer. She wore one of her many navy-blue suits, pumps, and held her briefcase. She glanced at her watch—two-thirty. For all his crimes, he was not an irresponsible drinker.

Roger sipped. "What's this all about?" she asked. "You're a wreck. And you're drinking in the afternoon?"

"Things haven't been exactly stress free around here," he said, taking a final sip and putting down the empty glass.

"What's wrong?"

"What's *wrong?*" he bellowed. "My wife damn near dies, then when she does recover she won't even talk to me, my son doesn't want to spend time with me, and what am I supposed to do? Huh? Huh?"

"Oh damn it, you're drunk."

"I'm *not* drunk. I want to be drunk, but I'm hopelessly sober."

Maggie walked into the room, but she didn't want to get too close to him. He was disgusting at the moment. So she took a superior position at the breakfast bar, leaning more than sitting on the high stool. "You and Clare are separated and she tells me there will be a divorce. This isn't news. I've seen you probably a dozen times since she moved out. You were holding up as your usual perky self." And then she added sarcastically, "Like you always do during your separations."

"Oh yeah? Well this is a little different, don't you think? She's *hurt!* I want to take care of her. Help her. And Jason." Then he rested his elbows on his knees and hung his head dejectedly.

"Look, Roger—I know what happened between you and Clare the night of the accident, so don't get all pitiful on me. You were doing some blonde when Clare stopped by the house."

He lifted his head to look at her, his eyes mean. "I'm not at all surprised you know about that. Clare usually can't wait to air my indiscretions."

"Don't make this about Clare! I don't believe she did anything wrong."

"We were separated. She wouldn't give me the time of day.

I didn't think it was against the rules. Besides, don't you see how that makes it even worse? I keep letting her down, over and over. All I want is a chance to help her. To make amends."

Breckenridge was a small town. It rested in the valley a mere half hour from Carson City, just eleven miles beneath Lake Tahoe and the snowy peaks of the Sierras. There were only fifteen thousand people, though a lot of tourists passed through on a regular basis en route to Reno, Tahoe or the Capitol. Residents ran into each other all the time and it was a damn hard place to keep a secret. Roger, despite his shabby marital habits, happened to be popular. He was extremely social. He was a respected insurance guy; he took good care of his clients. Sometimes too good, especially the women.

But this was a Roger she'd never seen before. He looked pathetic. She wished she could feel sorry for him.

"Well, Roger, as it happens you can help her. That's why I'm here. She sent me on an errand." He lifted his head. "Clare's been with my dad, as you no doubt already know, and she can't handle the town house she was leasing, so we let it go. The stairs, you know. She's going to be struggling with things like that for at least a couple more months." He dropped his head as though in agony. She tried to ignore him but found herself saying, "Hey, she's doing very well! Her physical therapy is coming along great! But—and you can probably understand this—she doesn't want to stay with Dad much longer. I think maybe Dotty is driving her nuts. She wants to be on her own. And she just isn't up to searching for and renting a single-level house. So she asked me to ask you if you'll give her the house."

This time when he lifted his head, he actually had a hopeful gleam in his eyes. "The house?" he echoed.

"Uh-huh. She can use the downstairs guest room and bath.

She won't have to go upstairs at all. And Jason can have his old room. It's already furnished, mostly by Clare, in fact. It'll be perfect."

He got to his feet and began tucking in his shirt. He ran a hand through his hair. "She wants to move home?"

"Well," she said, "not exactly, Roger. She'd like you to move out."

"What? Did she say that?"

"Oh yes. Very specifically."

"But I can *help* her! I can take *care* of her!"

Maggie straightened from the stool. "Roger, that's not going to happen. She's not interested in sharing a house with you again. Now, it's much easier for you to find your own place...You're going to have to do that eventually, you know."

"I'm not giving her the house unless she lets me stay, too. I'll stay upstairs. I'll be able to help out."

"Okay, now look," she said sternly. "I don't think she wants to expedite the divorce, given her condition, so let's not push it. All right? Here are the choices—you can refuse to vacate and we'll just proceed with the divorce settlement in which she will naturally be asking for the house along with other things, or you can be a good sport and let Clare and Jason move back in while you reside elsewhere. Those are the only two options."

"She said that?"

No, she hadn't. "Yes, exactly," Maggie lied. Well, Clare had implied it. What she'd said was that it was either Dad's or Roger's house without Roger. That business about expediting the divorce was along the lines of Lawyer's Privilege.

Roger hung his head again. He picked up his glass and walked over to the wet bar. He poured himself another slug and threw it back. Then he turned to Maggie. "Will you ask her one more time? If she'll let me take care of her?"

This was too funny. Roger taking care of anyone. To hear Clare tell it, Roger couldn't seem to ferry his own dirty shorts to the laundry bin, much less do something for another human being. He excelled at three things—looking good, selling insurance and banging women who were not his wife.

Clare had said, however, Roger could be very supportive when Clare was in need, though those times were very infrequent. Nonetheless...

"I will ask her one more time."

"Thank you, Maggie."

"God, you are so pathetic. Snap out of it, will you?"

"Maggie, I know you have no respect for me, but I love her, I do. I'm devoted to her. I'm a stupid idiot, I've treated her so badly, but honestly, the thought of losing her in that accident changed everything for me."

"You've got to stop drinking, take a shower and go to work," she said.

"But you'll ask her?"

"I said I would. And if the answer is still no?"

Head drop again. He turned and faced the bar, leaning on braced hands. "She can have anything she wants," he said.

She stood there watching his back for a moment, but he wasn't turning around. "Thanks, Roger. I'll be in touch."

Maggie went back to her office for the rest of the afternoon. She could have called Clare and asked her the loaded question, but wanted to be face-to-face in case Clare revisited earlier fits of indecision and even thought about giving Roger another chance. Maggie considered lying and not asking the question. The only thing that prevented her from doing so was the possibility of that conniving Roger telling on her. But, she fully intended to talk Clare off the ledge if she had to.

So she went to Clare.

"You are looking so much better," she remarked. And Clare really was. Those first few weeks after the accident she had become so thin, pale and wasted looking, her face in the constant grimace of pain. But that was easing now and she'd not only put on a couple of pounds, she was able to primp a bit. Her hair was shiny, her face had color.

"Thanks. I think I'm going to live."

"How's the pain?"

"I can't get through the night yet, but as long as I get a nap, my days are pretty manageable. Did you talk to Roger?"

They were seated in the family room. Jason was at the kitchen table with his schoolbook open while Dotty chopped vegetables at the counter. When Clare asked the question, everyone froze and silence hung in the air for a moment.

"Yes. He made me promise to ask you if he could stay and take care of you."

Jason slammed his book and shoved back the kitchen chair as he stood. He looked as though he was about to storm out of the room.

"No," Clare said without even glancing at Jason. "No, he has to leave. Did you tell him that?"

"Yes."

Jason looked into the family room and met his mother's eyes. He smiled somewhat sheepishly. He picked up the closed book and left the kitchen, not angry but mollified. Dotty went back to her chopping without comment, but there was no question she was listening raptly.

"And what did he say?"

"That you can have whatever you want."

"Well. That was nice of him. I think."

Maggie leaned forward and whispered so that Dotty wouldn't hear. "You should see him. He's a mess."

"Roger?"

"Dirty, greasy, wrinkled, drinking bourbon. Neat."

"No kidding?"

"A broken man," she said. Then sitting back she wondered what she was doing. It was dangerous to paint him that way and risk Clare's sympathy.

"Ah," Clare said. "The Broken Man game. Been there, done that."

"Is that how he gets?" Maggie asked.

"Ritualistically," Clare confirmed.

"But I've seen him here and there during your separations— I never noticed this side of him."

"I suspect he can put on a good face around his friends and clients. But I've seen him miserable and pitiful. Why do you think I always get suckered into one more chance?"

"Well, I knew you felt sorry for him and caved, but..."

"But you thought I was just stupid? Well, partly. But mostly it's that Roger is so good at convincing me he's sorry, that he's learned his lesson and he'll never do it again. I think I've recovered from that temptation now."

Maggie stiffened. "You mean it's all an act?"

"Actually, it's not an act. I think he really goes through it—the remorse, the guilt, the shame. The depression. The problem is, it has yet to modify his behavior."

"God, that accident. It really did shake up your thinking. You finally get him."

"Sort of," she said. "Probably it's more that I finally get me."

Maggie settled back in the family room, relaxed and had a glass of wine. Clare's was apple juice—the wine didn't go

well with pain meds. Maggie made time for the family gatherings but the rest of her life was always a rush; she always
had a million things to do. Now she seemed more at ease,
hanging out at her dad's during the workweek, than she had
in quite a while. Clare wondered if it was because they were
finally on the same page about her divorce.

Then Sarah came home, a little early, as she was doing these
days. It was almost as though she was desperate to make sure
Clare was all right, that the family remained intact. She was
clearly delighted to see Maggie. Before the accident the sisters
tried to carve out time for an after-work cocktail at least every
other week. "Oh boy," she said. "Happy hour." She poured
herself a glass of wine and joined them.

Sarah was wearing paint-stained overalls. Underneath was a
lime-green sweater, the sleeves so baggy that when she pushed
them up to her elbows, they just slid down again. Maggie
noticed that she had a piece of duct tape holding her glasses
together. "You didn't have to dress up for us," Maggie said.

"The paint doesn't care what I wear," she said, pushing her
glasses up on her nose. "What are you doing here?"

"Just dropping by."

"Good," she said. "I'll be glad when we can get back to our
regular happy hours."

"It's going to be a while, I'm afraid," Clare said.

"Sooner than you think," Sarah said, giving Clare's hand
an affectionate pat.

"Tell her about Roger, Maggie," Clare said. "She'll get a
kick out of it."

"Roger's falling apart," Maggie said.

"Really?" Sarah asked, leaning forward.

"I went to see him about getting Clare back in her house

and caught him drinking in the early afternoon. He's miserable. He's greasy and wrinkled and pathetic."

Sarah grinned. "What's he pathetic about? Can't he get a date?"

"He wants to take care of Clare," Maggie said.

Sarah sipped her wine and leaned back on the sofa. "Tell him to stick it up his ass. We can take care of Clare."

"Sarah!" Maggie said, laughing.

This, Clare thought, was why she loved her sisters so. Because they were dedicated, irreverent and sometimes hilarious. What more could a crippled, almost-forty-year-old, almost divorcée need?

When Maggie had gone and Sarah was busy in the kitchen, Clare crutched her way to Jason's room and tapped on the door.

"Yeah?" he answered.

"Can I come in?"

"Yeah," he said.

She found him lying on the bed with a Game Boy hovering over his face.

"I need to talk to you," she said.

"As long as it's not about him," he returned, his eyes glued to the game.

Clare entered slowly, careful not to get a crutch snagged on something left on the floor—clothes, shoes, books. She could get around pretty well now and was using the crutches only to give herself assistance, to keep the pressure off her pelvis. Walking no longer caused horrid pain but the ache crept back in as the day wore on.

She slowly lowered herself to his bed and he moved his long legs over to accommodate her, but he stayed focused on his game. She gently pulled it out of his hands. He released it and sat up, leaning against the headboard. "It's about him. I need a favor."

"Aww."

"Jason, the accident—it not only shook up my body, it shook up my mind. I can see that I need to make changes in my life, big changes. I have to heal my body, and also I have to heal my spirit. I have to get a life. And I need you to lighten up. I know you're mad. I'm not going to try to talk you out of it—you can work out those issues with your counselor. But I can't get better while I'm constantly faced with your rage. I can't move on. Understand?"

"But don't *you* hate him?"

"Actually, I don't," she said. She didn't even have to reach for the answer. "I'm really mad at him. Who wouldn't be? But Jason—he's the one who's losing out here. He had his last chance with me and it's over. He lost a good wife. And, I fear, a wonderful son. You have no idea how much hurt this is causing him. You have to trust me."

Remarkably, tears gathered in Jason's eyes. "You should hate him," he said, but he didn't say it in rage, he said it with pain.

"There was a time I did," she said, reaching out and threading some of that thick, floppy blond hair across his brow. "But I'm just too busy now. Healing is like a full-time job. And the second I'm better, I have to think about our own house, a good job and getting on with my life. My life with you."

"Sometimes I just can't take it," he said.

"Take what?" He shook his head in misery, looking down. "What, Jason?"

He looked up and a tear spilled over. Even though he was at that ragged and vulnerable age, seeing him cry was rare. "He's like his dad was, right?"

She shrugged. "I don't know. I guess so." She wasn't sure

of the details of Roger's family. He never bitched about his father. His mother, a widow for some time now, complained about what her life had been like, married to a man who was greedy and unfaithful and left her virtually penniless, but Roger's father had been dead for a long time and Roger took good care of his mother. Clare had met Roger's father, but couldn't say she knew him.

Just when you think your kid isn't paying attention. Apparently Jason had heard everything that spilled out of his grandmother's mouth.

"So? What if I'm like *him?*"

"Oh, Jason."

"Well? I *look* like him!"

True. When he filled out, gained some muscle, survived the pimples, he would be as handsome as his father. "It could be worse, Jason. You could be like me."

"That'd be okay!"

"Oh yeah?" she laughed. "Wishy-washy, do anything to please, passive-aggressive?"

"Passive what?" he asked, brushing impatiently at a tear.

"Passive-aggressive. I punish people by being late, by not speaking. Instead of being direct." Not giving sex, being coolly cooperative, acting like I'm back in the marriage when I'm really just counting the days or weeks or months 'til the next confrontation.

"You're not that way."

She was that way with Roger, and she knew it. That's why it was better for everyone if that cycle finally came to an end. "Or," she said to her son, "you could be like yourself. You could be exactly the kind of man you want to be."

"Didn't he see his own dad being a jerk to his mother and want to be better?"

"Can't answer that," she shrugged. "I don't know if he saw it, don't know if he wanted to be different."

"So what if you can't help it? What if I grow up to be a crappy husband?"

"Jason, if you don't want to be like that, you won't. Everyone has a choice about how they act."

"You think that?"

"I *know* that. Look, you can be mad, you can hate him if you want, but at the end of the day, you are who you want to be. You're in charge of your own life. Period. You don't have to waste one second worrying that you'll be anything but what you want to be. I swear."

Looking down into his lap, he nodded weakly.

She lifted his chin and looked into his eyes. "Jason, you should dump all this rage and fear of being a bad husband on your counselor. He's getting eighty bucks an hour—he went to school forever to learn how to help people deal with stuff like this. He might be able to help you move on, you know."

"Yeah, well, you're wasting your money as far as I'm concerned."

She smiled conspiratorially. "It's your dad's money. Knock yourself out."

Three weeks in the hospital, six weeks at George's, at least another two before Roger, who was not cooperating quickly by finding his own place. Clare was beginning to think that someday—within a few weeks—she would be living a life without crutches and pain meds. Right now she was moving around with all the speed of bureaucracy. But moving around, at least.

During the two-and-a-half months since the accident, Sam Jankowski had called a few times, asking how she was feeling, interested in the progression of her recovery. She found that when she heard his voice on the phone, it pleased her. He was so friendly and solicitous, wondering if there was anything he could do, anything she needed.

Today was no different. He called and asked how it was going, and she told him about her three trips a week to physical therapy, how many pain pills she was popping a day, how long it was taking Roger to get out of the house. "But I'm afraid I've never been very patient," she told him.

"Slow going, is it?"

"Oh, you have no idea."

"Getting out much?" he asked.

"Not getting out at all—except for physical therapy. But the worst of it is, I have no privacy. I am so grateful to my family for their help—I'd be doomed without it, but you can't imagine what it's like living with your father and sister after you've been on your own for years."

"Must be a little crowded there, huh?"

"The house is definitely shrinking. I'm having a brief reprieve. School's finally out and Jason grows inches a day, so I sent him with Dotty to do some shopping. I gave her strict orders not to try to dress him—he gets to pick his own clothes, however crazy they seem."

"He's gotta appreciate that," Sam said. Then, "Hang on one second, Clare." Slightly muffled, she heard him order an iced latte with whipped cream. "Okay," he said, coming back to her.

"That sounded good," she said. And she thought, it would be nice to get out for a coffee. With Sam or anyone.

"But tell me—how are you really feeling? Physically? You sound better every time I talk to you."

"I might be impatient with my progress—but the doctor says I'm doing great. And I have to admit, I feel just a little better every day. I get around without crutches most of the time and it's only after being up all day and tiring out that I have to rely on them. Not only that—I'm not all that sorry that I've dropped a couple of pounds, even if I wouldn't recommend the diet. And despite all my bitching, I think my housing situation is going to improve soon. It looks like by the middle of June I'll get to go home. I'll have to stay on the ground floor, of course. I still can't manage the stairs."

"Clare, how long have you been separated, if you don't mind the question?"

"Not at all. Going on six months. I would have filed for divorce by now, but it's a bad time to shake up all the health benefits, et cetera. And—should Roger be a pain in the butt about all the particulars, I have to be a bit stronger to deal with him."

"Are you sure this is final for you?"

"Absolutely. Not only is it almost six months now—it's the fourth time in ten years. I may be a slow learner, but I'm steady."

"Is it... Was it for the reason you gave me when I caught you speeding?"

"Unfortunately. Roger is a tomcat. Can't help himself. It'll never change. And even if it does, I'm moving on. Are you married? Single? Divorced?"

He laughed softly. "Clare, if I were married, I doubt my wife would be happy about how often I've called you."

"Oh, it's nice of you to check on me," she said. "Thoughtful. Sensitive."

"Single," he answered.

The doorbell rang. "Oh damn," she said. "Someone's here."

"You don't have to answer the door if you're not feeling up to it. No excuses necessary."

She groaned a little as she got to her feet. "No, I'm up to it. I'd just rather finish this conversation is all. Maybe I could call you back? I hear the radio in the background so I know you're on duty. But you could let me see who this is and maybe you could call me back?" She opened the door and there stood Sam, squad car in the drive, Starbucks bag in his hand. She smiled and clicked off the phone. "Or you could come in and bring that coffee with you."

"If you're sure I'm not imposing."

"You're not. I know I don't look very good. I haven't even—"

"You look great," he said, coming into the house.

"You knew where I lived? Where my dad lives?"

"Little things like that aren't very difficult to find out. I hope you like iced latte."

"Sam, you're a very nice young man. Let's go sit on the back patio. And don't run."

He let her slowly lead the way and from just a pace behind her said, "No crutches. That's a good sign, isn't it?"

"Steady as she goes. Right out here."

Sam stepped through the opened French doors onto the patio and whistled. The yard was lush and vine draped, a couple of chaise lounges beside a redwood table. There was a shallow, rock-filled stream that wound around the yard and opened into shallow pools in two different spots. A waterfall gurgled and at the far corner of the yard stood a ceramic birdbath and a gazebo.

"Clare, this is awesome!"

"My dad's pride and joy. He says the climate and fertile valley get the credit, but he's a master builder, and great with flowers. I'd take you out to the gazebo, but I'm afraid this is as far as I go today—I'm so sore. But go look around if you like."

"Just a glance," he said, leaving her to sit on one of the lounge chairs while he stepped off the patio and took the rock path along the man-made brook. "There are fish in here!" he exclaimed.

"Yes," she laughed. As he wandered back to where she sat, she said, "It's a little paradise, isn't it?"

"I think it's the most beautiful yard I've ever seen. Is your dad in landscaping or something?"

"No. He owns a hardware store on Granger."

"He's that McCarthy? I know George. Helluva nice guy."

"That's George. So, in all the weeks you've been kind enough to call and check on my progress, I haven't learned much about you. What's your story, Sam? Always wanted to be a cop?"

He answered easily. "That was an accident, a fortuitous one. I needed a good job with decent benefits and they were testing. I wasn't sure until I got into the academy. I have a daughter, Molly. My mom helps me raise her."

"So you're divorced?"

"No. Never married. I was going to college in Reno when my girlfriend got pregnant. Long story short, she wasn't interested in marriage or in having a baby, for that matter. She's from New Jersey and went home to her family and decided to have Molly adopted. That's before we knew she was Molly. If she'd had the paperwork sent to me right away, I might have signed off—but some time passed and I brooded. I wasn't ready to be a father, that's for sure, but I was less ready to have someone else raise my child."

"And how old is Molly?"

"She's almost ten."

Shock settled over Clare's features as she did the math.

"That's right—I was all of eighteen. Nineteen when she was born. And I had to fight to get her."

"Your girlfriend's family?"

He sat at the end of a chaise, facing Clare but not reclining. "This is just for you, okay? I haven't exactly explained this part to Molly. Can't figure out how. Her mother and grandparents didn't want to keep her, they wanted her adopted. Gone. Out of the picture."

"But you got her."

"My mother cashed in everything she had to help me fight a legal battle out of state, but yes, I've had her since she was two months old." He pulled the coffees out of the bag and handed her one. She leaned back on the lounger and carefully lifted her legs up. "That's life, huh?" he said. "How one stupid, irresponsible mistake can somehow turn into the best thing that ever happened."

They talked a little about their kids; she asked how he managed to work full-time and raise a child. With a lot of help, was the answer—his mother, a Realtor, was pretty flexible. And he worked four ten-hour days, giving him three off each week. They had a dog, Spoof, and Molly's best friend lived down the block—so they always had a safe place for her to go if Dad and Gram weren't home.

All the while he talked, the dispatcher sent messages by way of his radio, the receiver attached to his right shoulder, which was turned down, but she could see his eyes dart now and then toward it, keeping tabs on what was going on. And in the back of Clare's mind came this startling reality—in the past six months and in the previous times she'd been separated, she had never really been on her own. It was more of a respite before going back into that marriage.

This young man was doing so much better by himself

than she, so much older and with so much more experience, had done.

"I have so much to figure out," she finally said.

"Figure out getting on your feet. There's plenty of time for everything else."

"My biggest problem is that my son, Jason, is furious with his father. I mean livid. He won't even speak to him."

Sam whistled. "Ouch. Well, I hope they work that out. A young man needs a dad. Mine died when I was so young."

Just as she was about to offer her condolences, the front door to the house flew open with a bang and she heard Jason. "Mom! Mom!" And Dotty. "Clare! Oh, Clare!" The sound of running and shouting caused her to sit upright and Sam to stand by the time Jason and Dotty found them on the patio.

"Are you all right?" Jason, red-faced, demanded.

"Jason. Yes," she said, confused.

"The patrol car," Sam said. He stuck out a hand. "You must be Jason. I just brought your mom some Starbucks."

"Who are *you?*"

"Jason, this is Sam. He was the police officer at the accident." Dotty came up behind Jason before the handshake could be completed. Her hand twisted her sweater closed over her ample chest and there was a look of terror on her face. "Dotty, this is Sam. He was the police officer at the accident."

"Starbucks," he said, lifting his paper cup.

"Oh my Lord, I thought something had happened to you— and you called the *police!*"

"Everything is fine. Jason, it turns out I know your grandfather. Sort of. I go to his hardware store all the time."

Clare struggled up, getting to her feet slowly. "Sam has been kind enough to check on my progress since the accident. And today he surprised me with coffee."

He looked at his watch. "And my coffee break is more than over. Good thing we're not having a crime wave around here—I'd better get going."

"Let me see you to the door," Clare said.

"You don't have to. I know the way and I hate to make you move around too much."

"I'm supposed to be walking. Good for me, they say."

As they went to the door, they could hear Dotty and Jason settling their nerves with exclamations and deep sighs.

"You didn't tell them about me," Sam said.

"I guess I didn't," she said. "It never occurred to me that the police car would throw them into a panic. Sometimes I just don't think ahead."

When they got to the door, Sam looked at her and said, "Look, I don't want to throw any curves while you're trying to recover—but are you absolutely sure I'm being kind? Or thoughtful and sensitive? And that there's not another reason I've been in touch?"

The questions threw her. What would a handsome young man like Sam want with an older woman like Clare? came to mind. But all she said was, "I have a cracked pelvis."

He put his thumb and forefinger under her chin, looked into her eyes and said, "Well, it won't be cracked forever." And then he left her to think about that.

chapter four

· · · · · · · · · · · · · · · · · · · ·

"CLARE, I CAN barely hear you," Maggie said into the phone.

"Because I'm in the closet," Clare replied in a low voice.

"Did you say you're in your closet? Get *out* of your closet! So I can *hear* you!"

"Just a minute. Just a minute, it isn't that easy." The closet in question was not a walk-in closet. It was a mere cubbyhole with a sliding door. But she had to talk to somebody, and it was imperative that Jason and Dotty not overhear.

Once out, behind the closed bedroom door, she realized she'd gone over the top by trying to hide. This was her cell phone so there was no extension and Jason was probably either watching TV or in his room with his stereo turned up.

Clare sat on her bed. Still, she kept her voice down. "Did you hear anything I said?" she asked Maggie.

"You said the police officer who was at the accident came to see you?" she repeated by way of a question.

"The young police officer. Very young. Twenty-nine."

"Okay...?"

"He brought coffee. And..." She was momentarily speechless. She couldn't go on. It sounded so ridiculous even in her mind, it was impossible to comprehend.

"Clare! What?"

"He asked me if I was sure he was just being thoughtful. Was I sure it wasn't something more than that. Maggie, I think he's *pursuing* me!"

"Well now," Maggie said. "Any chance you might have sex again before you die?"

"Sex," she said in a slow, shocked breath.

Maggie burst into laughter. "For God's sake, Clare. You're just coming into your prime! You could teach the boy a few things." Silence answered her. "You haven't forgotten how, have you?"

"How can you talk about sex?" Clare wanted to know.

"Well, usually if things go well, sex follows. Good luck to you."

"Ugh. What I can't figure out is—why would a handsome young man his age be interested in someone like me?"

"Is this a trick question?" Maggie asked. Silence again. "God, I hate that you don't know things about yourself. Important things. You're attractive. No, you're beautiful. You're fun, you're sincere. You're ridiculously tidy, patient and wise."

"Tidy, patient and wise?" she asked, laughing suddenly. "Yeah, I'm sure this good-looking young buck has been searching high and low for a woman who's tidy! Besides, I'm not wise—I've made some of the dumbest choices for a woman my age." She thought for a second and said, "I am tidy, though."

"He probably just liked your face and body—the rest will come. Tell me about him. What's he like?"

"He's nice," she said. "Very conscientious. It seems that he got his girlfriend pregnant when he was just a kid—eighteen years old. And rather than go along with an adoption, he fought for custody. He's raising his ten-year-old daughter with the help of his mother. How many guys do that?"

"This the first time you've heard from him since the accident?"

"I didn't tell you? He came to the hospital right before I was discharged. He brought flowers. Then he called me. He's called me a few times. But I thought he was interested in my recovery. I thought he felt bonded to me because he saw the crash, then saw my wrecked body. I guess I thought that it was natural for someone like him to want to see how everything turned out."

"Clare, you're hopeless."

"Well, how was I to know?"

"Do you like him?"

"I don't know. I mean, sure, I like him fine. I never thought of him in that...*that* way."

"And handsome?"

"Oh Maggie, he's the kind of handsome that would knock you out of your shoes. He has a dimpled smile that can make you wet yourself."

"Jesus, Clare..."

"What?"

"What a lousy time to have a cracked pelvis!"

"This is simply ridiculous," Clare said, matter-of-fact.

"Aw, have some fun. How many times does something like this come along?"

"I'll think about fun later—when I have my life straight."

"You are such a drag," Maggie laughed. "I'd have been all over that. Even with a crack in my pelvis!"

Clare welcomed the distraction of settling into her old house, sans Roger. He'd found an apartment in a luxury complex complete with pools and gym where he could no doubt meet many lovely single women. By mid-June, Clare had moved home. Well, it wasn't as though *she* moved. She merely walked into the house. Jason, George, Sarah and her brother-in-law toted all their things.

To her great relief, the house seemed to welcome her. But then she didn't go upstairs to the scene of the crime. She stayed downstairs and if there was anything she needed, Jason fetched it.

Summer in Breckenridge was glorious. The flowers were full, the fields were green and there was still a little snow on the highest peaks. The haze of pain had lifted and Clare could appreciate the beauty of her town, her mountains. Ordinarily she would have taken care of the yard and garden, but she was forced to hire a landscaping service. So when they were there she pestered them, making sure everything was done to her satisfaction. It was such a relief to be outdoors again after that long, wet and painful spring.

Roger called all the time, sweet depression dripping from his voice. He surprised her by stopping by a couple of times, but while she was civil, she wouldn't let him stay long. She didn't want him to get too comfortable. He was filled with offers of help, begging to see her more often if only to be sure she was getting better. Something about seeing her limp a little must have worked on his conscience. He sent her generous checks very regularly, something she'd had to ask him for during past separations. And flowers—she hated when he sent her flowers! She could almost smell him, he was getting so close. So, she had the locks changed.

By the end of July she was hardly ever using the crutches, though she still had occasional pain. She could manage the stairs *and* the laundry, though she couldn't carry things up and down. There was a little complication with transportation—she didn't have a car anymore, and her little secret was that if she did have a car, she'd be terrified to drive it. But there were plenty of people from her dad to her sisters who would happily take her wherever she wanted or needed to go. She was still seeing the physical terrorist twice a week.

She had Jason bring her the paperwork stowed in her upstairs desk, including her records of all the schools in Breckenridge—not so very many, where she had done substitute teaching. She spruced up her résumé and got started.

Clare hadn't held a full-time teaching job since before Jason was born, only filling in from time to time. And you don't need the greatest teaching skills to do that. In fact the only real requirement is a whip and a chair; the little heathens gave the sub their absolute worst. She had faced each one of those days with anxiety and dread, but knew the wisdom of keeping her hand in. Not to mention a little money now and then that was entirely her own.

The nice thing about having kept her face in the school district of a small town was she was known and liked. There were two job offers almost immediately. Both were in the English department, one in middle school—eighth grade, and the other high school, though she had been hoping for younger kids. She was tempted to take the middle-school job just to avoid running into Pete Rayburn, who taught and coached at Centennial High, but Jason had turned fifteen over the summer and was starting high school in the fall, so running into Pete was going to happen, no matter what she did.

And…she had made that promise to herself, that she was going to seek Pete out and see if she could mend those embarrassing fences. After all, it had been nineteen long years. And they were grown-ups now.

She took the fifteen-year-olds and thought of all the advantages of being in school with her son every day.

"Aw, man, I'm gonna want to *die!*"

Jason did not.

In August Clare went up those stairs and looked into the master bedroom. She had always loved that room, but now all she saw was a blond stranger bouncing atop her unfaithful husband. So she called the consignment shop to come and take the furniture away and then called a local decorator. Ordinarily she would have done all the work herself. Growing up the daughter of a hardware store owner had many advantages and she was a master at everything from wallpaper and paint, to crown molding. But even if she felt one hundred percent most days, she knew the logic of not pushing her luck.

Just a couple of weeks later when she went back into the bedroom everything was changed, from the sheets to the window treatments. It was entirely new, without a trace of Roger's infidelities.

She gathered materials from her new employer and set about the task of preparing lesson plans for the year ahead, and as she did so she began to fantasize about doing any other kind of job than teaching. Why hadn't she become an architect? A nurse? Been a business major? How could she face one hundred and twenty fifteen-year-olds a day? One hundred and twenty Jasons and Jasonettes?

But surely they would be more tame if she was the regular teacher and not the sub....

She had all but forgotten about her flirty younger man. From his few calls over summer, he was all cooled down. She reminded him a couple of times about how sore her pelvis was and he moved back into his assigned slot as the local cop who was only concerned about how she was feeling, how her recovery was going. She did have one small handicap—she happened to enjoy talking to him.

And when he called she found herself eager to regale him with tales of her hectic days; of redecorating, job interviewing, shopping for work clothes, getting Jason ready for school, sidestepping Roger and working on study plans for her new job. She hadn't seen him all summer, since the day last June when he showed up with coffee. Five months had passed since the accident and she was nearly back on her feet. Only a little annoying soreness remained—she was ready to go back to work and get on with her life. Then one day Sam called and said, "You know, it's been weeks since I've seen you, and I bet you're just about fully recovered."

"I just about am," she said, surprisingly glad to hear his voice. "Feeling really great, as a matter of fact. Have you had a good summer?"

"I stay pretty busy when Molly's out of school—and we had a nice long vacation in July. Got a cabin on the North Shore of the lake and really relaxed."

"Your mom went along?" she asked.

"Sure," he said.

Clare surprised herself by thinking, then he wouldn't have taken a woman along. But she banished the thought as a ridiculous regression into dangerous fantasies. "It must have been fun," she said. And then the doorbell rang and she said, "Damn it. Can you hold on one second? Someone's at the door." Carrying the phone with her, she opened it and there he stood, not in uniform this time but in jeans and a sleeveless T-shirt that happened to show off his tanned and muscled arms. She gulped at his physique and kept herself from sighing at his hard good looks. "This is a cute trick you have," she said, clicking off her phone.

"I know," he said, treating her to that incredible smile.

"So, besides being very funny, what are you doing here?"

"On a mission," he said with a shrug. "Got a few minutes?"

"Actually, I'm right in the middle of...of..."

"Come on, I'm not going to kidnap you. Or maybe I should. You probably couldn't put up much of a fight." He dangled car keys in front of her. "I bought a new car. Wanna see?"

"Sure," she said amiably. How typical of a young guy, she thought. Car proud. There in her drive sat a Lexus SUV, a lovely deep blue color. "Wow," she said. "Breckenridge is paying cops pretty well these days."

"We get by. How about a spin?"

"Well, just a short one. I really am in the middle of something." But she was in the middle of absolutely nothing and Jason was out running around with his friends. She moved toward the passenger door and he said, "Clare."

She turned. "Hmm?"

He dangled the keys. "You drive."

"Oh! Oh, no, I couldn't! It's your brand-new car."

"I'd like to see how it feels in the passenger seat."

Her heart began to pound and her palms started to sweat. "No, really. I can't. I don't think I'm up to it."

He met her by the passenger door, slipped an arm around her waist and led her firmly to the other side of the car. "You haven't been on this horse in a while, Clare. I haven't missed that in all your running around, you've always had someone driving you. You start work pretty soon and you're putting this off. If you're scared, let's get it over with."

She tried to wiggle free, but he held her waist. "I can't," she said weakly. "I'm not ready."

"You'll never get ready this way," he said. He opened the

door and that new-car smell of polish and leather wafted out. "Take your time, but get in. Let's just do it. It'll be fine."

"It's been so long."

"I know. I don't think you should make it any longer."

"Really..." she attempted, pleadingly.

"Just around the block then," he said. "But it's time. You need a car and you have to drive."

Reluctantly, she slid in. Her dad had tried something like this a few weeks ago, but he'd let her off easy. Maggie had talked about it, her driving again, but talk she could handle. She swore to Maggie she wasn't phobic about it—she just wanted to pick out a nice car when her insurance settlement from the accident came in, and that would be that. But the truth was that Clare didn't need to wait to buy a car. She had plenty of money—both savings from her life with Roger along with the stipends he sent, not to mention her future salary from the teaching position. She could qualify for a car loan, no problem.

She sat behind the wheel while Sam got in the other side. She placed her hands on the steering wheel, massaging the leather cover. He waited a moment, then when she didn't move he reached across her and fastened her seat belt. "How's it feel?"

"It's very nice," she said. "I'd like to just sit here for a while."

He gave that about ten seconds, then he turned the key and started the engine. "Very uncomplicated car, Clare. Just put it in reverse, back out and take her around the block. You can do it. Simple."

"I can do that," she said. And in her head she said, *I can do it, I can do it, I can do it. I'd just rather not.*

One thing she knew for sure—this was going to have to happen sometime, and for whatever reason she was glad it was happening with Sam and not George or Maggie or even, God forbid, Roger. So she put the car in reverse and with her foot on the brake, adjusted the rearview mirror. She went slowly down the drive, changed gears and headed down the street. She signaled at the corner, made a right turn, signaled at the next corner for another right, and repeated the process a third time. She licked her lips, swallowed several times and gripped the wheel hard, so that it wouldn't fly away.

"How's that feel?" he asked.

"I don't know. Are you supposed to sweat this much?"

"Well, I do. But I think it has something to do with the payments." He chuckled.

She stole a quick glance at him and then got her eyes back on the road. He was smiling at her. Joking around with her.

Her house came into view. "Go around again," he commanded.

"Really, once is—"

"Clare! You have to get it up to fifteen miles an hour before we quit! Now drive!"

She eased down on the accelerator with caution and brought the speed up. "Jeez. All you have to do is ask."

After four trips around the block, her pulse began to slow. She wiped her hands on her jeans several times and then, miraculously, didn't have to anymore. Then Sam told her to take a left and another and that put them out on a nonresidential street and while she felt a little nervous, it wasn't too bad. "You have to do the speed limit if there are no traffic restrictions," he told her, sounding like such a cop. She sped up and navigated the road. She stopped at a light and when it turned green she looked both ways before proceeding. She drove as he directed and it began to come back to her, how she'd zipped around this little town with such confidence before. Not just the town but the country roads that wound around the luscious green farms and cattle ranches. But that was nothing—she'd been up the winding mountain roads and passes in the dead of winter to ski at Tahoe, and at night to have dinner at a wonderful small restaurant at eighty-five hundred feet at the top of Lander's Pass. And over the mountains and down the other side, all the way across the Bay Bridge to San Francisco.

Sam had stopped directing her and she was on her own. He popped in a CD and music wafted through the car on its wonderful sound system. She opened the window and felt the wind blowing her hair. She went through town, past her father's store and out into the country. She got on the highway and headed south right along with all the Tahoe tourists. Then she got off the highway and took the country roads back toward Breckenridge.

"Pull over at that field," he told her. "Please."

It never occurred to her to ask why; she did as she was told.

"Turn off the engine," he said, unsnapping his seat belt and getting out.

She was slow to respond, wondering just what he had in mind. He probably had to pee, she thought. Men—the world is their bathroom. There was nothing out here but a couple of big, old trees, a falling-apart structure that was once a barn, field upon field of what looked to be soybeans, and cattle grazing in the distance. Not terribly far away a tractor trundled along.

Sam just stood under the tree and looked westward toward the mountains. A breeze flapped at his shirt and he pushed his hands into his pockets.

She got out and joined him. "What are we doing?" she asked.

He nodded toward the Sierras. "There's going to be snow

up there in a couple of months. You going to be able to ski this year?"

You don't ask someone from Breckenridge or anywhere around Reno and Tahoe *if* they skied, because almost anyone who lived right beneath this gorgeous mountain range was born on skis. Her entire family had skied together, though George didn't go anymore. And Jason was a snowboarding pig who fancied himself an extreme snowboarder—something that challenged her sanity. "God, I hope so," she answered. "We grew up on skis. That's one of the things our family loves doing together."

"I do some part-time ski patrol," he said, not breaking his gaze from the mountains. "Molly is *very* grateful," he added with a laugh. "Free lift tickets." Finally he looked at her. He smiled that bright dimpled smile and said, "Nice driving."

One muscle in her stomach that had been tight since the accident finally relaxed. She had done it—the crazed fear was behind her. Oh, she might experience a tingling nerve or two, but it no longer seemed like something she couldn't push through. So she said, "Thank you, Sam. Whew. I might've put that off forever."

She noticed, not for the first time, that he had the bluest eyes she'd ever seen. And they bored into hers with heat and power. The smile was still there on his lips but without that flash of bright white teeth. He took one hand out of his pocket and reached toward her, threading his hand around the back of her neck under her hair. She was very still, not quite sure what he was going to do. Maybe just hold her there? But she couldn't deny that his large hand felt good, and for Clare, feelings like this were long ago and far away.

Then he pulled her to him and those eyes gently closed as he pressed his mouth against hers. But her eyes flew open and she held her breath. It was a soft kiss but demanded a little something, like a response. She was in shock. But why should she be when she'd suspected for a long time that his ultimate interest in her was romantic? Suspected? Hell, she'd *known!* She just couldn't figure out *why*.

He began to move against her mouth, giving her an idea that a deeper kiss was entirely possible, but certainly not more meaningful. Then he let go and looked into her wide startled eyes and said, "For God's sake, close your eyes, breathe and kiss me. It wouldn't kill you."

She had always been very good at doing just as she was told. She closed her eyes, leaned into his lips and gently breathed. Ah, that was what she remembered. It was very, very nice. In her head she was already pressed against that rock-hard chest, wrapped around him like her grandmother's shawl, but he didn't embrace her. So she embraced him, though somewhat clumsily. It must be hard for him to imagine that this almost-forty-year-old woman who'd been married for sixteen years was pretty inexperienced in this…this kissing men she barely knew.

But she did know him. She knew him well. They'd become friends during those phone chats. It was just that she'd been focused on keeping him at a respectable and platonic distance because there were two things that were glaringly obvious to her. One, she could fall into him and devour him like a hot fudge sundae, and two, she was a little too vulnerable to be in that kind of relationship right now. It held the potential for people to get hurt.

He pulled back. "That's more like it. You appear to be a little rusty."

"You don't," she said a bit breathlessly.

"I've been thinking about it a long time," he said with a shrug.

"Sam…"

"Me first. Are you dodging me, Clare?"

"No," she said. "No, really. I've been… Well, you know."

"No, I don't. Level with me."

She took a calming breath and said, "You're sweet, Sam, and I like you. Who could help but like you? I appreciate that you've stayed in touch since the accident. And what you did today—well, much as I resisted, it was wonderful of you."

"But…?"

"But any kind of relationship, with anyone, is way down on my 'to do' list. I have monumental things to accomplish, not the least of which is a divorce. I don't want to get hurt, and I don't want to hurt anyone. I'm not ready."

He pursed his lips and gave a sharp nod, as though he understood. "Fair enough, Clare. It's been a rugged few months for you."

"Thanks for understanding, Sam."

"No problem. I'm not here to mess with your head. That first night I met you, the one thing I could see was that you were a woman who could think straight even under stress." And finally he removed that hand, but not his eyes. And, she instantly missed the hand.

"Hah!" she laughed. "Me? I was speeding, remember? And a basket case at that!"

Unruffled, he just chuckled under his breath and said, "Do you know how many people actually shoot each other in situations like you found yourself in? Believe me, a few tears, ten miles over the limit—it was downright stoic."

"There was this ice bucket," she said. "At the foot of the bed? I doused them both," she admitted.

"Well good for you," he said. "I like you, you know."

"I like you, too," she said. "But I'm not ready for more than that."

"Okay then," he said, taking her hand and leading her back to the car. "Take me home—I have things to get done today. Since I'm not having sex."

"Yes, sir!" she said with a big laugh.

They didn't talk during the ride home. She enjoyed the driving and he, apparently, enjoyed the scenery and his sound system, though he did reach over and put his hand on her thigh. Common sense told her she should tell him to remove it, but she happened to like it there. What the hell, she thought. I should have something to look forward to. A fling with a drop-dead gorgeous younger man wasn't entirely out of the question. Was it?

Once they were back in her drive she left the car running as she unbuckled and got out. He crossed to the driver's side and she thanked him again. As he was backing out he lowered the window and said, "Clare? Get to work on that 'to do' list, okay? I'll be in touch."

Right after that drive, Clare rented a car. She had always hated the whole process of shopping for and buying cars and she just wasn't up to it. But one of the items in her "to do" list had to be taken care of right away, before the start of school. She had to see Pete, the football coach.

Jason didn't play football; he liked to save himself for snowboarding and varsity football players weren't allowed to ski during the season because of the risk of injury putting them off the team. Football practice started in early August, a month before the start of school. The team practiced all morning, every morning, and school would start in a few days. With nerves taut and heart hammering, she went to the field and watched what she judged to be nearly the end of their session.

Pete stood on the sidelines, his broad back moving with the force of his shouts, his raised hand and emphatic gestures. Every time she saw him over the years, she had quickly averted her eyes lest he see her, approach her, engage her. She hadn't allowed herself the luxury of watching and remembering him. She never let herself think about how handsome he was. Once they had been so close, such good friends, bonded by her relationship to his older brother. Then once they had been too close.

He shouted at the boys and dismissed the team. He turned toward the bleachers to walk off the field and spotted her almost immediately. He glanced, then stared, then tentatively raised a hand in her direction. She returned the brief wave. Well, she wouldn't have to chase him down or even find him in the parking lot as he prepared to leave. But she hadn't thought it would be this easy.

While the team ran off the field and the managers were busy stuffing supplies into big canvas bags, he walked toward her. She didn't think her heart could pound any harder, but it did. He leaned on the railing in front of the first row and said, "Hey. I've been wondering about you."

"Hey, yourself. I heard you called Maggie. That was nice of you."

"It made the paper—the accident. Jesus, Clare—that was an awful wreck."

"I came through it pretty lucky. You have a couple of minutes? To talk?"

"Sure," he said. But he stayed right there, the railing safely separating them and, with him standing on the ground and her sitting on the bleachers, he was looking up at her.

"I took a teaching job at this high school," she said. "English. Sophomore English."

His face brightened, no question about that. That gave her encouragement if not courage. So maybe he didn't hate her so much anymore?

"Wow," he said. "That's great."

"So—we'll be running into each other."

He smiled happily. "I wouldn't mind that a bit."

He was such a fine-looking man. Not like Roger, who was too handsome for his own good. But in so many ways Pete's good looks appealed to her more. His light brown hair was cut so short it wouldn't even need combing, and he had stayed fit—flat belly, strong shoulders and arms. Sweat stained his torn T-shirt and dirt and grass marked up his sweats, but he looked good like that. As though he'd been working hard. And there was rough stubble on his cheeks and chin—he hadn't shaved before coming to practice. Rugged looking, that's what he was. All man. She remembered. She shivered.

"Look, this is hard, but I want to talk about something. Something I know you don't want to talk about."

"Take your time. I'm not going anywhere."

"You know what it is. Nineteen years ago. We have to put that to rest."

He ducked his head uncomfortably for a moment, then looked back at her. "I'm sorry, Clare. I've been meaning to say that for nineteen years. I'm sorry for what I did to you— it was entirely my fault."

She was brought up short by that. "I... Ah... It's just that, I thought I did it to you. Put you in that position of hurting your brother. I know how much you worshipped him."

"You didn't do it to me," he said.

"Okay, maybe we were both at fault. And, I think, carrying around that guilt and pain all this time. I really want to let go of it now. I've been having trouble since it happened. Enough is enough."

"I'm sorry," he said again.

"Stop saying that, it was both of us." She took a breath. "Have you been struggling with the guilt, too?" she asked.

"Oh yeah," he said, with a chuckle that did not come from being amused. "But I don't think the same way as you. This isn't going to get me any points, I'm pretty sure, but I didn't have that much guilt over what I did to my brother. Some, sure, especially right after he died. I felt like a real slimeball, you know? But then he was gone and missing him was so much more real than feeling guilty about anything. The thing that worked on me for nineteen years was that it hurt you so much."

"I'm still not sure how it all happened," she said. He looked away briefly so she hurried on. "Wine, opportunity, loneliness—whatever." Then more quietly. "I'm sorry, too."

"There you go," he said. "We're both sorry."

Something about that was odd. She didn't understand. She said, "Every time I ran into you, you looked so damn uncomfortable, I thought you couldn't stand to look at me."

He looked totally shocked. "Me? No! No! I thought it was the other way around, that you hated me."

"Oh, no, I never did, Pete. In fact, you don't know how many times I thought if that hadn't happened between us, we might have been so much help to each other when Mike died. As it was, we avoided each other like the plague."

"Well, I doubt I'd have been much good to you...or anyone. I was pretty useless for a few years there. Later, though, when I got myself straightened out a little, I thought about you a lot, and how I never did anything to help you get through it. I hated myself for that, too. But honest to God, I thought if I even approached you, you'd freak out and snap. You...you seemed so hurt. So damaged by it. I knew I had to give you time. Space. And then—"

She waited for him to finish and when he didn't, she prodded. "And then?"

"You got married." He shrugged. "It made sense for me to keep my distance."

"I'm getting a divorce now," she said, and looked down as if she was ashamed of that, too.

"Oh damn, I'm so sorry! I went through that a few years ago. Me and Vickie—it was terrible." He put his foot on the bleachers' floor and hoisted himself up, leaping over the rail. Then he leaned back on it, facing her. "That's tough, Clare."

"Well, so it goes. This is for the best. So—you and Vickie now?"

"She remarried almost right away." Then he laughed. "Seemed like it to me, anyway, but I guess it was over a year later. Okay," he said, laughing again. "Two. Two years later. We do fine now. In fact, we're better with the girls than we were when we were married. And get this—I actually sort of like the guy. But don't tell anyone. I don't want to seem soft." And to that he added a large grin.

"That's good to know. So there's hope."

"Can I ask you something personal?"

"Sure, why not? I can always blush and run."

"You were never the blush-and-run type. It's just... Is there... Do you... Well, do you have someone else in your life?"

"Like a man?" she asked, astonished.

"Yeah, because that would mean you're leaving one relationship for another one and if you're doing that—"

She cut him off with her laughter. Suddenly it seemed so funny, after all the years of Roger fooling around, the very idea that anyone would come along and lure her away from her vows seemed ludicrous. What was even stranger was that she hadn't had an affair. Why hadn't she? "No," she finally said. "No, there was never anyone else for me. He had all the someone elses. So I left him." And then there was that little thing about how she'd been unfaithful once and that was so awful, she wasn't about to do it again.

"Oh," Pete said, somewhat taken aback. "I hadn't expected you to say that."

"Why not? It's not like it doesn't happen."

"Yeah, I know—but it shouldn't happen to *you*. He must be nuts."

"Thanks. I think."

He just looked at her for a long moment, a sentimental smile on his face. Finally he said, "I guess if we're both teaching here and you aren't in a relationship, it wouldn't be inappropriate for us to be friends."

"No, I guess it wouldn't." We used to be such good friends, she thought. Way back when they had classes together, when he was on the football team and she was a cheerleader, when they hung with the same crowd during her last two years of high school while Mike was in college. And though she hadn't seen much of Pete after moving to Reno, she still thought of him as a friend. It hadn't occurred to her until now just how much she missed that. "You know what? It was stupid for us to not be friends for so many years. If I hadn't been so ashamed and guilt-ridden, I could have gotten a lot of comfort from your family. And given it."

"Mom still asks about you. You were always her favorite."

"Tell her I send love, will you? And yeah, we should be friends." She stood up.

"I think Mike would have wanted that. Well, he'd have wanted to kill me at the time, but now, being dead and all, I think he'd be okay with it."

That startled a laugh out of her. "Pete!"

"What? I'm serious." Then he grinned again and this was what she remembered, that he had a light heart, that he was so much fun.

"That's something. Are you able to do that—joke about Mike?"

"Oh yeah, we all do. It gets you through, you know? We miss him, we always will, but most of the pain of it is gone. My mom said, 'Mike isn't hurting and we should let that part go as soon as we can and hang on to the good stuff, the fun stuff.' She's just amazing."

I miss her, Clare thought. "So, I'll see you around campus?"

"Looking forward to it."

She grabbed her purse and began to walk down the bleachers to the stairs. "Clare," he called out to her. She turned and he asked, "Why did you think I wouldn't want to talk about it?"

"Why? That note. 'It never happened. We'll never talk about it.'"

"Oh, that. That wasn't for me. You cried all night. I felt like a monster."

"God. We put ourselves through so much," she said. "What a sad pair."

But he said, "Thank you for doing this. I always wanted to and didn't have the guts."

She just smiled at him and waved him off like it was no

big deal, but inside she was remembering that it was her who couldn't face him, or let go of the hurtful parts of the past.

She drove home feeling fifty pounds lighter. She felt good down to the soles of her shoes.

But then later, alone in the house, right in the middle of laying out lesson plans on the dining room table, she was suddenly in tears. Racked with sobs and feeling a sense of loss more profound than she had in many years. All that time they hadn't talked, hadn't worked through their issues. God, she thought, it was *one* night! And neither of us meant to hurt anyone! We should have forgiven ourselves and each other so long ago. Gotten back the bond we'd once had.

So now, she thought, it's going to be okay. She dried her tears and embraced that invigorating feeling of starting over. With old and treasured friends.

chapter five

....

CLARE WAS AWASH in paperwork. It was the one thing that appeared to have increased tenfold since she had entered the teaching program eighteen years ago. It seemed there was a report to file for every phase of her program and for every student. She learned of all this in the week that preceded the first day of school; there were five days of training, one of which she missed for the doctor's appointment that deemed her physically fit to work. Two of the training days were dedicated to the new teachers. There were twenty-five of them in the district, a number that astonished her. And twenty-four appeared to be twenty-two years old. It seemed that Clare and the head of the English Department were the only two over thirty.

There was one young woman in the back of the room who attracted Clare's attention by the sheer tension she seemed to radiate. She was a tiny thing, probably a size two, and her clothes were a little too big, as if she'd recently lost weight. It was impossible to picture her holding off a class of strapping fifteen-year-old boys. Or girls, for that matter. Some maternal instinct kicked in and Clare sat herself beside her the next day and learned her name was Reenie, short for Maureen, and she was a wreck.

"I can hardly eat, I'm so nervous," she confessed in a trembling whisper.

"Don't get all worked up about this," Clare said, even though she herself was all nerves. "Just take it one day at a time and be sure to ask for help if you need it."

"I did my student teaching here. The high schoolers are brutal."

"If they sense you're scared of them, you're cooked," Clare said.

"We're *all* cooked," she said. "We have a new principal. And she has a *reputation.*"

"What?" Clare gasped. "Mrs. Donaldson isn't here? She hired me!"

"I hear she got a fabulous promotion to some state board job, and had to leave suddenly. The woman they hired to replace her has only been teaching about ten years."

"Well, she must have some incredible credentials to land in this job," Clare defended. "Best to keep an open mind."

As for asking for help—Clare soon learned it was every man for himself. She was short of textbooks and left to scrounge through the entire building, from storage rooms to boiler rooms, to find what she needed. Then there was the matter of preparing her classroom; it should be welcoming to the students. She decided on a theme—Fall Literature. She wanted to make huge letters shaped out of books and leaves that would set the stage for reading assignments with a strong sense of season, but when it came to finding supplies, she was on her own.

She had met some of the teachers before, during her substituting, and those she hadn't met were not unfriendly, but clearly she was the newcomer and without a clique. As it happened, Reenie had the room next door, eleventh-grade English, and it was obvious that Reenie was relieved to see her. As they compared schedules, reality hit home hard—six classes and one planning hour. Reenie's planning hour fell at the beginning of the day, Clare's at the end. There would be no honors classes for these new teachers—no getting by with the top students. Those kids, who were also the best behaved, took tenure. In fact, Clare and Reenie had two remedial classes each.

There would be lots of homework; very little time for paperwork on the job. And, with only thirty minutes, forget going out to lunch.

Right off the bat, there was whispering and sniggering about the new principal and once Clare met her she could understand why. She was a beautiful blonde and dressed in a manner very chic for Breckenridge, but she was unsmiling and cold as ice. When introduced to Elizabeth Brown, Clare frowned slightly. "You look vaguely familiar," she thought aloud.

"Do I now?" she returned, lifting one brow, her expression chilly.

"Well," Clare laughed uncomfortably, "in a town this size..."

"I'll be monitoring classrooms quite a lot during the opening weeks of school," she said. "Expect to see me in yours. And I assume you got my memo about the student handbook?"

"I'm afraid I have a memo for every day of the year, and school hasn't even started yet."

"This might be the most important memo of the first day. It's standard procedure for the students to bring a signed document from their parents saying they have read and understood the handbook, but in addition to that there will be a test that every student must pass before any other academic test is given. I'm not going to start out this year with excuses."

They're right, Clare thought in despair. She's hateful. But she said, "Yes, ma'am," to this woman who was younger than her. And spent hours asking herself where she had seen her before.

Clare had what she considered a great idea for her first day. She bought two crates of fresh apples; instead of an apple for the teacher, an apple for every student. Healthy and generous, in her mind. Something to warm them up a little before she threw this handbook test at them.

"Lame," said the first boy to walk in the room. He was dressed in drooping jeans, a T-shirt and leather vest complete with chains. On his hands were driving gloves, fingers bare. Right behind him was a girl in a skirt so short it looked like a napkin, bare midriff, belly button ring and boobs bigger than Clare's. There was multicolored hair in all crazy styles, everything from high-heeled boots to sandals, gum smacking, giggling and pushing and shoving. The few apples that were taken were being pitched back and forth across the room.

Oh, there were the quiet ones who took seats in the back of the class, a couple of serious ones who sat up front, but they were so overpowered by the raucous, they were hardly noticed. And, she feared, would never be heard.

But then it was going to be a trick for her to be heard. "Attention! That's enough now! Take your seats and quiet down!"

The quiet was brief. Very brief. There was whispering, note passing, laughter and the occasional girlish squeal. She said things like, "You're stuck with me for the whole year and if you want to get on my bad side right off the bat, you're doing fine!" and, "Would you like to copy this handbook, word for word, ten times?" and, "I'm going to start taking names and assigning detention!"

It was a battleground. In reality, there were only a few who couldn't settle down or pay attention, but that twenty percent made it so impossible for the rest she was on her last nerve and her head was pounding. Four one-hour classes later she thought she might have a raging migraine, something even Roger had never managed to inflict on her. She had spent her thirty-minute lunch in her car in the parking lot fighting back tears. I'm a bad, bad teacher, she thought in horrible despair. If I make it to my planning period, it will be a miracle.

That night she had to go to bed at seven, lesson plans halfdone. But what did it matter? It was going to take a month to even get to the lessons.

The second day wasn't much better. It seemed the rabblerousers had fifteen or so minutes of control in them before the room began to agitate like an old Maytag. Through sheer dint of will, she took her lunch break in the lounge with the other teachers where she hoped she would pick up a tip or two. What she found were teachers fantasizing aloud about what they would do if they weren't teaching. They'd open boutiques, work in a travel agency, learn to fly big jets, play professional poker. "I'd dance topless," one said, "if I had a chest."

She looked for Pete, for any port in a storm. There was a good chance he could at least make her laugh. But he was nowhere to be seen.

On day three there was a fight between two girls right outside her door. The teachers were told never to try to break up a fight, but to call the on-duty school police. But they were right there in her doorway! Hair-pulling, biting, spitting girls! She got in the middle of it and got scratched on the arm before she got them apart—and there on the sidelines were boys who could have easily pulled them apart, if they hadn't been getting the turn-on of their lives. And of course Clare was lectured to exercise more caution and patience and stay out of these inevitable battles. Chagrined and angry, she headed for her car again during the lunch break.

That's when she saw Pete, and had her first glimpse of their new principal's smile. She appeared to have him cornered by the locker room's back door and although Clare couldn't hear them, Ms. Brown was animatedly telling some story or joke that made her laugh, reach out and touch his forearm, pat his biceps and giggle like a girl. Pete's arms were crossed over his chest, the protective stance. It would have been nice to talk to him for a second or two, but no way was she going near the principal. She got into her car, which was facing the opposite way, so she didn't have to watch the display. Ms. Brown, so cold to the women, was not so icy when it came to a good-looking man.

Not even minutes passed when she was startled by knocking on her window. She jumped in surprise. Pete had braced both hands on her car door and gestured to her to put down the window.

"Hey there, how's it going?" he asked.

She shook her head dismally and glanced over her shoulder to see the ice queen standing by the back door, tapping her foot. "Not so good. They're eating me alive. Um, she seems to be waiting for you."

"Can I get in?" he asked. But he didn't wait for an answer. He rounded the front of the car and let himself into the passenger seat.

Clare chanced another look back, just in time to see Ms. Brown toss her head in annoyance and stomp back into the school through the locker room door.

"Oh boy," Clare said when he sat next to her. "You've pissed off the principal."

"Yeah? Well I barely escaped. She was in a playful mood. So—you're having some trouble adjusting?"

"I have no control of the classroom. They're wild. We were never like that, were we?"

"You weren't," he said. "I was pretty bad. I spent most of my life in detention. When I didn't have my assignments done, I found it distracted the teachers if I just cut up a lot. They found me hilarious. And I rarely had my assignments done. Which is why I had to redeem myself in community college before I could get in anywhere else."

"I guess I do remember that," she said. "Got any tips?"

"Hmm. Start out tough, demand respect, carry a bat and never turn your back."

"What do I do with the bat?"

"Try not to kill them." When she didn't smile he said, "They're wound up in the first days. It'll get easier."

"I was looking for you. I was looking for any friendly face. Pete, I hate it."

"You can't *hate* it. You're just starting!"

"I haven't had one manageable class. And her—" she said, nodding in the direction of the locker room door. "Whew. She looks at me like I just peed on her shoe."

He laughed at her. "I think she's trying to come on strong in the beginning."

"You call that strong?" she asked, indicating the locker room again.

"No, I call that flirting. Big mistake. That'll get her into trouble." He put his hand on the door. "Gotta go make sure no one's getting gang-raped in the showers," he said. And when she gasped he said, "Kidding!"

"God, don't leave me!"

"You'll be fine. Take them with a grain of salt."

"What did you tell her? To get away?"

"I told her I had to say hello to you, see how you're holding up. That you were an old friend. Now don't let the little devils get to you!"

And then he was gone, sprinting back to the building.

When she was on her way back to her class, she happened to see her niece Lindsey holding her books, her back against a locker, a tall and handsome senior with an arm braced against it, leaning over her. Lindsey was so beautiful, so darling. She had that sexy little girl's body and he…he was a big strong boy. A flash of her own youth came to her—Mike, leaning on the locker. Stolen kisses between classes.

The boy bent down and Lindsey rose on her toes and their mouths came briefly together, lips parted. Then he gave her a very familiar pat on the behind and she laughed. Total happiness and love. Lust. All that stuff.

For a moment she was nostalgic. Those carefree days, filled to the brim with emotion and joy. But she couldn't quite tell if she was happy for Lindsey or afraid for her. Sometimes life just didn't go as planned.

Clare didn't dare say anything to Jason about hating school; it would just get him all spooled up and complaining. But she dumped on Maggie. "They're killing me," she said of the students. "When I'm going to work in the morning, the minute the high school comes into view, my head starts to pound."

"It's got to get better," Maggie said. "Doesn't it?"

"If it doesn't, I could be suicidal by Christmas…"

On day four she was to give the Handbook Test. She read the test over. It had no known author, but whoever had put this beauty together was out for vengeance, or war. The questions were impossible. The easy stuff wasn't mentioned, just the most oblique and complicated. 'What is the grade point average under which varsity sporting team members must be suspended from the team?' The number of students who would get that one right would be equal to the number of varsity players. 'When is a conference with the counselor mandated?' 'Under what circumstances is absenteeism considered truancy?' And each question was followed by multiple-choice answers that all looked correct. Was that grade point average that bumped you off the team 2.0, 2.2, 2.3 or 2.4? If she were a betting woman, she'd wager half the class would fail.

And Ms. Brown was to monitor her class in the third period. The ice principal. "Class, this is Ms. Brown, our principal, if you haven't already met her. She'll be sitting in while you're testing so please try to impress her."

The class managed fifteen minutes of control as they buckled down to the test, but then it began. "Aw, this is such crap," someone muttered rather loudly from the back of the room. "Mrs. Wilson," a student called, waving her hand. "I don't even understand half the questions on this test!"

"Do your best and we'll go over it later," Clare said. "Don't overthink it, just give it your best shot. This is one of the few tests you'll get this year that you can retake."

"I read the stupid handbook," a usually quiet young man said. "I don't remember any of this shit. Oops. I mean stuff. Sorry."

"Now look, no more complaints. We're stuck with the test so take it, do your best, and if we have to—we'll go over every question and take it again. No more outbursts."

The hour was nearly over, the comments had subsided but the grumbling had not, and Ms. Brown's frown got deeper and meaner looking. Clare guiltily thought that it was diffi-

cult not to hate her just for her mannerisms, her lack of con-
geniality. Then Ms. Brown got up and went to the classroom
door to leave. She turned her back on Clare as she exited and
Clare felt as though the wind was suddenly knocked out of
her. She saw her life pass before her eyes, literally. It was *her.*
She had glanced at the face for a couple of seconds a little over
six months before, but the back of that head as she balanced
atop Roger was burned into Clare's memory for all time. She
leaned heavily on her desk as the principal left.

Fourth period was a nightmare. It was her worst class, and
they thought it the most ridiculous and punitive test they had
ever seen, the tantrums were rife with anger, and the students were animals. About halfway through the class one of
her most difficult boys stood up, ripped the test in half and
left the room. When the door slammed, Clare turned to the
blackboard and as serenely as possible, began to write: *See me
for test rescheduling after class.*

She had barely started to write, having forgotten the car-
dinal rule that teachers never turn their backs on the class,
when one of her complimentary apples found her head with a
thunk, driving her forehead into the blackboard. The class was
never more quiet. She was momentarily stunned. She kept her
brow pressed against the blackboard while she mentally and
emotionally assessed the damage. It hurt, but not terribly. She
wasn't dizzy or light-headed. But she was *mad.*

She straightened slowly, turned, pulled her purse out of the
bottom of her desk, and left the classroom. She went to her
car in the parking lot.

I can't do this, was all she thought. I've been out of the
classroom too long and I have dangerously little compassion
for the kids. If I ever become effective, I will hate every day
of my life while I try. And I cannot work for that woman.

She spent an hour there—the last thirty minutes of her class, while the abandoned students were probably tearing the classroom walls down, and her entire lunch break. Then, gathering her courage, she went to Ms. Elizabeth Brown's office and told the secretary it was an emergency. Ms. Brown didn't even bother to look up as Clare entered—she continued writing and said, tritely, "You seem to have very tenuous control of your students, Mrs. Wilson."

"I quit," Clare said.

Now she sat up straighter, folded her hands primly in front of her on the desk, and said, "In the middle of the fourth day. Now there's the fighting spirit."

"I've been gouged in a cat fight—"

"That you were strictly instructed to stay out of—"

"And just an hour ago I was beaned in the back of the head with an apple."

"I can't think of a more ridiculous gesture—to arm them on the first day."

"And now I can place you. Roger's birthday present."

She took a steadying breath and said, "I was given to understand the two of you were not together."

A few things became crystal clear in that moment. This was not a nice person. And while young and pretty, she was increasingly unkind. There had been a lot of blather about how she got her job, when there were so many older and more experienced contenders, and after seeing the way she behaved with Pete, Clare thought it might be true. And of course, Clare knew Roger. Roger had a real penchant for easy women. It was rare for him to latch on to one with actual standards.

Clare didn't care anymore who Roger slept with. The accident had made that all seem so long ago. Even if she had not accomplished a divorce yet, he was clearly her ex in her mind.

"I said I quit," she said.

"You have a contract," said the principal.

"Sue me," she said, turning to leave. She stopped. "But really, if there is anything, but *anything* you don't want to air in public, let's not go to court." She shrugged and smiled bravely. "But what the hell. Go for it."

By reflex, Clare drove toward her father's hardware store. He was the only person she could think of at this moment. But on her way there, she pulled over on a street in the older business district where the traffic wasn't heavy. She sat in her car, dazed, thinking, Oh my God, what have I done? Walking out on a teaching job in the middle of the day before the first week was complete was a death sentence in terms of getting another position. It was the only thing she was qualified to do—besides running a home.

Her cell phone chimed in her purse. She flipped it open and recognized Jason's cell number. Oh, God, how could she have ignored what this might do to him? "Jason," she said.

"Mom! Do you know what they're saying? They're saying you *quit!*"

"Oh, honey, I'm sorry! I should have pulled you out of class and explained!"

"You did? You *quit?*"

"I'm sorry, honey."

"Just like that? In fourth hour?"

"Can I explain later? It was kind of crazy."

"Sure, but did you? Really?"

She took a breath. "Yes."

There was momentary silence, and then he said, *"Hot!"* And he laughed. "Mom, you're cool."

"I am?" I'm jobless is what I am.

"Yeah. I'll see you later. At *home*."

"Okay then," she said. "Love you."

"Yeah," he said. Which was the best he could do while his friends might overhear.

She went to McCarthy's hardware. She'd practically grown up in the store. When she was little, she begged to go with her dad and when she was a teenager she worked there. So did the other girls, some. But they hadn't liked it as much as she had.

When she walked in her father was behind the cash register taking care of a customer. He looked up, saw her and said to a clerk, "Marty, finish this up for me, will you?" He wore a slight frown as he regarded her and without even saying hello, led the way to his office in the back of the store. George was the one person who could read all his daughters, no matter what. He might not know the details, but he could read the emotions on their faces and at that moment Clare was resonating shock and panic.

"Is Jason all right?" he asked.

"Fine. I just talked to him, and he's perfectly fine."

"Then what's the matter?"

"Dad, I walked out on my job. Quit in the middle of the day, four days into a one-year contract, and told the principal to sue me if she didn't like it."

George lowered himself into the chair behind his desk. Clare stood awkwardly for a moment, then sat in one of the facing chairs. "Well, you must have had a good reason," he said, but his expression was dubious.

"I can't do it, that's all. I'm a *horrible* teacher!"

"I don't believe that," he said.

"Oh, believe it. If I'd been subbing, I would've stayed out the week, blamed the lack of control in my classroom on the substitution. But I had to get out of there. By the second day I was hating them all!"

"Clare, you've had a lot of adjustments the past six months. You might be a little overwrought or something. Calm down. Maybe if you go talk to the principal later, after classes are out, you could negotiate—"

"I was in the middle of a fight on the second day," she said. "In my classes they were throwing things, cursing, muttering things about me that were less than complimentary...."

"Teenagers are tough."

"It was a war zone."

"I've heard it's gotten worse over the years, but—"

"I walked out after someone launched an apple, hitting me square in the back of the head."

He half rose out of his chair. "What?" he asked angrily.

She nodded. "It was very deliberate. The principal imparted that this was as much my fault, as I brought apples to the students."

He slowly sat again. "For the love of God," he said.

"So I quit. And I'm not going back, no matter what. The principal—young and pretty—is a viper. And she made it quite clear she hates me. Possibly she hates everyone. The women, at least."

"I just can't believe all kids are that bad," he muttered, shaking his head.

"Well, they're not," she relented. "But the new teacher on the block doesn't get any honors students who are actually interested in school. And in the remedial classes there are some real jerks with an ax to grind and the rest of the classroom isn't safe from them. It's easier for the others to go along with the disruption than to behave. It takes a special teacher to

make that many silk purses. I'm just not the one." She hung
her head pathetically.

"Don't cry in your beer," he said. "You made a decision—
stick to it. You must have been passionate, walking out like
that. I've been waiting a long time to see some of that."

When she lifted her eyes, she had tears in them. "Quitter,
that's what I am. You didn't see Reenie quit—and she's up
against way more than I am."

"Reenie?"

"This little bitty thing in the classroom next to mine—she
looks fifteen. And the kids scare her to death. But does she
cut and run?"

George leaned forward, stretching across his desk. "Maybe
she wants to teach," he said.

"What if I could've made a difference in just one kid's life?"

George drummed his fingers on his desk for a moment, then
stopped. "What if you can make a difference in your own?"

"But I feel like such a failure at everything I try."

He grinned. "You make a damn fine bran muffin. Keeps
me out of the Internist's office, that's for sure."

"This is no time to joke."

"Clare, I'm not joking. I'm sorry the job didn't work out,
but I'm tired of watching you stay with things that aren't
worth it. It's time to stop punishing yourself and start working for yourself."

"Dad, I really didn't think I was punishing myself. I have
a degree in education."

"That doesn't necessarily make a teacher, but never mind
that. I was talking about a lot of things."

"Roger, yes. I know. But how am I going to get my independence without a job?"

"You'll need a job, of course. You can always work here

until you figure things out. You know the store as well as I do." He sucked on his teeth. "Never could figure out people who could work for other people. I couldn't do it. This old store might not be so much, but I'm the boss."

"This is a great store. I'd give anything to have this store."

He grinned at her. "I don't suppose it comes as any comfort that you and your sisters will inherit it?"

"Not any time soon with you as healthy as you are. I'll be too old to run it when that time comes."

"It's imperative that I outlive Dotty at least," he said. "I don't want to have the biggest funeral in three counties."

She laughed at him.

"There's that smile. Don't tell anyone I said this, but of my three daughters, you have the most beautiful smile. Most expensive, too, as I recall."

Just as he said that, of course it disappeared. "What am I going to do, Dad?"

He stood up. "You're going to think, Clare. Think of the kinds of things that make you happiest in life. What gives you satisfaction. What do those things have in common with making a living? How can you find the right job or create the right job—one that makes you want to get up in the morning."

"I really enjoyed being a homemaker. I guess I could clean houses...."

"Try to use a little more imagination," he suggested. "And for God's sake, take your time. You need a little walking-around money?"

She kissed his cheek. "I'm fine with money. You're being awfully supportive. I half thought you'd go berserk—I know how you are about quitters. You never let us quit anything growing up. Eight years of piano lessons and I can still barely play 'Chopsticks.'"

"Ah, I don't know if this is the same thing, Clare. Sounds like maybe you chose wrong rather than gave up. It's at least fifteen years you've been subbing and I never once heard you say you were dying for a full-time position. You need a course correction."

She went home and took off the skirt and sweater, tossing it on the bed. What am I going to do with all the clothes? she asked herself. Most of them still had the tags on—they could go back. But the others were likely to gather dust. She pulled on a pair of jeans and lightweight sweatshirt. And she baked cookies.

Clare was amazed by how unpredictable her own son could be. Not only was Jason not embarrassed by her abrupt departure from his school, he thought it was cool.

"It totally rocks, how you just walked out like that and quit!" he said. "I wish I could do that."

"Well you can't, so don't even have fantasies about it. Besides, you don't hate school. Do you?"

He shrugged. "I guess I don't hate it. But I don't like it all that much."

"What don't you like?" she asked him. "Besides homework, that's a given."

The shrug again. "The kids, I guess. The jocks. Some of 'em are real assholes."

"Jason," she warned. "I didn't have as much trouble with the jocks."

"Because they're suck-ups."

"Well, maybe you'll have more success finding what you want to do in life. It turns out I had it all wrong."

"Why'd you do it then? Go to college for it and everything?"

The truth was, she was waiting to get married. She was

planning to be a wife and mother. An Air Force wife. "I knew I had to have a degree—that much is just common sense. You can't get a good job without one. And while I was in college, the only thing that snagged my interest was literature. What are you going to do with a love of reading without a teaching degree?"

"Dumb move," he said. "I could've told you being in a school for the rest of your life would suck."

She laughed at him. "Too bad you weren't around to warn me. We haven't touched on this one in a while—any idea what you want to do?"

Again the shrug. I guess at fifteen you're not sure of anything, she mused. "I'm thinking, maybe, pilot."

She shuddered. "What's your second choice?"

"I don't even have a for-sure first choice. Maybe I could take some flying lessons? I'm old enough."

"Um, let's think about that awhile," she said. She might have to tell him someday, she thought. At least part of the story.

Fortunately the phone rang. And it was Pete. She should have expected this, but it had never occurred to her.

"I heard," he said.

"Wow. Word travels really fast."

"It's a high school, Clare. By sixth period you were a legend. Now, is there anything I can do to help?"

"You mean like convince the principal to give me my job back? I know you have big testosterone points with her, but no thanks."

"Can you at least tell me why? I mean, besides hating it? Because half the people in America hate their jobs, and they still have to have one."

She took a deep breath and leaned against her kitchen counter. "Ah, you know, Pete, if I'd found myself in that spot a year ago, I probably would have stuck it out a long, long time. If I ever did get up the nerve to leave, it would have been planned out, nice letter of resignation, different job in sight—something very rational. But that damn accident shook me up. All of a sudden I'm almost forty, got a big lesson in how short life can be, and I'm not going to waste any time. It caught me off guard, really."

"But you're okay with the decision?"

"I was worried about explaining it to Jason, my fifteen-year-old son. But it turns out I'm a hero. The only thing he'd like better is if he could walk out."

"I can relate. I used to feel that way."

"Yeah. And you ended up a teacher?"

"If you remember, it was Mike who liked school, not me. I ended up a teacher because of sports and discovered I actually like it. Probably something about the difference between being in charge and being handcuffed to the desk. And I like the kids."

"Amazing," she said.

"There's only one thing about this that worries me. You came to me to talk because you'd taken that job. We made our peace because we were going to be running into each other every day. I don't want to go back to avoiding each other."

That made her smile. "Not a problem, Coach," she said. "I think we're in a good place."

"Great. So I won't see you around campus, but I'll give you a call one of these days. We should get together. Lotta lost time behind us."

"I'd like that. And thanks for the call. It's nice that you were concerned."

When she hung up the phone and turned toward the kitchen

table, she found Jason eyeballing her with a very grave expression on his face. "Who was that?" he asked very suspiciously.

"Oh. That was Pete Rayburn. The Phys Ed teacher. Football coach."

"You know him already?" he asked.

"I've known him for over twenty years. We went to school together, graduated together."

"Get out!"

"Absolute truth. Why?"

"*Be*cause, Mom! He *totally* rocks!"

chapter six

....

MAGGIE HEARD ABOUT Clare's walkout from Lindsey; Clare
was the talk of the school. "I can't believe you did that," she
said.

"You would if you'd been there. Here's a little tidbit that's
not being passed around the hallowed halls. The new principal? I finally remembered why she looked so familiar. Last
time I saw her was in my master bedroom, doing Roger."

"No!"

"I'm not working for her. End of discussion."

"Well. I guess you'll have to look for something else. I hope
you can find a job that doesn't come with the challenge of
working with or for one of Roger's bimbos."

Clare sighed. "He's had so many, that might be harder than
you think."

There was this favorite chair in her house that was perfect
for reading—she had upholstered that chair and made the
matching throw pillows. It was her love of books that drove
her to study literature and she learned, too late, that teaching
it was not exactly the same thing. So Clare was tasked with
the job of discovering what she loved. That would be the taste

of cookie dough, the smell of warm, clean laundry and freshly brewed coffee. She didn't enjoy scrubbing the floor so much as seeing it shine. And decorating had been easy for her—she had a way with color and design, and her goal was always the same—to bring comfort and beauty to her surroundings.

She was something of a perfectionist; things had to be just right. She had sanded and painted the doors in the house, replaced the baseboards and added crown molding to the living room, dining room and bedroom ceilings. George had taught her those things. There was a workshop in the garage and it wasn't Roger's. It was Clare's. She had painted, papered and plastered walls. She was hell on wheels with a staple gun— she'd once made her own upholstered headboard and matching cornices for over the windows. Nothing invigorated her like the smells of sawdust and paint.

She liked being a housewife, however antiquated the term. Maggie often said if she ever knew a true domestic engineer, it was Clare.

So, she thought—maybe someone wants to hire me to be their housewife? But doing all those things for someone else to enjoy at the end of the day just didn't sound like what she was looking for. And it was highly doubtful she could wring a paycheck out of the smell of cookies, sitting in her favorite chair to read, sniffing her clean towels and linens.

Clare was stuck. She knew she didn't have to come up with a life plan in three days, but she found herself wandering around her home, looking at all the improvements she'd made and realized that work had made her happy. Clare was skilled and talented enough to take a run-down house and turn it into a showplace. There were very few things she couldn't do—George had even showed her how to replace the garbage disposal.

Maybe, when the money from the accident came in, she could take some of it and buy a fixer-upper. Maybe her new career could be in remodeling and decorating to make a profit. And that wasn't the only money she had in her future—when she got around to divorcing Roger, they'd have to split the home equity and their investments. Nevada was a community property state—everything was fifty-fifty. The accident money, however, wouldn't go into the divorce settlement pot—they were already separated when that happened.

And then it came to her. She tossed off her sweatshirt and put on a white polo shirt with her jeans and drove to the hardware store. She went right to the hook by the office door and grabbed one of the green McCarthy Hardware aprons. To her dad's questioning look she said, "This. This is what I want to do. Until I can pull some money together and maybe buy a fixer-upper to sell at a profit, I'd like to work here. And if you like, I could give classes now and then—show people how to do their own crown molding or upholstering or tiling. Because I can do all those things—plus I'm a teacher."

George's eyes danced. He smiled approvingly. "Welcome aboard, then."

Sam had a training cadet in the patrol car with him, a kid about twenty-two who had a little too much enthusiasm. He was a talker, too aggressive on calls, too slow on reports. It had been a long day, finally winding to a close.

"What are the chances for a little overtime?" Jeffries asked.

"Zilch. It's quiet. We're going in."

"Aw, damn. I need the hours, you know?"

"Yes, I know. You've told me fifty times—you have your eye on this bike—a crotch rocket. Finish the report on that domestic. I need to stop at the hardware store."

"Yeah, okay," he said, a little pouty.

Sam parked in front of McCarthy's and got out of the car. The fall air was fresh and clean and outside it was far quieter than in his patrol car. He stretched his back. Then went inside.

He spotted her right away, up on a ladder, digging around in a box. Her chestnut hair fell forward, concealing her face, but there was no hiding the body, especially in jeans. She was slim with great legs, a tight fanny, narrow waist—all of which he'd love to get his hands on. Sam was a leg man. A leg man who didn't overlook breasts, especially medium-size perky ones just like Clare's.

Sometimes he could summon up her image in his mind and get a little worked up. There hadn't been too many women in his young life because he was the cautious type. He was a father. And he didn't just mess around. Substance and permanence were very important.

She looked so natural up there on the ladder. "What a view," he called up to her.

She looked down at him and unless he was totally crazy, her face lit up with pleasure at seeing him. "Hey, you! Run over another sprinkler head?"

"Yeah. I better get a few. I know where they are since I put 'em in, and I'm just hell on 'em with the mower. And a fistful of number ten nails."

"Building something?" she asked on her way down.

"Just some repairs," he said, which was a lie. So were the sprinkler heads. "You look better all the time. You're really having a good time here, aren't you?"

Her feet touched the floor and she faced him. "It's great. I worked here during high school and college. I'm right at home." She stuck her hands in the pockets of her apron. "How have you been? It's been—gosh—two whole days since you needed hardware."

"I told you, I come here a lot. A lot more lately." He grinned. "I have to admit, the scenery around here is getting better all the time."

She touched his arm and laughed. "You're so obvious."

"Good. So, how's that 'to do' list coming?"

"Actually, it's coming along very well."

"Need any more driving lessons?"

Her eyes twinkled and her cheeks might've colored slightly. She shook her head. "No, I'm good. I'd ask you to help me pick out a car, but my dad would be devastated. Tell you what, when I settle on something, I'll take you for a ride. Maybe let you drive."

"I'll hold you to it. And how about that other matter?"

"Huh?"

He leaned close and whispered, "Divorce?"

"Oh!" She almost jumped back. "That! No, I haven't gotten to that. But you'll be the first to know."

"You know, I don't care if you're divorced or not."

"Oh? Don't you?" she asked teasingly.

"You've lived apart for a long time. If he hasn't gotten the message by now, he's really dense."

"He's really dense," she assured him.

"We need to go out. You know—on a date. You're wearing me out. And I'm going broke on sprinkler heads."

"Be patient," she said, but she said it very sweetly. "You're very handsome in that uniform, you know."

He tilted his head and his eyes glittered. "Are you flirting with me?"

"Maybe a little. Just to see how it feels. I've been wondering if I've forgotten how." The door chime tinkled as it opened and Jeffries came into the store, his thumbs hooked into his gun belt as he looked around. He zeroed in on a young cashier—a sexy young thing all of sixteen with a belly button ring under her McCarthy's apron. "Is he *swaggering?*" Clare asked.

"Oh Jesus Christ," Sam swore. "My brick."

"Your—?"

"My load. My pain in the ass. My cadet." He took a breath. "How about those sprinkler heads. And a kiss."

"No kissing!" she whispered. "This is my father's store!"

"You know, you confuse me to death. You're all worried about how old you are, then all of a sudden you're fifteen."

"Yeah, well, my father does that to me sometimes." She went to the box full of sprinkler heads; he followed. She grabbed a few. "Four?"

"Two. I'll just go home, break 'em and come back."

"And how many nails?"

"Forget the nails—I have to get Jeffries out of here before he commits a felony. And can I call tonight?"

She nodded. "My cell," she said quietly.

"Of *course*. We wouldn't want anyone to think you're getting phone calls from a guy!" Then he grinned. "Later, gorgeous."

He went to the cashier that Jeffries was trying to impress. He put two dollars on the counter. "I don't need a bag," he said. "Come on, Jeffries." The younger man continued to talk to the girl. When Sam got to the door he turned to see Jeffries backing away from a giggling teenage girl, but doing so too slowly. "Jeffries!"

He turned. "Yeah, man. Take it easy."

When they were back in the squad car Sam said, "You know, Jeffries, that girl is too young for you to be fooling around with."

"I was just talking to her."

"Get her number?"

"No!" he protested. Then he turned and grinned at Sam. "But hey, I know where she works."

"She's too young. The sergeant wouldn't like it."

"Don't tell him, then. And I won't tell anyone that you're all hot for a woman with a tool belt."

Sam gave him a glare that should have told Jeffries he'd had about enough. But he was too green and goofy and just grinned. "Nice ass, though," Jeffries said.

Sam hit him in the chest, in the vest, with a balled-up fist. "Behave yourself." But he thought, yeah, it really, really is.

There was truly nothing to compare to fall in Breckenridge. The September air turned crisp and the trees in the valley began to change color and soon would burst into flamelike breathtaking color right up the sides of the Sierra Nevadas. It was Clare's favorite season. She also loved spring, when the new green growth and brightly colored flowers decorated the valley, which this year she had missed almost entirely; the accident happened in the wet drizzle of late winter and the next three months were a blur of pain and pain medication while during the summer she slowly came out of her cocoon of misery. But now, in fall, she felt reborn. Vital. And for the first time in forever, she had a goal.

Things fell into place rather neatly. She left the house right after Jason in the morning and was home by six. She wasn't on the clock, so if she had errands or shopping, she could dash out of the store when things were slow. Whenever she was running around town, she found herself glancing at the For Sale signs in front of houses that looked as though they could use work. Her plan almost seemed meant to be.

Maggie called almost every morning before work, usually from her car while Clare was just getting ready to go to the store. "I'll be getting that check soon. You're going to be coming into a large amount of money and we should talk about your future," she said one morning.

"I'm trying to live my future," Clare said.

"I mean investments. Retirement. A portfolio. And maybe something more permanent than working in a hardware store for your father."

"There isn't anything more permanent than that store, Maggie. It got three of us through braces and college, not to mention two ostentatious weddings."

"But it's just the hardware store. God, I remember when he made me work there and how much I hated it…."

"I'm thinking about buying a fixer-upper and doing some remodeling, too."

"Before you do anything like that…"

Clare picked up yesterday's pile of mail from the countertop and began leafing through it while Maggie droned on and on in her ear. She heard things like *estate planning, bonds, mutual funds*. She stared at the envelope in her hand—from Centennial High School where she had so briefly taught.

She opened it and as she read, stopped hearing Maggie. It was from Ms. Elizabeth Brown. She was filing a complaint against her for breach of contract and while the district considered further action, wanted immediate restitution for the training days the school district had paid for Clare to take.

"Further action?" she said aloud.

"What?" Maggie asked.

"Uh. I'm sorry, Maggie. I have to go. Need to make a couple of phone calls." And she hung up without a goodbye.

So that's how it was going to be—Ms. Brown was pissed. She was going to come after Clare.

Clare called Mrs. Donaldson, the principal who had originally hired her. She heard exactly what she expected—there were plenty of experienced teacher applicants in the district and her abrupt departure following more than one potentially dangerous episode with students was not something the district would ordinarily pursue. The amount of money invested in Clare for a few days of training was minimal and she was not paid once she walked out. It appeared, unsurprisingly, to be a vendetta.

"I don't know what her heartburn is, Clare. If it were me, I might've tried to get you to reconsider, but I wouldn't have gone this route."

But Clare wasn't perplexed. This was more about Roger than Clare. And she'd be happy to hand over Roger.

Her next call was to that fine fellow. She'd been avoiding him long enough. It was time for a frank talk. She asked him if he would meet her for lunch and he was disgustingly elated.

She chose for their meeting a small, quiet, dark Italian restaurant and she set the time at 2:00 p.m. when it would be less crowded. When she arrived he was already there—seated in a corner booth, a long-stemmed rose lying across her plate.

She stood just inside the door and looked at him. A wave of nostalgia came over her at the sight of that floppy blond hair, tanned cheeks, toothy smile. Sometimes it seemed like just yesterday that she felt he'd saved her life. When he plucked her out of the gloom and brightened everything, giving her a reason to live, titillating her with his smooth moves and humor and charm. She had fallen so completely in love with him, right at a time when she thought she'd never be visited by that emotion again. Had that been love, or gratitude? It didn't matter—it had been powerful enough to motivate her to marry him and get instantly pregnant. After all her grief and pain, she had never felt more alive, more desired.

He had made her so happy. She remembered walking into restaurants with him and seeing the stares of envy on the faces of other women—it was a little like winning the lottery. Then when her mother died after a brief and terrible illness, it was Roger who had really been there, holding her through what seemed like long months of tears and she wondered how she would ever have made it without him.

Then she remembered the odd phone calls, the hang-ups. The late nights and missed dinners and unrecognizable scent on his clothes. She hadn't wanted that to be happening, but had known it was. And she had been so devastated.

She hadn't left him after the first affair, but more like the third. That she knew of.

As he noticed her arrival, he stood. She stopped reminiscing and walked to the booth, a little hint of tears in her eyes. Clare let him kiss her cheek, briefly, and slid into the booth opposite him. As she sat, she moved the rose onto his plate. "Clare..." he said in disappointment.

She wasn't going to let him do this to her anymore. The trust had gone years ago, and so must the marriage go.

"Sit down, Roger. This isn't a reconciliation lunch and I want the flowers to stop. We have a few things to discuss."

"Good God, Clare, what more can I do?"

"That's just the point, Roger. There's nothing you can do so stop doing it. Save your money." She handed him the envelope addressed to her. "Tell me if you think you can do anything about this."

As he opened it, the waiter was at their table. "Cabernet," he said. And pointing to Clare said, "Chardonnay."

She didn't argue, but had already decided she wouldn't drink her lunch with him. She was going to keep her head. "Water," she added. "And you can just bring the antipasto for two and bread."

The waiter nodded and disappeared. Roger read. It wasn't a long letter, but apparently it took him some time to absorb. Then he looked over the page and asked, "What do you want me to do? Pay it for you?"

"Don't you recognize the name?" She held her tongue to stop from adding, *you moron.*

"I don't understand," he said.

She leaned toward him and kept her voice low. "Roger, that's the woman I found you in bed with on your fortieth birthday. She's the principal at the high school. She threatened me when I quit. She hates me devotedly, and I assume it has something to do with you."

He handed her the letter. "I haven't seen her in ages. If she hates you, I doubt it has anything to do with me. Besides, Clare—you know you don't have to work. I'm taking care of everything."

She leaned back in her chair and chose to ignore his last statement. "I did a little checking. Although Ms. Brown is one tough cookie, this is unprecedented. The former principal, the woman who hired me before her promotion, said this sort of thing is never done. I think it's a vendetta of some kind. I bet Ms. Brown thinks you dumped her for me."

"It's only two hundred and eighty dollars. It's the last you'll ever hear from her. Make it go away," he said. He accepted wine from the waiter.

When they were once again alone Clare said, "Our son goes to that school, Roger, and if Ms. Brown has some idea that you broke off your little romance with her to get back together with me, she might extend her harassment to Jason. Or," she said with a shiver, "she might try sucking up to Jason to get your attention. I don't know which is worse. She needs to be put in her place. Here's what I'd like you to do," she said, spelling it out for him. "Go see her, preferably at the school and not at a bar or restaurant. Tell her that there is no possible way we're ever getting back together and if you've stopped seeing her it has nothing to do with your family."

"But it does!" he protested. "That night, the accident, everything that happened, God almighty, Clare, I've changed!"

"Roger," she said, leaning toward him, "I don't care. Don't you understand? It's too late. That's what I want you to tell her. Ask her to tear up the letter, unfile the complaint or whatever it is, and if she refuses, write her a check."

"Why? Clare, I really don't understand you...."

"Because, Roger, I simply don't believe she'd be doing this if she didn't think I've taken you away from her. Because, Roger, I believe you brought this on me. I could write the check—it's not that. In fact, if you insist, I'll reimburse you. But I think this is your mess, not mine."

He sighed heavily. "Whatever," he said, lifting his glass. He took a gulp. "I haven't even seen her in a long time," he repeated.

"Has she called you from time to time?"

He waved his hand impatiently. "That's totally irrelevant," he said.

"You've seen her since that night," she said, just realizing it must be true.

"Not lately," he said.

But for Roger, not lately could be as recently as last week. "God," she said. "She's pissed. She wants you back."

"I'll talk to her. Get her to back off. If that's what it takes."

"If that's what it—? Oh, God," she said, resting her face in her hand. She shook her head in frustration. It was her own fault—this was so long overdue. But there was that little matter of being nearly killed.

The appetizer and bread arrived at that moment and Roger ordered another glass of wine, though his first was not yet empty. As the waiter left and she looked at the delicious antipasto, she found she had no appetite. She didn't touch it. She did, however, and against better judgment, lift the glass of Chardonnay to her lips and take a sip. She thought it might quiet the homicidal urge she was feeling. "Okay, Roger, it's time to talk about our divorce. Do you want to use lawyers or just do it ourselves? Because I can ask Maggie to help me with a settlement agreement and draw up the paperwork."

"I don't want a divorce. I want another chance."

"I know that. But fortunately you don't have to want a divorce for me to get one. So—you want my lawyer to call your lawyer?"

His fist hit the table and set the dishes to rattle. "I've seen my son five times in the past eight months! I haven't spent a whole weekend with him! I've sent money at the first and fifteenth of every month and I've paid all the bills! There is absolutely no reason for this!"

She took a tiny sip and put down the glass. "You sleep around."

He leaned his face close and she noticed his cheeks were flushed. "I'm in *counseling* for that!"

This was a mistake, she found herself thinking. All of it. The restaurant, the attempt at a civilized meeting, the request for help. She grabbed the envelope and said, "I'd better not hear that this woman is bothering our son in any way." She stood up and quickly exited the restaurant even though he tried calling her back three times.

Clare went to the car and was just about to get in when she felt a hand on her shoulder. He had followed her. She shook him off.

"Clare, I'm going to get you back!" he shouted desperately.

Calmly, though her heart was hammering, she said, "You have to back off and leave me alone, Roger. I'm done talking about this."

"We *haven't* talked about it yet! You've refused to talk!"

"I'm not talking about getting back together!" She gave him a little push so she could get in the car.

"Mr. Wilson?" the waiter called from the door. "Was everything all right?"

He whirled. "No! It is not all right! My wife wants a divorce!"

Oh brother, she thought. She got into the car and locked the door.

Fortunately he didn't try to further accost her, so she backed quickly out of her parking space. It was drizzling and sloppy and she just drove around for a while, ending up at the edge of town in front of a dump of a house with a For Sale sign in front of it. She just sat in her car and thought. About Roger and divorce. It appeared he wasn't going to make this easy.

When her cell phone rang, she looked at her watch. An hour had passed. Clare saw that it was Sam calling—the one person she had told she would be meeting Roger, and only because he had asked her if she could get away for lunch. "Hi, Sam," she answered.

"Are you still in the thick of it?" he asked.

"No, it was very short and probably unproductive."

"Are you back at work?"

She sighed deeply. "No. I'm sitting in my car. Pouting."

He laughed at her. "Where are you?"

Clare looked around. "I don't know. Jefferson Avenue." She looked at the run-down house. "Fourteen-fifty. Unless some numbers have fallen off."

"I know where that is. Stay there. I'm on my way."

"But—" She was about to say, But I want to be alone. Except he'd clicked off.

It was only a couple of minutes before he pulled up behind her. She glanced in the rearview mirror and saw him walking toward her car, head down in the drizzle. He jumped in the front seat beside her. "You all right?" he asked.

"Yes," she said. "Roger isn't going to make things easy. He's still begging another chance. I get so sick of it."

"What are you doing here?" he wanted to know.

"I was just driving around and I saw the For Sale sign. I've been thinking about getting a house to fix up and either sell at a profit or rent. So I pulled over—but my mind wasn't really on the house."

"Have you looked inside?"

"No, it was completely spontaneous."

"Come on, let's peek in the windows. It's empty."

"How do you know?" she asked, though he was already getting out of the car.

"I patrol this area. Come on."

Sam was up on the front porch out of the drizzle before she got out of the car. Well, why not? she thought. She joined him there and they looked inside. The foyer, part of the living room and wide, open staircase were in view from the little front-door window. Under the trash were hardwood floors, though the banister was a wreck. Wallpaper was peeling in large sheets off the walls. "This has possibilities," she said. "Think we can see the kitchen from the back?"

"Let's do it," he said. He got them through the back gate and fortunately there was a small porch over the back door that kept them out of the rain. The yard was large and private; there was a detached garage. She looked in the back-door window, framing the glass with her hands to see inside. Behind her he asked, "Tell me about it. Roger."

She turned around and leaned against the door, her hands behind her back. "I think I tell you too much...."

"Don't stop now. You've got my curiosity roaring."

"I made a big mistake not getting a divorce faster. I thought I was being cautious and certain, but that wasn't it. I have to own up—I can just be so damn passive-aggressive. I was just avoiding it. My hesitation has Roger willing to do anything for another chance. Probably because I've given him so many chances in the past."

"Well? Have you thought about that?"

"Out of the question," she returned. She ran a hand through her hair, gathering it up and letting if fall. "It's been over for so long, I can't even remember when I last had feelings for him. My God, I'm not even angry with him anymore! Just annoyed...that's all I can summon up. I just want to settle with him and not have to deal with him anymore."

"You have a son," Sam pointed out. "You'll always have to deal with him."

"Jason's fifteen now. Whatever he has to work out with his father is between them. I can't do much beyond using will-power not to call him names and put him down."

"Clare," he said, "why didn't you move on a long time ago?"

"I don't know," she said, shaking her head. "I'm a gutless

wonder sometimes. I have issues, as they say. But emotionally I left that marriage so long ago, it's like it was another lifetime."

He seemed to laugh to himself as he moved toward her. He pulled her hand and drew her into his embrace. "I love hearing you say that." Her arm went around his shoulders very naturally. He touched her lips softly. "You ready to move ahead now? Maybe give a new guy a chance?"

"I'm worried about—"

"I know, I know—you're worried about the fact I'm younger than you and I live with my mother."

"It does seem a tad awkward."

"What I want is for you to worry about how you feel when I do this," he said, covering her mouth in a deep and powerful kiss that parted her lips for his tongue. God, but he was a good kisser; strong and slow and delicious. "And this," he said against her open mouth as one of his hands found her behind and pulled her hard against his groin. "And this," he whispered again, as his other hand found her breast. And then he captured her mouth once more, demanding a response.

She went instantly weak in the knees and felt a fluttering take the place of her regular heartbeat. She drew him closer and a hunger she hadn't felt in some time took over. She nearly trembled with it, it was so strong. She knew, long before he kissed her under the tree the day of their ride that this was where they were headed. She might have been trying to ignore it, but he had never tried to conceal it.

The taste of his mouth was woody and natural, his scent was of wool and leather and some divine aftershave. She sighed against his open mouth. "Listen, I really appreciate that you've been so patient," she said. "But..."

"You were almost dead there for a while," he reminded her.

Dead inside, she thought. But Sam was reminding her that her body had needs that had been ignored for too long. She clung to him and moved her mouth under his, welcoming his tongue.

After another kiss he said, "About that marriage, Clare. I don't care that it's not final, as long as it's over for you."

She pulled back slightly. "And what if it's not over for *him?*"

"That could be a pain in the ass. But nothing worth having is easy."

"And so what is it you have in mind? My son lives at my house and he's a little vulnerable—I really can't have guests, if you get my drift. And you don't have your own place, either. So—do we go on dates and make out in the backseat?"

"Boy, once you decide, you decide! I've been practically nuts just wanting to hold you, but you're already worrying about sleepovers!"

"I just don't know how things like this work."

"I have a punch card for the Motel 6. Stay ten times, get one free." She gasped and he laughed. "God, you'll buy anything."

She wanted more of him, more of his lips, his arms, even though she wasn't sure it was such a good idea. And certainly not on this little back porch. "You really get me riled up," she admitted.

"That's a good thing. It's mutual. But let's get out of here, okay?" He took her hand and led the way back to the street, but to his SUV.

"Where are we going?" she asked nervously. Her whole body was ready for the Motel 6, but in her mind she was still miles from being ready. She hadn't even come to grips with the very idea that there was a man in her life; a lusty, funny, sexy man.

"Don't worry. I'm in complete control."

Well I'm not, she thought.

She locked her car and got in his. He drove through the misting rain just a few blocks to a hamburger stand that fea-

tured carhops who delivered meals on trays to the windows
of cars under a covered roof. It wasn't a meal hour and the
weather was objectionable, so theirs was the only vehicle. He
ordered burgers, fries and colas and said, "You haven't eaten,
have you?"

"I ordered, but didn't eat," she said.

"I figured as much. Did you come here with your boyfriends in high school?"

"Boyfriend," she said. "Mike."

"Ah. The guy you were calling to at the accident."

"You remember that, huh?"

"At the time, I thought you were asking for your husband. I
was relieved to know that wasn't the case. But you must have
been pretty locked into this Mike, for him to be around your
subconscious for so many years."

"Uh-huh. We started dating in high school and got engaged
in college. He was a little older and went into the Air Force.
I was planning our wedding when he finished flight school
and was training in the F-16." She looked down into her lap.
"He was killed in the jet. I'm still not really sure what happened. I think mechanical, the Air Force says he lost control
of it. There was nothing left, of course. Nothing to bury."

He reached out and touched her cheek. "You were so young
when that happened. It must have been awful."

"Pretty awful. Now I see that it explains a lot. I graduated
in spite of my state of mind and started teaching. I hated it,
but I hated everything so I blamed it on grief, not on having
made the wrong career choice. And then there's Roger. This
handsome flirt came into my life at just about the time I decided to go on living and bam! I was so relieved to smile, to
sleep through the night, to actually look forward to things, I
went ahead and married him. And my family and friends, so
happy to see me come out from the dark cloud, never took

a closer look at Roger. We all should have. He and I weren't right for each other."

"But was it always bad? The marriage?"

"Of course there were bright spots, not the least of which is Jason. But you know what was the very worst part? When it became evident—at least ten years ago—that I was in a hopelessly bad relationship and really didn't do much to save myself, the people around me, the ones I love the most, began to give up on me."

"Aww," he said in protest.

"No, it's true. The first time I separated from Roger, there were cheers that could be heard for miles! But three months later I took him back. I felt I owed him a chance to redeem himself, to be the husband and father he said he wanted to be. It was like I was the only one who didn't know it was virtually impossible for him change. They all tried to be supportive, but then came the second time, and the third, and they seemed to collectively throw up their hands in helplessness." She took a breath. "I think my father and sisters were as unhappy as me. That's why..." She found the right words difficult, but for once she was going to be strong and follow her instincts. "That's why it's so important to me, now, not to make bad choices."

"You mean—me."

"I mean a lot of things, but you definitely fall into that category."

Instead of looking dejected, he dazzled her with that grin. That decidedly boyish grin. "Don't worry so much, Clare. Roger pushed. I'm going to give you all the time you need."

She just shook her head in wonder. "Are you sure you're only twenty-nine?"

"My mother says fatherhood grew me up fast. Actually, she said *too* fast."

"You don't have a mother-thing, do you?"

"You are not old enough to be a mother-thing." The carhop brought the food and he passed her a burger. "You know, if you were dating a man ten years older than you, you wouldn't think twice about the age difference. Get beyond this. If it's right, it's right. If it's not—we'll move on. Undamaged."

"What about broken hearts or severe disappointment? I think that's overly optimistic."

He pulled his fries off the tray. "You're lucky to be alive. You were given a second chance. Focus on what's really important and enjoy your life a little. Follow your gut. Take a chance." He put a long fry in his mouth, leaving the end out. He leaned toward her, inviting her to bite what was left up to his lips. She smiled, then obliged.

"How's that feel?" he asked.

She chewed the fry. "Everything about you feels nice. That doesn't mean I'm ready to get serious. We can only keep this friendship if you understand that I don't know when or if I will be ready to get involved on a deeper level."

He popped a fry into his mouth and smiled at her. "Okay. You have issues. I don't. You handle your issues, I'll try to behave."

"Thing is—you tempt me."

The smile broadened. He lifted her chin with his thumb and forefinger. "Try not to hold that against me. Okay?"

Then she said, "You could have taken advantage of me back there. I'm a little vulnerable and you're... Well, you know what you are."

He put the cardboard carton of fries in his lap and put his hand against her cheek. He threaded his fingers into her hair at her temple. "I intend to take advantage of you, Clare. But when I do, you're going to welcome it."

chapter seven

· ·

CLARE HAD A very big day. Maggie called her to say the money from the insurance company had been deposited in Clare's checking account, so Clare asked Maggie to meet her for a glass of wine after work to celebrate. Then she called and invited Sarah to join them. And then she agreed to go out to dinner with Sam.

The Fireside was one of the few fine dining restaurants in Breckenridge, so named because of the strategically placed fireplaces in the restaurant and lounge. It was one of the Mc-Carthy sisters' favorite places to meet for a drink, especially once the weather cooled and the hearths were ablaze.

It was only six when Clare arrived at the restaurant, but already it was dark outside. The late-September evening was cold, promising that in a few weeks the kids would be trick-or-treating with jackets and snowsuits under their costumes.

She checked her coat and looked around for her sisters. She had assumed she would be first to arrive. Maggie was always delayed by some legal business and Sarah, well Sarah could get so easily absorbed in a work of art that time would elude her. They called it keeping Sarah-time.

To Clare's surprise she saw that Maggie had beaten her. She was already seated in a comfortable chair at a low table. As Clare started across the room, she saw Maggie's mouth fall open slightly as she noticed Clare. Clare wore an elegant, slim-fitting, long-sleeved black dress, dark stockings and pumps. Her only jewelry were diamond stud earrings and a gold chain. She was most commonly seen in jeans. She seldom dressed up and when she did, preferred slacks, but this was a special occasion. She'd even done her nails.

"Look at you," Maggie said when Clare arrived at their table. "Wow. You didn't come from the hardware store."

"I left early today. After I made sure the check was there, I made an offer on an old house—a fixer-upper."

"You didn't!"

"I did. It's in a neighborhood that seems to be renovating—it's the worst one on the block," she said almost proudly.

"Are you sure that's wise?" Maggie asked.

"Oh, I'm sure. If they accept the offer, I'm stealing it. I can't wait to get in there and start working on it."

"You sure got dressed up to make an offer on an old house."

Clare laughed. "There's that, and I think we should toast my very first date. And I'm not even quite single yet."

"You finally gave in. To the young stud, I presume?"

"Sam," she said. "It feels a little strange." Clare took a breath, wishing she had a drink to steady her first-date nerves.

"Sorry," Sarah said, rushing upon them. She took a seat, brushed at her dress which was loose fitting and matronly, pushed her glasses up on her nose and rattled on. "I was giving a class that ran over and as I was ready to lock up, a customer came in and just about bought out the store. Then I had to cover the sculpture I'd been at work on and get the lights and— Oh, well, you know how it goes." She looked down at her hands. Her nails were choppy in places and there was still some clay around the cuticles. "God, I'm a mess. I thought I got it all off." She looked at Clare. "Wow. Did I RSVP for the wrong party?"

"Date night," Maggie said. "Clare is being pursued by a young stud."

"Date night? No kidding? You're dating? Is it awful?"

"I don't know yet. This would be my first."

"He's been chasing her for months," Maggie further explained.

"Does everyone know about this but me?" Sarah asked. "No one ever talks to me!"

"He hasn't been chasing me. Not really. We're friends."

"I bet he wants to be more than friends," Maggie said.

"No, really. His name is Sam, he was the police officer at the scene of my accident and he came to the hospital to see how I was. Then about a month after I was discharged, he dropped by Dad's with coffee from Starbucks, we've talked on the phone now and then over the past six months, and there you have it. We became friends. He asked me out."

"This has been going on for months?" Sarah wanted to know.

"She's been in denial," Maggie explained. "He wants her."

"I was in physical therapy for five of the last six months," she reminded them. "He's a very nice guy, really. Good-looking, too. But I don't see this going anywhere serious. Just a date. Just friends."

She was answered with dead silence and calm stares. It was Maggie who broke the silence. "You can have sex with friends, can't you?"

A waiter arrived just as the women were melting into laughter. He took drink orders and disappeared.

"So where's he taking you on this date?" Sarah asked.

"Right here," Clare said. "I thought I'd meet you guys for a drink to celebrate getting the insurance check, and to settle my nerves, then have dinner with Sam."

"When are you meeting him?"

"About seven," she said.

Maggie and Sarah exchanged glances, looked at watches and settled back in their chairs. Clare burst out laughing as it was all too clear they weren't going anywhere until they got a look at him.

When their drinks arrived, Maggie lifted hers and said, "To sex."

"You don't have sex on a first date," she said.

"Where's Jason?" Maggie asked.

"Football game. He's got a ride and should be home about ten."

"Ah, the house is empty," Sarah pointed out, sipping her wine. "My big sister has a shot at sex." She sipped her drink and said, "I can't remember when I last had sex. But I remember thinking it was a nice invention."

"You know," Clare said, "I could hook you up. It sounds like you might have more of what he's looking for."

"You know I would do anything for my sister," Sarah returned.

Clare told Sarah about the house and she was much more enthusiastic than Maggie had been. But then, the artist in Sarah could envision creative changes and had taken closer notice of Clare's work in her own house than Maggie had. Maggie hired things done. There was no question that if anyone could make a fixer-upper pay off, it was Clare. And any work she couldn't do herself, she'd have done. Given her connections through the hardware store, she'd get the best deals, not to mention discounts on all her supplies.

When the topic had been exhausted and Clare leaned back in her chair, Sarah asked, "So. How often does he call you? This Sam?"

"Come on, you guys," she said, frustrated.

"I call her a lot. As much as she'll let me," a strong male voice said.

They turned as one and looked up. There, standing right behind Clare was a young, dark-haired Adonis in a navy-blue sweater atop a crisp white shirt and gray wool slacks. When he smiled, his dimples came out to play. His shoulders were broad, his waist trim and his twinkling eyes a cornflower blue that teased.

"Sam!" Clare said.

He bent down and gave her a peck on the cheek. "Don't let me interrupt. I wanted to get here early and have a beer while I waited for you. I had no idea you'd be meeting friends."

"Don't be silly, pull up a chair. These are my sisters and they're dying to get a look at you. There could be a brief interrogation."

"You're sure? Because really…"

"Absolutely," she said, pulling on his hand. "I was just telling them about that house we looked at—the fixer-upper. Not that they care in the least."

"If you're sure," he said again, pulling a chair from an empty table nearby and sitting beside Clare.

"This is good," she said. When he was settled, she patted his hand and turned toward the women. "This is—" She stopped short. They were staring at him in shock and awe. All big wide eyes and open mouths. Sarah pushed up her glasses again. They seemed mesmerized. Clare surmised that Sam was younger and more handsome than they had imagined. And she said, "Jeez."

Sam turned toward her and in a whisper asked, "Do I have a booger or something?"

"No," she laughed. "Give them a second, they'll snap out of it. Maggie! Sarah! This is my friend Sam. Sam, meet Maggie my sister, Sarah my other sister."

Maggie and Sarah left the Fireside at seven, although Clare and Sam had graciously invited them to stay. They hadn't interrogated him after all, but asked him things about his job and family, polite things that were nonthreatening. And he was open and friendly. Good disposition. He had a very natural charm about him—and he was clearly wild about Clare. He reached for her hand several times and held on to it until she pulled it away.

It was possible Clare was uncomfortable. Maybe with this affection around her sisters, maybe with how much he wanted her. It was almost palpable. He was hot to trot.

Maggie was so jealous she could spit.

She couldn't remember the last time Bob came on to her. In fact, she couldn't remember the last time he'd rebuffed *her* advances.

Maggie admired her house as she drove into the cul-de-sac. She always did. It was one of the bigger homes in Breckenridge and she'd labored over every detail in the design when they'd built it ten years ago. The lights shone from the ground floor; the upstairs bedroom lights were off. Bob's office light was on. Of course.

She pulled into the four-port garage and parked her BMW next to Bob's Mercedes. When she walked into the kitchen— the immaculate kitchen—she was treated to the delightful aroma of the meal Ramona had prepared. She put her purse and briefcase on the kitchen desk and glanced into the dining room. On the days Ramona worked for her, she always made dinner before she left and laid the dining table. She saw that on this occasion it was set for two, tall tapers ready to be lit. That meant Ramona had given the girls something to eat earlier and Bob had waited for her.

She shed her coat and hung it in the front closet. As she did so, she could hear Bob's voice coming from his study. On the phone again, which might explain why he hadn't had his dinner. She glanced at her watch—it was only seven-fifteen.

By the time she made herself a cup of tea and went to his office, he was off the phone and on the computer. Bob was a lawyer and lobbyist for several environmental groups in the Northwest. He kept an office in Carson City, but he was well set up here and could work from home, especially when the legislature wasn't in session. Like Maggie, his hours were long and he was extremely successful.

She reminded herself that they were lucky. *She* was lucky. Bob was a wonderful man; a fabulous and devoted father. An extremely supportive husband; a good partner. He was tall, handsome, growing sexier with age. So what was wrong? What was happening to them?

She put her tea on the desk and embraced him from behind. "Hi, honey," she said. "How was your day?"

He didn't turn, but rubbed her hand and reclined against her. "Long. Yours?"

"Interesting. My sister is dating. A younger man."

That made him turn. "Really? How much younger?"

"I'm not sure—I met her for a drink and he showed up there to have dinner with her before I could get more details. I think at least ten years."

Bob laughed. "Good for her. And here I thought she was going to pine away for Roger." He laughed again.

Maggie leaned a hip on his desk. "You know, we need a break. We should try to get away."

"We have that trip to Hawaii planned right after Christmas...."

That was a family vacation during the girls' holiday break from school. "I was thinking...just you and me."

"I don't think I can get away before Christmas."

"How about a weekend? How about one night?"

"What's up? You have trouble at work?"

"No, Bob. I have trouble at home. We haven't... You know."

He reached for her hand and stroked it lovingly. "What's the matter, honey?"

She touched his cheek just as affectionately. "Why don't we make love anymore, Bob? Is it me? I'm not attractive to you?"

"Come here," he said, pulling her onto his lap. "Don't be silly, Maggie. You're gorgeous. I'm just overworked, is all. You know how much I love you."

"It isn't something like someone else, is it?"

Shock registered on his features. "Shame on you. You know there could never be anyone else." He kissed her lips, but it was one of those brief husbandly kisses. Then he rubbed her back a little. "It's been twenty years, honey. It just hasn't been the priority it was when we were younger. But don't we have a good life?"

"Perfect," she said. "But I think I could use a little special attention, if you know what I mean."

He smiled knowingly, with a superior smirk. "You saw Clare being pawed by some good-looking young guy and had an estrogen surge, didn't you?"

"I think I did," she admitted. There was no *think* about it—she wanted to feel someone's hands all over her.

He laughed roguishly and pushed her off his lap. "Come on, honey. Let's have a drink, a nice dinner—I waited for you. And then a little later, we'll take care of Miss Maggie's hormones."

She slipped an arm around his waist as they walked to the dining room together, comfortable and safe against him. "That would be nice," she answered. But she didn't dare get her hopes up. Very likely by the time she primped and came to bed, Bob would be asleep with the light still on and a book spread across his chest. This wasn't the first time she had asked and he had promised.

Sarah didn't go home. She went back to her shop. She let herself in, locked the front door and went to the back, to her studio. She pulled the damp cloth off the sculpture—a little boy and his dog. She ran her fingers along its curves and in so doing, got another look at her chipped and dirty nails. She lifted her hands, splayed the fingers and grimaced.

She had never seen Clare look so lovely. Elegant and almost regal. And the glow on her cheeks suggested that she was stirred up inside, filled with that passionate surprise that is love and explodes into lust and fulfillment. Would she do it with him? Sarah wondered. Surely she would. It was all over them.

Sarah had never had that. Well, she'd had plenty of lust when she was a kid, but only a glimmer of love. She remembered thinking she was in love several times, but knew in the aftermath the feeling had been nothing. Nothing.

Since her mother's death, she had only had a couple of relationships, both very dreary and pretty much meaningless. There was Hal, a very quiet and unstimulating accountant from Carson City. They had actually dated for five years, but Hal was not very interested in sex. Just when she had decided she couldn't stand him any longer, he broke up with her and instantly married a hot blonde from Lake Tahoe. At that point Sarah decided it must have been her. Sarah was the dull one.

Maggie and Clare had felt so sorry for her when she lost Hal. "Oh please," she had said. "He bored me to tears."

One of her customers became an affair for a while. He lit her up inside and she had a hint of what Clare might be feeling right now—excited and nervous and hungry inside. She wanted him. She had him. Very soon after having him and finding him more than a little satisfactory, she found out he was married. She actually shed tears—but she was so grateful that she hadn't told her sisters about him. They would have hovered and fussed. Since that depression episode, they still thought of her as broken and needy.

If she had a man like Sam—sweet and handsome and so physical—she wouldn't be able to contain herself. But, she thought as she looked at her blurry reflection in the studio's window, she couldn't have a man like Sam. Look at yourself, she lectured. She took off her glasses and saw only a worse blur.

She put the glasses back on and was instantly disappointed. She closed the blinds.

She pulled the tie from her hair and shook it out. It was so limp and flat.

I used to be sexy, she thought. Then she heard Maggie's voice in her head saying, "Sarah, this is not sexy—it's trashy! There's a difference, for God's sake!"

A tear slowly escaped her eye and she brushed at it impatiently. Sarah would give anything to have a man like Sam look at her the way he gazed at Clare. Ache for her that way. Want her in such a hard, passionate way that the air around him was electrified.

But that would never happen, she reminded herself. Better paint something.

★ ★ ★

Clare and Sam were seated at a small table in the corner. He pushed the candle and flower out of the middle and reached across the short space to take both her hands. "That was nice—the way you brought me right out of the closet. Almost like you're not hiding me anymore." He tried to keep his face from beaming, but he doubted he was successful.

"I had just been telling them about you. Of course they wanted to know everything."

"You were being grilled," he pointed out.

"You can tell, can't you—that they thought I'd never have a real date."

"With someone who's so hot for you, he's almost explosive."

"There's that talk again. Want me to run?"

"Clare, aren't you just about done running from me? Aren't you getting comfortable with this? With us?"

"Sam, you might be the best-looking guy in town," she said. "And you're a good guy on top of it. Sweet. Funny. You could have any woman you want. Why on earth do you want me?"

He took a deep breath and folded his hands in front of him.

"I'm not fishing for compliments," she said. "I'm serious. I really don't get it."

"Clare, I don't have any trouble picking up girls, but it isn't easy to find a woman who's solid. Who knows her mind. I like that you're mature—I don't see that as a handicap. I know you've had some tough times, but instead of being a victim, like some women younger than you might be, you've let it give you character. You probably think all men find sex appeal in boobs, but some of us find humor and strength and wisdom to be sexy. And," he said, treating her to that grin, "it doesn't hurt that you're also very beautiful."

She just smiled for a moment and then said, "Something wrong with my boobs?"

"I love your boobs," he laughed. "But that's not all I love." He held his breath. Was that too much? He was trying to be careful not to push her. She didn't respond well to being pushed. Another thing that turned him on.

She shook out her napkin and draped it over her lap just as their salads arrived. She smiled again and picked up her fork.

He watched her for a minute. Her movements were so graceful. He loved the way she'd give her head a delicate toss and her rich brown hair would bounce. He was aching to grab handfuls of it. "You look gorgeous," he said. "I didn't think you could get any more beautiful, but you did."

"Thank you, Sam. You're very good for my ego." Then she did something she rarely did—she reached for his hand. It was almost always the other way around. "Why were you here early?"

"I told you—I thought I'd grab a beer and wait for you."

She took a bite of salad, then said, "You weren't calming your nerves, were you?"

"No," he said. "I was a little anxious, but not nervous." Not for dinner, no, he thought. But for later. He hoped she would let him take her someplace where they could be alone, and it wasn't Lover's Lane he had in mind. But he hadn't been at all overconfident—hadn't done anything like book a room. It wouldn't be hard to get one, however. If she agreed. "I've just been looking forward to this. Did you have nerves?"

She shook her head. "I got a big check today—the settlement from the accident. We were celebrating. And I decided it was time to tell my sisters about going out on an actual date with you. That had me wound a little tight. Just so you know, it's out now for sure. They'll probably tell the town."

"Okay by me," he said, digging into his salad, telling himself not to eat like a pig and devour his meal to get it over with quickly. Dessert. He'd like to have Clare for dessert. He heard himself moan and was appalled that it was actually audible.

"Are you all right?"

"This…this is really good."

They talked about food for a while—finding their likes and dislikes remarkably similar. He asked about the house they had seen, was she really considering it? She told him she'd made an offer, then about her plans to remodel. She explained all she had done to the house she lived in. He tried to be patient through her descriptions of spackling, painting and papering. Their steaks arrived with a bottle of red wine.

"If you waited this long to tell your sisters about me, either you're not exactly best friends or you had reservations about trotting me out in public," he said.

"I had mentioned you to Maggie earlier, but the subject hadn't come up with Sarah. She's almost seven years younger than me. We're nothing alike. To tell the truth, we have nothing in common—we're all different as night and day. We didn't get really close until after college, but we were at least loyal when we were younger. There was this one time—my mother was waiting up because Maggie and I were both out on dates. We got home about the same time and were sitting on the couch with Mom, it was pretty dark in the room—only the fireplace and television providing light. She was asking about our evenings, what we'd done, where we'd gone, all that. All of a sudden Maggie burst out laughing so hard she fell off the couch. She was pointing at me with one hand, holding her stomach with the other, tears rolling down her cheeks. I couldn't figure out what she was laughing at until I looked at myself. My sweater was on inside out. My mother said, 'Oh honey, did you have it like that all night?' My face went so red I thought I'd faint and all I could say was, 'Boy, how embarrassing.' Maggie has never let me forget it."

He looked perplexed. "You had it inside out on your date?"

"No," she laughed. "When I left the house, it was on right."

"Oh," he said. Then a slow smile grew on his face. If there's a God, he thought, she'll go home with that sexy black dress on inside out.

"Mrs. Wilson?" The restaurant manager, Frank, stood at their table. He was a man about a dozen years older than Clare and had been with the establishment for many years. "Clare?"

"Yes?"

"There's a situation. I'm sorry, this is very uncomfortable...."

"What is it, Frank?"

"It's Mr. Wilson, ma'am. He's in the bar. I'm afraid he's had a bit too much to drink. I've never seen him—"

They were interrupted by the sudden slurring presence of Roger, swirling a drink in his glass. "Well, well, well, isn't this a pretty picture. My wife is out for the evening."

"I'm sorry, Clare," Frank said. "We'll just—"

"Roger! What's the matter with you?"

"I might've had juss a tad more than is imprudent... But what'd'ya 'spect—when I'm sitting there just washing you grope this...this kid here."

Clare, completely dumbfounded, looked at Sam. There she saw an entirely new face—grim, stony, dangerous. This would be the cop's face, not the sweet young man who'd finally gotten her to agree to a date. His eyes glittered, looking a little as though he might've recently eaten human flesh. There were no dimples but a very scary tic at the corner of his mouth. And there was a pulsing vein in his left temple. This was *not* a kid. This was a serious man. And he was very protective of the woman in his company.

She had not once in her entire friendship with Sam imagined him in a conflict, and now she wondered how she could have known about his job and not conjured up such a picture. But here it was—and Sam was very large and strong. If he got into it with Roger, Roger would be severely damaged. Thank God Roger was a lover, not a fighter.

"Sorry, Mrs. Wilson. Clare," Frank said, nearly wringing his hands. He raised a hand and snapped his fingers. Two young waiters were at his side immediately, escorting Roger away from the table.

"Frank, we've been separated pending divorce for months," she tried to explain.

"So I've gathered, yes. I'm so sorry for the interruption. Please accept our complimentary dinner. We'll escort him out."

She looked at Sam desperately. "I have no idea what that's about. Of all the headaches Roger has given me, he's never been a lush. He just doesn't overdo it."

"It's about him seeing his wife out with another man," Sam said, but he didn't look at Clare. He watched Roger's departing back.

"God," she moaned, lowering her head to her hand. "How many ways can I humiliate thee—let me count the—"

Sam was on his feet.

"Where are you going?"

Sam looked down at her. His expression was still forbidding. "Clare, he can't drive," he said.

She had no idea what she was supposed to do. "Well... Should we call him a cab?"

"Maybe the restaurant will," he said. "I'll be right back." He walked away from the table, following Roger.

Clare sat at the table and noticed, suddenly, that the restaurant was so quiet you could hear a stomach growl. The only noise was the distant singsongy voice of Roger protesting his ejection from the premises. She looked around and saw that every set of eyes was on her. "Oh, jeez," she said. She grabbed her purse and bolted after Sam.

Roger was outside, the two young waiters were preventing him from going back inside and Sam was standing just outside the door with Frank. "Did you ask about a cab?" she asked them both.

"We offered a cab and he said he won't have it," Frank replied. "We couldn't get his keys away from him."

"Damn it! What's the matter with him?" she said, more to herself than to the men.

"If he gets in his car, I'm going to make a phone call," Sam said.

"What'll happen to him?" she asked.

"He'll be picked up," Sam said. Tic. Pulse. His eyes, usually deep blue, were steely. Icy. He did not look at Clare. "Probably before he can even find the ignition."

Roger wandered around the small parking lot, a little lost, lurching from one side of the aisle to the other. He had his keys in his hand and, swaying, he managed to click the control so that the lights of his Pontiac blinked. Sam took his cell phone out of his pocket.

"What will they do to him?"

He looked at Clare. "I imagine they'll hook him and book him. Drunk driving. Leave him alone, Clare. This is not your problem."

"They'll put him in jail?"

"It's what they do to drunk drivers, Clare."

Roger leaned against the hood of his car for a moment. He obviously kept pressing the button on his remote because the lights on his car kept blinking on and off. She looked at Sam—no solution there. She looked at Roger—he was trying to get the key in the door of the car as if he didn't know he had unlocked it with the remote about a dozen times. She looked at Sam—he had his cell phone to his ear.

"Shit," she said. She took off across the parking lot, disappointingly aware that Sam did not call after her or join her. She caught up with Roger and pulled him away before he got in the car. "Come on, Roger. Come with me—behave! I'm going to take you home. And then I'm going to *kill* you!"

"Clare," he said in a whine. He put out a hand as if to stroke her cheek.

"If you touch me, I'll coldcock you!" She looped her arm through his and walked him to the other side of the parking lot. She poured him into the passenger seat.

"Clare..." he said again. "Oh, Clare..."

"Oh shut up!"

She slammed the door and went around the car. She got in the driver's side and pounded the steering wheel a few times. Then she looked at him. Roger was slumped in the seat next to her, humming some off-key tune as though oblivious. She reached across him and buckled him in.

"Thank you, Clare," he slurred contritely.

When she drove out of the parking lot she saw Sam and Frank standing just outside the restaurant door, watching. She made sure she signaled.

Roger was singing. She could recognize the lyrics if not the tune. "Can't smile without you... Can't laugh, can't sing..." She wanted to stop the car and push him into a ditch and leave him there. Tonight was special—she'd spent the last few months of phone calls and stolen kisses working up to having a real date and now *this*. And if Sam hadn't been so stony and cold, she might've made plans to just take Roger home then meet him for an after-dinner coffee that might have led to an after-dinner make-out session to end all make-out sessions, but his demeanor left no room for something like that. Sam clearly wanted to kill Roger and did not endorse the idea of Clare helping him.

Don't be so hard on Sam, she told herself. Because I want to kill Roger just as dead.

"Clare, I didn't mean to," he said. "It was just seeing you like that... So happy with another man...."

"Oh really? Well, welcome to my world, Roger!"

"Clare, don't be mad, honey—"

She slugged him in the arm as hard as she could. "Don't call me *honey!*"

"Ouch! Jesus, Clare! Whatsa matter with you?" Then, he started singing again.

What a disastrous end to a promising evening, she thought. But it had taken her only moments to realize that she could either drive him home or bail him out of jail, and with the rift between Roger and Jason still so wide, having him booked into jail was not going to serve their healing in any way.

She looked at her soon-to-be ex-husband and thought, no jury would convict me. It didn't take long to pull up to the complex in which Roger had taken a small apartment. Luxury Apartments, the sign said. It was gated. "What's the code?" she asked him.

He rattled off some numbers and went back to singing. She pulled through the gate and stopped the car right inside. "Roger, where is your apartment?"

He looked straight ahead, had a confused look on his face and said, "Gee, they all look the same, don't they?"

"Roger!"

"Okay, okay. Gimme a sec. Hmm. I think it's right over there. Yeah, over there." Then he smiled at her. "Wanna come in?"

Clare parked and got out of the car. She opened his door for him. He struggled to get out of the car but failed—his seat belt was still hooked up. If she weren't so furious with him, she'd laugh. Clare simply hated him too much to laugh at him. She popped the seat belt off and he nearly fell out of the car. When he righted himself, he said, "So? Wanna come in?"

"No!"

"O-*kay!* Sheesh."

Roger wove his way up the walk toward an apartment door. He fumbled with his keys for quite a while, then the door opened and he lurched inside.

Clare sighed in relief. And went home. She never even considered going back to The Fireside to see if Sam was there. She could tell he was very unhappy with her helping Roger and didn't feel like trying to explain. Besides, Jason might already be home.

She found the place deserted. It was only nine-thirty. The message light on her answering machine was blinking. She thought it was pretty likely that Roger was already calling her and she considered not listening to her messages. But it could be Jason so she pressed the button.

To her complete astonishment, Pete's voice rang out in the room, completing the trifecta of men in her life. "Hi, Clare. I meant to call you long before this, but football season keeps me pretty tied up. Anyway, can't help thinking about how we were going to get together—you probably thought I forgot. Not hardly—you've been on my mind. I was wondering if you'd like to meet for coffee or something on Sunday? It's about the only time I don't have a game or a practice. Give me a call. Let me know. I…ah…can't wait to hear from you."

He didn't even say his name. Didn't leave a number. He didn't have to say his name; didn't have to leave a number. Her annoyance over the disastrous evening vanished.

Clare played the message again. And again. And again. She felt herself smiling.

chapter eight

....

BEFORE CLARE COULD contemplate whether it was too late to return Pete's call, she heard her cell phone twittering in her purse. She heaved a sigh—that had better not be Roger, drunk dialing. She wished a major hangover on him as she plucked the phone out of her purse and looked at the caller ID. Sam.

"Hello."

"You're home now, I assume?"

"Yes."

"Any reason you didn't call me to see where I was? So we could finish our date?"

"I was finished," she said.

"Hey! Are you putting this on *me?*"

"You weren't exactly helpful," she said.

"And why would I want to help your drunk ex-husband? He got tanked up, made a scene and was about to put the whole town in danger by driving impaired!"

"Are you raising your voice? Because I can just hang up if that's what you're doing."

He took a breath. "Okay. All I want to know is why you did what you did."

"Because my life isn't going to be any easier if Roger goes to jail. I don't expect you to get it."

"That's good, because I really don't. You're either over him or you're not."

"You think I did that for Roger?" She laughed bitterly. "I was this close to pushing him out and leaving him in a ditch! But I have a son—his son—and things are bad enough between them, without giving Jason any more reasons to refuse to make amends with his dad!" She sighed. "I'm *over* him, I'm just not *done* with him. Apparently."

"You said anything they had to work out was between them," he said, his voice irritable.

"It is. And the sooner the better, because I need to have someplace for my son to go once in a while so I can have a little privacy!" She hung up on him.

Clare sat heavily on the couch. She couldn't believe she yelled at him, then hung up on him. As if it was his fault. She picked up the remote and turned her gas fireplace on. She clicked on the light by the sofa. She was holding a phone in each hand—the cell and the house phone from which she was contemplating calling Pete.

She sat. And sat. She should call Sam back, apologize. This should be nipped right here because regardless of what Sam had said or done, it was Roger who had acted like an ass and screwed up their evening.

The cell phone rang. Sam. Again.

"Hello," she said, much more calmly.

"Okay, we had our first fight. Check that one off. Now we can kiss and make up."

"I was just going to call you to say I'm sorry. Do you see how crazy Roger can make people? God!"

"Can I come over?"

She hesitated. "Jason will be home anytime now."

"He's not there right now?"

"No, but he'll be home any—" The doorbell rang. "You did it again, didn't you?"

"I did."

She put both phones on the hall table and opened the door to Sam, who rushed in and immediately grabbed her like a starving man. She gasped, which served to give him her slightly opened mouth, of which he took full advantage. He devoured her mouth, his tongue probing and hot inside. He turned her so that her back was against the front door; he flipped the dead bolt. He pressed into her.

Sam's hands were on her face, his fingers laced into her soft brown hair, his mouth moving passionately over hers. As he plastered her back to the door, she felt the full measure of his desire against her pelvis. If this were happening any other place, even in the backseat of a car, she would be lost. Her whole body ached to be satisfied; she virtually trembled with longing. She heard her own moan, deep in her throat.

"I'm sorry I yelled," he whispered against her mouth. "It was stupid. I was disappointed. I wanted to be with you."

"Okay. I understand. Let's not get all worked up—Jason will be coming home soon."

He ground against her, kissing and nibbling her neck and she moaned again. It felt so good. "Let's get a little worked up," he whispered. "God, Clare, do you know how badly I want you?"

She did. She directed his mouth to hers again, filled herself with his kiss, moved her hips a little against him. Tempted. Awfully tempted. But she said, "Not tonight."

"We could make a run for it," he said. "Get your coat."

His hand found her breast and she put her hand over his to hold it there.

Clare actually thought about doing just that. Grab her coat, go anywhere he wanted, *do* anything he wanted. She enjoyed him, was attracted to him; she was more than a little flattered by his attention; she could *easily* sleep with him and she bet he was fabulous in bed. He turned her on. Except... Her feelings for him were not growing or showing signs of permanence. Their relationship wasn't becoming love. She wondered if it ever would... And she doubted it. It was showing signs of being a fling. Period.

"What's the matter?" he asked her.

So here was her dilemma. She was going to be forty soon— did she have to love him? What did that matter, really? There wasn't anyone else interested in her. She'd be monogamous, naturally. She was excellent at monogamy. And as he had said, enjoy life and if it works out, fine, and if not, no harm done.

Oh, but she knew better. He wanted her too much. So much that Roger, who wasn't a threat sober and was even less of one drunk, had made him very angry with his ridiculous little scene.

She couldn't do it. She had to be in love, or at least think she was in love. She had to believe the affair was going somewhere. And Sam, for all his playful spirit, was intense. He would devour her. If she let him in, he would not let her go. It was too soon, way too soon for her to get into a hot and serious relationship, especially since she would be hot and he would be serious. She couldn't keep him at bay any longer while she struggled with this. She wasn't sure they could even continue to be friends.

Feeling him against her, his hands on her body, it was very

difficult to give this up. It was too tempting to forget her scruples and just go for it.

"Clare?"

"Okay, look, I'm going to make us some coffee. We'll sit by the fire for a while. We'll settle down a little, okay?"

"You sure?" he asked. "Because I think we can still make a break for it before—"

There was the sound of a key in the lock. Sam braced a strong hand against the front door to prevent it opening and whispered, "Bathroom?"

"Right there," she said.

He disappeared around the corner instantly. Jason pushed the door open.

"Hi," he said. "Who's here?"

"Sam Jankowski. We had dinner together tonight. I'm going to make us some coffee."

"Cool," he said.

It was eleven-thirty and Clare was under the covers, phone in hand. She had managed to get Sam out of the house about an hour before without any more clinches, citing concern that Jason might discover them and be traumatized. "He's probably getting more than you are," was Sam's insightful remark.

So she lay here, thinking about the situation. One of the things that had kept her from going full tilt into bed with Sam was some instinct that told her despite what Sam said about having all the time in the world, he was running out of time. And patience. She had thoroughly enjoyed his flirtation. It had been fun being wanted like that, being tempted. Desire had all but dried up in her, and he had brought it back to life. And she hadn't been particularly worried about how he might react when she ultimately said, "So, Sam—this isn't working for me—let's not see each other any longer."

But she should have been. He was falling in love with her. If she didn't do something about this, he would get in too deep and experience an awful lot of hurt getting out. It might already be too late. She'd had hints of this intensity in him, but hadn't been able to put a name to it.

She wanted to talk to someone about it, but there was no one available to chat at eleven-thirty. Maggie and Sarah would have gone to bed long ago.

She clicked through the caller IDs to see if anyone had called but left no message. Pete Rayburn's name popped up four times. She clicked on the number and put the call through. The answering machine came on. "This is Pete..."

Clare started to leave a message. "Oh. Of course it's too late, I'm sorry. Just wanted to tell you that I'd love to—"

"Hello? Hello?" a man's tired voice said. "You there?"

"You were sleeping, I'm sorry," Clare said.

"No, no, no! I was, ah, screening calls."

She laughed at him. "You were sleeping," she said.

"Okay, but I'm up now. How are you?"

"Fine, fine. I got your message. I'd love to go out for coffee. Or something."

"Great! That's great! So—how you been? Busy?"

"Kind of, yes. Would you believe that tonight was my very first real date in my almost single new world?"

There was a pause before he said, "Really? Um, how was it?"

"It was a complete disaster," she said. "Try to picture this— I'm having a very nice steak dinner with a man who happens to be one of our local police officers when my soon-to-be ex, Roger, sees us from the restaurant bar and proceeds to get himself plastered. I mean, *steenking*. The manager is trying to eject him, but he comes to our table, makes a little scene, the police officer date threatens to make a phone call and have him locked up if he attempts to drive, which Roger, who can barely walk, insists he is going to do. So instead of having a nice first date, I drove my drunk almost-ex home."

Pete was laughing. "God, you couldn't have made that up!"

"Oh, it's the truth," she said.

"That's priceless! Think you'll get a second date with this guy?"

"We'll have to just wait and see," she said evasively. "You've been single awhile. You any better at this dating thing?"

"Well, my ex-wife doesn't show up drunk." A pause. "No, I'm lousy at it. I haven't been out on a date since... Since... Hell, I can't remember," he said. A long silence followed. "This police officer. You like him a lot?"

"Oh," she hedged, "he's a nice guy, but...I don't know."

"Don't know what?"

"I just realized something. He's intense. I think he's looking for a lot more in a relationship than I am. Probably not a good thing. At this point, anyway. I'm not officially divorced, though Roger and I have been separated for months. And months. And tonight I almost made myself a widow."

"What's holding things up? Is he giving you a hard time? Roger?"

"As a matter of fact, he's being a huge pain in the ass, but the thing that really stalled this out was the accident. I just couldn't take on a divorce while I was recuperating."

"You have a clean bill of health yet?"

"One hundred percent. Cleared to ski, though I've been warned to take it easy. Sounds like the bunny slopes for me."

"But that's great. We used to have such fun skiing, didn't

we? I was remembering some of the things we used to do," he said. "Remember when we were sophomores and it was homecoming and we were out at Sorenson's farm making the float for the parade?"

"Yeah?"

"And everyone was working really hard, but we snuck off to the pasture with a bridle and hooked up the horse? And we were riding around the corral and around the barn, irritating all the hardworking seniors. We were bareback—you were hanging on to me and kept slipping. So we got to laughing. We got the stupids."

"We used to do that a lot. Get the giggles and not be able to stop."

"And the homecoming king, my big brother, got really pissed…"

"Oh, God, he was so mad at us. Screw-offs, he called us."

"I was a screw-off, that much we know. I was a bad influence on you. Got you in trouble with your boyfriend, who was sooo reliable and responsible."

"I wasn't all that hard to influence, though."

"Yeah, but you're a girl, so you always tried to behave. Me? I was hopeless. Behaving never really turned me on. You know?"

"I know," she laughed. "You were a bad boy. But you had so much fun."

"I stayed in trouble. That's probably how I deal with these teenage boys as well as I do. I relate."

She was quiet for a moment. "It's nice. Remembering some of the good things. The funny things. For a long time I could only remember that terrible time—when his plane went down. Too long. I was stuck in that time frame too long."

"It's so good to hear you laugh. We had some great times

back then." He paused and then said, "Clare, it's so good to hear your voice."

She was cradling the phone next to her ear, getting sleepy. "I can't believe how it feels like no time has passed."

"Remember when we all went to my grandpa's cabin to ski?"

"Oh, God," she said, laughing again. They had built a snow fort, a snow wall, and lay in wait for some of the others and hammered them with snowballs. *Waled* on them! Beat the tar out of them! "We teamed up a lot," she said sleepily. There was a smile on her face as she drifted.

"Remember the time...?" he said. He went into another story. But before the end of it, Clare was asleep, the phone beside her ear.

"Clare?" he asked. "Clare, are you there?"

She made a little snort, followed by a snore. She rolled over. She had the most lovely dreams in which she was a girl again—a happy girl, surrounded by friends, laughing, dancing, singing. They had a most magical teenage experience in the shadow of the glorious Sierras—the football and basketball games, the dances, hayrides and ski trips, the long days spent at Lake Tahoe. They used to sun and swim all day and then build a bonfire on the beach and cook hot dogs and sing songs and make out.

The sun streamed into the window and Clare slowly roused. The first thing she remembered was a wonderful, long conversation she was having with Pete before she fell asleep. Then she rolled over and saw the phone lying in the bed beside her and she jerked awake with a startled yelp. "Pete!" she cried. She picked up the phone and saw that the line was still open. She'd fallen asleep on him! "Pete?" she yelled into the phone.

"Huh?"

"You're *there?*"

"Huh?" Clare heard a little rustling around and then he said, "Clare?"

"You're still there?"

"Uh, I think you fell asleep during one of my more entertaining stories," he said sleepily.

"Why didn't you hang up?"

"If you were asleep, I didn't want the phone to go aaa-aaa-aaa-aaa."

She said, "I'm sorry!" But she was laughing. "Oh, God, I can't believe I did that!"

"Clare? Listen…Sunday. The weather's so great—meet me at Barkley Park at two. I have the kids this weekend, but will drop them off in the early afternoon. I'll bring us something. I'll bring a thermos."

They used to hang out at Barkley Park. Play touch football. "Sounds perfect," she said.

The phone was ringing as Clare stepped out of the shower. She wrapped a towel around herself and answered it in the bedroom.

"Clare? Hi," Sam said. "Everything okay?"

"Sure. Why?" she asked.

"I tried calling your cell phone and home phone. I'd get your voice mail on the cell, but the answering machine never came on the home line."

"Oh that," she said. She laughed an embarrassed laugh. "I'm sorry. The phone was off the hook and I forgot about it. I fell asleep. And of course the cell is in my purse in the closet downstairs, where I couldn't hear it."

"Well, at least you're okay. I was a little worried. Why was your phone off the hook?"

She thought fast. "Um... I was just avoiding any drunk dialing from Roger."

"Gotcha," he said. "Just wanted to tell you, I'm working a little overtime this weekend. I have to work swing the next two days. But I'd really like to try that date thing again. What are you doing?"

Clare bit her lip. What she needed was not to see Sam for a couple of days; his overtime this weekend was fortuitous. "Let's see... I promised to take Jason to the electronics store for an upgrade on his computer this morning, then I'm going to work at the store for a few hours this afternoon. And tomorrow I'm having Sunday brunch with the family. I've got to get together with Maggie about the divorce. Roger has to be put out of his misery."

"It kind of looks that way," he said.

"Later tomorrow afternoon I'm meeting an old friend from high school for coffee."

"How about Monday night—let's try again. Maybe we can make the evening end better."

"I kind of like to hang close on school nights, Sam. But how about lunch? I'm not on the clock—I can take as much time as I need."

"Good. I'll plan something nice. Something special."

She chewed her lip. Special wasn't exactly the right word. Only she knew that she was about to break his heart. "That'll be good," she said. "I'll talk to you later."

She hung up the phone and it rang. She picked it up and Roger said, "Do I owe someone an apology?"

"Me, my date, all the diners at The Fireside and the management. I hope you're miserable and in excruciating pain."

"You have no idea...."

"Good. I can't talk. Take aspirin and consider more therapy." She hung up on him.

Clare got dressed and went downstairs to make coffee. On her way to the kitchen, she took her cell phone out of her purse and looked at the call record. Five missed calls; as many messages. If she wasn't sure before, she was now. Sam, bless him, was in over his head. With her usual penchant for putting things off, she had let this go on too long, let him get too close.

She should have seen this coming, but she was naive about the dating world and hadn't realized what was happening. It was one thing to chat with him on the phone during her recovery—she was out of reach and he was held safely at bay by the crack in her pelvis. But lately he'd moved closer. Sam had been heating up and she hadn't exactly discouraged him. He was starting to sizzle. She felt it last night when he pressed her against the door. He was committed to getting her in bed.

Clare had a sticky little problem here. And she knew it. She hated to have to hurt him. Five missed late-night calls suggested this was going to smart.

Family dinner time varied on Sundays, according to what was going on in everyone's schedule, and fortunately for Clare, her nieces had afternoon commitments, as did she. They had their meal together at noon, after which George and Bob took their coffee to the living room to watch football, the teenagers dispersed and the sisters washed up, letting Dotty go home and relax.

Maggie carried the dishes from the table. "Okay, spill," she said. "What happened with your young stud on Friday night?"

"Stop calling him that," Clare said, not looking up from her rinsing chore. She passed a plate to Sarah to put into the dishwasher. "It was a disaster." She told them about Roger's drunken antics.

"Oh my God," Maggie said. "I think Roger's losing it. He's not going to calm down until he realizes it is irrevocably over. We'd better do that divorce."

"I think you're right," Clare said. "Will you please help me with that?"

"Absolutely. Damn, I'm sorry about Roger. I had it in my head that you were going to… You know. Get so, so lucky."

Clare passed another plate to Sarah. "I could have killed Roger," Clare said. "But in the end, he might've done me a favor. This thing with Sam… It just isn't for me."

"What?" Maggie and Sarah said in unison.

"I should have seen this sooner, but what do I know about dating, about relationships? I've been playing do-si-do with Roger for sixteen years. It's very clear that Sam is ready for something serious. Something…intense."

Sarah shivered visibly. Both sisters looked at her. "What's wrong with him?" she asked.

"Nothing. Absolutely nothing. He's great—he's got it all. Looks, personality, charm—and have you seen his arms? Woo. Clearly, he could have any woman he set his sights on. But what I saw as friendship has obviously grown in his mind, and hasn't in mine."

Maggie leaned one hand against the kitchen counter, the other on her hip. "Clare, he's gorgeous. Young, energetic, and so hot for you he's almost smoking! Are you crazy?"

"There's something about Sam that I never realized. Something not apparent in a few months of casual phone chats. He's not capable of playing around. He's passionate. There's allure in that—the sheer power of his passion. Maybe I'm making a mistake, maybe I'll regret it, but I think I'd be taking a big chance getting any more involved with him. It isn't going anywhere."

"Except maybe a thoroughly fabulous roll in the hay," Maggie said. "Here I was, jealous, and you're going to have this sudden attack of conscience and mess up your one opportunity for what appears to be unrivaled ecstasy."

"I know—I think I've lost my mind," Clare said. "A little unrivaled ecstasy sure would feel good right now. But the picture I can't get out of my mind is the look I'd see on Sam's face when I tell him—as I eventually will—that I can't see him anymore. He doesn't deserve to be my middle-age experiment."

"Are you sure?" Sarah wanted to know.

She looked at her younger sister. "Honey, no matter how tempting, he feels a lot like a sweet younger brother. I just can't get the term boy toy out of my mind. And believe me, Sam is no boy toy. You saw him, how he behaves. He's not the kind of guy who goes into anything halfway. He's already invested a lot of emotion in this relationship—and we haven't even spent that much time together."

"But how do you know it won't develop into something— you know—that you're as passionate about as he is?" Sarah asked. The look in her eyes was so earnest it was almost pleading.

"Here's what I know. I should say here's what I *remember*. When you fall for someone, when you fall in love, you can't wait for his calls, yearn to be alone with him, ache to have him touch you, hold you—it's unmistakable. It's impossible to keep from calling him first. You don't sleep, your heart skips beats, you think about him constantly, you live for the next kiss." She took a breath. "It felt very good to have his interest. His attention. It would be very easy to go along with this and have some pleasure, too. But I'm not serious about him. I don't think we can even be friends—it will encourage him, and that would be cruel."

Sarah sighed. Maggie threw down the dish towel and started to leave the kitchen.

"Hey," Clare said. "Where are you going?"

"I think I'm going to take Bob home and tie him to the bed."

When Clare got to the park Pete was already there, sitting on top of a picnic table. He had a small picnic basket and beside it a thermos. Her heart lifted. She had felt morose knowing she was going to have to tell Sam she was breaking it off, but seeing Pete, her old friend Pete, brightened the day considerably. She had missed him so without realizing it. He stood as she approached and gave her a welcoming hug. "Good to see you. So good," he said as he embraced her.

"Pete, you reconnected me to a part of my life I'd forgotten, and I can't tell you how good that feels. I'm sorry about the other night, about falling asleep like that."

"It's okay." He grinned at her. "I wasn't that insulted."

"What did you bring?"

"A hot rum drink—just like at the lodge. And cookies," he said, flipping the lid on the basket. "Made 'em myself."

"You *bake?*"

"My daughters like to bake—I supervise so they don't burn the house down. I just dropped them off at home." He poured her a drink in a mug. "Catch me up on your sisters and dad."

They sat on the top of the picnic table, feet on opposite benches, facing each other. Clare filled him in on Maggie and Sarah, told him about life at the store and the house she'd made the offer on, which she expected to hear about on Monday.

She asked him about his daughters, they gossiped a little bit about the high school that had so briefly employed her. An hour passed in what felt like seconds. They reminisced about the good old days and the laughter that had caught them up then was back. Clare didn't want the day to end.

"You'll never know how much I regret that I avoided you for years. What seemed so disastrous before, now feels like just a misunderstanding. Honestly, I didn't think I'd ever get past it. And here we are, friends, like old times."

He hung his head briefly, as though that bothered him.

"I'm sorry," she said. "Did I say something wrong?"

When he looked up, his eyes seemed troubled. "I'm glad, too," he said.

"Um, something about that didn't seem completely glad."

"Clare, I have to tell you something. I'm a little nervous. Afraid it might be a mistake—might be purely selfish. But I don't want to mislead you."

"Uh-oh. Now you're scaring me."

He took a deep breath, then poured himself a small amount of hot rum from the thermos and took a bolstering drink. "I did this on purpose—the rum. I wanted to loosen us up. Well, I wanted to loosen you up and give me some courage."

God, she thought. He's getting married. He has a terminal illness. He's moving to Costa Rica. "You don't want to mislead me how?"

"I want to cleanse my soul," he said gravely. "Clear my conscience. That night—nineteen long years ago. Clare, that wasn't an accident. It wasn't just too much wine. Not for me. It was the greatest moment of my young life."

"What? I don't understand."

He put his hand over hers on the tabletop. "What I did was wrong and I knew it, but it was intentional. I had a huge crush on you. Since I was about fourteen, I guess. I was in love with you."

"You couldn't have been..." she said, shaking her head. They goofed around together. Laughed insanely. There had never been a hint of romance in their relationship. She pulled her hand out from under his.

"Oh-ho, I was so gone, it was almost tragic. But I was this skinny freckle-faced kid and the only way I could get your attention was to make you laugh. Then you got hooked on my brother—who was older, bigger, smarter, better-looking. And I think I stayed this kid brother in your eyes all through high school, so I just kept making you laugh."

"You never let on," she said in a soft breath. "Not once."

"Are you kidding? I liked living. Mike would have killed me. But he was gone, we were alone, and I could tell you were warming up to me in a brand-new way." He shrugged. "What an asshole, huh? It turned out I took complete advantage of you. Then felt completely ashamed of what I'd done to you."

Clare was flabbergasted. This possibility had never occurred to her, not once in nineteen years. She held her mug toward him and he tipped the thermos over it. "How did you expect things to turn out?" she asked him.

"Ah. Well. In my fantasies I thought you'd realize you were marrying the wrong brother and we'd break it to him. He'd be pissed, but by the time we'd had our second or third kid, he'd be over it. Or, I thought it was possible you'd stick to your original choice—but have no regrets about what we'd done. You'd have let me down gently—you always were a really nice person. Then there was always the chance that you'd go ahead and marry Mike and struggle not to be unfaithful again even though you were constantly tempted—and the strain would be with us through forty years of family dinners. The one thing I never considered was that you would be shattered by it. And hate me."

"I never hated you."

"And never did I consider that Mike would up and kill himself in a jet. And screw us all up even worse than we were already screwed up."

"I just don't believe it," she said, shaking her head.

"It's absolutely true. I wanted you. For years. I was about as desperate as a tortured young man can be."

"My God," she said. "I just don't know what to think."

"It never crossed your mind? In all these years?"

"Not once."

"And you thought—?"

"That we drank too much wine, were too alone, did what came naturally without using one single brain cell in the process." She looked down. She cleared her throat. "Wow. Now I'm going to have to remember this in a whole new way. From an entirely different perspective."

"I've been wanting to get together since we talked in August, but knowing that I had to do this—it took me a long time to get up the nerve to call you."

"Why did you feel you had to tell me this? You really *didn't* have to."

"Because I just couldn't let you go on thinking that I was as innocent as you were. For you it was a mistake—which you only made because I went after you with everything I had. I wanted you to know the truth because…"

"Clare," someone shouted. They both turned and looked as Sam approached. He was uniformed and his cruiser was parked behind Clare's car. As he recognized Pete, a broad smile broke over his face. "Hey, hey, hey," he said, sticking out his hand.

Pete stood and accepted the handshake. "How you doing, Sam?"

"Great, Coach. Great!" Then he moved closer to Clare, leaned toward her and gave her a proprietary peck on the cheek. "Hi. Is *this* your old friend from high school?"

"As a matter of fact," she said. "You two obviously know each other."

"I coached Sam in varsity football," Pete said. "About a dozen years ago?"

"At least! What a hoot! I thought you'd be getting together with a girlfriend!"

"Pete and I grew up together," Clare said. "We graduated in the same class." She forced a smile. "And taught at the same high school for four whole days." *And made mad passionate love nineteen years ago that I just found out was premeditated.*

"That kind of put us back on the same path," Pete explained. "We were just talking about old times. What brings you out here?"

"Oh—I saw Clare's car and wondered what she'd be doing here. So I stopped." His radio sputtered and he turned it down. "I'm not one to pass up a golden opportunity. So, how are Vickie and the girls?"

"Girls are great. Vickie and I have been divorced about five years now."

"Oh man, I'm sorry to hear that, Pete. Jeez."

"It's okay. She's been remarried quite a while now."

"So—you seeing anyone special?"

Pete shrugged. "I go out now and then. Pretty casual, I guess you'd say."

"Got someone you can call, go out with me and Clare?" Sam asked. He reached out and rubbed her arm. "That'd be fun."

Clare didn't respond. Sam's radio sputtered some more, but he didn't seem concerned.

"That would be great," Pete said.

There came a whoop-whoop-whoop from the police car and the lights suddenly flashed. "I'm being paged—I guess they seriously want me. Gotta run." He leaned toward Clare and kissed her cheek again. As he backed away, he pointed a finger at Pete. "Great seeing you, Pete!"

Pete nodded. Hands plunged in his pockets, he just watched Sam as he turned around and jogged back to his squad car. He waited till the car pulled away, lights flashing and siren screaming, before he turned back to Clare.

"We've been out on one date," she said.

"Clare, he was marking his territory. I'm surprised he didn't pee a circle around you."

"I have a little problem here," she said. "I think I made a mistake. I think I led him on. I'm going to end this now before it goes any further. And I know he's not going to take it well."

"What happened?" Pete asked.

"He was the police officer at the scene of my accident. He came to the hospital to check on me, then he called, then he dropped by." She took a deep breath. "More recently he started asking me out, let more and more of his feelings be known. But he always had a light touch—just relax and enjoy yourself, he said. If it's right, great, and if it's not, we move on." She took a deep breath. "Even as he said that, I knew it wasn't that simple. To tell the truth, it's the first time in a long time someone has paid attention to me. And it felt good. I wanted to think it could be casual. It can't."

"But you were considering it," he said.

"Well, who wouldn't? But I'm in no condition for that kind

of relationship. I'm not even divorced yet. I need time to figure out my life, which seems to get more complicated by the day."

"I have a feeling I just added to your complications," he said.

"Well, yes you did. But we might as well have the truth between us."

"Don't spare me now—does that truth make you hate me more?"

"No, Pete. I never hated you. I'm determined to have your friendship back. Regardless of the mistakes we made—and we both made them—there is more good stuff in our past than bad. I just need a little time to digest this."

"Just say you forgive me."

"I think the one who has to forgive you is gone."

He smiled a small smile. "It's been a long time. I've made my peace with Mike."

chapter nine

· · · · · · · · · · · · · · · · · · · ·

CLARE WENT HOME and got busy in the kitchen making Jason's favorite meal—homemade macaroni and cheese and chocolate cake. When he was finished with dinner and had the chocolate cake in front of him, she said, "Jase, I have something to tell you. It won't come as a surprise, but it still might be hard to hear. Tomorrow your aunt Maggie is serving your dad with divorce papers."

He slowly looked up from his cake. "Why would that be hard to hear?" he asked her.

She ignored that. Instead she said, "You know, an old friend of mine taught me a lesson I wish I'd learned years and years ago. About how to remember the things that are really important. Your dad hasn't lived with us for a long time now, Jase. And from now on we're going to be friends, not husband and wife."

"Fine by me. But I don't want to—"

"Okay, stop. Just listen to me for a second. The marriage is over, but the family isn't. Whether you love him or hate him, he's your dad and he *was* my husband. There were times he came through for me in such a huge way, I don't know what

I would have done without him. When your grandma died, I was devastated. Totally wrecked. I cried and cried and cried till I was so pickin' sick of crying I'd want to die, and then I'd cry some more. If the roles had been reversed, I'm not sure how much patience I'd have had—but your dad just held me and said, 'there, there, I know it hurts.' For days. For weeks. Maybe months.

"He was there when you were born and he cried, he was so happy. Remember how he loved to take you skiing? And he was the one who insisted you have a chance to learn to ride that sinful four-wheeler I hated, and *he* bought the snowboard, not me. I don't think he ever missed a soccer game. And even though I have plenty of complaints about the kind of husband he was, he never missed my birthday or anniversary—he gave me beautiful presents. Wonderful cards. He took you shopping for Mother's Day. And since the day we separated, he has paid all the bills and sent money. Do you know how many men leave their marriages and their children and have to be chased down by the courts to support their families?"

"So what are you getting at?"

"I have plenty of negative things to think about, to remember, if I want to. But I've decided I'm not going there. There are things I treasure that I wouldn't have without your dad—starting with you. So from now on, I'm going to work on remembering the positive things. The good things. I don't want the last sixteen years to have been a waste of time."

He stared at his cake for a minute. Then he said, "Well, good luck." He picked up his plate and took it to his room.

Well, that little speech wouldn't have worked on me six months ago, either, she thought.

It was ten-thirty and she was in bed with a book when she heard Jason's bedroom door open. He tapped gently at her half-open door and she waved him in. He stood at the foot of her bed and she could see that his eyes were red rimmed from crying. She wished he hadn't cried alone, but boys his age are so stoic, so isolated. "He used to dress up like Santa," he said. "Like I couldn't tell who it was."

"He did," she said. "Come here," she invited, patting the bed beside her.

He was already taller than she was, but he sat on the bed beside her, then up came his long legs as he curled up on the bed, his back to her. His head on her pillow, his shoulders shook just slightly as he cried.

"It's going to be all right now, honey," she said. "We're going to be fine. All of us."

Sarah couldn't remember when she had wanted something so badly that she'd be willing to risk so much. She took a hard look at herself in the mirror and made a conscious decision— she was going to make changes. Major changes. She couldn't expect any man to look at her the way she was. Her natural beauty, and there was some, was buried beneath this veneer of neglect she had adopted. It had not been as deliberate as it appeared—it had been born out of her complete absorption in her work. That, and her need to change that tawdry, cheap persona her poor mother had so despised.

Clare and Maggie used to try to coax her back into beauty and style. "How about a better haircut," one would say. "Or highlights. Blond streaks would light up your face." She had heard things like, "If you must wear the glasses instead of contacts, let's at least get you some more fashionable specs," and "Honestly, Sarah, you have such a perfect figure, why not dress in clothes that show it off." She tried to remind them that when she had tried showing off her assets, it upset everyone, especially their mother, but they were quick to point out that there was a happy medium.

Her sisters had long since given up as Sarah appeared to be committed to plainness.

It was time, she reckoned. And it might not work at all, might not pay off, but she had to give it a chance. Sam would never glance her way as she was—and why should he? More than beauty was required, of course, but looking as if you just don't give a damn was no way to get a man's attention.

Every time she thought about him, she trembled. This was what Clare was talking about. Tossing and turning, feeling your pulse race, your cheeks suddenly brightening from the sheer heat of a fantasy. According to Clare, that wasn't happening to her. But it was sure as hell happening to Sarah.

This would take time, she decided. She meant to effect her superficial changes quickly, the rest would come later. It was imperative to sit quietly and watch, to be sure that Clare had no lingering interest in Sam. If it appeared that Clare was waffling, Sarah would do nothing. Her sister's love was everything to her and it was finders-keepers. But if it was truly over between them, after a respectable amount of time, she was going to hunt him down and see if she had a chance. Was two weeks respectable? Oh, God, she hoped she could wait even that long.

There was a little voice in her head that said, You might be very, very disappointed. He might not have the slightest interest in you, even prettied up. Or he might do to you what Clare refused to do to him. Toy with your feelings; break your heart.

So I'll cry, she told the voice. So I'll feel a little sorry for myself. There is no guarantee, but you never know unless you try.

There was a time, in her young years, when she would sleep with anyone. Then in later years, no one. Since she'd turned twenty-one, there had been exactly two men in her life, and neither of them had caused her heart to pound the way the mere thought of Sam did.

She put up a sign in the shop—Closed For The Day. She went to the beauty shop without an appointment. Bonnie, the beautician she and her sisters had been seeing for years, was usually instructed to trim an inch or two off the bottom of Sarah's light brown hair. But when Sarah was in the chair she said, "I'd like to do something different today, if you're up to it."

"Well, hallelujah!" Bonnie said.

"Do you think you can make it…I don't know…pretty?"

"Girl, I can make it beautiful."

Bonnie got to work, cutting, coloring and perming. Sarah was in the chair so long she was about to call Maggie and tell her to pay the ransom. Three hours later Sarah looked at herself in the mirror and smiled. Her long, straight, lank hair was now cut in a layered shape, streaked with soft blond, curling around her face and onto her shoulders. It was fluffy and soft. Full and thick.

"You want my advice?" Bonnie asked. But before Sarah could answer she said, "Let's wax your brows into a nicer shape. Say goodbye to that monobrow."

"Sure," she said, taking off her glasses.

It only took minutes and when she looked in the mirror again, even though her new brows were surrounded by pink skin from the hot wax, it made all the difference in the world.

"Girl, look at those eyes. You have the most beautiful eyes I've ever seen. You and your sisters—you green-eyed hussies. You have to get rid of those glasses. Any reason you can't wear contacts?"

"I…ah…I stopped wearing the contacts because my eyes

would get so dry and scratchy from long hours of painting. Weaving."

Bonnie twirled the chair around so that Sarah faced her. "Let me just say something. You have your work on display here and there. From time to time…"

"Exhibitions," Sarah supplied.

"I would think it would be better, help you sell your stuff, if you spruced up a bit. I'm not saying glamorous. Just, you know—"

"Professional?"

"There you go."

"I'm sure you're right."

Sarah hadn't needed Bonnie's advice. Only thing was, she wasn't doing this to be more professional looking. She wanted a man. She had everything else.

On Monday Clare was able to blame her distraction and nervousness on the fact that Roger was being served with the divorce papers. That fine fellow took it better than she expected. Of course he called her at once. In a watery voice, he asked her to reconsider. But he didn't make her endure too much of that before he said, "If you ever change your mind, even for a second…"

"I won't," she said firmly. "But Roger, we need to get back on track with Jason. I want us all to get along."

"I want that, too, Clare. I promise you."

"I'll do what I can to help," she relented. "He needs you in his life."

"Even if you don't?" he asked.

"I need you to be my son's father."

A couple more hours dragged by, and then it was time. Sam

picked her up at the hardware store at noon. She had wanted to take her own car and meet him somewhere, but he insisted.

When they were in Sam's car, he asked, "How'd it go with Roger?"

"Better than I expected. It was Jason who surprised me with a few tears. I take that as a good sign. He might be softening up." It might be better to just tell him in the car, she thought. Before we get to some restaurant where we'd have no privacy. She cleared her throat. "Where are we going?"

"Look in the backseat," he said, smiling.

She turned to see a picnic basket and carefully folded blanket. Oh, God, she thought. We're going to be alone, probably isolated, and I'm going to rip his heart out. This is going to be horrible.

"The leaves are getting awesome," he said. "It's such a beautiful day, why be cooped up in a restaurant? Is this okay with you?"

"Sure," she said, her voice small.

"You okay?"

"I might be a little moody," she answered. "It's kind of a strange day."

"You don't have second thoughts about Roger, do you?"

"No. But even knowing you have to end something doesn't make it easy." She stole a guilty look at his strong profile. "Especially something that's been going on for…a long time."

He reached across the console and squeezed her hand. "You'll get through it, Clare. God, your hand's like ice."

"Maybe a little sunshine will warm me up. We aren't going far, are we? I don't have to rush, but I do have to get back to work."

"Not to worry," he said. "It's not far."

She was quiet the rest of the way, but it wasn't long before

Sam turned off the road and down a dirt drive at the end of which was a small park. A very private place. He got out, taking the basket and blanket from the car. She followed more slowly. There were two picnic tables, but he spread the blanket on the grass under a large tree that had begun to display its fall colors. By the time she reached it, he was kneeling, picnic basket open. A bottle of wine appeared and he popped the cork.

Clare sat on the blanket, cross-legged, and Sam handed her a glass of red wine. The wine was probably a good idea, she thought. But she doubted they would get to the rest of the basket. He lifted his glass in a silent toast; she touched his glass with hers, but knew her eyes told too much. She knew she couldn't put it off, but it was he who said, "What is it, Clare?"

"Sam, you will never know how hard this is for me." She dropped her gaze, unable to look into his eyes. "Sam, I have to end whatever this is between us."

A moment of silence drew out. He took a sip from his glass. "What brought this on?"

"There's no way I can make this easy. You're great, and you've been wonderful to me. I'm very fond of you. But my feelings for you are just not as strong as yours are for me, and I think it would be best if we let this go now. Before it gets more complicated."

He stared at her, his lips parted slightly. Then he smiled a small smile. "That's not what your body says."

"I know, that's why I'm stopping it here and now. My feelings just don't match." She shrugged. "I'm sorry. It was never my intention to lead you on."

"Okay," he said, shaking it off. "I admit I was moving a little fast. You're right—we'll slow way down. I'm not going to pressure you. I've got all the time in the—"

"No, Sam, you weren't moving fast. You've been extremely

patient, and it's been months. It's just not growing for me. I don't have…" She cleared her throat. "I just don't have it."

"Clare, I don't care," he said. "I haven't asked you for anything. I haven't asked you to make me promises. I know better than that."

"You have to listen to me. I'm not asking you to slow down—I'm saying we're going to end this here and now, before it drags out any longer. What started as a friendship has clearly grown more serious for you. But it hasn't for me. I don't want this to get any more involved, only to have it end bitterly."

Sam reached out a hand, touching her knee. "Clare," he said softly, earnestly. "You responded to me. When I put my hands on you, you come alive."

She shook her head sadly, laughing without humor. "Only a dead woman wouldn't respond to you, Sam. I think you might be the sexiest man I've ever known. And having you want me has been fun. Flattering." She shrugged again. "But I don't want to lead you on. I'm not in love with you."

"Clare," he said, a hint of desperation in his voice, "shouldn't we just give it a chance? We've had a good time together, I couldn't have mistaken that. Neither of us has any other commitments, so there's no harm in—"

"But there is harm in it, Sam. You're not the kind of guy who can just have a fling and walk away unscathed. It would hurt. And I'm really not that kind of woman, either. I can't go any further. I'm sorry."

"When did you decide this, Clare? Because Friday night we were close to consummating this relationship. I wanted to, you wanted to—"

"And it would have been a terrible mistake."

He stood up, walked a few feet away and turned his back

on her. She watched as he took a few short sips from his glass and let some time pass, sought composure. Clare realized this was so very different from anything she'd ever done in her life. It wasn't as though they had some crushing disagreement or betrayal, as had happened with Roger. Painful as it was to leave her husband, this somehow hurt more, for Sam had done nothing wrong. He'd been sincere, caring and sensitive. What woman wouldn't want his vitality and passion for her own?

When he came back to the blanket, kneeling, she could see that his eyes were moist and it tore at her heart. "Are you absolutely sure, Clare? Because I think you know—I'm falling in love with you."

"I suspected that, and it frightens me. This is hard enough, Sam. I don't want it to get any harder."

"But if I can respect your space and give you the time you need—?"

"You would become more invested and I, less. I know what I feel, Sam. And what I don't."

He shook his head and gave a huff of rueful laughter, then tossed the rest of his wine on the grass. He put the glass in the basket and looked at her, his hands in fists on his thighs. "It was going to be today, you know. Right here, under this beautiful old tree. I was going to give you a glass of wine and make love to you. I was going to do things for you that no one has ever done. Make you beg for more. I wanted to tell you, finally, that the worst day of your life was the best day of mine. The day I found you and almost lost you, all in just a few minutes. I don't think I've ever felt this way about a woman before."

She felt the tears on her cheeks and wiped them away. "You are entitled to so much more, Sam. A younger woman, for one thing. Someone who's as passionate as you are. A woman who could add to your family, if you wanted that."

"I don't need that," he protested. "You've had that cheating husband all those years—and I would have given you love you could trust. One that would be true."

"I never doubted that. But you know I have to share that desire for it to work."

He swallowed, glanced away, looked back at her. "Tell me one thing, and please don't lie to me. Is it Pete? Pete Rayburn?"

"What?" she said, confused.

"There was something going on yesterday, when I found you with him at the park. I could sense it."

"Oh," she said, letting out her breath. "Yes, there was something going on. We were talking about old times, just as he said. One of the old times was his brother's death. Mike was Pete's older brother. We shared a devastating loss."

"I didn't know."

"Of course not. It never occurred to me to mention it, but then I didn't know you two knew each other." Sam stared at the ground. "I never meant to hurt you, Sam. You must believe that."

He raised his eyes. "I never meant to fall in love with you. Some things, it seems, are beyond our control." He stood. "We better get out of here. I don't think there's going to be a picnic." He held out his hand to help her to her feet.

"Will you be all right?" she asked.

"I'll live," he said, giving her a wan smile. "Kiss me, Clare. Kiss me goodbye."

"I don't think that's such a good—"

"It's all I'm asking. When I think about this day, I want to remember one nice thing." He pulled her into his arms and covered her mouth with his. At that moment she knew she had done absolutely the right thing. She felt his lips, as skilled and passionate as ever; she felt that familiar temptation. But nothing else. Then she felt his tears on her cheeks and her heart was ripped to pieces.

He pulled away and ducked his head, so that she wouldn't see. He stooped to collect the basket and blanket and as he walked to the car, he swiped impatiently at his eyes. "Let's go," he called. "No point in making this any harder."

She caught up with him and before he could get in the car, she grabbed the sleeve of his shirt and turned him toward her. "Sam, there's someone out there for you. Someone wonderful and devoted whose passion for you will match yours for her. I promise you."

He gave a dubious little laugh. "That's the last thing on my mind."

Clare didn't know where to go. She was in no shape for work and rather than go into the store and tell her dad she was taking off for the day, she just retrieved her car and called him from there. Finally, at a loss for what to do, she went to Maggie's office, hoping her sister would be there alone.

The minute she got into Maggie's plush office and closed the door, she burst into tears. "What in the world...?"

"Maggie, it was horrible. I broke his heart."

For a small, trim woman, Maggie exuded power. It was probably a lawyer thing. She was a rock, and seemed fearless. "Stop crying!" she demanded. But that only made Clare cry harder. Maggie tossed the box of tissue at her and said, "Stop crying and tell me what happened."

"He took me on a picnic in a deserted little park. He had big ideas of what would happen on that blanket—and instead

I told him that I couldn't see him anymore, that I just don't have those kind of feelings for him."

Maggie was almost knocked back in her chair and she said, "I don't know how you could not."

"Well, what can I say?" Clare sniffed. "It's true—I responded to him. I had plenty of lust. I just didn't have love in my heart."

"Hell, *I* responded to him. I don't think that proves anything."

"He was planning to tell me that the day he met me was the best day of his life."

"And you couldn't just…? You didn't have to make a commitment to him, did you?" Maggie shook her head. "Women. Couldn't you have enjoyed him for a time? While you're getting back on your emotional feet?"

"And then, after using him for a while, tell him to hit the road? Oh, Maggie—"

"All right, all right." Maggie relented. "It was a kind thing you did for him, Clare. He's twenty-nine. He has lots of time for meaningful relationships."

"I should have been kinder faster," she said, and blew her nose heartily.

Maggie got out of her chair and walked around to Clare, leaning a hip on the desk. One of her least favorite things was weeping women. She, herself, never cried. She couldn't remember the last time. But being a lawyer and handling the occasional divorce put her in the company of tearful women fairly often. "I'm going to say something to you, and you'd better hear me. You did *noth*ing *wrong*. Women date men. They flirt, respond to flirting, experiment with their emotions to determine whether they have the chemistry to go further. Women and men have sex, often before they know whether there's enough substance for the relationship to go the distance. There's no possible way to find the right person without exploring these things. If you don't take the risk, you chance the other extreme, which is closing yourself off, and that makes less sense than a good old-fashioned cry, when and if it has to be ended. I'm proud of you for doing what you know to be the right thing. So don't beat yourself up for not doing it sooner."

"He was shattered. It was the most painful thing I've ever seen. Done."

"Well, who knew? It might've worked. It was worth giving it a shot. But generally we say at least six months of autonomy between relationships. That whole rebound thing is not fiction."

"I just wish there was something I could do to make this easier on him," Clare said.

"As it happens, there probably is," Maggie said. "If you've made up your mind, which apparently you have, make it a clean break. Don't play around with this. If he calls or drops by, be kind but firm—it's time to move on. He'll be better off. And so will you."

"He asked me to kiss him goodbye. I could feel the dampness on his cheeks," she added with a miserable hiccup.

"God, he is such a *hunk*," Maggie said. "Not only the big, tough, good-looking guy, but sensitive. How is he single? There must be something wrong with him!"

"It might have to do with being a single father. And living with his mother."

"He lives with his *mother?*"

"His mother helps him raise his daughter. It's probably just a practical thing."

"Still, that must impact his sex life in a very negative way."

"You're sure this wasn't my fault?"

"Absolutely not. If it doesn't fly, it doesn't fly. You can't force these things."

"Is it what you would have done?"

"Me?" Maggie asked. "Oh hell no! I would have had tons of meaningless sex!"

Maggie called Sarah. "We might have a bit of a problem here. She did it. Clare broke it off with Sam."

"She did?" Sarah asked, trying to keep the hopefulness from her voice. "Is she okay?"

"She's pretty messed up, actually. But not because she has regrets. Because she said he was very upset. And last Saturday, none the wiser, I called him and invited him to her surprise birthday party in two weeks."

"You didn't tell me you were doing that."

"Sorry, I didn't think of it. I asked Jason for some names of friends he thought she'd like to have come and he came up with a few, including Sam. Should I call him, tell him not to come?"

"Well, that would be pretty rude," she said.

"I advised Clare to make a clean break. This is no way to do that."

"Maggie, if he's upset and doesn't want to see her, he won't come."

"And if he does?" Maggie asked.

"Well," Sarah said, "I trust him to be polite."

And I want him there, Sarah thought. I want to see how he is, how he looks at Clare. At me. Let's see what he's got.

Throughout the week, Clare was often caught completely lost in thought. She missed things said to her at the store and at home in the evenings she would find that while she stared at the TV, she couldn't remember much of the program she'd been watching.

She had kept her eye on the front door of the hardware store, expecting Sam to walk in for sprinkler heads, but he didn't. She checked her cell phone for messages, afraid there might be one and all those painful feelings visited on Monday might come rushing back. He didn't call.

Clare was glad of this, of course. Except that she was worried about him. It was possible he'd shrugged it off and already found himself some young babe, more his type. More likely, he was suffering and hurt. That whole thing about the clean break was hard to commit to—faced with his pain, she would be tempted to take him in her arms, hold him, tell him it would be all right. That it was better this way.

She prayed he wouldn't put her to the test.

Sam wasn't the only man who occupied her thoughts. In a far different way, she thought a lot about what Pete had told her. She tried to remember the past in a new way, looking back through the years for a time she might've known her buddy, her pal, was harboring this secret crush. She just couldn't see it.

When Mike had graduated and began taking classes in Reno, Pete and Clare were together constantly. It was like Pete was protecting Mike's interests. For the first time she wondered why he hadn't had a girlfriend. He had dates, but nothing seemed to click for him. Why had she never noticed? They talked about everything—why hadn't they talked about that?

When Mike wasn't away at school, it was very often the three of them. In fact, the only time Pete wasn't included was at their make-out sessions. They'd go to ball games, movies, parties, skiing, beaching and hangouts together, then drop

Pete off at home and park, steaming up the windows. How that must have tortured Pete, just knowing.

She spent a lot of time wondering how things might have been different. If that night hadn't happened, Pete and Clare would have remained close in the aftermath of Mike's death. They might've ended up together; Clare had loved him like a brother. That love could have easily been transformed, as she had learned that night in her apartment.

What if Pete had told her while he was making love to her? That he had always loved her, wanted her? Would that have shocked her out of the act like a cold shower? Or would it have made the whole thing seem less sinful?

But probably the most profound question was this—what if Pete had been stronger and smarter than she and had confronted her about their guilty tryst before she met and married Roger?

For the first time since it happened, she realized that Pete's pain must have exceeded hers. His actions had been both deliberate and wrong. The burden must have been immense. Clare couldn't decide if she was glad Pete had come clean about that childhood crush, or not. He certainly hadn't had to—they had worked through the event and got their friendship back on track. Except that the other person who didn't walk into the store door or call was Pete.

And, inevitably, Roger crossed her mind. She couldn't help but wonder how he was holding up, now that it was official— she was divorcing him. But even he hadn't called. It was a long and empty week, full of many questions and no answers.

Friday morning when Clare entered the hardware store, she found George at the back counter wearing a very troubled frown. "Something's going on with your sister and I want you to find out what it is," he said.

"Maggie?"

"No, Sarah. She's changing. At first I didn't notice—I don't notice things like that."

"Things like what?"

"Like hair and clothes. Everything is changing."

"What? I just saw her on Sunday. Nothing was different."

"It is now," he said, and then he went back to his office, brooding.

Clare got a sickening feeling in the pit of her stomach. She would never forget Sarah's transformation.

When they buried their mother, Sarah had cried the hardest. But then she seemed to almost sink out of sight. She couldn't get out of bed, barely ate. When Dotty came on board, she forced the girl up, shoved her into the shower, nearly spoon-fed her, but her morose mood was a terrible thing.

Maggie and Clare were not in the best shape to be objective, for their grief was terrible, as well, and they had small children who needed them. Ironically it was Roger who came to the fore. "She's sick, Clare. We have to get her to a doctor. This isn't just normal grief. She needs help. And fast."

Indeed, that was confirmed immediately and Sarah was hospitalized. It was very fortunate for her that medication eased the darkness quickly and she was only in the hospital for two weeks. But change was not over for their family. While Sarah got great comfort from her counselor and her new hobbies of painting and weaving, she stopped caring about her appearance. It would have been obvious it was some sort of defiance if it hadn't been so gradual. As she slowly replaced her clothing, she chose the plain and dull clothes that hid rather than accentuated her figure and she stopped wearing makeup altogether. Next, the contacts disappeared and the old glasses came out. Her hair, which she used to spend countless hours grooming and teasing into a high hussy mound was left thin and flat. There was a time you wouldn't know what hair color Sarah would show up with—black, red, white-blond, or some combination. Her natural color, which was not a particularly fetching kind of dirty blond, became her new preference. It was as though she wanted to become invisible.

She would spend hours and hours in front of an easel or at her loom and could barely be coaxed away. But then she decided to go back to school and relief flooded the McCarthy family. From that point on, this new Sarah was what they were going to have. "I only wish I had made a few sensible changes before Mama died," she said when her sisters voiced their worry over the way she looked.

"Mama wouldn't want you to stop paying attention to your appearance completely," they assured her.

To which Sarah said, "I bet she'd prefer this look to the previous one." And she'd go back to her painting or weaving or art studies.

Well, if those were the only two choices, they'd rather have Sarah at least doing something productive, as long as she was healthy, which her doctor assured them she was. All that loose and wild behavior has a heavy price. A far heavier price than looking plain.

Clare didn't waste any time in getting over to Sarah's art shop. Sheer dread accompanied her. She just couldn't imagine what image Sarah would present next. Had she gone to sackcloth and ashes? Was she sick again? When she opened the door and the little bell tinkled, a young woman she barely recognized came out of the studio in the back. Clare gasped and took a step backward. "Sarah?"

Sarah just smiled, giving her head a little tilt. "Hiya," she said. Her hair was highlighted and shaped in a bouncy cut that framed her face and curled at her shoulders, her eyes were an almost mystical green, and she was wearing slimming jeans with a crisp white blouse, tucked in and unbuttoned to al—most—but not quite—her cleavage. On her feet—boots! Stylish boots with slim, high heels!

"Sarah!" Clare gasped. "Oh, God!"

"What do you think?"

"What do I think? I think you scared ten years off Dad's life!"

"Well that's certainly not what I intended."

Clare came closer. "What in the world happened to you? Have you been hypnotized or something?"

"No," she laughed. "It's actually your doing, Clare."

"Me? I haven't said a word!"

"You did something much more significant. When I saw you last Friday night at the restaurant, you looked incredible. Unbelievable. I mean, you always look great, but you usually look great in your jeans. I don't know where I've been—but I haven't paid much attention to how striking you are all dressed up. That dress…"

"I've had that dress for three years!"

"Okay—it was a combination of things. That dress, which by the way is very sexy, but in a very elegant and chic way. Your boobs weren't hanging out or anything. And you had that good-looking man drooling. And it got me thinking—here is my big sister, not even divorced yet, having a *life*."

"Oh, Sarah," she said, feeling the threat of tears come to her eyes. "Please tell me this is totally sane! You're not, like, going through some manic thing…?"

"God, I hate that you all think I'm crazy. I had a very bad

time when Mom died, but I got help and I've been happy since then. I know it seems boring to you—my pieces, my little shop. But this is my world! I just decided I'm going to expand that world. I can sculpt and weave in clothes I don't look so homely in."

Clare walked to her sister and touched her pretty hair.

"You know what would be so nice, Clare? If when I met you and Maggie for a glass of wine, a waiter hit on me."

"Honey…"

"It came to me when I saw you last week—life can be bigger than this. It can be beautiful and fun. I think I've been hiding—just afraid to take a chance. Afraid that if I emerge, I'll be out of control again."

"Well, promise me you won't take too many chances."

"I'm thirty-three, Clare."

"You'll always be my little sister."

"But I'm not made of glass. Have you any idea how taxing an exhibition is? How stressful trying to land a big sale that will keep me in business? I'm not a baby. I'm strong."

Clare smiled at Sarah. "I guess I just don't give you enough credit. This is good," she said, relenting. "Maggie is going to die."

"Well, I just hope she dies of happiness and doesn't freak out."

chapter ten

....

FOR CLARE'S FORTIETH BIRTHDAY, Sarah and Maggie took her to a day spa where the three sisters indulged in massages, facials, manicures, pedicures and had their hair done. They brought along nice clothes to change into for dinner later.

Sarah had a new dress for the occasion. A sleek, dark green knit that hugged her curves and lit up her eyes. When she put it on, she was so beautiful that Clare almost wept. "The best birthday present I could possibly have is you back, Sarah. I've never seen you more stunning."

"I've always been like a hangnail on the middle toe, standing between you two," Sarah said.

"Does this make you happy?" Clare asked her. "This gorgeous new you?"

"I'm kind of amazed it didn't occur to me sooner—how good it might feel. Maybe tonight's the night," she said. "Maybe a waiter will hit on me, or something."

"Well, not so fast," Maggie said, holding out her cell phone toward Clare. "Your phone must be turned off. It's Jason. He locked himself out of the house."

"Well, how in the world," she said. She spoke to him for a

moment and handed the phone back to Maggie. "I'm sorry, but can we swing by the house and let him in on our way to the restaurant? He says he can't find Grandpa."

Not a problem, they assured her. And so they went. When they got to Clare's neighborhood, there were cars parked up and down the street. "Someone's having a party," she observed. Her house was dark and Jason was standing outside, shuffling his feet back and forth, shivering in the cold. "Sorry, Mom," he said.

"You lose another house key?" she asked him.

"I might've," he said.

"I swear, I'm going to have one imbedded in your head," she said, unlocking the door for him.

The houseful of people yelled "SURPRISE" and almost knocked her off her feet. There were over thirty people in the living room. Her entire family plus some neighbors, employees from the hardware store, a couple of girlfriends she'd kept up with since high school, and there, at the back of the room by the table of food, Sam and Pete. Standing together. Not far from those two was Roger, standing next to Bob. Oh boy, she thought. This should surpass interesting.

She turned to her sisters. "How'd you do this?"

"All we had to do was manage the guest list and order the food. Dad, Bob and the kids did the rest."

"And a very comprehensive guest list it is, too," she said, stepping into the house. She greeted every person, including the three men who had been most on her mind lately. Someone pressed a glass of wine into her hand, which she drank perhaps a little too quickly. The stereo was cranked up, the dining room table was covered with food and there were balloons and streamers all over the family room and kitchen. The patio doors were open and the fire pit outside was lit and flaming, around it the young people—Jason and friend, Stan, Hillary and girlfriend, Lucy, Lindsey and boyfriend, Christopher.

On her second glass of wine, she was able to actually brave a conversation with some of her more controversial guests, Roger first. "How are you, Roger?" she asked.

"I'm sorry about this, Clare. I wasn't actually invited. I just came by to wish you a happy birthday and Bob said I should stay."

"That's okay, Roger. How's Jason taking it?"

Roger shrugged and looked toward the patio. "He's giving me a wide berth. Can I steal you away from the crowd for a second? I have something for you, and I don't want to be overheard."

"Oh, Roger…"

"Now, don't do that to me. I know where we stand. Just come over here," he said, taking her hand and pulling her toward the hallway, out of the earshot of guests. He pulled a small gift-wrapped box out of his pocket and said, "You should have something special for turning forty, and for putting up with me for sixteen years."

She wouldn't take it. "I wish you hadn't…"

"Clare, call it a divorce gift. Whatever. Sell it, pawn it, I don't care. I want you to know that I'm moving on, which is what you want. Still, it just wouldn't be right for me to let it go unsaid, you were wonderful to me. I wasn't so wonderful to you and I regret that. I'd at least like us to be friends." He pushed the box at her. "Please."

Reluctantly, even fearfully, Clare took the small box. She opened it very slowly. Inside was an absolutely irresistible diamond pendant necklace on a platinum chain. "Roger, this is out of the question. Too much."

He closed his hand over hers that held the opened box. "You

deserve it. And don't worry—it's not an attempt at begging you back. By now I know—it's out of the question. Just the same, Clare. Thank you for sixteen years and a son."

"Roger. That might be the loveliest thing you've ever said to me."

"Hmm. Well, I regret that, too." He looked over his shoulder toward the buffet. "I suppose I owe your young man an apology."

"He's not my young man—we're just friends. But that would be a nice gesture. If you're up to it."

"Yeah. Okay."

She put her hand against his cheek. "Thank you, Roger. Not so much for the gift, but the thought. It's very nice."

"Would you like to put it on?" he asked.

"Why not?" she said, turning for him so that he could fasten it around her neck. When that was done, she said, "Come on, I'll take you over to Sam."

She pulled his hand and led him to the far corner near the back door where Sam stood, slowly nursing a beer. "Sam, this is Roger, who you didn't quite meet under very unfortunate circumstances."

Roger stuck out his hand; Sam slowly and perhaps reluctantly took it. "I apologize, buddy. Terrible thing I did. Believe me, it's not habitual."

"That's good to hear. If it were, I'd worry about you." He looked at Clare. "Nice necklace," he said, nodding toward the diamond.

She touched it and smiled. "Divorce bauble. Right, Roger?"

"Yeah. It seemed like the right thing to do—after all Clare has put up with from me. The least I could..."

Pete joined them and pressed a glass of wine into Clare's

hand. "I noticed the birthday girl has an empty glass, and we can't have that."

She laughed at him because she had had enough wine now to not be uncomfortable about anything. She was, in fact, growing a little giddy. "I'd better slow down—who knows what might happen." And she hiccuped.

Across the room, Maggie took a seat next to Sarah, who was staring at Clare. Maggie stared, as well. "Look at our sister," Maggie said. "Look at those men. Look at those three incredible men making her laugh and hanging on her every word. Lord above."

"Yeah, but one of them is Roger," Sarah said.

"You have to admit—they're all drop-dead gorgeous. Even Roger. When she comes out of her shell, she comes all the way out."

It was a sight to behold—the men, so different, but certainly equally handsome. Sam had that pitch hair and dimpled smile, Pete with his light brown hair and tan face, and the blond and sadly beautiful Roger.

"It's her birthday. Think she'll pick one?" Sarah asked.

"If she has another glass of wine, she might pick all three," Maggie said.

They stared impolitely, leaning to the side as their view was blocked by a guest passing through the room. "Isn't it amazing?" Maggie said.

"Amazing," Sarah concurred.

But what Sarah was focused on was Sam. She'd been watching him all night. She watched how he looked at Clare. She thought there might be longing there. Perhaps sadness—it was hard to tell. What was easy to see was that when someone didn't engage him in conversation, his eyes would drift to Clare and watch her intensely.

Well, it had only been a couple of weeks. The important thing was that Clare didn't look at him with longing. She was busy having a birthday, enjoying her party. When she did connect eyes with Sam, she smiled at him, but not in a way that suggested heartbreak.

That made it official in Sarah's eyes—Clare was finished, and Sam was healing. Sarah wouldn't mind helping him get past that. If she ever got the chance.

Clare was having fun with Roger, Pete and Sam. She'd been circulating and visiting and hadn't had more than a tiny morsel of food, so she was feeling a bit frivolous and light-headed. Then, with a sudden whack of clarity, she realized she was standing in a circle with three men she'd known in the biblical sense! Okay, she told herself, she hadn't actually been that intimate with Sam, but it had been a serious enough dalliance that she knew what he *had,* what he was capable of doing, what he almost did. Little difference. She blanched. Holy shit, she thought. Look at me! Am I crazy?

She faked a smile. "You'll have to excuse me," she said somewhat lamely. "I should circulate."

"Sure," Roger said.

"Of course," said Pete.

"Clare? I'm going to head out," Sam said. "But thanks for including me."

"And thanks for coming," she said, putting out her hand.

He rejected the hand and, grabbing her upper arms, gave her a peck on the cheek. "Forty looks great on you. Happy birthday."

Sam grabbed his jacket and walked out the front door. He was halfway down the sidewalk when he heard his name.

"Sam?" He turned to see Sarah coming toward him. She hugged herself in the cold.

"Hey," he said.

"I wanted to say goodbye, and thank you for coming."

"Thanks for having me, Sarah."

"I hope you had a good time. Clare told me that you and she… That you're not dating anymore. I thought maybe you wouldn't come, but I'm glad you did."

"Hmm. Me, too. You know, I have to admit, I didn't even recognize you. I guess I wasn't paying much attention the other night, when we met."

She laughed at him, but she shivered, as well. No matter, she thought. She would brave an arctic blast just to have a few minutes alone with him. Especially if she could get an insight on where he stood. "I was pretty wiped out that day. Long day of work. I didn't have time to primp or anything before meeting my sisters. I looked like hell, probably."

"No," he said, shaking his head. "I think it was the glasses."

"Oh, that. I wear them when I work long hours. To keep my eyes from getting dry, tired and itchy."

"What is it you do? Clare probably told me and I just forgot…"

"Art. I'm an artist. I have a small shop with a studio in the back for working, and in the front I sell art supplies."

"Yeah, I think she did mention that," he said, and he thought, they're all beautiful, these three women. Then she smiled at him and he thought, yup. Beautiful. Lethal. This one was perhaps the prettiest. Younger than Clare. What had she said? Seven years? She shivered again. Though he really wanted to get away, he whipped off his jacket and put it around her shoulders, then watched as she hugged it to herself. No way, he thought. I'm not about to get kicked around by another one of these women.

"Now you'll be cold," she said.

"Actually, I have to get going. Let me get you inside before you freeze. Then I'll take my jacket and head out." He turned her and with a hand to her back, pushed her gently toward the front door.

"You probably have a date or something."

He laughed. "Not hardly," he said. They were sisters. They knew everything, so why pretend? "I think there's going to be a little break in the action for me."

She turned around and faced him. "Are you okay, Sam?" she asked.

"Sure, Sarah," he said. He shrugged. "It takes two, you know. Apparently there was only one. So? Life goes on. But I wanted to come tonight so Clare would know there are no hard feelings."

"That was very nice of you," she said.

"Yeah, I'm a helluva guy."

She slowly removed the jacket and handed it to him. "Thanks again," she said. "See you around." And she went in the house.

Sam went to his car, got in and drove. He didn't have the slightest idea why things didn't work out with him and women. He tried to be a gentleman; the kind of man a woman would want to be out with. It had always been important to him to put a woman's needs above his own—he hadn't had any complaints in that department. As a date, as a lover, he thought he was passably good. Yet here he was, twenty-nine and still unattached. When he found someone he thought he could make a life with, for some reason it just didn't stick. He

kept hearing that boring old line—"you could have anyone."
Being good-looking was no free pass.

Okay, there hadn't been that many. Most of the women
who let him know they were attracted to him were much
younger and it was he who couldn't get that interested. Cops
tend to attract these giddy girls—it was the uniform. A couple
of times since Molly's mom, he had been in love, or thought
he was in love. There was only one long-term relationship—
two years—and the end of that had been so hard on Molly
that he didn't take dates home anymore. Molly had gotten attached and when Roxanne had said she was through, it hurt
Molly as much as it hurt him.

It's just that he had thought with Clare it might be different.
She was mature, steady, and obviously needed a man in her
life she could trust. Someone she could depend on, someone
who could give her all the pleasure she'd been living without for so long.

But—it had just been too soon. After Roger. God, what a
piece of work he was.

Sam was going to swear off dating. Enough with the
women. Clare's departure had hurt so much it had brought
tears to his eyes—and that was something that Sam, the big
and tough, could hardly bear to think about. So fine—he
was good without a woman. His life was full and he was
mostly happy. He had his daughter, whom he adored, and
a good home life. He loved his work, ski season was almost
upon them and he got almost as much pleasure from skiing as
from policing. So okay, he thought. It's very clear that Clare
is done. There was nothing there and he wasn't even going
to test her feelings once more. Bite me once, shame on you.
Bite me twice…

I'm fine on my own, he said to himself. And he said it to
himself over and over.

★ ★ ★

By eleven, people began leaving the party. Maggie and Sarah were cleaning up and most of the teenagers had found better things to do than hang out with the folks. Pete saw that Clare was outside by the fire pit, alone. She was sipping on a glass of wine. He went to her.

"Well, you certainly had a big birthday," he said.

She raised her eyes to him and smiled a slightly lopsided smile. She touched the pendant. "How many women do you suppose get divorce gifts?" she asked him, and her words were slightly slurred. He laughed at her.

"Get enough to drink?" he asked her.

"Well, what do you expect? Here I was, celebrating my big day with three men I've been intimate and almost intimate with. For a while there I was worried there might not be enough wine at this party to get me through it."

Pete could do that math. So, Sam hadn't scored. He considered that a plus. Less messy that way, if she had had to end it. Less fallout.

She put a hand on his chest. "Better be careful, Pete. You know what happens when I get a little too much wine in me."

"I feel pretty safe," he said. "At least while your sisters are still in the kitchen." She swayed against him slightly. He put an arm around her waist and, holding her steady, pulled a lawn chair closer to the fire. "Here, birthday girl," he said. "You'd better sit down."

"'Kay," she said.

He pulled a chair alongside and sat down beside her. She leaned against him and he put an arm around her. "Clare, I think you're drunk."

"There is no think about it," she said, snuggling closer. "I guess my sister called Sam and invited him before she knew I had to—you know. God, that was the awflest day."

"He seems to be holding up all right," Pete said. "He's young. He'll bounce back."

She turned her head and looked up at him. "How'd you get your invite?"

"Jason, I think. Maggie said she asked Jason for some ideas. That's my guess."

"Ahh," she said, snuggling back against his arm. "I'm glad of that. Really, if they'd asked me, you would have been the only one I'd've said. Certainly not *Roger.*" Pete chuckled. "'Course," she said, touching the diamond. "He gives very nice divorce gifts. I'm thinking of divorcing him again."

"I doubt it would work twice."

"You never know. Roger's a lamebrain with a lot of money." She looked up at him. "Know what Maggie said? She said, 'That better not have come out of the settlement.'"

It felt so good to hold her. He just wished she would stop talking.

"Did you get me a present, Pete?" she asked him.

He'd been standing right there when she opened the card that held the tickets. "Yes," he said. "Tickets to the Billy Joel concert in San Francisco."

"Thas right," she slurred. "Are you taking me to that?"

"You have two tickets," he laughed. "You can take anyone you like."

"Well, I think it should be you!"

"Whatever you want, Clare," he said, pulling her a little closer.

"Pete? Tell me one of those stories? From when we were kids. You know."

"Hmm," he said. "I remember the time during Christmas

break one year. I think it was the year after graduation. Yeah, we were about nineteen, you and me. Mike was twenty-one, I remember that, because he was legal. A bunch of us went skiing. We rented a cabin so we could spend the night. We went to Utah, remember? Couldn't just go to Grandpa's place in Tahoe—too close to the parents. They might pop in. I think there were ten of us. We packed up food, booze, skis. Mike bought the beer. Lotsa beer."

"Mmm," she said.

"We had a little cabin that had one bedroom, but that didn't matter. We had sleeping bags. We spread them out on the living room floor, in front of the fire. After skiing all day and drinking beer all night, we just lay on the floor in front of the fire."

Clare's wineglass tipped from her hand and Pete caught it. She had fallen asleep. Or passed out. He put the glass on the ground.

"I wonder if I should worry about the fact that when I tell you these stories, you fall asleep?" She snored softly. "There must be something about me." She snuggled closer. Her head lolled slightly. "After all that beer," he went on, "it didn't take long for everyone in the cabin to be asleep. In fact, you fell asleep on me then, too. Mike was sprawled out on the couch, you and I were lying on the floor. You put your head on my shoulder, kind of like this, and went to sleep." He gently touched her cheek. "I didn't sleep all night. I just held you. Once, while you were asleep, I snuck a little kiss. Wasn't much of a kiss, since you didn't respond. It was kind of like…" He lifted her chin with a finger so that her face was tilted up. He touched her lips lightly with his. "Like that. I could've… No, I couldn't. I wouldn't take advantage of you. Especially with Big Mike right there. Never mind Big Mike. I treasured you."

He bent his head and put a soft kiss on her forehead. "Ah, Clare," he said. "What are we gonna do?"

After a few minutes, he carefully disengaged himself and, putting his hands under her arms, lifted her to a standing position. She was limp as a noodle. "Come on, Clare. I think you've had enough."

"Hmm?" she asked, eyes still closed.

He put his arm under her knees, the other behind her back and lifted her easily in his arms. He went into the house and saw that Maggie and Sarah were just about done in the kitchen. They turned to look at him, mouths open slightly in surprise.

"Where would you like me to put the birthday girl?"

There was a roaring inside Clare's head. She opened one pink eye and saw her sister Sarah, dressed in one of Clare's nightgowns, using the blow-dryer to style her hair. The blow-dryer must be broken—it sounded like a jet engine. Clare picked up the TV remote from her bedside table and threw it at Sarah, hitting her in the butt with it.

Sarah turned off the blow-dryer and turned around. "Morning," she said.

"What are you doing here?" Clare whispered.

Sarah put down the dryer and went to sit on the side of Clare's bed. "Someone had to stay and make sure you were all right. There might've been a little titch of alcohol poisoning last night."

Clare groaned. "Did I have a good time?"

"You tell me. You passed out on Pete Rayburn."

She sat up suddenly and a pain shot through her head. Head down, her face canopied by her hair, she rubbed her temples. "Oh, God. Please tell me you just made that up to punish me." Slowly, carefully, she lay back down on the pillow. "Where?"

"Outside. By the fire. He carried you to bed."

"Oh, God," she moaned.

"What happened?" Sarah asked. "One minute you were a little tipsy, the next Pete was asking, 'Where would you like me to put the birthday girl?'"

She put the back of her hand to her forehead. "Who undressed me?"

"Not Pete."

"Did I… Did I do anything really, really embarrassing?"

"Well, you were outside alone with Pete when you passed out. Last time I peeked out the door, you were leaning against him and he had his arm around you. Hey, do you have a thing for Pete Rayburn?"

"I obviously have a thing for chardonnay…."

"He's very cute. In fact, the place was dirty with cuties last night. Maggie and I were watching them flock around you. I keep trying to imagine what that must be like. You could have had your pick."

"I think I did," she said. "Only I can't remember it."

"Were you fooling around with Pete Rayburn?"

"Sarah, how many ways can I say I don't remember? I had on all my clothes, right?"

She nodded. "Right down to the panty hose."

"If I live through the day, do you think I have to call him and apologize?" Clare asked.

Sarah shrugged. "He didn't look all that unhappy, Clare. God, I've always wanted to be carried off to bed," she said wistfully.

"Did you want to be carried to bed because you were trashed?" Clare asked.

"Well, at least you didn't get sick," Sarah said.

Clare's features froze. She paled. A strange look came over her face and her complexion slowly went from white to ashen.

"Uh-oh," Sarah said, moving out of the way.

Clare threw back the covers and bolted for the bathroom, slamming the door.

That night just before ten, Clare called Pete. When he said hello, she said, "I'm so, so sorry."

"Not necessary," he said. But he laughed.

"Was I completely obnoxious?" she asked. "No, don't tell me. I don't even want to know. Was I?"

"You were hysterical," he said. "You're a cute drunk."

"Ugh."

"Hangover?" he asked.

"You can't imagine."

"The sad truth is, I sure can. I was carried off to bed once in my younger days. But I was dragged up the stairs by my heels—by one of my teammates. I think he bounced my head off every stair. I was bruised from head to toe. It was a nightmare."

It was her turn to laugh.

"You said finding yourself surrounded by all your ex-lovers drove you to it," he told her.

"That was discreet of me," she said. "How many people overheard that remark?"

"We were completely alone. Sitting out by the fire while your sisters cleaned up."

"What else did I tell you?" she asked, holding her breath.

"Aw, you just babbled. You did mention how much you liked your divorce gift and said you were thinking of divorcing Roger again."

"*He* didn't see me passed out, did he?"

"Almost everyone was gone. Only your sisters saw you— and I left so they could put you safely to bed."

"Then I should say thank you in addition to I'm sorry."

"You keep falling asleep on me. Do you think I should take that personally?"

"I think it means I feel safe," she said, and once the words were out, she realized they were true.

"I'll take that as a compliment," he answered. "And say good night before it happens again."

Clare got the old house, and at a bargain even Maggie admitted was superb. She asked George if she could go on a part-time schedule at the store so she could remodel the house and to that end, she took George over there to see it. Clare had to push the warped front door with all her might to get it open. They entered a foyer just left of a large living room, littered with debris. To the left of the foyer was a wide-open staircase with a banister that was literally falling down. The dingy, old wallpaper was peeling off the wall and the baseboards were scraped, dented, broken and horrible looking. Walking straight ahead brought them to a small kitchen with no appliances and old, yellowed linoleum that was cracked and peeling. A swinging door on the far right wall of the kitchen took them to the dining room, almost as large as the living room. There was a large hearth in the living room, some of the bricks of which were missing or broken. An old wrought-iron chandelier dangled crazily in the middle of the room and looked as if it might crash to the floor any second. The paint—very likely leaded—around the window frames and sills was cracked and peeling.

George stood in the middle of the living room and turned in a circle, looking at the damage. And Clare said, "Dad. Isn't it *great?*"

chapter eleven

....

THIS WAS THE time of instant divorce. Roger had been served three weeks ago and according to the paperwork he would be a single man in one more week. He stared at the documents knowing there was no longer anything he could do to turn this around. Clare had left him shortly after Christmas and it was already October; the holidays were just around the corner. Had it not been for her accident, the divorce would have been accomplished much sooner. Roger knew what Clare thought—that his regret and guilt were contrived just to get her back into his life for reasons even he didn't understand. But that wasn't true. His regret and guilt were completely genuine and he knew exactly why he wanted her in his life. She was pure and classy and sincere, while he was a shallow, weak idiot. She had given his life substance. Only a fool would cheat on Clare and risk losing her.

Clare had given him more chances than he deserved. Their marriage was over. He had meant everything he said to her at her birthday party—that he understood it was time to move on; that he was grateful for the years and their son. All he could do now was try to repair his relationship with Jason and maybe, in the end, earn some respect.

He didn't bother to call Jason—if Jason answered the phone when he called, it was by accident. If Jason was home when Roger stopped by, he tried to avoid him. But Roger was going to go to the house and keep going until he convinced Jason to spend a little time with him. Even if it was miserable, he would keep doing it. He intended to show Jason that he was important, that even if he couldn't have Clare in his life he wanted his son.

It was Sunday, sunny and crisp. People had started putting out scarecrows and pumpkins. Little farming towns like this one really got into the harvest. Halloween was a big deal. He drove over to the house and went to the door. Jason answered and jumped in surprise when he saw Roger. "Hey," he said, stepping back a step.

"Hey, yourself, pal. I thought maybe we could do something today. Go-carts? Movie? There's a game on… I bought a big screen. We could swing by the store, get some snacks—"

"Um, I'm kinda busy. I…um…I kinda have some plans."

"Want to take a friend?" He shrugged. "I'm flexible. Whatever."

"You shoulda called. Aren't you s'pose to call?"

"I don't know," he said honestly. There was no custody issue—Jason was fifteen and made up his own mind. "I'll do whatever I'm supposed to. Want me to go back out to the car and call?" he asked, trying to make a joke.

"Maybe next week. Or the week after, depending on, you know, homework and stuff."

"Jase, holidays are coming up. I want us to spend some time together, have some fun, get back on track, if possible."

"Yeah, well…I might need to think about that."

"You could think at the movies. If we take in a movie, you won't have to talk to me," he said, smiling lamely. "Or we could go out and practice driving. You're going to want that learner's permit pretty soon."

Roger saw Jason's eyes light up a little, though he could tell the kid tried to hide it. "Yeah, I could think about that. Maybe you should call next week."

"Are you sure? Because I can wait till you finish whatever you're doing, or if you have plans with friends, we could take a whole crowd out. Pizza?"

"I think you should maybe call next week. Okay?"

"Jason, just so you know, I miss you, man. I'm going to keep pestering you till you give me a chance. It's been a really tough year for you and I know you're still pissed, but—"

"Naw, I'm not that pissed. But I am kinda—"

"Yeah, I know. Kinda busy. But I'm not giving up, son." He reached out to grab Jason's shoulder and give an affectionate squeeze, but the kid jumped. Roger made contact, but it didn't come off as cool as he planned. "I'm not going to fight you, son. I'm just going to keep trying and trying."

"Yeah, okay," he said. "See ya later, then." And he backed into the house and closed the door.

Well, that wasn't far off from what Roger expected. It still stung. This was exactly why it was so hard to keep asking, keep trying. Every time Jason rebuffed him it had taken Roger weeks to put himself out there again. But this time it would be different. He'd call Jason every day this week and try to get something set up for next weekend.

He turned to leave just as Pete Rayburn was pulling up to the house. Just what he needed, competition with Pete for Jason. It caused him to frown darkly.

"Hey, Roger," Pete said brightly. "What's up?"

"Not a lot, Pete. What are you doing here?"

"I came to see Clare. You here for Jason?"

He let out a breath. "I tried, but he's... You know..." He shrugged.

"Ah." Pete thought a minute. "Hey, I know. Come here." He turned and walked back to his car, opened the trunk. He took out a football and tossed it in the air. "Let's throw the ball around."

"What for?"

"Trust me. I have a little experience with this."

"With what?" Roger asked.

"Divorced father of two," he said, and then he grinned. "Believe me, if you think boys are tough, you oughta try a couple of pissy little girls."

"Yeah?"

"Whoa," was all Pete said. He backed out into the street at a trot and fired the football at Roger, who caught it clumsily.

"Pissy little girls, huh?" Roger said, firing it back.

"They were horrible. Even though it was a mutual split and I decided it was best to leave, it was somehow all my fault. I had to crawl on my belly like a snake and plead for mercy." He shot the football back at Roger, who caught it better this time. And laughed.

"How long did it take?" Roger asked.

"I don't know. Months. Maybe a year. They still have their dark moods." Pete caught the ball. "I've always had a hard time understanding girls. The boys, I get. Go out for a long one," he told Roger, and Roger complied.

"You're having a good season," Roger yelled. "Winning everything."

"Yeah," he said, and then to Roger's adequate catch, "Good one!"

Roger came a little closer—he wasn't about to try a long pass and look stupid. After all, Pete did this every day. "So," he said. "You and Clare?"

"Old friends," Pete said, noncommittal. "We kind of remet during her, ah, teaching career."

"Yeah, I suppose. I think she's seeing that young guy," Roger said.

"Um. I don't think that worked out," Pete said.

Without meaning to, Roger actually hung his head. "I probably screwed that up."

"Don't be so hard on yourself, Roger. Go deep. Farther. Farther."

"You're showing off," Roger said with a laugh, but did as he was told. And caught the ball admirably. Then, braving humiliation, went for the return of the long pass. And made it.

"Whoa! Look at you!"

"What are you doing?" Jason yelled from the end of the drive.

Pete immediately trained the ball on Jason and fired it at him. Jason caught it, then stood there with it. "Your dad went to the trouble to come over…he should have someone to play with."

Jason turned toward Roger and threw it to him. Roger to Pete. Pete to Jason. In less than thirty minutes there was running, falling, fumbling, tripping, laughing, one pair of jeans torn at the knee, one jacket tossed on the curb. And Pete yelled, "Hey, Jason—your mom home?"

"Yeah."

"Let me out, you guys. I wanna ask Clare something." And he jogged toward the front door, leaving father and son to their football.

Clare answered while he was still knocking. She had a confused frown wrinkling her brow. "What did you do?"

"It's not a very secret formula—introduce a ball and all
boys will play."

"Amazing."

"I think Roger and I bonded. As divorced men are wont
to do."

"Further amazing."

"I went through the ex-husband to get to the ex-wife," he
said. "I must be freaking fearless."

"I haven't heard from you in…" She wrinkled her brow,
but she knew exactly how long it had been. "Since my fortieth birthday. I finally decided you were just being kind and
I was totally obnoxious. And you hoped to never run into
me again."

"You had some serious stuff going on," he answered. "I
didn't want to get in the way."

"Like what?"

"Like breaking the hearts of virile young cops and divorcing rich dimwits like Roger." He smiled. "Plus, it's football
season. They're killing me."

"What are you doing here?" she asked.

"I thought it would be okay to get in the way now." Grin.
"I want to take you someplace, if you can get away."

"Where?"

"Secret. What do you think?"

Before she could answer, the front door opened. Jason stuck
his head in and said, "Mom, I'm going with Dad to get some
dippin' strips. That okay?"

"Sure. Take house keys. I'm going out with Pete for a little
while. How long, Pete?"

"Couple of hours," he said.

Jason didn't seem to think there was anything unusual about this. He ran past them and up the stairs to his room to get his keys. Then in a flash he was back and out the door.

"Completely amazing," she said.

As they drove, Clare told Pete a little bit about Sam. Not the details like the goodbye kiss, or the shattered look on his face when she told him. If she recalled that, it still caused a little ache to creep into her heart.

"He's a tough kid," Pete said. "Don't worry about him."

"Did you know he has a daughter?" she asked.

"Yeah, I know. He was really young."

"He's still really young," she said. She looked at Pete's profile as he drove. It didn't seem as though he had changed so much in twenty years. Suddenly she could picture him the way he was that night in her college apartment. The details came flooding back—that first tentative touch, the way he cautiously leaned toward her and gently touched her lips, as if anxious to see if she would respond or slap him. That light kiss, barely there. The way his arm slipped around her waist, hesitatingly. How his breath caught when she invited a deeper kiss. Oh, she remembered it now. He had moved so slowly, so carefully. She could even remember the taste of his mouth— Chianti and desire. And yes, his hand trembled slightly as it crept to her breast, giving her every opportunity to stop him, to push him away. But she had put her hand over his and pressed it down harder, and he made a sound of such longing it shook her. Stirred her.

She should have known then what she knew now—he had adored her. He wanted her fearfully. Had he been making a conquest, even one born of wine and darkness, he would have taken her acquiescence and swooped down on her. He would have taken her quickly before she could change her mind. But he had not. Instead he was gentle, giving her the time to be sure. Time to respond. Until she begged him to be less gentle. What she also remembered, it had been *good*.

"Hey," Pete said, stealing a look at her. "You okay?"

She shook herself. She'd been staring at him openmouthed. "Oh sorry," she said. "You haven't changed that much. Can you believe we're forty?"

He laughed and said, "Me first."

"Where are we going?" she asked again.

"We're almost there. Haven't you figured it out yet?"

"Does it have anything to do with football?"

"There could possibly be some football involved, yes," he said.

"Thanks for doing that with Roger and Jason. Brilliant."

"They need each other. Jason just doesn't realize how much yet."

"Are we almost there?" she asked.

"Almost."

Suddenly she recognized a street they turned down. She held her breath without meaning to. Pete pulled up in front of his parents' house and she slowly let out her breath. She looked across at Pete.

"Is this okay?" he asked. "Are you up to it?"

The house looked the same as it had twenty years ago—brown with yellow shutters and trim, a long porch. Not a fancy house, and the neighborhood was about forty years old, but kept up nicely. It didn't look as if it had aged a day. It brought tears to her eyes. "Give me a second," she said.

"They want to see you," he said. "They've been begging. Especially my mom."

"Sure," she said, but she said it a little weakly. "Maybe you should have asked me. Or at least told me."

"We don't have to go in, it's up to you. We've spent a lot of time talking about the past. I thought it might be a good idea to move into the present. And I was afraid you'd say no." He patted her hand. "It's okay if you cry. I won't take it personally."

"I'm not going to cry. Maybe."

"Then come on. They'll be waiting, trying not to open the door before you get there."

Sophie and Fred Rayburn met them at the door; they had aged some but were still young and fit in their sixties. They were small, this couple who had bred up two large boys. There were emotional embraces. The last time she'd seen them was at her mother's funeral a dozen years ago. Fred had been in the hardware store, but Clare hadn't worked there until recently and it wasn't as though they went to the same churches, restaurants or grocery stores.

The football game was on TV, naturally, but Fred had the volume down and Sophie had put out snacks in the family room. The fire was lit in the hearth and the room cozy and welcoming. The furniture had been updated, but it was almost comforting to note that the smells in the house were familiar—furniture polish, glass cleaner and freshly-baked cookies.

Sophie took her by the hand and led her to the kitchen where she poured her a cup of coffee. "When Pete told me that he ran into you and you two were back in touch, I just can't tell you what a lift it gave me! It's been too long, Clare."

"I agree. It's so good to see you. The last couple of times were not happy ones."

"How is your father doing?"

"He's great. Strong, feisty, working too hard as usual."

They went around the dining and living rooms, coffee mugs in hand, looking at the framed photos. There were Pete's girls at all ages, a couple of gatherings of extended family, and of course high school photos of Pete and Mike. Ah, she remembered. Pete was very young-looking, even when he graduated. And there on the mantel was a picture of Mike in his Air Force uniform. He seemed to be looking away, as though he was already leaving her. She picked it up and held it. "I put away my pictures of Mike."

Sophie touched her arm. "Of course you did, dear. You got on with your life, as you were meant to do."

"This brings back such memories."

"Embrace the good ones, sweetheart. Let any unpleasant ones go."

Sophie and Clare sat at the dining table with their coffee and caught up on family matters. Clare told Sophie about going back to the hardware store to work, now part-time, about the fixer-upper, about her son, about her divorce. Sophie filled Clare in on her granddaughters. "It's such a joy to have girls, I can't tell you. Like my reward for raising two boys."

"Do you go to the football games?"

"We used to go all the time, but we miss some now. The cold gets to Fred. And to me, if I'm honest."

When Fred told Pete to come outside with him to get firewood, Sophie seized the moment to say something she didn't want her son to overhear. "After we lost Mike, I had this farfetched hope that you and Pete would find each other—but you both went in other directions. You know, he had such a crush on you in high school."

Clare was momentarily shocked. Did everyone know but her? "He did?" she said.

Sophie nodded. "The way he looked at you. The way he looked at you and Mike—I could tell he was just in agony.

But I knew." She shook her head almost sadly. "It must have been hard on him. He loved his brother so."

"Did Mike know?"

Sophie laughed in absolute amusement. "Darling, Mike was just a guy. There are a lot of signals that guys are immune to until they're much older."

"I guess that's probably true."

"Promise me something, Clare. Now that you've come by for a visit, don't be a stranger."

"Count on it, Sophie. I've missed you, too."

When Pete was driving Clare home, he pulled over at a crimp in the road beside a farmer's field. He killed the engine, took her hand and held it and asked, "How are you doing?"

"A little emotional," she said honestly. "But good."

"Thank you for doing that. It means a lot to my mother."

"Means a lot to me, too. Your mother told me she knew you always had a crush. I think I might be the only one who didn't know that."

"My mother," he laughed. "How she can still surprise me."

"Pete—I've been remembering that night. I don't want you to take all the blame. I responded to you. That whole thing… It was very mutual."

"I know." He smiled. "That's the special part."

"You could've let it remain in the past."

"No, I couldn't," he said. "You had to know the truth. I planned it for years. How I was going to seduce you, get you all turned on and go for it. I knew you might think it happened because we were alone, had wine. It was a setup, Clare. I set it up. I want you to be real clear about that."

"Because…?"

He lifted her hand to his lips. He pressed a soft kiss into her palm. "Because if I happen to see that opportunity again,

if I try again, if I give you wine and darkness and try to seduce you, you'll know. It's deliberate. It's not an accident."
He shrugged. "Maybe then if you respond, you won't regret
it later."

She shivered at the thought.

He started the car and drove her home, leaving her with
lots to think about.

The end of October came with a shock of cold, and the
high-school Homecoming. Over the years Clare had managed not to pay too much attention to the way the town was
charged with excitement during Homecoming, and she realized now that was partly due to the fact she would not allow
herself to remember all the joy during that time of her life.
But having a son in high school invited her back.

She hadn't been to a Homecoming celebration since right
after her high school graduation, but this year's was like a
family reunion. With Jason and his cousin Lindsey in their
sophomore years, not only did Clare attend the festivities, so
did George, Maggie and Bob and Sarah. There were banners
all over town, the teenagers in Breckenridge so wired with
excitement, it was exhausting just to watch them. And Clare
had an added reason to be interested in all of this—a secret
no one knew. A secret she had barely admitted to herself. She
had a thing for the football coach.

The festivities started out with the crowning of the king
and queen. Then there was a huge bonfire on the school
grounds the night before the game. On game day the high
school students held a parade featuring their royalty, floats
they constructed themselves, a marching band, dance team,
pom-pom girls, the riding club, and some representation of
virtually every student organization.

The parade and floats wound up at the football field for a trip around the track. Thousands of people swarmed the grounds and bleachers; buses were lined up in the parking lots, emptied of their fans who accompanied the opposing team from out of town. After the game would come the dance—a glamorous affair reigned over by the king and queen, chaperoned by teachers, parents and the coach.

When Clare arrived for the game with Sarah and George, she immediately scanned the field for a sign of Pete, but the team wasn't out yet. Their opponents were from Fallon—a bunch of big farm boys who were reputed to be ruthless killers. But the Centennial boys had been winning all season and there wasn't anything small or timid about them.

Clare stopped her dad before they went into the bleachers. "Why don't Sarah and I wait here to see if Maggie and Bob are coming—you can go ahead and see if they're already here, or save room."

"Perfect," he said, going on without her.

"I'll get us something from the concession stand," Sarah said. "Want anything?"

"Coke, please," Clare asked.

Clare watched Sarah as she walked away, her blond hair bouncing on her shoulders. She must be going broke on the new clothes, but she looked so darling in her fitted slacks, sweater, scarf and boots. She kept her makeup light and tasteful and admitted that she had been shocking her customers with her new look. Whatever this was about, Clare and Maggie were very grateful.

The opposing team ran onto the field and the bleachers opposite where Clare stood exploded into cheers while behind her she heard boos and hisses.

"Clare?" a voice asked.

She turned around to find herself face-to-face with Sam. He held a cardboard carton holding three Cokes and a bag of popcorn. He smiled at her. She looked for that sadness in his eyes, but to her relief saw none. Instead he seemed cheery, all dimples and teeth. Maybe Pete was right—he'd bounce back without a problem. "How are you, Sam?" she asked.

"Good. You?"

"Good. I've thought about calling to see how you're doing, but I didn't want to…you know…"

"It's okay, Clare. Really, I'm fine. You shouldn't worry."

"I'm glad. Have you been…have you been going out?"

He shrugged. "Not really. Hey, there's someone I'd like you to meet. Got a minute?"

"I have to wait here for my sister. She just went to get drinks."

"I'll wait with you. If it's okay."

"It's okay."

"So. How's it going at the store?"

"Good. You haven't been tearing up the sprinklers lately."

"We're about done mowing for the winter," he said. "Have you been…you know…going out?"

"I… No. My divorce is final now. But you know what they say. You should go it alone for at least six months."

He grinned at her. "Is that what they say? What's that about?"

"That old rebound thing, I guess."

"Is that how long it takes to heal?" he asked. And there it was, a hint of sadness in those typically bright, dancing eyes.

"I guess so. Approximately."

"I'll have to remember that."

The home team ran onto the field with a roar and Clare was grateful for the interruption—the conversation with Sam stopped for the cheers and the band blasting out the school song. There he was, the coach and his assistants. She raised up on her toes, but all she could have of him was his back. He would be focused on the field the rest of the night.

"Here you go," Sarah said, handing Clare a cola. "Hi, Sam. How've you been?"

"Good. Good to see you. Come with us—I want Clare to meet my daughter."

Sam led the way, Clare and Sarah following. They exchanged furtive glances behind him, Sarah with a question in her eyes and Clare answering with a shrug.

Not very far into the stands sat a woman and little girl. The little girl was a darling, freckle-faced sprite with long reddish-blond pigtails flowing over her shoulders. She was holding a tiny dog wrapped in a plaid throw. Just his little head with spiky, out-of-control hair and a little black button of a nose stuck out. "Clare and Sarah, this is Molly, my daughter, and Joan, my mom. This is Clare and Sarah, friends of mine."

While Clare just said hello, Sarah bent closer to the little girl and said, "I know Molly. I gave an art class at your school, remember?"

"Miss McCarthy?" she asked. "You look *beautiful*."

Sarah laughed and straightened. "I usually tie my hair back when I work or teach," she said to Sam's mother. "Nice to meet you."

"And you."

To Molly, she said, "I remember you really liked art. I give little classes at my studio, if you're ever interested."

"This is Spoof," Molly said, holding up the dog.

"You should paint him," Sarah said. "He'd make a great model."

"I bet he wouldn't," Sam laughed.

"We'd better get going," Clare said. "We have to look for Dad." When they walked away, Clare said, "That was weird."

"How so?"

"Meeting his family? After breaking it off?"

"Well, he appears to be doing just fine. You're not disappointed, are you?"

"Absolutely not. I just think it's weird, introducing us like that."

"He was just being polite," Sarah said. She strained to look up into the stands. "There they are. Up there."

The game had been a huge victory for Centennial. The kids were all charged up. Jason went to the dance with his buddies and was spending the night at Stan's. Lindsey was going to the dance with Christopher, in a car, an event that did not fill Maggie and Bob with comfort. The adults left the kids to the rest of their celebration and went out for pizza and beer.

It was only eleven when Clare got home. She didn't turn on many lights, but settled back on the sofa in the semidark and put her feet up. Her insides were still vibrating from the noise at the game and pizza parlor and the quiet was welcome.

She wondered if Pete had any idea how often she thought about him. Ever since going with him to his parents' house, ever since that memory of the past had come back to her so sweetly and he'd confessed his reasons for making sure she knew how deliberate his seduction had been, he had hardly left her thoughts for a second. Yet in the week preceding the homecoming, she hadn't heard from him.

She had started thinking about Pete in the way she had described to Sarah one should think about a man one loved—constantly, with a little patter of the heart, a lift, a feeling of euphoria and elation. Expectation. And not just at that moment of his touch—but at the mere thought of it.

She decided to leave him a message, telling him that the game was great and congratulate him. But he answered the phone, startling her and putting her off guard.

"Pete! You're home!"

"Just barely walked in the door. I got a reprieve from the dance since I put in such a long damn day."

"I was just going to leave you a message, congratulating you."

"Would you like me to hang up and you can leave a message? I'll hear it right away."

"No," she laughed. "Good game. Congratulations."

"I saw you there. I was glad you came."

"I haven't been to a Homecoming in years. But with Jason in high school…"

"Most important, it was a fun game," he said. "Football season is almost over. When it is, how would you like to go out? Dinner or something?"

"I'd love that."

"I'd take you out this weekend, but I have the girls. What are you doing?"

"I'm going to work on my old house. It's going to be more than a renovation. It's going to be a huge remodel. I'm going to start by cleaning up. I'll have the heating and plumbing repaired first—so I can work in the house this winter, but I already had a chimney sweep pronounce the fireplace safe, so I can use that right away. Then in spring, I'll work on the outside."

"You're amazing, Clare. Wish I could do that kind of stuff."

"You do other stuff," she said. "You do wonderful football stuff." You do something to me, she thought.

★ ★ ★

George would have loved to help Clare in the old house on Saturday, but he had to run the store as usual. She was just as happy about that; she didn't want her dad to overdo it. He wasn't a young guy anymore, after all.

Clare lit a fire in the hearth on Saturday morning to warm as much of the downstairs as possible. Then she started on the upstairs, sweeping up trash and finding the occasional dangling torn sheet of wallpaper irresistible. She'd grab it and tear, adding that to the other debris. She'd filled a couple of trash bags when there was a banging at the front door. She ran downstairs and peeked out the diamond-shaped window to see Pete.

She tugged on the warped door until it opened. He smiled at her and lifted a broom. "Pete! What are you doing here?"

"My plans with the girls got canceled—some kind of birthday thing for their stepdad's side of the family." He grinned. "Normally that would really irritate me, this last-minute stuff, but it frees me up to give you a hand. If you're interested."

"Wow," she said, stepping aside so he could come in. "This is great of you. I started upstairs. It's really cold up there, but I'm nearly done and it's warming up down here. Come on," she said. She took him by the hand and led him up the stairs where she had a nice big pile of debris in one of the bedrooms and in the hall, a box of giant trash bags.

Pete took heavy work gloves out of his pockets and said, "Looks like you can sweep and I can haul. We might be done in time for lunch somewhere."

He bent to the task of scooping trash into a bag and Clare found herself just standing there, watching his back and arms as he did this chore, though she couldn't see his muscles work— he wore his heavy jacket. But she could imagine them. When he stood and hefted the heavy bag over one shoulder, he asked, "Where are we putting this stuff?"

"Backyard," she said.

He smiled at her and said, "You'd better sweep. If you have a little help, there will be more time to play."

She moved the broom. Play. Yes, she thought. I'd like to play.

An hour later they were downstairs, which the fire had warmed considerably. She swept up in the living room while he got busy in the dining room. When he removed his jacket and wore just his V-neck sweatshirt, she found the expanse of his back and shoulders most distracting. But not nearly so much as his butt in those jeans!

She took off her jacket, as well, but suspected it was not the fire that made her warm.

Clare wasn't the only one stealing hot little glances; Pete found his eyes drawn to her all morning long. The curve of her jaw; the small, compact butt; the way her soft hair would swing around her shoulders. He wanted to get his hands all over her.

"Where's Jason today? Why isn't he over here helping?" Pete asked.

"He's with his dad. They're getting along real well these days, thank God," she said. "I think I owe a lot of that to you."

"Nah. They'd have gotten around to it. Roger was pretty determined."

"Still, that whole football thing… Jason wouldn't have been invited to help anyway. All I need is a complaining fifteen-year-old over here, making my life miserable." Besides, she thought, I want you all to myself.

By noon, the living-room floor was cleared with a big pile of trash in the foyer. Pete took a bag of garbage out to the backyard and when he came back into the kitchen, Clare was rinsing off her hands in the kitchen sink. His eyes warmed over as he looked at her back. Well, more specifically, her butt. She had that leggy, tight-bottom look about her; a killer in jeans. The very same that had been turning him on since he was about fourteen. It hadn't changed all that much.

"I thought the plumbing was out?" he said, taking off his gloves.

"No hot water heater. We can rinse and flush—that's it."

He tossed his gloves on the counter and came up behind her, putting his arms around her, his hands under the cold water with hers. He covered her hands with his under the icy water, massaging them, and she leaned back against him. He bent his head, nuzzling her neck with his lips, inhaling her scent. He wasn't sure he could get close enough.

She pulled their hands from the water and turned off the spigot. She dried their hands together while he concentrated on her neck. This wasn't exactly what he'd planned, but feeling her against him was so good, he didn't care. Then she lifted his hand to her mouth and licked his fingers, gently sucking on one, and he thought he might lose his mind. He turned her around to face him and slipped his arms around her to hold her. She tilted her chin up and he lowered his lips to hers, slowly, gently, touching them softly. He pressed gentle kisses against her lips before covering her mouth in a kiss that was demanding and serious. Deep and hot. And her lips opened beneath his, inviting his tongue. He kissed her long and hard, and then he said, "Ah. You taste too good."

"You taste pretty good yourself."

"It's been awhile."

"Probably too long," she whispered against his mouth.

Probably, he thought. Yet things always seemed to happen

in their own time. He was a little older now; not necessarily in a rush. There was a part of him that wanted to fall into her in a hurry and experience her body, but a stronger part that wanted to savor every touch, every sensation. He realized, devouring her mouth, that he hadn't forgotten how delicious she was. His hands moved over her. He threaded his fingers into her hair to pull her mouth hard against his. Then down her neck and over her shoulders to her arms, to her back, over breasts and bottom, pushing her against the sink and pressing against her.

She was coming to him with heat, with passion, thrusting her small tongue into his mouth hungrily, sighing deeply. Yes, he thought. Yes, this is what I want. What I've always wanted—this woman in my arms, her mouth open under mine. He ran a hand down her back, over her bum, down her thigh to the back of her knee. He lifted her knee up to his hip and pressed himself against her. He was hard, ready for lovemaking, moving against her. Grinding against her. And she gyrated her hips against him, knowing.

Against her lips he said, "The last time I tried this, I broke your heart."

"The last time, we didn't know anything."

"You know what I want." He kissed her deeply. "I want to love you like mad. If you want it, too, you have to tell me."

"I want you," she said. "Take me somewhere."

"Are you expecting anyone to come here?"

"No."

"Does the door lock?"

"Uh-huh. But…"

He dropped her knee and pulled away. He put a hand under her chin, a soft kiss on her lips and said, "Go stoke the fire. I'll be right back."

He walked through the front of the house and out the door. Not clear what he was up to, she did as he asked. She was on her knees in front of the fireplace when he returned, a sleeping bag under each arm. He locked the door behind him and crossed the room, kneeling beside her. Together they wordlessly spread the sleeping bags, zipping them together.

Pete sat and pulled off his boots, setting them beside the fireplace, and Clare did the same. Then he pulled her into his arms and lowered himself to the floor, his lips on hers. He rolled, pulling her on top of him. She began to move on him at once, pressing and wriggling against him, until he groaned with pleasure.

He locked his hands into the bottom of her sweatshirt and pulled it over her head. Then he unhooked her bra, tossing it aside. He cupped her breasts and ran his thumbs over her nipples bringing them to life until his attention turned them into hard little pebbles. He rolled with her onto their sides so he could get rid of his shirt, then pulled her against him, feeling her breasts brand his flesh. "Ah, Clare," he said. "God, you feel good."

"You have no idea how good I feel," she whispered.

She sighed deeply, moaned with longing. She moved her hips against his erection and nearly whimpered. He reached for the snap of her jeans, opening them. Running his hands down her hips, he slid them down and helped her out of them. Next went the thong, cast away. The second they were gone, she was straining eagerly against him again, and with his hands on her bum, he pulled her to him, holding her there. Then he slid a hand between their bodies and down. Over her flat belly, slipping into that place that was dark and wet. He put a hand on her, probing with his fingers. She was as hot as a pistol. He hadn't even had the luxury of getting her worked up. She was ready and hungry. Needy. All riled up and about to explode.

"Whew, Clare. I better take care of you right away," he murmured.

"Oh… You better…"

"I had a vasectomy years ago, but I brought condoms."

"You've been planning this," she whispered against his lips.

"For years, Clare. Years. But I was going to invite you home, to my house, to a bed…."

"I never would have made it," she said. "Now hurry up."

He rolled her onto her back and, kneeling between her legs, he got rid of his jeans. He put himself against her, right where he would enter. With her small bum in his hands, he pressed himself slowly into her, sighing deep in his chest as he felt her hot, tight body surround him, as he felt her pull him in. He'd been waiting to feel this, waiting forever. And it felt every bit as wonderful as he imagined. Remembered.

"Pete," she whispered. "Oh, Pete. I'm not going to last a minute."

He brushed the hair back from her brow. He moved within her, stroking deep and long and slow. "Let it go, baby. I've got you." He moved some more, smiling as he heard her purrs and murmurs, her sighs, his name on her lips. She wasn't a quiet one, this woman. These sounds were music to his ears. She had more passion inside her than she might realize, something he had always known. She was writhing beneath him, reaching. "Let it go, baby," he whispered. He could feel her quivering everywhere and knew she was so close, so ready. "Ah, Clare… Almost there," he whispered, pressing himself into her, rocking with her. He wanted to bring this to her, this magic made between a man and woman. And he wanted to be there, inside, when it happened. He held her bottom against him and pressed himself deep. She froze, gripping his shoulders, clenched around him and the spasms came, so tight and hard it almost knocked him out. She was amazing; her orgasm was phenomenal, and he felt it all over him—wild and wonderful. It was hot and powerful and long, as if it wouldn't let go of her. "God," he whispered, overwhelmed. He had barely to touch her and it came to her, as though she'd been waiting for years. As he had. And finally she began to relax in his arms, panting, kissing him in soft, sweet, tender little kisses while she recovered. It was magnificent, what he felt surrounding him. It took her quite a while to rest easy in his arms.

"Clare," he whispered, kissing her lips, chin, neck, shoulder. "That was nice."

"I want you to feel nice, too," she said, breathless.

"Don't you worry about me," he said. "I know what I'm doing."

She shivered in his arms. "My God. You certainly do."

He kissed her neck. His lips slowly moved to her breast, gently drawing on one nipple, then the next. As he progressed lower, he carefully withdrew from her body and he kept kissing her—down her body, over her tummy, over her soft mound, until he reached the center of her body and he gently kissed the inside of her thighs. Then deeper, his tongue growing more urgent as he found that hard knot that was the most pleasurable, most vulnerable part of her, and he went to work on it, gentle at first, and then with much more determination, until he could feel her begin to quiver against his mouth. She pressed into him, she moaned above him, and he rose to her, pushing himself into her again. He grabbed her hips and slid in, pulled back, slid in again, each stroke bringing the movement of her hips harder against him. She was killing him, it was so good. He lowered his lips to hers, de-

vouring her with his urgent kiss. Her pelvis tilted up to bring
him deeper; her hips moved harder and faster and he matched
her rhythm. Her legs wrapped around him, she strained toward him. Greedy, he wanted to feel it again and he waited.
Waited for her orgasm, which came quickly and was just as
wonderful as the first. This time, when she was gripped in the
peak of it, when it was at its most relentless, he pushed into
her and let himself go in a tremendous blast, not sure he'd be
able to stay conscious through it. "God," he said in a breath.

She pulsed for such a long time, breathless, he just held
her until the storm passed, kissing her, loving her, caressing
her. "God," he said again. Until she was complete. "Clare,"
he whispered.

"Holy cow."

"Nice," he said softly.

"Nice?" she asked. She laughed.

"You're incredible," he said, covering her face with kisses.
"I knew you would be like this. Amazing."

Her fingers on his face, she pulled him down to her lips
again. "That was unbelievable. Pete, you've been holding out
on me."

"Well, not intentionally." He rose above her, looked into
her eyes and said, "I never stopped loving you. I managed to
stop thinking about it for a while, but I never stopped."

"I wish I'd known sooner. How you felt."

He shrugged. "It didn't seem possible. We had other lives."

She brushed a hand against the hair at his temple. "Well.
We have this one now. And it's very, very good."

He nibbled at her lips. "It is. I'm not letting you get away."

"You'd have trouble getting rid of me…"

"I have an idea. Let's dress, grab some lunch and take it to my house. Let's have a naked picnic in the bed and then make love until curfew."

"Curfew?" she laughed. "Jason's with his dad till tomorrow night."

"Oh, God," he said weakly. He started kissing her again and before even minutes had passed, his lips were on her neck, her breasts, her belly.

Her hand slid down to him, closed over him, bringing a deep, lusty moan. He heard her softly laugh. "I have a feeling I'm not going to get lunch for a while."

"Not for a while," he answered.

"So," she whispered. "This is deliberate?"

"Not anymore," he said, seeking and finding her again. "Now it's beyond my control."

chapter twelve

. . . .

THE LEAVES COMPLETED their change of color, setting the hill-sides of the Sierra on fire, then they fell, leaving the branches bare before Halloween. The clouds of winter came in No-vember, drenching Breckenridge in rain, but covering the mountains in a fresh blanket of snow. Locals and tourists alike flocked to the slopes, and for the first time in years Sarah had a renewed excitement about skiing because of a certain part-time ski patrol.

She had done a lot of skiing as a kid, but later when she was so into her art and operating her shop, had taken only the rare trip to the mountains with her sisters and their kids.

It took no time for Sarah to sharpen her skills. After a cou-ple of days, she was mastering the expert slopes she had visited as a young woman. She closed her shop a few times during the first good snow and went to Afton Alps, Squaw Valley and Alpine Meadows. When her father asked her if she could afford to do this she said, "Of course. Selling that big tapes-try to the Afton Alps Lodge set me up. And don't you think I should visit it?"

Sarah bought new gear—a bright pink ski bib, darker pink

jacket, skis and poles, awesome polar boots. And it only took a couple of trips to the mountains, which were less than a forty-minute drive, to learn that a certain ski patrol by the name of Jankowski worked on Mondays at Afton Alps.

Well, Monday was an excellent day to close the store. She posted her new hours on the door and waxed her skis.

Ski patrols roamed the slopes, looking for spills and problems, driving around on their snowmobiles, dragging toboggans to ferry injured skiers, marking the restricted areas and posting signs where avalanche was a danger. Every time she saw a red jacket with a white cross on the sleeve, she looked to see if she recognized the face. She skied all day without seeing him, and then on what was to be her last run of the day, she spied him at the top of the expert hill. Ah, he was so beautiful. She made her way toward him and yelled, "Sam! Hey, Sam!"

He turned and squinted in her direction.

"It's me, Sarah," she said, popping up her goggles and laughing.

He pulled off his goggles and smiled at her. "What's up, Sarah?"

"I heard you did some patrol. Busy day?"

"Nah. Everyone's behaving. We just have to keep the bad boys under control. And bad girls," he added with a grin that almost brought her to her knees.

"Sounds like a perfect job for you."

"You up here alone?" he asked, looking around.

Was he looking for Clare? she wondered. "Yes. I decided to take a mental-health day. This is going to be my last run."

"Big mountain for a little girl."

"Who are you calling a little girl, big shot? I was raised on this little hill."

"That so?" he said, grinning again.

Sarah thought she could die a happy woman if she could just look into those blue eyes as she went. It was true she'd been raised on this mountain. They'd done plenty of skiing as kids, but she was clearly the best in the family. Jason was going to pass her soon—on his snowboard—with Lindsey a close second behind him. "When do you get off work?" she asked.

"In about a half hour. I'm going to head in now."

"Have a drink with me?" she dared, though she was quaking inside.

"Um...I don't drink at the lodge. Image, you know."

"How about the pub at Lander's Pass? Not too far out of the way."

He hesitated, thinking about it for a second.

"Just a beer, Sam," she pushed.

"Why not?" he finally said.

She got an impish gleam in her eye, snapped her goggles into place and said, "If you can catch me!" She pushed off and headed down the difficult slope at a rate of speed that frightened even her. He was right on her heels, keeping up with her effortlessly. When she came upon the moguls, she jumped, landing soft as a feather. She bent at the waist, her poles tucked under her arms, and flew. "Slow down!" he yelled, but she was not for going slow. No more holding back. She was, literally, throwing caution to the wind. She shifted her weight right, then left, then right again, traversing the steep slope, carving turns in the soft powder. She could hear him jumping each mogul behind her. And it was exhilarating.

It took them a few minutes to get down and when he pulled up beside her, she was laughing.

"You're good," Sam said. "You were showing off."

"I was," she chuckled. "I wanted to see what you had."

"No," he said, the smile huge. "You wanted me to see what you had. You could be a little more careful."

"Why? I had a ski patrol on my tail. I felt safe as a kitten. Should I meet you there?"

"I have to change out— You'll beat me."

"Take your time. I'm sure the fire is warm and cozy."

"See you in a while," he said. And she watched him as he made his way to the patrol station.

Sarah's heart was high as she drove down the pass to the pub. He didn't appear to be dying of a broken heart. It was good that he was going to follow her in a few minutes. She'd use that extra time to fluff her hair and make sure her makeup was perfect, concerns that hadn't even occurred to her a couple of months ago. It would also give her time to slow the hammering of her heart and appear composed, though she was far from it.

By the time Sam arrived, she was sitting by the fire in the pub, nursing a glass of white wine. Sarah reminded herself not to sigh in longing just at the mere sight of him. It completely escaped her how Clare could give him up. Sarah had not been this moved by a man in her life. Now, if the angels were on her side, the snow would fall, the pass would close and they'd be stranded for the night.

He pulled off his gloves, stuffed them in the pockets of his jacket and hung it on a peg inside the door. There weren't many people in the bar and she had secured a cozy, private spot near the fire.

"This is a good idea," he said. "Thanks."

"I like this place. Do you come here very often?"

"Only once in a blue moon. I'm usually in a rush to get home and relieve my mom of Molly, but I called and she said to take my time."

"When do you work at Afton Alps?"

"Mondays. Then I try to take Molly skiing on Saturdays or Sundays. Saturday, Sunday, Monday are my days off from the department."

"Do you like being a cop?"

"I love it. Almost as much as skiing. Policing is good work. And how long have you been an art teacher?"

"About eight years—but teaching isn't my primary job. The studio, store and my own art is how I really support myself. I have some of my work hanging at the Afton Alps Lodge. That big tapestry? I did that."

"No kidding? You *made* that? That's amazing." The waiter appeared and Sam ordered a beer. "I'm surprised I haven't run into you before now. If you ski a lot."

In fact, she hadn't before she went on the Sam hunt, but she was blessed with a skill that looked as if she was there a lot. "You only work one day a week, Sam," she said.

Sarah asked him questions about Molly and his mother, told him about her work and exhibitions. They talked a little bit about where they went to school, who their friends were in town, and not wanting it to end, Sarah ordered a second glass of wine. But Sam didn't have another beer. She sipped slowly, hoping he would, but after a little more than an hour had passed he said, "I guess I better get going."

"Me, too. I suppose."

"Let me get the tab and I'll walk you out."

"It should be my treat," she said. "I invited you."

"Naw, get your coat," he said, disappearing toward the bar.

She stood by the door, watching his back, his shoulders broad under his heavy sweater. God, he was magnificent. And sweeter than a puppy. Those hands, large and strong and neat.

He turned toward her and smiled. With that face and body, he should be on a coin.

I don't stand a chance, she thought.

"Ready?" he asked, grabbing his jacket.

He took her arm as they walked to her car and she thought, this is probably going to be the most I ever get from him. A little friendly conversation, a walk to the car. But I'll take it.

"Thank you," she said. "And thank you for not asking about Clare."

He shrugged. "I assume she's fine?"

"Great." She pulled her jacket tighter. "I think I'll plan on Mondays being ski days. Maybe we can do this again some-time?"

"I'll watch for you," he said, opening her car door. "I'll follow you down the mountain. Make sure you don't have any problems."

"You don't have to. I've been down this pass a million times."

"It's narrow in places. And I already know you have a need for speed."

"Just on the slopes," she laughed. "I trust skis a lot more than cars."

"That's probably smart," he told her, shutting her door.

All the way down the mountain she grinned like a Cheshire cat. And asked herself how she could last until the next Monday.

The next two Mondays were like heaven at Afton Alps. Sarah managed to find him during the day, let him know that she was there, even ski with him a bit and ride the lift up with him a few times. She longed for a phone call during the week, but it appeared those Mondays of skiing with a beer afterward were all the time he had for her. She tried not to be discouraged, but it was hard. She wanted to ask him if he was seeing anyone, but fear of the answer kept her silent.

She cautioned herself not to pursue him too dramatically; there was an expression that sometimes crossed his features that told her he could be frightened away easily; there was definite caution in his eyes. Besides, Sarah was still a little shy with him. Her renewed style had helped her gain some confidence, but not so much that she could summon the courage to throw herself at him, which she thought was a good thing. While they had their drinks, she did manage to work into the conversation questions like why hadn't he married, and answered the same question with, "I've been too consumed by work. But I've decided it's time now to venture a little farther from the studio, be a little more social."

When he left her at her car, she would tilt her face up toward his, ready. But he would only open her car door and say good night.

The last Thursday of November was Thanksgiving, held at George's house as usual. It was the typical loud affair with three teens, six adults, televised parades and football. When dinner was done and the sisters were cleaning up, Maggie said to Clare and Sarah, "Something's going on with you two."

"What?" they asked in unison.

"Oh, now that was almost guilty. Someone's having sex." Both displayed heightened color on their cheeks. "Oh!" Maggie exclaimed. "You dogs!"

"*I'm* not!" Sarah insisted. And she thought, *damn it!*

But Clare looked away.

"Clare?" Maggie said.

She looked back and in a whisper said, "I haven't told Jason yet. Or anyone for that matter. Can you keep it quiet until I do?"

"Of course! What are you hiding?"

"I've been seeing Pete Rayburn."

Dead silence answered her. Maggie finally asked, "How long has this been going on?"

"Well, hard to say. We reconnected last August when I took that teaching job. We got together for coffee, had a few conversations, and it just sort of grew from there. Out of friendship. It came into full bloom Homecoming weekend."

Maggie leaned closer. "Are you sleeping with him?" she asked in a whisper.

Clare smiled devilishly. "There's hardly any sleep involved."

"Is it...? Is it...?" Maggie couldn't make herself form the question.

"It's unbelievable," Clare said with an involuntary shiver.

This news caused the sisters to squeal. Sarah couldn't have been more relieved—this meant that Clare had moved on and had no lingering feelings for Sam. But Sarah wasn't talking. She didn't want to jinx it. Her mind was made up, she wasn't going to tell about Sam until he professed his undying love for her. And at the rate they were going, that could be a while. She just hoped and prayed it would occur to him to kiss her before the spring thaw. So far there had been only the touch of his hand on her arm as he walked her to her car.

Another Monday of skiing came and went. Then, a couple of days later, early in December, Sam came into the shop and she beamed with pleasure when she saw him. It was the first time he'd made any contact with her besides those Mondays. He was on duty and she almost fainted at the sight of him in that dark blue uniform. "Oh Sam, look at you," she said.

"Are you propositioned every time you try to give a woman a parking ticket?"

He favored her with a wide smile. "That's against the law, Sarah."

"*That* wasn't an answer, Sam," she said.

He ducked his head a little, as if shy. "I wonder if you could help me out. I'm shopping for Molly's Christmas and I heard you say she liked art. Maybe you could pick out something I could give her? A painting set? Markers? I don't know...."

"I know exactly what to do. I can make up a kit for her— the right kind of paints and brushes, charcoals and paper, stuff that matches her skill level."

"Will it take long? I have to get back," he said, glancing out the door toward the squad car.

"You can come back for it later, or tomorrow. How much do you want to spend?"

"Fifty? Is that enough?"

"That's great. When do you get off work?"

"Not until ten. Maybe I can swing by before then, if there's a break in the Breckenridge action."

The twinkling of an idea made her smile. "You don't have to. I'll be here till after ten. Come after work... If you can...."

"I thought you closed at six."

"I do. I go home, have dinner with Dad, and come back here in the evenings. Sometimes I teach a class when the shop is closed, sometimes I just enjoy working without the interruption of customers. I often stay till midnight. Right now, I'm working on a painting. I'll make you up something special. It'll be ready for you tonight."

For the rest of the day she prayed he wouldn't find time to pick up the kit any earlier. She didn't rush back to the shop after dinner because what she wanted was for him to be finished working when he came in. Tonight, she vowed, she would somehow let him know that it was all right to kiss her, to touch her. To be in his arms for just a moment would be like a dream come true.

She primped and changed into a crisp white blouse and midi-length lightweight skirt, something she hoped looked feminine. As she was leaving, George asked, "You going out, honey?"

"I'm going back to the shop," she said. "I think I'll be late."

He wrinkled his brow. "You don't usually shower and change before going back to work."

"It was a gritty day. I needed a little pick-me-up," she returned, finding it curious that her dad even noticed.

That night as she painted, she didn't get lost in the work. Instead, she watched the clock and her heart sank as ten came and went, then ten-thirty. At eleven she assumed, in complete disappointment, that he had probably gone home and planned to pick up his daughter's present the next day. Maybe he just isn't interested in me in a romantic way, she thought. It hadn't been hard to coax him into a friendship, but he gave no indication he wanted to go any further.

Just as hope had all but vanished, there was a knock at the shop door. She came out of the studio and saw him standing there, wearing civilian clothes.

"I didn't know if you'd still be here," he said. "We had a little fender bender right at ten. Tied me up awhile."

"You're fine. Come in. I think you'll like it." She bolted the door behind him and he followed her to the back room. There on the counter amidst a lot of supplies was a green metal box that she had painted some sweet little flowers on earlier in the day. She opened it for him and gave him a little inventory. Brushes, pastels, watercolors, charcoals, a booklet

on drawing. Under the box, a couple of small stretched can-
vases and a drawing pad.

"This is great, Sarah. You take plastic?"

"Sure," she said, her voice dripping with disappointment.
He was going to pay and dash.

Sam pulled his wallet out of his pocket and, looking over
her shoulder at a painting on an easel, he said, "You doing
that?"

"Uh-huh." It sat next to her still life of an empty bottle of
wine, two glasses, a white linen napkin, a papier-mâché loaf
of bread. "Wine, bread and thee," she said.

He moved closer to the painting. "You're really good. I can't
even draw a straight line, much less something you'd recognize." Without really planning to, she was reaching toward
his back, his shoulder. Reaching out to touch him. Aching
to touch him. "I admit, I haven't tried to paint anything but
a wall, but…" As he turned around to face her, her hand was
stretched toward him. "Sarah?" She started to pull back but
then, seizing on what little courage she could muster, she put
her hand on his chest and looked up into his amazing blue
eyes. Then she took a step toward him, so close she could feel
his breath on her face. Another step brought her against him
and she thought, if he pushes me away, I will die. She laid her
head on his chest near his shoulder. "Sarah?" he asked. She
didn't move. Her cheek lay on his shoulder next to her hand.
He just stood, his arms at his sides.

Sam put an arm around her waist and she drew in a con-
tented breath. He held her for a long moment, then lowered
his head to her hair and deeply inhaled the scent. He moved
lower and, lifting her hair away, softly nuzzled her neck, bringing a sigh from her. She felt his lips on her neck, under the

collar of her blouse. She felt his tongue there and she trembled. "Sarah," he said in a hoarse whisper. "You're delicious."

Sarah turned her head and rubbed her cheek against his. His other arm went around her and he held her closer, nibbling at her neck, then burrowing farther, to her bare shoulder beneath her blouse. Her sighs filled the studio and she embraced him, held him to her. He lifted his head and softly touched her parted lips. "Sarah, what are we doing?"

"Mmm," she murmured, claiming his mouth again.

He pressed his lips harder against hers, pulling her closer.

"You're delicious, too," she whispered.

"Should we be doing this?" he asked her.

"I think so, yes," she said, a little breathless, her eyes closed. And his mouth moved, opened, his tongue probed, kissing her deeply. Passionately.

It was exactly as she dreamed it would be, to be in his strong arms. Her emotions soared and the heat of desire filled her. The feel of him, the smell, the texture of his mouth—how could it be so familiar when this was her first taste? His hands caressed her back while his mouth devoured hers. Then his lips were on her neck again, kissing and teasing her. He moaned with deep pleasure, then took her mouth again. And again, and again. This is what she had lived for. Never in her life had she wanted something so much.

She pulled away from him slightly and looked into his eyes, his hands still on her hips as though to keep her from getting away. He wasn't smiling, for once. "You're full of surprises, Sarah."

Her fingers, trembling slightly, went to the buttons on her blouse. She undid the first, the second, his hand grasped her wrist as she touched the third. "Do you want to think about this?" he asked, his voice husky.

"No," she whispered. "I don't want to think." He let go of her wrist and she undid the third, fourth and fifth.

"Are you sure?" he asked her. "Because I can not think, too. In fact, I'm probably better at it than you."

Her eyes softly closed. "We'll see," she whispered.

He didn't hesitate. He put his hands inside the blouse and spread it. Eyes closed, she dropped her head back and let out a long slow breath as she felt his hands on her breasts. Then his lips were there as he kissed, nibbled, then sucked and her knees threatened to give out. He tongued her lips apart again, in a long demanding kiss. "I think we're playing with fire here," he said.

"I know," she whispered against his mouth. "Oh, God, I know." And then she demanded as much of his lips as he had of hers.

He pulled away from her to shrug his jacket from his shoulders to the floor. He ripped his sweater off over his head and held her again. He turned with her in his arms and flipped the light switch so that the large overhead light was out and the room was lit by only the soft glow of the night-light under the supply cupboard. He pushed the blouse from her shoulders, letting it drop, and crushed her against his bare chest, both of his hands on her buttocks so that she could feel his desire, too, had risen. Then he began to crunch her skirt into little fistfuls of fabric in his hand until he had raised it and beneath he found the warm flesh of her thigh. He explored her, finding nothing more than a thong to get in his way. "God," he whispered. He pushed it down easily and it rested around her ankles, so she stepped out of it. Then she dared put her hand over his erection and he groaned against her open mouth, pushing against her hand.

They stood, rocking, fondling, their mouths locked together in a hot wet kiss that seemed to go on forever. He dug his hands into her hair, pulling her face hard against his, then under the skirt again, caressing her soft bum and lower, to her delicate insides. Pleasure shot through her as he touched her there. She enjoyed the sensation of the smooth muscles of his chest under her fingertips, his flat, muscled belly. His breathing was labored and excited as she struggled with the snap on his jeans and finally, getting inside, slipped her hand down, closing it around him in a firm caress that caused his breath to catch in his throat. He answered by grinding closer to her as he kissed her.

Sam embraced her again, looking down into her eyes. He lifted her onto the worktable and stood between her spread knees. He lifted her skirt to her thighs, rubbing them. Pulling her to the edge of the table, he kissed her again. "I can still stop, Sarah," he whispered against her lips.

"If you stop, I will die."

"Someone should put out this fire," he said.

"Oh, Sam, please…"

"Are we okay here? Safe?"

"Yes." She ran her fingers through the hair at his temples, drew him back to her lips.

He freed himself from his pants and slowly, neatly, pulled her onto him. She gasped as he filled her. With his hands under her bottom, he lifted her so that he held her off the table, her legs wrapped around his waist. Kissing her deeply, he lifted her up and down gently. She held his shoulders, feeling the tension of his muscles at work, and rocked with him. Her pleasure was rising and rising until she thought she would scream, and then it exploded inside her, showering her with the greatest bliss she had ever known. In her ecstasy, she bit down on his lip, startling a small noise out of him. While she was gripped in orgasm, she heard him whisper, "Oh…God…" Spent, she began to go limp, but he said, "Hold me, Sarah. Tightly." He thrust once, twice, and then exploded inside her.

He gently rested her back on the table, but continued to hold her tenderly as his kisses began to come softer, sweeter. She wouldn't let him go, but returned his kisses for a long while, and then he gently slipped out of her.

"My God, Sarah," he said. "Did you know that was going to happen?"

She shook her head, smiling. "But I'm glad it did."

He touched her hair. "You're really something."

"You did all the work. I've never experienced anything like that in my life." She laid her head on his shoulder and he held her, quiet and close, until she shivered.

Sam fastened his trousers and reached to the floor for her blouse. He held it for her to slip into and then he slowly buttoned it. "I'll need a minute," she said. He helped her off the table and into her shoes.

Sarah went into the little bathroom in her studio to freshen up. She heard him rustling around in the studio. He'll go now, she found herself thinking. Then she heard the soft sound of music—the slow melodies of late-night radio. When she opened the door, she found he was still bare chested. He held a hand out to her, pulled her into his arms and danced with her, taking tiny steps in the small space.

Nothing could have prepared her for this. She knew he would be an extraordinary lover, but she hadn't counted on him being so romantic. As she held him, moved with him, kissed him to the strains of soft jazz, it wasn't long before his kisses became deeper, more demanding. His hand went again to her breast, but this time he managed the buttons. His mouth on her was sheer heaven; his hands were magic. And her hands were all over him, caressing his shoulders, down his arms, past his flat belly. Again she was lifted to the worktable. He nibbled at her lips and said, "Try not to bite me this time. Unless you have to." He brought her onto him again, again bearing all her weight as she enjoyed a thundering climax in his arms, and when she was done, he matched her. The only thing he said when he caught his breath was, "We need a bed."

It was almost five in the morning when she locked the shop door. "Will your father be worried about you?"

"No. It's not uncommon for me to get caught up in something and stay here all night. How about your mom?"

He shrugged. "I work overtime sometimes," he said. He kissed her and said, "I'll follow you home, make sure you're in safely."

The next afternoon, a floral bouquet arrived at the shop. There was one word on the card. "Wow."

Sam called Sarah once that week, asked how she was, but when the weekend came she didn't hear from him. The following Monday afternoon when she found him on the slopes, she passed him an envelope. Inside was a key to a room in the small motel at Lander's Pass near the pub they had frequented. When he opened the door she was already there, in the bed. Beside her was a bottle of wine and two glasses. The sheet was pulled up to cover her naked breasts.

"Damn," was all he could say.

As Christmas drew near, Sam's life was changing. Ten years of tension fell from his shoulders and a mysterious smile played so often at his lips that cop friends asked, "What's up with you, man?" All he could do was grin.

The first day he'd seen her on the slopes, he warned himself about getting mixed up with another one of these McCarthy women. Especially this one—clearly the most beautiful. The sexiest. But instead of pushing him away, Sarah seduced him and in her arms, in her body, he found a thrill like nothing he'd ever known. She was an incredible lover.

He started calling her every day, stopping by the shop, buying her little things. He found a green cashmere sweater that just lit up her eyes, and lit up his eyes when he took it off her. He found some cloisonné combs for her pretty hair. He took her to dinner in Lake Tahoe and halfway through the meal, slid a room key across the table to her. They didn't finish dinner.

When he had her in his arms, he felt like the world's greatest lover. She melted to him like hot butter and he found that hardly any effort was required to bring her to climax after shattering climax, the sound of her purrs and sighs, the sound of his name as she reached her pinnacle again and again, causing him to answer with a deep, lusty laugh. It filled him with some kind of male pride to work her body so well. And brother, did she have a way with his body. It caused him to shiver involuntarily in the middle of the day. He wasn't sure he'd ever been with a woman so passionate; he'd never had so much sex in his life. He thought he'd been cursed with an overactive libido until Sarah; hers was a definite match.

As he held her in the aftermath, looking down into those bewitching green eyes, he said, "You like sex, don't you, baby?"

And she laughed.

"Is that funny?"

"Sam, I haven't had sex in years...."

"Huh?" he said, stunned.

"In the last twelve years I've had two boyfriends. One for five years, one for five weeks, and neither of them could hold a candle to you." She touched his face. "I haven't been with a man in ages. Whew. I had no idea what I was saving up for."

"I'll be damned," he said. "You're practically untouched."

"Not anymore," she said.

Monday nights they stayed over at Lander's Pass, but there were other times. There were rooms available in Breckenridge, and he frequently found himself at that art shop for some groping and kissing, and sometimes more. That little table in the back room was getting a workout.

While he was in bed with her one night, looking down at her, smoothing her hair back from her face, he asked, "Have you told your sisters about us?"

The question clearly took her by surprise. "No," she finally said. "Why?"

"I thought you three told each other everything."

"Not everything," she said.

"Why haven't you told them about us?"

"I don't know," she answered. "Maybe I just want you all to myself. Why are you asking me?"

"Well, I'm not trying to keep you a secret, but I have something to tell you," Sam said. "To explain. It's about my daughter. She's just a kid, you know. Molly doesn't have a mother in the picture, and she'd like one. That's why I can't…" He struggled, so he stopped talking and just kissed her. Then he said, "I can't let her get attached to you until… I can't have her get all hopeful and then it doesn't work out between us. Do you understand?"

She nodded, but the look on her face told him he had just frightened her. He smiled into her eyes. "We've only been together a few weeks, Sarah. And I don't have any reason to think it won't be a lot longer. But once, some years ago, the first serious relationship I had after Molly came along, something went wrong. I'm still not sure what happened. Roxanne and I were together a couple of years and then she decided it wasn't what she wanted. Molly was crushed. I think she took it harder than I did."

"Oh, the poor little thing," Sarah said. She touched his face with her hand. Finally she said, "You're going to wait for two years?" she asked.

He laughed and kissed her, bit at her lip playfully. "That's not why I'm telling you this now. I have to spend Christmas with my family. If it weren't for Molly... Or if she were quite a bit older, I'd invite you to join us. I would have already brought you home to meet the family, but she's so young. I have to be so careful with her feelings. Her expectations. She's tenderhearted."

"It's okay, Sam. I'll meet them soon enough. I've already met them, actually. Remember? Homecoming."

"I mean as more than a friend. You know."

That made her smile. "I know."

"But I want to see you. I want to be with you. If I get us a place—will you meet me? Christmas night? After all the family stuff is over?"

"Yes, Sam."

"Will you spend the night?"

"The whole night," she said.

Pete went to Clare's house, just two days before Christmas. She let him into the house and into her embrace. She gave him a little kiss, nothing passionate. Jason was just down the hall. "Are you sure you want to do this?" she asked him.

"I'm sure," he said. "Is he home?"

"Right in the family room. Nervous?"

"A wreck. Wish me luck."

"Good luck, Coach," she said. As he headed for the family room, she gave him a swat on the butt.

Pete found Jason half sitting, half lying on the couch. The boy had awfully long legs, he found himself thinking. Huge feet. "Hey, bud," he said.

Jason straightened up. "Coach?"

"Got a minute?"

"Yeah, sure," he said. "Wassup?"

Pete sat on the love seat that made an L with the couch. "I want to ask you something. Permission, as a matter of fact." He cleared his throat. "I wonder if it would be all right with you if I date your mother?"

That really put a rod in the kid's spine. "Huh?"

"Your mother, Jason. I'd like to date your mother. But only if it's okay by you."

"Why you asking me?"

"Well, because it's just you and your mom here. And then it's you and your dad over there," he said, gesturing with his chin toward another place, another home. "I don't want to disrupt your family life. You know?"

Jason got a goofy grin on his face. "What if I say no?" he asked.

Oh, he's going to torture me, Pete thought. And enjoy every second of it. "I was counting on you saying yes," was all the answer he could think of.

"Yeah, I don't care," he said. "Man, that's too weird. Having some guy wanna date your mom!"

"Thanks, bud."

"How come you never dated her before?"

"Simple. She was never available before." He stood up and put out his hand. "Thanks, man. I'll let you get back to your show there."

Pete left the family room most gratefully. He met a grinning Clare in the foyer. "So?" she asked.

"Whew," he said, pulling her into his arms. "He really made me sweat. I wondered how I was going to get around it if he said no." He kissed her. Then he kissed her again. Then he wrapped his arms around her and really gave it to her.

"Hey!" Jason said.

They broke apart and looked at him.

"I said you could date! I didn't say nothin' about *that!*" But he had a stupid grin on his face.

"You date your way," Pete said. "I'll date mine."

chapter thirteen

....

THE FIRST TWO hours of Sam's shift was like a mini crime wave, in the nastiest wet weather they'd had in a while. He worked swings—2:00 p.m. till ten, and he'd already helped recover a stolen car, stopped a fight in the Target parking lot and booked a man who'd been knocking his wife around. Sometimes he thought that rain made people do things.

As he drove through Breckenridge, he looked up at the mountains. Snow. A soft fresh blanket. It made him think about Sarah. The last really good snowfall had been two weeks ago at Christmas. The memory of that night made his pulse race a little. It had been perfect.

For reasons primarily nostalgic, he had taken Sarah to the inn on Lander's Pass where the snow had cooperated beautifully by falling in thick white drifts, closing the pass. Sarah had made an excuse to her family that she was going to the house of a fellow artist in Reno for a Christmas evening open house and would stay the night there. So Sam brought champagne and gave her a beautiful gold bracelet, which was the only thing she wore as she pushed him back on the bed and, leaning over him, said, "And now it's time for your present...."

It had only been a little over a month they'd been intimate, but in his mind it seemed as though he'd been born in her arms. It was as if they had a long, long history when in fact it was all new. And he loved that she was getting bolder with him—a little aggressive from time to time. When she made some lusty move on him, it would cause him to laugh in loud, surprised delight and let her have whatever she wanted.

He looked at his watch—almost five. The winter sun would be setting soon. He pulled into the grocery to get a drink and some flowers for Sarah. He was standing at the checkout with bottled water and a bouquet wrapped in cellophane. Peeling a few dollars out of his clip, he glanced up into the security mirror. Aw, Jesus, he thought. There were a couple of teenage boys loitering near the liquor department. They were fidgety and goosey; they were about to commit a smash-and-grab for a six-pack.

Sam said to the cashier, "Keep this here, I'll be right back."

The boys had obviously entered the store ahead of Sam. Had they seen the squad car out front, they would've crossed this particular store off their list. He went around a store display of canned goods, staying out of sight. He circled around to the back of the liquor aisle, coming up behind them. His timing was perfect. Just as one of the boys grabbed a six-pack, he grabbed the collar of the other. Boy number one dropped the six-pack and fled the store while he shook boy number two as he would a bad puppy.

"What're you doing, boy?" he demanded. He turned the kid around and came face-to-face with the startled expression of Jason Wilson. "Oh, brother," he said.

"Hey, please. I didn't do anything," Jason pleaded.

"I'm not buying that," Sam said.

The store manager was upon them at once. "What's going on?" he asked.

"Just a close call," Sam said. "There's your beer. The thief got away and his accomplice here is going to come with me."

"Aw, Sam," Jason whined. "Come on, man…"

"I'm gonna let go of your shirt, Jason, and if you run I'll be waiting at your house for you when you get home. I'm not chasing you in this rain, but I *will* get you. You copy?"

"Yeah," he said in total disgust. "Yeah, I *copy*!"

Sam kept a hand on Jason's elbow as he went to the cashier to retrieve his water and flowers. Then he took the boy to the car, but he put him in the passenger seat rather than the back. The flowers he threw in the back. "So," he said to Jason, "gonna have a little after-school party?"

"We just wanted a beer," Jason sulked.

"Drink a lot of beer, do you?"

"No! We don't!"

"I have a choice here," Sam said. "I could just take you to the station for petty theft. Or I could take you home."

"I think I'd rather go to jail," he said. "It's going to be prison one way or another."

"Let me ask you something, Jason. Why didn't you boys just pilfer a little beer from the icebox at home? Why'd you decide to steal some from a store? Which, by the way, is a misdemeanor."

"Because Stan's old man doesn't drink beer, and my mom drinks so little, she'd know if some was missing."

"There you go," he said. He put the squad car in gear. "Where is Mama today? The store? Home?"

"Can I just go to my grandpa's?" he asked.

"Nope."

Jason sighed and got smaller in the seat. "She's at the old house she's fixing up."

"Address?"

"I don't know."

Sam gave him a little swat in the arm.

"Jefferson Avenue. Fourteen something."

That old house, he thought. He keyed his radio. "Control, DP-thirty-five, I'm out at fourteen-fifty Jefferson Avenue, returning a juvenile to his mother."

"DP-thirty-five, copy."

As they rode, Sam said, "You might want to go ahead and think about what you're going to tell her. Since I'll be right there, eavesdropping, start with the truth."

"You're killin' me, man."

"No, snookums," he grinned, and he hoped he grinned meanly. "I'm taking you to the woman who's gonna kill you."

By the time they pulled up to the old house, Jason was so small in the seat next to Sam, he was all but disappearing. "Come on, pal," Sam said. "Let's get this over with. You'll feel better."

"I doubt that," Jason said, getting out of the car.

"Look," Sam said, "it's not like your mom has it that easy. You might try cutting her some slack. At least keep your skinny ass out of trouble, huh?"

"What do you know about it?"

"I lost my dad when I was just a kid, younger than you. My mom did it alone. It's hard. At least you have a dad around."

"Yeah," he said, hands plunged into his pockets, walking toward the house, head down. "And when she's done killin' me, he's gonna start."

"That's comforting," Sam said, not displeased. This was not what Sam would consider a serious crime—not compared to what he dealt with daily. But it was a golden opportunity for the parents to get control right here, right now.

Jason pushed open the front door. "Ma?" he called.

She was working in the living room but apparently hadn't seen Sam pull up to the house. She had a ball cap on, a sweatshirt and jeans and wore heavy work gloves. In her hands she held a crowbar. Lying around the floor were pieces of baseboard that she'd pried off the wall. A fire blazed in the hearth. "Jason?" she said, confused. Sam stepped into the house behind him. "Sam?" she said, even further confused.

"Ma, I'm in a little trouble."

"What?" she asked, shaking her head.

Sam just stood back by the door, his thumbs hooked into his gun belt. There was a part of him that wanted to laugh at this kid's predicament, but he wasn't about to crack a smile. He kept his expression stony, drawing his brows together.

"Hey, Mom—could you lose the crowbar? Makes me a little nervous. When I tell you what I did, you might, you know, snap."

She took two steps closer to her son. She did not put down the crowbar. And she was wearing an expression that Sam had never seen on her face. Whoa, that was the mother-look if ever there was one. Very scary to be fifteen right now.

"Me and Stan, we were going to pinch a six-pack of beer, but Sam caught us."

"What?" she said again. "Why would you do a stupid thing like that?"

Jason took a breath. "Because we couldn't buy it." He shrugged. "I swear, it was Stan's idea."

Now it became actually hard for Sam to keep a straight face. He looked down at his feet to regain composure. Oh, sucks to be Jason, he thought.

"Is that it?" she asked. "Where were you going to drink this beer?"

"We thought maybe Stan's. His folks don't get home till like after seven."

"Oh crap," she said. "Sam? Is he going to be charged?"

Sam shook his head. "I figured you could take it from—" Behind her, on the floor near the fireplace, he spied a rolled-up sleeping bag. It was wider than normal. He knew what it was—it was two sleeping bags zipped together. It was very doubtful that Clare was taking naps or spending the night in this old wreck of a house. He looked back at her eyes, but he knew his expression had changed. "You can take it from here," he said. "You might want to call Stan's parents. He got away from me."

"You bet I will." She looked over her shoulder, more or less confirming that she had seen what he had seen. "Jason, go wait for me in the car. I want to talk to Sam."

Jason skulked out the door and Sam said, "I recommend you not let this slide, Clare. It's just a dumb-shit fifteen-year-old boy stunt, not nearly as scary as some of the stuff I deal with every day. But, you don't want this to be the beginning of a bad streak. Take a firm hand now and it might save some heartache later. Get his dad involved—let Jason know you have a united front."

"Sam," she said, walking toward him. "I want to tell you something."

"You don't have to tell me anything," he said.

"You can give me a minute. I think it's important. It's important to me, anyway, that you know I never lied to you. When I went out with you, when I broke it off with you, there was no other man in my life."

"What could it possibly matter now?" he said, knowing he sounded sarcastic.

"It matters a great deal to me. Sometime after the Homecoming game, I started dating Pete. After you and I— Well, I just want you to know I didn't lie. That day in the park—Pete and I really were talking about Mike. His brother."

"Why worry about it? We've moved on. So?"

"So? So the look on your face says that I just hurt you. Again."

"Let it go, Clare. You made yourself clear. And I haven't bothered you."

"No. You haven't."

"You and Pete," he said, laughing hollowly. He shook his head. "You don't have to be psychic to have seen that one coming."

"I didn't," she said. "We were like best friends in high school, Sam. When I was engaged to his brother. It somehow makes strange sense. And it's kind of stranger that we didn't discover each other sooner." She tilted her head. "It has nothing to do with you."

"Course not," he said. "So—you found what you wanted. Good for you. I gotta go. Take it easy," he said. He turned back to her. "Don't take it easy on Jason."

Sam left the house, then the neighborhood. He had some kind of an ache in the back of his throat that he couldn't explain. They had moved on. So? If she was telling the truth, and he had no reason to think otherwise, he had found Sarah as quickly as she had found Pete.

But there was something hurtful about the days and weeks and even months he'd invested in trying to woo her, unsuccessfully, only to have her go to Pete so easily. Is it just pride? he asked himself. Ego? Because that's stupid. After all, as reluctant as Clare had been, Sarah had molded to him like soft clay in his arms—sweet, responsive and pliant. He'd never been more comfortable. Or fulfilled. Wasn't this better? For everyone?

Still, the ache. If not for Clare, then for the expectation that had been Clare, and had been wiped off the slate somewhat painfully. And maybe, just maybe, some concern that Sarah would tire of him.

He drove to the art store almost out of habit. When he walked in, there was a customer, so he hid the flowers behind his back and pretended to poke around, looking at things. Sarah took the customer's money, bagged the merchandise and said goodbye. He brought the flowers out from behind his back.

"Isn't this a sweet surprise," she said. "I'll get a vase."

He followed her into the studio. While she filled the vase with water, he embraced her from behind. He nuzzled her neck, drank in the sweet smell of soap and vanilla lotion.

She put the flowers in the vase, the vase on the counter and turned in his arms. "Are you having a little coffee break?" she asked.

"I'm having a crappy day. Let me hold you."

"Would you like me to go lock that door out front?" she asked.

"No, I just want to hold you."

She laid her head on his chest. "What's the matter, Sam? Is something wrong?"

"Does something have to be wrong for me to want to hold you? Just be still a minute." He inhaled her fragrance, felt her small frame inside his arms. Sometimes he thought she was so little she might break and other times she reminded him that she was actually very strong, very powerful. Powerful enough to bring him to his knees. He kissed her neck and she put her arms around him.

He couldn't feel her against him while he wore his vest. But what he felt inside surpassed that. The sight of those sleeping bags drifted further and further from his mind and he knew he was in the right place. Home. This was where he belonged; this woman wasn't going anywhere. There was no ache in his throat. "Sarah," he said against her neck. "I'm starting to have a better day already. Where will you be when I get off work?"

"Wherever you want me to be."

When she got home, Clare called Roger and he immediately came over. When Clare let him in, she was rather surprised by the angry look on his face. Impressed, when it came down to it.

"Where is he?" he asked.

"In his room. Quaking."

"Jason!" Roger yelled. "Get down here!"

Response was immediate. The door opened and he came down the stairs. As his father came into view, Clare noticed that Jason's expression grew more fearful. He got a little paler.

"Family room," Roger snapped, letting Jason go first.

Jason sat on the couch while Roger paced in front of him. Long seconds passed. Then Roger stopped pacing and bore down on Jason. "What the hell were you thinking?"

"It was stupid," Jason said. "I told Stan it was stupid."

"Drinking at your age is bad enough—but stealing? Jason? *Stealing?*"

"I said, it was stupid."

"I just can't believe it. Not you. I never thought you would do that."

"I'm sorry."

"Not as sorry as you're going to be." He turned to Clare, who was actually very pleased with this. "Have you called Stan's parents?"

"Uh-huh. They went straight home."

"Get your jacket," Roger said.

"Aw, Dad..."

"Come on, we're going over there."

It was a tense meeting that lasted about an hour. Jason had never looked more miserable in his life. The adults decided that the boys were not allowed to hang out together for at least a couple of weeks. Stan, who had recently scored his driver's license, was losing use of the car for the rest of the month. Jason, who was ready to take his test for his permit, was not going to get to do that for another month.

On the drive back home Roger said, "Clare, do you think your dad would go along with Jason working at the store after school for a while?"

"Probably."

"Aww, man," came from the backseat.

"You obviously can't be trusted to stay out of trouble after school, so I want you to go to your grandpa's store until your mom is either done at that old house or done at the store. For at least the rest of the month. Then we'll reevaluate."

When they got home, Jason headed straight for the stairs. He was halfway up when Roger said, "Jason?" He turned around and looked at his dad. "Jason, I'm disappointed. I trusted you to at least never break the law. I hope you learned something from this. I hope you're going to turn out better than that."

"Yes, sir," he said meekly.

Roger nodded. Jason fled.

Clare put a hand on Roger's arm. "Thank you. You handled that very well. I couldn't have managed as well without you."

"Oh, you probably could have," he said. "But I'm glad you called. I want to be in his life—in the good times and the rugged." He took a deep breath. "I'm exhausted."

She smiled. "How about a beer?"

Having a grounded fifteen-year-old and a boyfriend who kept his daughters almost every weekend would have had a definite negative impact on Clare's love life, if it weren't for Roger. God bless him, he was serious about mending his fences with Jason and wanted to spend more quality time with him, especially since the shoplifting episode.

"I just can't stop blaming myself for that," he said. "I was absent too long."

Tempting as it was to let Roger wallow in guilt, she knew it was pretty likely not his fault. Jason was a good kid and had a very close and supportive family, and he'd begun to patch things up with his dad before getting in trouble. She'd had many long talks with Pete about it, and Pete was something of an expert on teenage boys. So she said, "Lighten up, Roger. Boys his age do lamebrain stuff like that. They also drive too fast, skip school and get into trouble with girls. Let's just try to stay on top of it. He's basically a real good kid. And with both of us paying attention, letting him know his parents aren't going to let him get away with anything, we might be lucky."

But she convinced Roger that he should spend a couple of evenings during the week with Jason. Having a grounded teenager at home was such a ball and chain, she was afraid to leave the house in the evenings. Afraid he might plot something, maybe slip out, get himself in trouble again. So Roger agreed to pick him up after work at around six a couple of weeknights, take him out for a bite and back to his place to do homework. Home by ten, in bed by eleven.

When that happened, Clare went to Pete's house.

On this particular night, she had called to say she was on her way, then let herself in with her own key. She found him in his family room at the wet bar, mixing two drinks. The room was dimly lit, the fire ablaze in the hearth, and Pete was wearing only his slacks. No shoes, no shirt. She stopped as she entered the room and just filled her eyes with him. That broad chest; the nice, neat mat of hair; the flat belly and broad shoulders. She especially liked his strong forearms, big hands.

He passed her a drink. She took a sip, he took a sip, and then they tasted it on each other's mouths. She ran her fingers through the hair at his temples. "You're getting a little gray here," she pointed out.

"I can't see how it's possible. I feel like a teenager."

"Why aren't you dressed? Getting a head start?"

"I took a quick shower. How much time do we have?"

"Three hours. Four."

"I can keep you out of trouble for that long."

He slipped an arm around her and she looked up into his eyes. "A year ago I was leaving my husband. Leaving my house. I was lonely, kind of scared and thoroughly pissed off. Now I have you, the deepest friendship I've ever known, not to mention the kind of love life I didn't think existed. I really believed it was too late for me to have this in my life."

"It's just the beginning, Clare."

"I've been meaning to tell you—when Sam brought Jason home to me after his little shoplifting adventure, he saw the sleeping bags. I don't think Jason noticed, but Sam did."

Pete shrugged.

"I felt like I had to explain to him—that we came together after. After I ended things with him."

"How'd he take it?"

"He was a little snotty, but he said it didn't matter."

Pete surprised her by laughing. He leaned down and put a soft kiss on her lips. "It's a good thing it was Sam you had to end it with. I don't think I'd have gone away quietly. I don't think I could have."

"I'm in love with you, you know," she told him.

"I've been waiting for that," he said with a smile. "And it feels just as good hearing it as I thought it would." He took the drink from her hand and put it, with his, back on the bar. He lifted her into his arms and said, "I love you, too. Let's get you out of these clothes so we can make love until curfew."

chapter fourteen

....

CLARE AND SARAH had entered the new year rosy with love and drunk on fabulous sex. No one knew Sarah's little secret, but if anyone had looked closely, they would have seen she had that same flush and glow that Clare was sporting.

However, Maggie's perfect life began unraveling. The first thing to go terribly wrong was when thirteen-year-old Hillary's best friend, Lucy, was diagnosed with juvenile cancer. The prognosis for Lucy was very optimistic—the doctors gave her a ninety percent chance of a full recovery, but poor little Hillary was terrified and constantly plummeted into hysterical tears. She began to show real fear and signs of depression.

As for Lucy, she was instantly admitted for chemotherapy and by the second week of January had started losing her hair. This further upset Hillary and keeping her spirits up was a constant challenge for Maggie.

Hillary began to devote all her time to her best friend, studying her disease on the Internet, obsessed with her treatment. And Maggie was devoting all her mothering to Hillary, possibly failing to notice anything different about Lindsey.

Then, when Maggie came home from work one evening

in the third week of January, Lindsey uttered those words mothers never like to hear. "Mom, I have to talk to you. In my room," she said gravely.

Oh, how Maggie hated this. She didn't even take off her coat. Her mind went wild on the way to Lindsey's room. She couldn't be flunking anything—the girl was a perpetual honor student, shattered by an A-minus. Was it a fight with a girlfriend, had she skipped school, shoplifted a belly ring, got caught smoking…? Or, please God, let her be breaking up with Christopher.

"I'm not a virgin anymore."

Maggie actually grabbed her heart. "You're *fifteen!*"

"I know this," Lindsey said.

"Was it Christopher?" she asked angrily.

"Well, of *course* it was Christopher! He's my boyfriend!"

"Don't you dare yell at me," Maggie said. Because I'm practically a virgin again, she thought. "Could you be pregnant? Did you use anything?"

"We used a condom. Once."

"Once? You mean you've done it more than once?" Maggie sat on the bed beside Lindsey.

"Well," Lindsey said. "Yeah. More than once."

"How long has this been going on?"

"Mommm," she whined.

"Well? How long?"

"It's been a couple of months. Since about October."

"October?"

"Or September," she said in a quieter voice. "But I always got my period. And most of the time he'd remember to, you know, pull out."

"Oh, God! Are you late now?"

"I might be a day or two late," she said.

That's why she's telling me, Maggie thought. This could have been worked out much more neatly if she'd mentioned she needed birth control before she and that boy had started messing around, as they'd discussed ad nauseam. She glared at her daughter. Her beautiful, brilliant, fifteen-year-old daughter who was about to plunge herself into disaster via the vagina. "I should never have let you out after dark!" She stood up. "I'll take tomorrow morning off. We're going straight to the doctor. I'd take you now if the office wasn't closed. And in the meantime, pray. Pray very, very hard!" She stomped toward the door.

"Mom?"

Maggie turned back toward her. Lindsey finally had a contrite look on her face, tears in her eyes. "Do you have to tell Dad?"

Maggie wanted to be understanding and helpful—girls Lindsey's age had raging hormones and those of boys Christopher's age raged even hotter. But this pissed her off to her very core. They had talked this to death. She told her daughters that there was no excuse for getting into this kind of trouble. If they were afraid to ask for birth control, they should insist on condoms. They talked about STDs and she stressed that condoms should always be used anyway, even if there was other birth control in place. During these discussions Hillary said, "Eww," and Lindsey looked completely bored.

She wanted to be sympathetic, but she just wasn't there yet. "Of course I have to tell Dad," she said. "And then I'm going to have to tie him up to keep him from going straight to Christopher's house and killing him!"

"It wasn't his fault, Mom. He didn't make me."

"Well, did you make him?"

"Of course not," she said, a large tear running down her cheek.

"Start praying," Maggie said, leaving the room.

She went to her bedroom and sat in the big chair by the window, in front of the fireplace. How could this have happened? They were so strict, and Lindsey was so smart. They always knew everywhere she was. She couldn't go to Christopher's house if his parents weren't home; they were only allowed to double date; Lindsey never went to anyone's party unless supervision was assured. They checked everything.

Well, dum-dum, clearly your daughter lied to you, that mocking voice in her head told her.

We lied to our mother, she thought. But Maggie hadn't been fifteen, for God's sake!

But Sarah had been just fourteen. How had that girl kept from getting pregnant all through her teenage years? And Maggie had actually been only seventeen.

Maggie drew herself out of her chair and went back to Lindsey's room. She was hoping to find her daughter crying, but she was, more predictably, talking on the phone. "I'm going to run an errand. Do not go out. Keep an eye on Hillary. I'll be right back."

She drove to the drugstore and hunted through the aisles for the home pregnancy tests. Reading the backs of some, she made a discovery—you could now determine pregnancy at about four minutes after conception. She held the pack in her hand for a long time. The news might not be good. She could be throwing away the last good night's sleep she would have literally for years. Oh hell, she thought, who's going to sleep?

She purchased and took it home. Lindsey was still on the phone. "I need you to hang up now." For the first time in her memory, Lindsey said goodbye and hung up without so much as a peep of protest. She handed her the bag. "Read the instructions, pee on the stick. I'll be in my room. Please do it right now."

She turned and left her daughter. Back in her room, she slumped onto the bed, still wearing her coat. "God," she said out loud. My daughters are both in crisis, she was thinking. One is terrified of losing her best friend to cancer and the other might be pregnant. "God," she said aloud again.

A few moments passed and then she was jolted upright by a piercing scream. Oh, God, she thought—it's *positive!* On her feet and racing down the hall, she saw Lindsey standing in front of the open bathroom door with a stricken look on her face. She'd gone completely pale. Maggie peeked into the bathroom and then *she* screamed. There stood Hillary, her head completely shaved.

"My God, what have you *done?*"

Hillary's eyes met her mother's in the mirror. All of her glorious long blond hair lay in a heap on the floor around her feet and on her face was the most serene expression she'd worn in a few weeks. "I did it in support of Lucy."

"Couldn't we have *talked* about it first?"

"Oh, like you'd've said yes." She rubbed her pale bald head. "It'll grow back. And so will Lucy's."

Maggie looked at the ceiling. "Am I being punished for something?" she asked the higher power beyond her roof. "Okay, get out of the bathroom right now. You sister has peeing to do."

"You are a serious whack job," Lindsey said to Hillary.

"And you're a butt hole," the little bald one said, brushing past her older sister.

"They're going to come after me with a net," Maggie muttered to herself as she went to her room.

She threw herself facedown on the bed, still wearing her coat. She beat the mattress with her fists for a little while. Where the hell was Bob? Carson City—legislature was in session. That'll teach me to come home early. I should have found somewhere to hang out until I wasn't the only adult in the house.

What am I going to do if this child is pregnant? She thinks she's in love with this big lunkhead, Christopher, who apparently is walking around with all his brains in his dick. Don't worry about that, she told herself. He'll run like his ass is on fire. But what about Lindsey? Girls her age, even incredibly smart girls, have all these romantic illusions about having a baby. Oh, God, Lindsey had been talking about medical school! There was a good chance she'd be valedictorian! She'd been in accelerated classes since she was seven.

"Mom?"

Maggie was lying in the shape of a crucifix, feet hanging off the bed, arms stretched out wide. She lifted only her head. Lindsey was smiling. "It's okay, Mom. One line, not two."

"When was the last time you had sex?" Maggie asked from her tortured position.

Lindsey shrugged. "A week or so, I guess."

"Well, I hope we're all right. I'll take you in the morning."

"It's probably okay, Mom." Lindsey sat in the chair facing her mother. Maggie lowered her head. "I'm sorry, Mom. It's just that, you know, I really love him."

"I can't talk about that right now," Maggie said, not looking at her daughter.

"Now do we have to tell Dad? I mean, it's okay. And this is a girls' thing. Huh?"

Maggie lifted her head and glared at Lindsey.

"Jeez, you're acting so weird," Lindsey said.

"Go to your room. Study something. You are grounded for *life!*"

By the time Bob came home it was after nine. Maggie had finally discarded her coat and was wearing a comfortable sweat suit, sitting in her big comfy chair, working on her second scotch. "Hi, honey," he said. "Have you eaten?"

"I don't have much appetite. Have you seen the girls?"

"Not yet. I just barely got home."

"Well, you might want to go downstairs, fix yourself a very large drink and come back up here to talk to me before you talk to them."

"This doesn't sound good," he said.

"*Large* drink," she advised.

Not terribly far away in another bedroom, Sarah was looking at a pregnancy stick, except on hers there were two lines. How was this possible? she asked herself. She'd been on the Pill forever, even when she didn't think she needed it. And since setting her hopeful sights on Sam, she'd been very diligent about her pills. But she had only had a bit of spotting her last period, and lately she'd been feeling queasy in the mornings.

She had managed to remain in denial for a few weeks, but the queasiness had persisted. Disbelieving, she bought the home pregnancy test and was blown away by the results.

In a near panic, she called her doctor the first thing the next morning and after begging, pleading, they found a way to sneak her in.

When she walked into the waiting room, who did she find but Maggie and Lindsey. For a moment she was embarrassed, then remembered that pregnancy wasn't the only reason to visit this doctor. "Hey, you two. What are you doing here?"

Lindsey looked away and Maggie said, "Checkup," but she didn't say it happily. "You?"

"Ah...checkup." Sarah sat down next to them, and then she remembered. Fourteen. She'd been only fourteen when she'd lost her virginity. She looked at Maggie, her mouth opened slightly in shock, her eyes wide. Maggie's eyes dropped slowly closed and she nodded grimly. "Shit," Sarah said.

"Oh, this is *great*," Lindsey huffed.

Lindsey was the first one into the exam room, Maggie waiting outside with Sarah. "I don't even want to ask," Sarah said.

"No, you don't *have* to ask. You *know*."

"Damn. I thought if anyone was on top of that, it was you."

"I was," she returned. "Apparently it was falling on deaf ears."

"How'd Bob take it?"

"Better than I did. When I told him our daughter was officially having more sex than we were, he said, 'It was bound to happen someday, honey.' *He's* lucky to be alive. And if you think this is interesting, you should see Hillary. She has shaved her head in support of her best friend who is losing her hair through chemotherapy."

"Aw. That's kind of sweet."

Maggie's eyes teared. It was something one never saw. She was so tough and strong, she never cried. "All that beautiful long blond hair, lying on the bathroom floor."

Sarah squeezed her sister's hand. "It'll grow back, Maggie. At least she's not having sex."

"Yeah. That bald head might buy us some time."

Sarah laughed in spite of herself.

"Go ahead. Laugh. Great Aunt Sarah."

She gasped. "She's not..." A sudden, horrible image of she

and her fifteen-year-old niece going into the maternity ward together suddenly flashed before her eyes.

Maggie shook her head slowly. "I don't think so. But we're here to find out for certain and rectify what we can."

"Did you do one of those home tests?"

"Immediately. It was negative."

"Well, that's something. I guess."

The nurse stuck her head into the waiting room. "Mrs. Traviston? You can come in now."

Maggie leaned toward Sarah. "They should just call me Mrs. Travesty." Then she went with the nurse.

Dr. Corvis was a lovely woman of about forty. She seemed made up of comforting lines, safe brown eyes, unpanicked mouth. She was behind the desk and Lindsey, dressed again, was sitting in one of the two chairs in front of it. Two chairs. They should be for the husband and wife, hearing the happy news. Not for the mother and daughter.

"Have a seat, Maggie. I think we're all set here. I did a thorough exam and pap and told Lindsey that once she becomes sexually active she'll need to be examined annually. I also tested for STDs and we'll have those results back right away. I've prescribed emergency birth control that will take care of any pregnancy that may have occurred during the past few days, and a prescription for a very reliable contraceptive pill. However, and I can't stress this enough, Lindsey, so I hope you hear me. Condoms are necessary—these pills will not prevent sexually transmitted disease and people do *die* of them. It's not worth it to do without. Not worth it." She started writing on the chart. "Now, you'll need about two weeks for these pills to become effective, so if you please, no unprotected sex."

"Believe me," Maggie said.

Dr. Corvis folded her hands on her desk and looked at Maggie, then Lindsey, then said, "Ladies, you cannot unring this bell. This happens to most women at some point in their lives. We like it not to happen to women who are too young, but the only thing we can do is act responsibly. The best situation is to have children you plan. Are we all on the same page here?"

"Yes," Lindsey said.

"What about a little lecture on Lindsey being too young for sex?" Maggie wanted to know.

"I believe she is," Dr. Corvis said. "And I said so. But we're beyond Just Say No. We're right up against, Do Not Skip A Pill. And, thankfully, Lindsey appears to be completely healthy." The doctor stood up. "It would be in your best interest to tell your daughter that if she ever feels nervous talking to you about a medical issue like birth control or a sexually transmitted disease, she can always call me. Any questions?"

Maggie didn't have any. Case closed.

But in her heart she was sick that her daughter had crossed this threshold so young, and she knew the doctor was right, there was no going back. She might have celibate periods in her young life, but once the nectar had been tasted, it was drunk whenever it seemed right. Much as she hated this, to Lindsey, this young high school senior seemed right. Bllllkkkk!

"Lindsey, give me a second with Dr. Corvis? Please?"

"Don't plot behind my back," she said sternly. And left.

"What's up, Maggie?"

"God," she said, rubbing her forehead. "I don't know how to do this."

"Something I should know about Lindsey?"

"No. Something you should know about me. Bob and I haven't… It's been… I don't know if it's me…? I don't know…"

"How old are you?"

"Forty-three. And coming into my prime, they say."

"And Bob?"

"Forty-sex. Forty-six."

Dr. Corvis chuckled. "Get him to the doctor, Maggie. He needs a physical. And if there is a problem, it's probably easier to fix than you realize."

"I don't know," she said, shaking her head. "It isn't that he can't. It's that he just isn't in the mood. He works so hard, gets too tired…"

"Oh bull. Men can do it in their sleep. Make a doctor's appointment."

Sarah sat on the exam table, whimpery though she wished to be strong. "How can this happen?" she asked the doctor.

"Ninety-nine point nine percent effective, Sarah. It's extremely rare."

"Why couldn't the point one percent be some nice married lady?"

"You have many choices, but let's talk about that later. For now, let's do an ultrasound. Lie back down, dry your tears. It's not the end of the world." She revved up the machine, punched a few buttons and gelled up the probe. Dr. Corvis inserted the wand slowly and carefully; the machine bleeped in harmony. "Sarah, turn your head. Look," she said softly, almost reverently. "There he is. This little mass here has a beating heart."

She saw this little tadpole moving around inside of her and gasped. "It's a boy?"

"We can't tell yet. But what I can tell is that you're actually about six weeks. Six weeks and change. At three months you'll see arms and legs."

Sarah, in awe of the squirmy little creature, did the math in her head. Dear God, she probably got pregnant that first time. She hoped that meant something—like it was kismet or something. "My God," she said, reaching a hand out toward the monitor.

"We'll print out a copy of what you see on the screen. Everything seems perfect, Sarah." The doctor looked at a chart. "How does August twenty-fifth sound?"

"Like a million years from now."

"You won't believe how fast it will come round."

"Right now, I'm a little more worried about the next couple of days."

For once, time played on Sarah's team. Sam worked overtime on Saturday, so she only saw him briefly when he stopped by the shop. There was only a little kissing in the back room. Sunday he took Molly to the slopes. Monday was ski day, after which they would meet at the inn.

All afternoon as Sam patrolled and Sarah skied, he was randy and playful. He'd sneak up on her and whack her on the butt, grab her and pull her behind a tree and plant a deep kiss on her, treat her to that dimpled grin, and the twinkle in his eye said that, as usual, he couldn't wait. Couldn't get enough. Oh boy, did she hate to throw a wet blanket on this party.

Sam didn't seem to notice that she was somewhat preoccupied. But then, probably all the blood had drained from his brain to keep that powerhouse between his legs serviceable. They rode the lift together and he licked her ear and said, "I am dying for you."

"Well, stop it. You're no good to me dead."

When she got to the inn, she didn't wait in her usual inviting lack of attire. She was fully clothed. When Sam entered, he seemed not to notice. He rushed to her, grabbed her, lifted her up into his arms, whirled her around and devoured her with kisses that were hot and strong. He fell with her onto the bed and asked, "Want me to undress you with my teeth?"

"We have to talk," she said.

He froze. "When a woman says that, it is almost always unpleasant."

"I have absolutely no idea how you're going to take this, Sam. I had an accident. I'm pregnant."

Again, he froze. Shock registered on his handsome face. "How?"

"I was on the Pill. It didn't work. I don't know why."

"Well...how long have you been on that pill?"

"Years. But...I wasn't putting it to the test."

"Okay, you said it had been a while since your last boyfriend, but—"

"Years, Sam. Years."

He swallowed hard. "How far along, Sarah?"

"As near as the doctor can determine, it might have happened that first night."

Sam sat up on the bed. His feet were planted on the floor and with his elbows resting on his knees, he dropped his head into his hands. "Well, that figures. I think we set some kind of record. I think my biceps are actually bigger." She touched his back. He glanced over his shoulder at her. "This sucks."

"Yeah. I'm sorry."

"It's not like you did it on purpose. Just give me a second to absorb this."

"Take your time. I've had a couple of days."

"Why didn't you tell me right away?" he asked. "The minute you knew?"

"Because I wasn't going to tell you on the phone, and when I saw you on Saturday, you were on the job. Today you were working. I didn't want this on your mind, with what you do—you just can't afford to be distracted. I thought we could probably use some time alone."

"Jesus. Let me think." He put his head back in his hands. "Let me think why it never occurred to me to use a frickin' condom!"

"Well, it was pretty spontaneous. And I doubt you could have carried enough of them in your wallet for that particular night."

"Yeah," he said. "I was like a runaway train." He turned and looked at her. "Do you want to have it?"

Now it was Sarah's turn to look shocked. Before she answered, she asked, "Do you want me not to?"

He shrugged. "Well, it's an option. It would give us a fresh start."

She put her hand on her flat stomach. "I saw it. On the ultrasound. I saw it moving around inside me. Its heart is beating. I'm thirty-three and I really didn't think I'd ever have a baby. Yes, I'm having it."

"And that's another option," he said. "Not real convenient, but hey."

Well, that was a relief. She sighed audibly; it almost sounded like "whew." "Tell me something—how would you feel if I'd said I wanted to have an abortion?"

"I wouldn't feel good about it," he said. "But at the moment, I don't feel good, period." At the look on her face he said, "I'm sorry, baby. I know you don't feel good about it, either. Do you want to get married?" he asked.

"Is that what you want?"

He raised one leg onto the bed, turning toward her. "Sarah, what I want isn't exactly a factor here. We have a situation."

"You haven't said you love me," she pointed out.

He smiled and touched her hair. "I will love you every night, until you beg me to stop."

She sat up. "That goes without saying. You're insatiable. But do you love me enough to marry me? I think that's a *factor* in this situation."

"Sure, Sarah. Of course."

She stared at him for a long moment, reading his eyes. "No, you don't."

"Sarah, we've been together about as long as you've been pregnant...."

"There were some weeks before that. Drinks at the pub. You know. Getting to know each other...."

"Sarah," he said almost sternly, "six weeks and four hours. But that's not the issue—I love you. We can do it. I'll make you happy. I already make you happy. I can give you a good marriage. A secure marriage. When I give my word, I don't break it. You don't have to ever be afraid that I'd change my mind or screw around."

"Oh, God," she said. She punched the bed. "This is *exactly* why women make men say they love them before they screw their brains out! Because point one percent of the time the damn Pill doesn't work!"

"Hey look, we're going to be all right," he said, trying to console her. "The rate we're going, it's only going to get better. Stronger." He rubbed her arm. "We're good together. We'll be okay."

"Okay," she said. "I'll wait for that."

"Well, hell, I haven't heard you say it."

"Don't you know *anything*? Don't you know you were being chased down like hunted prey? I was after you, you idiot! I stalked you! God, the second I saw you I nearly fainted. Sam, you had to have known!"

He had a very serious look on his face. "Maybe you did do it on purpose."

She slugged him in the arm. "Asshole."

He rubbed his arm. "Okay, I guess I did know," he said. "Because I'd just sworn off women for life, and you came along, getting more irresistible by the hour. Okay, here it is. You're having a baby. Our baby. We'll do whatever you want."

"I don't know..." she said, shaking her head.

"We have to do this together, one way or another. If you're going to have it, it's going to have a father."

"Well, I'm not going to marry you just because I'm pregnant. I'm not marrying anyone who thinks we'll be okay!" She huffed and thought, if I cry, I'm going to be very pissed. "Is this just about Clare? Are you still stuck on my big sister?"

"Oh, don't even go there!"

"That would be great. Marry you and have you look at my sister like you want to die of heartbreak at every family dinner. No thanks."

"I said, that's *not* an issue. It has nothing to do with us."

"Oh, God, you still want her."

"No!"

"Sam," she said pleadingly, "at least be honest with me."

He reached for her, but all he got of her was her arm. "You want to know if it hurt, Sarah? Yeah, it hurt, okay? But it's in the past. It's over, and I don't have any illusions about it— I'm never going back that way. It's never gonna happen. You don't have to worry that I'll make hurt little puppy dog eyes at my wife's sister. I'm a man. A responsible man." He took a breath. "I probably suffered more hurt pride than loss, because I've been really happy. With you. You know I'm not just saying that."

She looked away from him and he grabbed her chin and made her look back. "You've been happy with me, too. I know you have."

Her chin quivered. She couldn't speak.

"Come here, damn it! Let me hold you!"

"I *can't!*"

"Well, why *not?*"

"Because you're going to make me cry and I don't want to cry!"

Of course, that was all it took. The floodgates opened and she began to sob. Sam gathered her up in his arms and held her on his lap while she cried. And cried. And cried. He tried kissing her tears away, but ultimately he had to grab the tissue box off the beside table and give it to her.

While he held her, he thought about their short history together. He was already more comfortable with her than he'd been with women he'd known far longer. The very few women he'd known longer. There was something symbiotic about it—as if it was just right. Something about this was working for her, too, because it hadn't escaped his notice that she was growing more beautiful, more lush each day. She was blossoming under his attention. Her cheeks were rosy, her eyes sparkled, her laugh was quick and infectious. And yes, he was insatiable. But so was she.

When she finally stopped crying, he said, "Sarah, you know how I came to have Molly. How it was an accident and the best thing that ever happened to me." She nodded, her head still resting against his shoulder. "I don't want to be unhappy about this. We're having a baby—I want us to be happy. No more tears. We'll work this out."

She lifted her head off his shoulder and looked into his eyes. "We don't have to get married because we're having a baby. Marriage is serious. We should be sure."

"Having a baby is serious, too."

"I know. And we'll treat it seriously. I think we need a little time for the rest. I need a little time. To be sure."

"Okay, baby. You take the time you need. I'll be right here. In this all the way." He lifted her in his arms and laid her gently on the bed. He settled down beside her and gathered her close.

"I don't think I can tonight, Sam."

"It's okay, honey. But I have to have you close. At least let me be close to you." He kissed her temple and she curled up in the circle of his arm and before long, slept. Probably exhausted, he thought. From skiing and nerves and crying. Plus, pregnancy made a woman tired.

He kissed her brow and held her. Held them both.

It was the middle of the night when Sam followed Sarah down the mountain. It was close to morning when he got home, but he still helped himself to a couple of beers. He wouldn't be able to sleep anyway. He called Sarah from his cell phone to make sure she was all right. She said she was, but her voice was thick and he suspected she'd been crying again. "I'll call you in the morning," he said. "Later in the morning."

He stayed in his room when he heard the sounds of his mother getting Molly off to school. When the house quieted, he went to the kitchen. His mother had the paper spread out in front of her on the kitchen table. He sat down opposite her. He rested his elbows on the table and looked down, hanging his head. When he looked up, his mother was staring at him. "Remember the women I introduced you to at the game?" he asked. "Clare and Sarah? Sarah is the younger one. The artist. Art teacher. I've been seeing her."

"She's very pretty."

"She's pregnant."

"Oh dear," she said.

"I asked her to marry me, but so far she says no."

Joan folded her hands on top of the newspaper. She stared at her son. "Well. At least you're consistent."

chapter fifteen

. . . .

SARAH KNEW ONE of the first things she had to do was tell her sisters, but it took a couple of weeks to work up the courage. No one seemed to have noticed that she was acting a tad differently. Clare was too busy knocking boots with her new boyfriend and Maggie was constantly hovering over her daughters, watching one's hair grow and monitoring the other to make sure she wasn't having sex.

It seemed as though Clare's house was the best bet, because Sarah wasn't ready to tell George yet. That might take a couple more weeks. She asked if they could meet there for an after-work drink. Jason had no idea how well he cooperated with Sarah's plans. He walked into the house, saw the women gathering, and said, "Oops, girls' night. I'm outta here." And he fled for his room.

Maggie helped herself to a glass of wine. "Who called this summit?"

"I did. I have something to tell you. I'm pregnant."

Stunned silence and wide eyes answered her. She sat on the family room couch while her sisters just stood there, staring down at her, dumbfounded.

"With child," Sarah said, looking up at them. "Bun in the oven. Knocked up."

"Sarah," Clare said. "You've been seeing someone?"

"Oh yeah, every inch of him. I was keeping it pretty quiet."

"So, who did the honors?" Maggie asked, still a bit in shock.

"Okay, you'd better sit down." When they did, she said, "It was Sam. Sam Jankowski."

Another vacuum of silence. Then Clare shot suddenly to her feet and said, "That son of a bitch! He did my little sister! I'm going to kill him!"

"Well, there are couple of things you should know before you kill him," Sarah said. "I went after him. I stalked him. I chased him like a crazed and wanton maniac. That night I saw him with you at the restaurant, my heart about burst out of my chest. Love at first sight. Then when you said you had no interest in dating him any longer, I thought—oh, my God, he's on the loose!" She shrugged. "I couldn't risk someone else getting him."

"Your makeover," Maggie said.

"Uh-huh. Seeing Clare and Sam like that—all that lust just emanating from them, I thought what I'd give to have some of those feelings in my life. Especially with a guy like Sam. I took a hard, painful look in the mirror. I didn't stand a chance the way I used to be. Hell, even *I* couldn't stand to see myself like that. So I fluffed up and went looking for him. I found out he's a ski patrol at Afton Alps every Monday." She smiled. "I've been doing a lot of skiing lately. Among other things."

"This is just unbelievable."

"When did all this happen?" Clare asked.

"It started in November. Around the first good snowfall. I don't think he ever saw it coming." She shrugged. "Turns out I haven't lost my touch after all."

"How far along are you, honey?" Maggie asked.

"A couple of months. He got to me right off the bat. Potent little devil."

"And are you well? Feeling okay?" she asked.

"So far. Baby seems to be perfect."

"Have you told him?" Clare asked.

"Yeah. He said, 'That sucks.'"

"The son of a bitch! I'm going to kill him!"

"And you're having the baby?" Maggie, always all business, wanted to know.

"Uh-huh. You know, I never thought I'd have a child. If you had asked me six months ago what the rest of my life looked like, I would have said, just more of the same. Art, the store, dinner at Dad's on Sunday. Now I have this whole new life in front of me." She touched her stomach. "Inside of me."

"Do you love him?" Maggie asked.

"I love him so much it makes my head swim. And he's so good to me—treats me like, God, I don't know. Like I'm precious. Royal. So considerate of my feelings. Romantic, even. He asked me if I wanted to have the baby and when I said yes, he said, 'Okay, we'll get married.' There's just one hitch. He doesn't love me."

"He *told* you that?" Clare demanded.

"No, not exactly. He said he loved me—but he didn't say it real convincingly. I asked him if he loved me enough to marry me and he said, 'Sure. Of course.' Sure? Not, I love you so much I'll die if you don't marry me, but sure. So I had to press the issue and he hemmed and hawed and came up with some lamebrained comment like he was positive it would grow, given time."

"Oh, see? He has to die!"

"You said no," Maggie said. It was not a question.

"I said no. Well, specifically what I said was that I thought we should take the time to be sure, because no matter what he might say, I just don't think he's there yet. I admit it, I'm scared. I don't want to marry someone just because I'm pregnant. What if it's a mistake? What if I look into his eyes in five years and see misery and regret?" She swallowed. "I think I could be happy with Sam. Right now, he makes me happier than I've ever been in my life. But I don't know. Am I crazy?"

"You don't have to marry anyone, Sarah. You have a very supportive family."

"Have you seen him since you told him? Or did the bastard cut and run?" Clare asked.

"Clare, you know better than anyone, he's not a bastard. He's an angel. His problem is he's a lousy liar. And no, he didn't run. He checks on me every day. Several times a day. He calls, stops by the shop, wants to know how I'm feeling, whether I've told the family. He offered to come with me to tell you. In fact…" She stopped and tried to collect herself as tears threatened. "He took me to dinner in Tahoe Saturday night and when we were finishing dinner, he slid a hotel room key across the table. And I thought, what the hell, I can't get pregnant. And he was…"

She had to close her eyes and purse her lips together to try to keep control. She swallowed convulsively. That night he had been so wonderful. So tender. Their lovemaking, usually so tempestuous, adventurous, wild, was slow and careful and sweet. He kept kissing her belly, and other places. He usually made her body scream, but that night he'd made it sing. It sang many choruses, as it turned out. When it was over he said to her, "Sarah, I'm going to take care of you whether you like it or not."

"…he was so gentle. So tender and careful." And then she

lost it. The tears descended on her and she fell into a full-blown cry, burying her face in her hands.

Maggie and Clare bolted out of their seats and rushed to her, arms around her, holding her and comforting her.

"God, I'm sure doing a lot of that lately," Sarah finally said. "I bet this gets old after about nine months."

"When are you going to tell Dad?" Clare wanted to know.

Sarah shuddered. "Do you think he's going to be totally ashamed of me?"

"Honey, he loves you. He knows you're not a bad person. These things happen to people."

"It's a lot more convenient when they happen to married people. Or at least people who are sure they're mutually in love. It looks like I could be a single mom. Anyone have any pointers?"

"Pointer number one—you could choose an easier job. Like neurosurgery."

"Well," Maggie said, going back to her chair. "It's official. Everyone is having sex but me. And I'm the only one who's married!"

George McCarthy was nodding off in front of the TV when Sarah went to him. "Dad?"

He popped awake. "What, honey?"

"I have to talk to you about something. If you're not too asleep?"

He grunted and straightened in the chair. "Wasn't sleeping," he said. "It's okay. What's on your mind?"

"This is pretty tough. I'm afraid you're going to be very disappointed in me. It's about that cop—the one who kept coming into the hardware store when he had a crush on Clare? Sam?"

"I know who Sam is. But she said—"

"Clare stopped seeing him quite a while ago. In fact, she only had one real date with him. And after she stopped seeing him, I started. Well, a couple of months after."

"That a problem?" he asked. "Cause I don't know what kind of problems you girls have...."

"It's not a problem for us, Dad. Thing is..." She cleared her throat. "You know all those art projects and exhibitions I wanted to see that were taking so much time? So many late nights? Staying out of town? They weren't art projects or exhibitions."

"Oh," he said, catching on immediately. He grunted. "You live with your old man. Not a lot of privacy in that."

"I'm pregnant," she said, and instantly the tears sprang to her eyes and she thought, Oh hell—this is getting ridiculous. I'm a fountain.

His eyes widened and his mouth turned down into a frown. "Is he going to be responsible?"

"He has offered to marry me," she said. "But I don't think I want to marry him."

"What about the baby?" George asked.

"I want the baby," she said through tears.

He looked at her for a long hard minute. Then he said, "Come here, duckie." He used to call her that when she was a little girl. Duckie. She went to him, kneeling on the floor beside his chair, laying her head on his shoulder. He put his arms around her.

"I'm a little old-fashioned," he said. "I think when you're having a family, you should be husband and wife. But I don't want you to be with any man you don't want to be with."

She could tell him all about it, about how Sam could act as if he loved her, could touch her as if she was the most loved woman alive, but when it came down to it, she wasn't convinced he felt as deeply about her as she felt about him. But why complicate things any further—this was all messy enough.

"Children are to be loved," George said. "I love my girls, I love their kids." He lifted her chin. "I'll love this one. No matter what."

"I'm sorry, Daddy."

"We never apologize for new life. It's our sweet compensation for losing the ones we love."

Jason had served his time and was getting along better with his dad. Maybe there was truth to that business about kids wanting limits. So Roger, pleased with his son, had called and asked Jason if he wanted to go skiing on the weekend, and Jason, probably suffering from a bad case of cabin fever after being grounded, leaped on it. He also asked if Mom could go. "Sure she can, if she wants to. But don't be too surprised if she doesn't."

But Pete was busy with his girls, it was Sunday, and she had nothing better to do. To be safe, so that Roger wouldn't get the far-fetched idea she wanted to spend time with him, she called Sarah and asked if she was still cleared to ski. "The doctor says for a few more weeks, and try to take it easy. But you know—if I hurt anything out there, which I don't plan to, it's not going to be a uterus."

"Problem is," Clare said, "they want to go to Afton Alps."

"I can't go to Afton Alps, Clare," Sarah said. "I'm certainly not avoiding Sam—he hardly lets me out of his sight. I'd just rather not run into him when he's skiing with his daughter. He hasn't sprung me on her yet and I don't want to get involved with his family until a few things are settled. Let's go to Squaw Valley."

Clare, Sarah and Jason were excused from Sunday dinner at George's and up the mountain they went, with Roger.

Roger was pretty good on a pair of skis, Clare was a little better, but she was playing it safe because of her pelvis injury—wouldn't want a repeat of that. It was Sarah who could cut it up. So Jason, who fancied himself an extreme snowboarder, hooked himself up with her and wanted to do the big runs. He was wedging it down the advanced Black Diamond slopes with speed and ease. She could still stay ahead of him. She regretted that it took Sam in her life to rediscover this sport—out there on the slopes with the wind in her face and speed under her skis, she felt alive, exhilarated. And not worried about what was going to become of her.

They took on the advanced slopes, then moved to the expert hills.

"Let's go over there, where it's new powder," Jason begged.

"No way, buster. Red flags. It's restricted."

"It's no big deal," Jason said. "C'mon, Aunt Sarah, don't be a wimp. You can handle it."

She grabbed the front of his jacket. "Listen, bub. That's no game, the red flags, the warning signs. There's no ski patrol over there. It could be junk on the hill, a weak snow ridge threatening avalanche, anything. You never cross the flags. Never."

"Wuss," he said.

"Tell you what, if you can handle this expert hill, I'll stand amazed." She popped her goggles on. "Last one down is a rotten egg." And she shoved off. She gathered speed, skated the skis, bent over and got her center of gravity low, tucked the poles and went for it. She shifted her weight and cut right and then left around a mogul, but the next one she jumped, going several feet into the air and landing soft and sweet on her skis, perfectly. She tucked and flew. She chanced a glance and to her delight, Jason was right behind her, wedging around the moguls skillfully; the snowboarders didn't jump them. She was going to slow down and let him have the race. Aw, but then she just couldn't. She went for it. Forty miles an hour. She felt as if she was sailing. Flying.

When she got to the bottom of the run, Jason came up alongside her. "Aunt Sarah, you're hot."

"And you're not—beat you by a mile."

"By a few feet."

"Okay, so this hill is good—you don't need anything past the flags."

"Yeah, yeah."

Jason moved off toward the lift and a skier came up fast and hard from behind her, showering snow as he stopped. He flipped up his goggles. "What the hell are you doing?" Sam asked her.

"What are you doing here?"

"Sarah, for God's sake—do you know how fast you were going? And jumping? Jesus—what are you thinking? If you fell—"

"I wasn't planning to fall, and air is a lot softer than hard pack, which is why I jump. Why are you here? Are you following me?"

"I brought Molly out. We get lift tickets on all the local slopes—just for being part of the search-and-rescue team. She's taking a lesson. Do you understand, I just don't want anything to happen to you? To the baby?"

She took off her glove and put her hand against his frosty cheek. "Sam, I'm going to ski while I still can. I'm not going to hurt the baby."

He took a breath. "I think I'm getting too old for this," he said. "You scared me to death."

"Let's go up," she said. "I'll race you down."

"No! I'll go up with you for another run, but only if you promise not to race me, because first of all, if I apply myself, I can beat you. And second, if you fall, you could do some serious damage."

"Okay, let's go up. You can race Jason down—he's still getting it figured out."

"I saw him. He's got it pretty well figured out."

The three of them went up. Jason and Sam pushed off while Sarah lagged back a bit. Then when they were ten feet in front of her, she launched herself, and with all the strength in her arms and legs, working the poles and skating the skis, she went for it. When she approached their backs, she let out a woo-hoo, got to their left, took a small hill, got down and dirty and, tucking her poles, left them in her dust. She heard Sam behind her as he said, "Shit!" She didn't have to look to know what was happening—he was coming after her. Her laughter almost cost her the race she wasn't supposed to be having. They came in—Sarah, Sam, Jason.

Sam moved his goggles to his head atop his stocking cap. "Woman, you are going to drive me to an early grave."

She couldn't help but chuckle at him. She made the *L* sign with her thumb and index finger on her forehead for *loser.* Sam, at a loss for words, grabbed her and kissed her. Kissed her hard. And long.

"Whoa!" Jason said. "Aunt Sarah! What is going on here?"

They broke apart and Sarah said, "Just compensating the loser, kiddo."

On Tuesday afternoon, Sam went into work and dressed out for duty. When he was on his way to briefing, his sergeant snagged him and said, "There's a lawyer here to see you."

"What case?" he asked.

"I don't know. I put her in interrogation. You can catch up on the briefing from one of the other officers."

It never occurred to Sam that anything was wrong. The officers went to court regularly to testify on their arrests and therefore had lots of traffic with attorneys. They were in constant touch with the D.A.'s, being prepped for court.

But that wasn't it. He opened the door to interrogation and there sat Maggie, prim and proper in her lawyer suit. Seeing her there, so sternly serious, so attractive, what came to mind was George. How had he done it? Raised these beautiful, hardheaded daughters and kept his sanity?

He entered and closed the door. "Well, I guess the family knows."

"The family knows," she said. "Be glad I insisted on talking to you alone. Clare basically wants to kill you."

"Please tell Clare that my death right now would be a disadvantage to her sister. Much as Sarah resists me, she's going to need my help."

"Sit down, Sam. There are a few things you don't know about my little sister."

As he sat, he touched his lower lip. He could still almost feel the spot where Sarah bit him as she came to a crashing climax in his arms. And he thought, I bet there are lots of things *you* don't know about your little sister. "Shoot," he said.

Maggie's lips curved. "You shouldn't say that to the older sister of a woman you just made pregnant. What you should say is 'don't shoot.'"

"Are you here to chew my ass? Because if you are, let me assure you that I feel as bad about this as you do. We didn't plan it."

She stared at him hard, then shook her head in frustration. "What were you thinking?"

He leaned toward her. "Maggie, obviously I wasn't thinking about anything I can share with you."

"Well, that much is obvious. Okay, I came here to tell you that Sarah is more complicated and vulnerable than you realize. Fragile. You better watch yourself."

"I'm doing everything I can to support Sarah. I won't abandon her."

"Has she told you about her nervous breakdown? Ah, I can see by the look on your face that she hasn't. Our mother died of cancer, quite suddenly, when Sarah was only twenty-one. Prior to that, Sarah and Mom were locked in a pretty fierce contest of wills—not that unusual for young women who are testing their independence at the expense of their mother's strong desire that they settle down and act like proper young ladies. They didn't exactly get that issue resolved when Mom died. It threw Sarah into a terrible depression. She had to be hospitalized."

This was hard for Sam to grasp. Sarah didn't seem to be vulnerable, other than the recent occurrence of pregnancy tears. Sure, she had been shy with him at first, but that hadn't been a weakness in his eyes. And she'd become bolder. More self-assured. In fact, she seemed to be stronger than most women. She knew what she wanted and wasn't afraid to go after it. She went after him—chased him until he caught her. When she was with him, she wasn't shy anymore, wasn't hesitant. She was like a comet in his arms. It could make him shiver in the middle of the day, just thinking about her.

"She went through a complete personality change at that time," Maggie went on. "When she was young, she was a wild child. Sexy, adventurous, a risk-taker."

He felt something in his chest expand. That's my Sarah, he thought.

"When she came out of her depression, she lost herself in art. She was consumed by it. Got her degree and opened that shop and studio. And in the process, she gave up most of her interest in the outside world. I'm not sure if it was her art or some notion that she could yet gain Mom's approval by giving up her old ways, but she just got frumpier and frumpier. It drove me and Clare crazy. We finally gave up trying to get her to pay closer attention to how she looked, because she seemed at least happy, if a little lonely."

That made him frown. He didn't know that frumpy person. Sarah was sexy and alluring. Gorgeous.

Maggie smiled at him. "You don't remember what she looked like when you first met her, do you? Well, your sights were pretty locked on my other sister. And Sarah was practically invisible. Let me jog your memory—she wore a gray, loose dress. Her hair was straight and uninteresting—probably pulled back and clipped. No makeup. Her beautiful green eyes were hidden behind thick, black-framed glasses that were held together on the left side by a piece of duct tape."

"I remember the glasses...." he said.

"Well, here's how it went down. It all made sense once I knew the time line. She took one look at you and Clare and became inspired. She had a hard stare in the mirror and got herself together. She pulled the contact lenses out of storage, got her hair fixed up, bought makeup for the first time in years and new clothes, more stylish and flattering than what she used to wear. All spruced up, and bam. She made you notice her."

"I noticed," he said. "She's very beautiful."

Maggie leaned toward him. "I don't want her heart broken. I don't want you to hurt her any more than she's already hurting. She tells us she is declining your proposal of marriage because you don't love her."

"Maggie, with all due respect, that's between me and Sarah."

"Are you getting my drift here? Because if my little sister is thrown into some terrible depression because you just can't step up to the plate, I'm going to let Clare have a crack at you."

"You McCarthy women," he said. "You're all a pain in the ass, you know that? I'm doing everything I can to step up to the plate here."

"Somehow, that's not entirely convincing."

"Well, you're not the one I have to convince," he said. He stood up. "That all?"

"One more thing, Sam. Clare. Does this hesitancy Sarah is worried about—does it have anything to do with your feelings for Clare? Because with sisters…"

Sam's expression darkened and he drew his brows together. "Sarah is having my baby," he said. "I can assure you, I'm over Clare."

Sam saw the studio light on in Sarah's shop and pulled the squad car up in front. He tapped on the door and she came from the back. She opened the door and said, "Hi. Coffee break?"

"I just wanted to see how you're doing," he said.

"Sam, you don't have to check on me so much. I'm not sick."

"Okay," he said. "I wanted to kiss you."

"And that's all?"

"That's all for tonight," he said. Oh, he could get into the idea of more, but he wasn't going to throw her around the studio with their baby in the middle. He was feeling more protective than that. It had become important to him that she be comfortable. Safe. Plus, he wasn't at all unhappy with the new tempo of their lovemaking. "I don't have that much time," he lied. "Can I see what you're working on?"

She smiled and took him by the hand, leading him to the back. "You're such a liar. You don't care what I'm working on."

"I care," he said. But the second they were in the back room he drew her into his embrace and covered her mouth with his. Her arms went around his neck as she yielded to his powerful kiss. Heavy breathing, hot tongues. He was instantly hard. This was the only part he didn't particularly love. God, but she turned him on. There wasn't anything he could do about it tonight, under the circumstances.

"This vest," she said, pounding on his chest. "It makes you seem so much bigger than you already are." She put her hand over his erection. "Oh, Sam, what you do to yourself."

"Actually, I think it's what you do to me."

She tickled him under his chin. "I know the cure."

"I know you do. I'll let you show me Saturday night. I'll take you to dinner, get us a room."

"All these rooms—it must be depleting your fortunes."

"You live with your father, I live with my mother. It's money well spent. Believe me." He kissed her and asked, "Have you given it any more thought? Getting married?"

"I think about it a lot," she said.

"Have you reconsidered?"

"A couple of times a day I do," she said.

"Well, we're making progress, I guess." He kissed her again and said, "I'd better get going."

"Okay. I don't mind, you know. That you stop by, get me all worked up and leave me. Although, I think I sleep better when you finish what you start."

"Yeah? Me, too."

He took her hand so that she might walk him out, lock the door behind him. When they got to the studio door he turned suddenly and asked, "What are you working on?"

"That," she said, pointing to a painting. "Another still life."

"Nice," he said, turning to leave. He gave her a little peck at the door. "I don't think I like you here, alone, late at night."

"I've only been assaulted once today. Now go."

"Lock the door. If you have any problems—"

"I'll call the police."

"You do that."

Sam actually had more time than he let on. His mission was to see where Sarah was, and knowing she was in her shop, he drove to George's house. He rang the bell and when George answered and saw Sam, his frown was unmistakable. Well, Sam thought, he's pissed at me. Small wonder. But he's in his sixties, I can probably take him if it gets ugly.

"Sir, I wonder if you have a minute to talk," he said.

George left the door open and walked back into the house. Sam followed. In the living room George sat in what was clearly his favorite chair. Sam looked around and found a chair facing George. He sat on the edge.

"Sir, I want you to know that I won't abandon Sarah. I take full responsibility for the pregnancy and I've asked her to marry me."

"I heard," George said.

"She isn't ready for that, I guess. It's up to her. But no matter what she does, I'll stand by her. You should know that."

"You'd better," George said. "Weren't you seeing my other daughter?"

"Well, that. That was over before this... It turns out that Clare and I were only friends. Not— Well, suffice to say, this situation could not have occurred with Clare. Believe me, sir, I was never seeing two sisters at the same time."

George gave a nod. "That's good. Because I might have to kill you for that." Sam sat up straighter, kind of surprised. "Okay, maybe not that. I might have to file a complaint or something. It has to be against department policy."

"I'm pretty sure it would be frowned on," Sam said. He stood up. "I just wanted you to know that I intend to act responsibly toward your daughter. I hoped that at some point we could be friends."

"I'm not quite ready to be your friend," George said. "She's still my little girl."

"I understand." He shuffled a little uncomfortably. Mission accomplished, he told himself. Sam didn't expect him to be happy. "I'll say good night."

Sam turned to go and to his back George said, "Maybe someday."

He turned around.

"Lot of adjustments to make right now. But maybe when the dust settles, we'll get along all right."

"Thank you, sir," Sam said. And took his leave.

chapter sixteen

....

Bob Traviston gave Maggie a diamond necklace for Valentine's Day and she was moved to tears. Maggie had been getting consistently more emotional since Lindsey's and Hillary's escapades, and since Sarah had gone public with the pregnancy. And, he thought secretly, there might be a little something else going on with her.

Maggie had been asking Bob to see the doctor about his apparent lack of interest in sex, but Bob—being a man—preferred to see a doctor only if a limb were actually falling off. "I've been to the doctor," he said. "I'm in perfect health."

"But you've never mentioned this," she argued.

"How do you know?" he returned. But he was thinking, of *course* I never mentioned this! Besides, it wasn't as though he didn't have erections. Well, in reality, he rarely had them anymore, and they were usually those early-morning events that went away pretty quick.

But because Maggie had been getting a little tearful lately, and Bob had to admit that he'd almost completely lost interest in sex, he made an appointment. For a checkup. The prospect of telling the doctor he wasn't getting it up anymore surpassed daunting. He could face Congress with less tension.

At the doctor's office, all his vitals were checked, he peed in a cup, an order for routine blood work was written up. "Anything else we should check?" the doctor asked.

"Hmm," Bob said. "Let me think…."

"Anything your wife wants us to check?"

Bob sighed deeply. "My wife has been complaining about the infrequency of…" He couldn't go on.

The doctor flipped through the chart. "How infrequent?" he asked without looking up.

"Never," Bob admitted. What the hell, he thought. It's going to come out eventually.

"Hmm," the doctor said. "Hmm. Here's one thing. Let's change that blood pressure medicine you've been taking the past couple of years. And if there's no improvement, we'll get you to the urologist. You're too young to give up erections."

The prospect of going to the urologist for this problem filled Bob with dread. If there was one thing a man never wanted to own up to, it's that he was having trouble getting it up. Anything else, okay. But not that.

The whole thing just depressed him. Quieted him out. He was starting to come out of his denial, aware that it wasn't the job, the hours, the pressure. That perhaps accounted for his blood pressure being elevated, but not the rest. He began taking the new blood pressure medicine, knowing in his gut that he was going to end up dropping his drawers for another doctor pretty soon, admitting the unadmittable.

But at least things were getting a little easier in the family arena. Hillary had a soft cap of new hair on her head and announced she was trying out for cheerleading. Lindsey brought home a progress report from school that boasted straight A's in all honors classes.

He thought a lot about how much he actually loved his wife. He found her incredibly attractive; he considered her his best friend. No matter how hard this situation was, he made a decision he would pursue a cure.

He got into bed with his book while Maggie scrubbed her face and brushed her teeth in the en suite. He could hear her in there, changing. It was cold in the room, so he turned on the gas fireplace with the remote at his bedside. She came out of the bathroom wearing her long, concealing, decidedly un-sexy flannel nightgown. She's given up on me, he thought. I've given up on me. She's going to have an affair before long, if she hasn't already.

Then an idea occurred to him, for the first time in at least a year. She got into bed and turned off her light. She leaned toward him, kissed his cheek and snuggled down into the bed, her back to him.

He put aside his book, turned off his light, and lay down.

"Don't fall asleep with the fireplace on," she said sleepily.

"I won't," he said. His pulsed picked up. Hope I don't have a heart attack, he thought. But no, that heart rate was not a medical thing. It was caused by a vaguely familiar emotion.

He rolled over and spooned her. His hand crept under her arm and she snuggled against him. He cupped her breast, kissed her neck and voilá! The old boy sprang to life!

"Bob?" she asked, a little weakly, feeling something against her bottom. Something hard and strong, something she had greatly missed. She rolled onto her back. "Bob?"

He kissed her. One of those short sweet husbandly kisses that had become routine for them. And then, uncharacter-istically, he covered her mouth in a hot and serious kiss. She opened her lips under his and answered in passion. Then he rose above her and said, "I've been to the doctor. Turns out, it was probably my blood pressure medicine, which I changed about a week ago."

"You didn't say anything," she said, startled.

"Well, I wasn't all that optimistic that the cure would be an easy one."

"Oh my God, Bob! You did this for me!"

He kissed her again. "I did this for us," he said, lifting that boring old granny gown and snaking his hand underneath. "I think we need to spend more time together," he said.

Late February arrived and Pete was invited to Sunday dinner at George's. "Aunt Clare has a boyfriend," Hillary said in awe.

"It is too totally weird, seeing your mother kiss the football coach," Jason said, and Pete reached out and palmed his head, giving it a rough shake, making him laugh.

When it was just the sisters in the kitchen, Sarah put a hand on her still-flat tummy and said, "I'm going to have to trot my boyfriend out pretty soon. I should probably spring him on the kids before I start to show."

"Which is just around the corner," Clare pointed out.

"Did you know he came over here one evening and talked to Dad?"

"When did that happen?" Maggie asked, picking up plates.

"A few weeks ago. Right after I told Dad about the baby. He wanted to be sure Dad knew he wasn't running for his life, I guess."

"How'd it go?"

"Well, there weren't any punches thrown," Sarah said.

"Are you still skiing every Monday?" Clare asked. "Because I'm not sure that's such a great idea."

"Sam worries about that, too. I'm just about done skiing."

"I like the sound of that, that he's concerned."

"He's a little overprotective," she said.

Was it solicitude and courtesy? Sam just being responsible? Clare wondered.

"I suppose I could go a little easier. Tomorrow will probably be my last Monday chasing the ski patrol around the slopes."

"I could wangle a day off from Dad," Clare said. "I worked six straight days last week and I'm supposed to be part-time now, so I can work on the old house. Why don't I go with you? If you ski with me, you'll take it lots easier." And, Clare thought, it's time to see them together. She believed she would be able to tell much from the way they interacted, the way they looked at each other.

"Have you gotten over your urge to end his life?" Sarah asked.

"I think I can control myself now."

"Then okay. That would be fine," Sarah said. "I might not go home with you, however."

Maggie fluffed Sarah's curls. "Are you happy, honey?"

There was no hesitation. Her smile was quick and genuine. "I am." She shrugged. "My timing could be better, but my life couldn't. He makes me very happy."

Clare took the day off from the store and picked Sarah up at ten in the morning. They stuck to the tamer slopes, skiing for a couple of hours without seeing Sam. Clare was looking for him, eyeballing every ski patrol who crossed their paths. "Did you ever wonder if they hire these guys by looks?" she asked Sarah.

"Ski patrol and firemen," Sarah said. "Calendar boys. Here

he comes," she said, pointing up the hill. Sam was traversing down the slope in sleek, wide turns, punching through the powder, a rooster tail of white crystal flying up behind him. It was a magnificent sight. "The best-looking one out here."

He came to a stop in front of them. He popped up his goggles and with that heart-melting grin said, "Hi, girls." He leaned toward Sarah and gave her a little peck on the cheek. "You're behaving. That makes me happy." Then, "Clare. How's it going?"

"Good. And she's only behaving because she's with me. I just don't have any stamina this year. I'm already exhausted."

"You'll get it back."

The sound of distant twittering could be heard. Clare popped off her glove and reached into her snow pants to find her phone. She scooted away a bit to take a call from Pete. She put the phone to one ear and covered her other ear with her hand. While she listened, she watched Sam and Sarah. He looked down at Sarah and Clare saw her sister had his complete attention. She couldn't see Sam's eyes, but she thought if she could she would see something more than solicitude there. She watched as Sam took off a glove and touched Sarah's face, tilting it upward to say something that made Sarah smile, then laugh.

"What?" she said to Pete. "What did you say?"

"I said, Jason cut school. The gossip is that he's up there, snowboarding."

"How would he manage that?"

"Stan drove to school today. Did you tell him you were going up there with Sarah?"

"No. Since we haven't said anything to the kids about Sarah and Sam, he wouldn't know they're up here on Mondays. And I haven't seen him."

"Well, if he saw you, he probably ran for his life."

"Oh, he's in so much trouble!" she said. "Thanks for the tip."

She put the phone away and went back to Sarah and Sam. "My confidential informant at Centennial tells me Jason skipped school and is rumored to be up here snowboarding."

"I haven't seen him," Sam said. "They groom the hills on Tuesday—so Monday's a pretty light day. Not that many people out there."

"He'd be bored on these hills," Clare said.

"That little brat," Sarah said. "Bet I know where he is. Rest a minute, Clare. I'll be right back." She took off for the lift on the other side of the intermediate hill she'd been skiing with Clare.

"You be careful!" Sam yelled after her.

"I'm always careful!" she yelled back.

Sarah moved quickly toward the lift. Jason would have headed for the harder, longer slopes, probably the expert runs or snowboard park. And Sam would have spent much of the day around them, too, so if Sam hadn't seen Jason there were only two possibilities. Either Jason saw one of them—Sam, Sarah or Clare—and left before getting caught, or went into the restricted areas to stay out of sight.

She looked over at Sam and Clare as the lift scooped her up and carried her upward. Good, she thought. Let them talk awhile. Get any unfinished business sorted out and behind them. They all had many, many years ahead of them as family. There was no point in being haunted by old romances. And Sam would have to be sure, once and for all, whether he could move ahead without having any feelings stuck in the past.

It was impossible for Sarah to love any two people more—

Clare and Sam. She needed them both in her life, and without the slightest hint of complications.

She got off the lift at the crest of the hill known as the Crown, a challenging slope for advanced skiers and snowboarders. She looked around and down. She didn't see Jason's purple stocking cap anywhere. To her left were red flags and a warning sign, no ski patrols beyond this point. She had no intention of skiing in a restricted area—she just wanted to look down the slope and see if anyone was there. She moved cautiously across the ridge past a small stand of trees and scanned the landscape. Nothing. Thank God. Maybe he did have a brain.

Just as she was about to go back to the expert slope and make a run down to Clare and Sam, she caught something out of the corner of her eye. And it was purple. There were two of them. They were coming from the far south of a hill that when it was open was known as Big Bear. The stupid little fool. She was going to go get him and when she caught him, beat him senseless. He was about halfway down when she pushed off.

As Sarah neared the lift, Sam looked back at Clare, and she saw a wistful look in his eyes. She immediately thought, oh no! He can't still be pining! "My sister is very happy, Sam."

"I think pregnancy agrees with her," he said. "Want to go sit down for a while?"

"I don't want to keep you from your job," she said. "I'm fine. I'll just wait here."

"You look content. Happy. Life must be treating you well."

I'm not real content at the moment, she thought. I don't know how to handle this. She looked in the direction Sarah had gone and saw her getting on the lift. "Yeah," she said, somewhat absently. "Great. I'm great."

"Okay, you're not that happy," he said. "Well, I'm sorry about that, but I think we're all doing pretty well, considering how awkward this has been—me and Sarah. You. Maggie. Your dad. Did Maggie tell you she came to see me? At work?"

"Yeah, I knew that was going to happen. How'd it go?"

He shrugged. "It was half an ass chewing and half a warning that Sarah might not be as rock solid as she appears. Maggie told me about the nervous breakdown. It's really hard for me to grasp. She's not like that with me." His voice had become soft. Almost soothing.

"She hates that we think she's fragile. It makes her furious. Did you tell her what Maggie said?"

"I did. You're right, it makes her furious. But I talked her down—I think she understands Maggie meant well. I'm glad to have a chance to talk to you about it. Sarah told me everything—from those crazy growing-up years and all the wild oats, to the time following your mother's death. She's been through a lot, but I think she's stronger now." He chuckled. "She must have really been something when she was a kid. Now that, I believe."

"I'm amazed you told her."

"Of course I told her, Clare. We had a couple of very long discussions about it and I'm confident that she's all right. I don't think you have to worry about that anymore. Let me worry about it."

"Sam, she is so in love with you, it's almost painful to watch. If you hurt her, I don't know what it will do to her."

"I'm not going to hurt her, Clare. You have to believe me. I'm going to do the right thing. I *want* to do the right thing."

"Good," she said.

He cocked his head to one side and said, "It seems like there's something you want to say to me. Let's get it out."

"No, there's nothing."

"For Sarah, Clare. She's completely devoted to you. If there's anything you wonder about, let's clear the air."

"Well," she said, hesitatingly.

"Say it."

She took a breath. "You seeing Sarah… It didn't have anything to do with me, did it?"

His brow furrowed. "In what way?"

"You weren't trying to get back at me? By taking up with my little sister?"

"How would that get back at you? I guess I don't get it."

"I know you thought you were in love with me and I hurt you. You might've been needy. Or, I don't know. Angry."

His grin was suddenly huge. "Aw, Jesus, the way you women think."

"Well you have to admit, it's pretty strange that we'd only broken it off by a month or so when—"

"When Sarah laid her trap for me and I fell right into it?" He laughed. "Clare, you're a great catch, no kidding, but if you hadn't cut me loose, I wouldn't have Sarah." He whistled. "You have absolutely no idea what I have now. All that I have."

Whatever that look was that had crossed his features, she must have mistaken its meaning. God, it wasn't for her! she suddenly realized. It was for Sarah! "You almost sound as though you're in love with her."

"Do I now?" he asked. "I never believed you for a second, you know—that there was someone out there who would be perfect for me. Breaking it off was the best thing you could ever have done for me because I would have never even looked at Sarah if we were together." He shrugged. "I'm just a plain old one-woman man. And...I didn't know I could be this happy."

"Oh, God," she said. "Oh, Sam!"

"You knew what you were doing, Clare. It wasn't right. This is."

"Sam, that's wonderful." Clare threw her arms around him and hugged his neck. "That's so wonderful!"

He almost fell over from her assault, but righted himself and laughed at her. "Does this mean you're not disappointed that I'm completely over you?" he asked.

"You'll just never know—"

His radio sputtered. "We've got skiers in restricted areas. Big Bear."

"Sarah!" He bent and popped the bindings, stepping out of his skis.

"She wouldn't go in a restricted area," Clare said.

He put the skis over his shoulder and started to jog away from her. "She would if Jason were there!"

A couple of ski patrols ran out of the pro shop and headed for snowmobiles. A couple more jumped on the lift Sarah had used. They'd go up to the ridge, but these patrols were not going to go into restricted areas. Skiers knew they went there at their own risk. Sam ran to a stand of snowmobiles, propped his skis on the back, strapped them in and fired up the machine. The advanced hill nearest Big Bear was too steep for the snowmobile; he could better access the area from the ridge above the intermediate grade. Skiers were coming down the hill and he kept his ride as close to the trees as he could without grazing any of them. When he got to the top, he drove along the ridge and up the next slope to a higher one. When he got to the top of the expert hill to the north of Big Bear, he got off and put on his skis. Going through the red flags, he made his way as quickly as possible to the top of the Big Bear run.

About halfway down the hill he saw a skier and snow-boarder, stopped. Talking. Sarah had gone in pursuit. He wasn't going to follow her, but watch her descent, and when she was out of danger, he'd take the expert hill down. And spank the daylights out of her. "That damn woman," he muttered. Then he heard a loud crack and a rumble and said, "Son of a bitch!"

Jason was wedging right and left when he saw his aunt Sarah's pink bib and jacket—coming down the hill after him. He put a little speed into it and then asked himself why bother—she'd catch him anyway and his ass would be in a sling. So he wedged right and stopped. Stan kept going. He was going to get out of harm's way.

She came upon him easily, sending up a spray of snow as she stopped. She whacked him right up the side of the head with one mittened hand. "You little jerk," she said. "You're an idiot."

"Hey, Sarah, cut me some slack."

"Slack? In your dreams. When we get down I'm going to have to hold your mother back."

"I saw you guys—and we'd already spent a bunch of money on the lift, so we just thought we'd stay outta sight and get a couple of runs in before going home."

"You cut school! You're on a restricted hill! You're history!"

There was a loud boom. They turned and looked up. A heavy shelf of snow had broken off the ridge and hit the hill above and just barely to the right of them. If they stayed where they were, it was going to bury them.

"Go, go, go!" she yelled, though she could barely be heard

against the thundering noise of the avalanche. "Outrun it, Jason! Go!"

Sarah couldn't do anything but fly. She jabbed her poles into the snow, flipped around and took off. She couldn't help Jason, couldn't give him speed. All she could do was pray that he'd know what to do. It was every man for himself. The avalanche was coming down to the right, so she cut down and left, tucked her poles and prayed. She neared the tree line that separated the runs and cut as close as she dared, as far from the avalanche as she could get and keep going down. She weaved in and out of the widely separated trees near the run, but where they got thicker, she was forced to stay out. There was too much growth, rocks and junk to go through the bush to the run on the other side of the tree line that separated the slopes.

Sarah expertly maneuvered, shushing around the trees, the barrage getting ever closer. Inside her mind was screaming, Please, Jason, please. Run, run, run. Outrun it. She cut left, right, left, right, barely dodging the trees. She felt the wind of the falling tonnage of snow whip at her from the side—it must be right next to her. She was clear of it or it would have buried her by now, but the bottom was not yet in sight. And then it happened; all the dust from the snow was blinding. A whiteout. She could barely see and was too close to the trees to continue skiing. She slowed, came up to the tree line and hung on to a trunk. She looked to her right. If it wasn't passing her, she was toast. She heard the rumble as it roared by.

The avalanche seemed to have spared the very left side of the slope, which meant only half of that weak shelf had let go. She prayed Jason had cut across to safety, but she highly doubted he would dare the trees. And if he had, he might not be able to handle them as well as she had; he was getting good, but not that good. She must get down and see if he made it.

It was hard to see. It would be a little like skiing by braille. And she'd have to get out of the trees.

She pushed off and was moving through the trees when her ski went over something—a rock hidden in the snow per-haps—giving her left ski a fast, erratic turn. And she felt it—her knee seemed to pop and snap. She went down. A tendon, she thought immediately. Probably a torn anterior cruciate ligament, a very common skiing injury.

She dragged herself against a tree. If any more of that snow shelf let go, she was sunk. Trapped. Dead. The trees wouldn't keep her safe; there was no shelter out here. She was going to rest a minute before doing anything. She thought about going down on one ski—she could do that. Or maybe it would be better to slide. She could sit on her skis—but it was impos-sible to bend her knee. Maybe she could crawl or roll the rest of the way. But at the moment there was just too much pain. And she still couldn't see anything as the whiteout slowly, so slowly, settled to the ground.

Sam saw Jason and Sarah take off like the seats of their pants were on fire, but it was only a few seconds before their images were obscured by the dust of the rapidly descending flood of snow. He saw Sarah's bright pink jacket as she cut left, toward the trees, but he lost sight of Jason in the white cloud.

As soon as the thunder subsided, he keyed his radio. "Con-trol, I made one skier and one snowboarder on Big Bear, try-ing to outrun the avalanche." The air was thick with snow, slowly settling to the ground, but so gradually he still couldn't see anything down there. The fallout hung in the air for what seemed like forever. He waited until he could see a path near the top, and it was the longest few minutes of his life. By the time the cloud was somewhat settled, there were two more ski patrols off the lift and beside him.

His radio answered him. He tipped his head to the left to listen to the transmitter attached to his shoulder. "We don't have them down here. Yet."

"Damn it," he muttered.

"It was a boy on a snowboard and a woman on skis," he told the patrols. "The woman cut left and I lost the boy. She might've taken refuge in the trees. I'm going down."

"It's unstable, man," one of the patrols said. "You shouldn't chance it."

"Yeah, well, if she's down there, I'm going to get her out of there before the rest of it goes," he said.

"We'll go down The Crown and work our way up with a toboggan and search poles," the other patrol said.

Sam didn't even bother to respond. Enough of the snow had settled so that it looked more like thick fog than a white-out. He pushed off and skied down. He prayed as he went, and he skied as slowly as he could make himself. He didn't want to miss her; he didn't want to hit a tree. Those trees, he found himself thinking, just have no give. The powder was deep and too soft, the air was white with fallout from the avalanche. He stayed close to the tree line. At about the place he thought he'd seen her cut over, he slowed to a near stop and peered into the trees. He was afraid to shout, afraid he might create an echo that would dislodge more of the weak shelf.

If I lose her, I'll die, was all he could think. I can't live like that. I'll never make it without her. Not now.

The fresh dusting of snow had covered any tracks, and then he saw a couple. Around this tree, around that. Damn, she was good. At the speed she was going, to clear those trees in the middle of that horrendous avalanche was astonishing. Then he saw a flash of bright pink, crumpled up against a tree. "Skier versus tree," he said into his radio.

He made his way cautiously into the trees, shushing between them slowly. Her head was down, one knee bent up and the other leg straight. Move, he was thinking. Let me see you move! It seemed to take forever to get to her, but at last he was next to her. He knelt down. "Sarah!" he whispered.

She looked up at his face, tears of pain streaming down her cheeks. "'Bout time," she said. "The service around here sucks."

He put his gloved hands on her face. "God, Sarah! What were you doing?"

"Going after my nephew. Please. Tell me he made it."

"I lost sight of you both, but I saw you cut toward the trees. I died a hundred times. Did you hit the tree? Your head? Anything?"

"No. I was doing pretty good, then my knee went out. I think I blew a tendon or ligament. Oh man, it hurts."

"Thank God it's just your knee. We gotta get out of here," he said. "A big piece of that weak shelf broke off. It's just a matter of time before the rest of it goes."

"I can't ski. Sam, you shouldn't be here. It's dangerous."

"You think I could leave you? Come on, up on the good leg. We can't wait for rescue—we're gonna do this the old-fashioned way." He picked her up and leaned her against a tree, balanced on her good leg. He popped the bindings on her skis and once off, they began to slide down the hill. He braced himself against the tree and said, "Put your arms around my neck, and let me do the work—if you try to help, we'll fall." He lifted her into his arms. She let a small yelp of pain escape as her knee bent over his arm. He kept his shoulder against the tree. He kissed her cheek. "Just trust me, Sarah. Stay very still."

"You're crazy. You just skied into the path of an avalanche."

"*I'm* crazy? When we get off this stupid hill, you're going to stop doing these insane things. I can't take it." Then more quietly he said, "Aw, baby. You scared me so bad."

"Sam, put me down. We should slide. Or roll."

"We're going to do this, Sarah. I'm getting you down."

"But it's so hard to see."

"Then don't look. I know this hill," he said. "You just hang on and try not to move, try not to throw me off balance."

She buried her face in his jacket. There wasn't a wind and the air began to slowly clear. He pushed off the tree carefully, putting him out on the run. Heavier now with his burden and without the use of his poles, the soft snow nearly covered his skis and their progress down the hill was agonizingly slow. "I don't know what you were thinking," he said. "Don't you know how much I love you?"

She kept her face buried against his chest. He nearly lost his balance once, but Sarah, trusting him, remained perfectly still as he straightened again.

"I know you need time to figure this out, but damn it, I can't live without you. It's too late for me to change course now—I need you. I've never…" He stopped talking as he wobbled slightly. "Halfway, honey. Stay still. That's my girl."

She tightened her arms around his neck. "I never thought I'd have anything like this in my life," he said. "If I lost you, I don't know what I'd do. You're my world, Sarah."

The two ski patrols he'd left up top were making their way up the slope from the bottom on a snowmobile dragging a rescue toboggan. He met them halfway and decided not to hand her over. "She's pregnant," he said. "Bouncing down on the toboggan or snowmobile isn't going to cut it. Follow me down."

"We gotta get off this hill," one of them said.

He continued his slow, careful descent. "If you want to go ahead, I'll understand," he told them.

They stayed behind him, braving another avalanche to pick them up if they fell. But Sam exercised all the caution he could muster, kept his speed slow and went carefully down the hill. "Almost there, Sarah," he whispered. "Almost there."

At the bottom of the slope he stopped. One of the patrols jumped off his snowmobile and stooped to pop off Sam's bindings. Sam stepped out of the skis and left the patrol to pick them up. He settled Sarah against his chest. Carrying her now on terra firma, he walked as quickly as he could away from the offending hill. The snowmobiles carrying the other patrols whizzed by, one with Sam's skis balanced over his shoulder.

"I can't believe you're doing this," she said to him.

"And why can't you?" he asked. "You're the best thing that's ever happened to me. I couldn't do anything else."

Sam saw that the area had been evacuated and the skiers were all down, gathered around the lodge. An ambulance stood waiting, its red lights a strobe on the white hills. At the front of the crowd he made out Jason and Stan with Clare. "They made it down, honey. They're fine." He headed for the lodge as quickly as he could.

"Thank God," she said in a breath. She looked up at his face and said, "We're safe now, Sam. Put me down. I'm too heavy."

"I'm not putting you down." He kissed her forehead as he walked. "God, I was scared to death." He glanced at her tearstained face. "Is the pain terrible?" he asked her.

"I don't have any pain." She touched his frosty cheek. "I love you, too. I can't live without you, either."

He hugged her tighter. "Then why do you make me beg?" he asked.

"I like the sight of a good man groveling," she said through her tears.

"Well, then you must be ecstatic. I'm completely desperate for you. All I want is to lie beside you every night for the rest of my life. Sarah, I love you so much."

She put her hand against his cheek and just drank in his beautiful face. But Sam didn't hesitate—he didn't waste any time looking dreamily into her eyes. He made fast tracks toward the lodge.

There was a loud crack, a boom, and Sam turned back toward the dangerous slope to see the rest of the weak snow shelf let go and fall with explosive force to the hill below, its weight and girth crashing into the trees where only a few minutes before, Sarah had heard the words that made her life seem complete. The voices of the skiers gathered in front of the lodge rose as one in awe of the avalanche's power.

Sarah grabbed the front of Sam's jacket and gave it a hard yank to get his attention. She kissed him. Long and deep. Then she said, "Okay, then. Marry me. Right away. I want to do it now. Before you change your mind."

"I'm never going to change my mind, baby," he said. "Never."

epilogue

....

November

FOOTBALL GAMES HAVE a special significance, when you're in love with the coach. Plus, Clare considered Homecoming to be a kind of anniversary, even though it didn't fall on the same day as the year before when her love affair with Pete had come into full bloom. And what a year—so full and lush.

Many things had fallen neatly into place. Roger proved himself to be a dedicated parent, something he was better at now than during their marriage. Sam and Sarah brought into the family a son, Casey. Jason traded Stan for a young lady, Beth, who seemed to have a more positive impact on his manners, his grades, his appearance.

But for Clare, the highlight of the past year was learning about Pete all over again. He gave so much of himself, worked so hard, was so completely dedicated. He was greatly loved in the town, in the school, and not just during football season. The students and other teachers depended on him, the community took pride in him. Rather than being boastful, he was humble. But he wasn't modest about his team, his boys—he brought them to victory after crashing victory and celebrated every win as if it were their first.

The entire McCarthy family, even Roger, sat in a tight, proud knot in the bleachers, right down front, for every game. George lived for them and even baby Casey was there, packed tightly against his father's chest, warm and snug in an infant sling. If Clare didn't know better she'd think they were all as proud of Pete as she. But that was impossible. She loved watching him in action; she loved it when he turned from the field, found her in her usual spot and smiled at her. And as she became known as his steady, his woman, his love, she glowed. It seemed as though their families, their friends, were as pleased as they were.

Watching the town light up at Homecoming held new excitement for her, for her man was at center stage. The electricity in the air, the exuberance of the teenagers, the fun and happiness that seemed to radiate through the whole town—it filled her up. Something about this brought her full circle— her life with him had begun in high school and although it had been derailed for a decade or two, when they rediscovered each other, the pure intensity of their new love made up for lost time.

Another Homecoming, another new year, another gathering of family, and she stood and cheered her lungs out at every good play, every touchdown. She shivered through her whole body when he turned her way and briefly, so briefly, met her eyes. She beamed with nostalgia when the floats came out at halftime, when the Homecoming King and Queen strutted their adolescent stuff in front of the bleachers, when the marching band claimed the field and blasted out their game music.

Then suddenly, she saw Pete standing in front of the bleachers, looking up at her. He was out of the locker room a little early; he usually didn't come back on the field with the team until after halftime. He stood, hands in his pockets, head tilted up, watching her, while behind him, the marching band played.

"Clare," Maggie said from behind her. "Clare, look." Maggie pointed over Clare's shoulder toward the scoreboard.

CLARE—MARRY ME!

It brought her slowly to her feet, her mouth open in surprise. She looked down at him and dipped her chin in a little nod.

Pete jogged toward the bleachers, grabbed the rail and hefted himself up and over. He reached for her hand, pulled her into his arms and covered her mouth in a powerful kiss. The fans erupted in a loud and wild cheer. He didn't let go quickly; for all the heat in his kiss, they might have been alone. When he did release her lips, he hung on to her still and whispered, "I'll take that as a yes."

"Yes," she whispered. "Of course, yes."

"Good. See you after the game."

He kissed her again, more quickly. He jumped over the bleacher rail and ran back toward the field, his arms stretched up over his head just as his team came running out.

On the scoreboard it flashed, SHE SAID YES!!

★ ★ ★ ★ ★

NEVER TOO LATE

ROBYN CARR

Reader's Guide

MIRA®

1. The three sisters in the novel are facing different challenges in their lives. With whom do you most identify, and why?

2. How important is your family's support when making big life decisions?

3. Was Clare punishing herself for her past mistakes by staying in a marriage with a serial cheater?

4. Would you be able to forgive your spouse for an infidelity? Do the circumstances matter, or is cheating always unforgiveable?

5. What effect does grief have—especially a young woman losing her mother?

6. What are your thoughts on an older woman dating a younger man? Would you be comfortable with that kind of relationship? Are women judged for that in a way that men are not?

7. What are your thoughts on Roger? Will he finally be capable having a faithful relationship with the right woman, or does a leopard never change its spots?

8. Pete and Clare share a powerful history. Given the chance, would you reunite with a past love, or should the past be left behind?

9. Do you believe it's never too late to start again?